Previous novels by D. M. Samson

Silent Violence

In 1984 Dawn Marie travelled with her husband to Saudi Arabia. He had secured a job replacing the outgoing foreman of a secluded farm near Riyadh. Almost two years later she would return home. Alone. Broken.

In *Silent Violence* she tells us of her journey: a long downward spiral. From the first inklings of things not being right, a pet killer in the expatriate compound, clandestine excursions by the farm crew, through to the rising hysteria within the expatriate community, then the killings at the farm, the ensuing imprisonment, moral deterioration, government procrastination and eventual deliverance.

Without question her story is harrowing. Yet it contains a great deal of humour too. For humour was the life jacket that kept the displaced person buoyant in a strange culture.

After years of psychiatric treatment she was persuaded to write her story. The road to publication is a story in itself. Ultimately the book was suppressed in the interests of international relations.

Silent Violence should be a warning to prospective expatriates. Its portrayal of Arab mentality could help policy makers too.

Nails

There is little one can say about the plot. Succinctly put, it is the story of one day in the life of a car mechanic. Admittedly, not much in itself. But it's hard, raw, violent, sexy, sensitive, funny, poetic and philosophical to boot. It's a page-turner that grabs you by the short and curlies.

Bottle

In *Nails* Kevin was a prisoner of frustration, middling, but waiting for who knows what. In *Bottle* he's liberated with the proverbial "kick up the arse" he needs.

This book has got everything. Even the kitchen sink! It's teeming with life and death, tears and laughter, sex and violence, parents and children, brutality and tenderness, anger and contentment... But why should I go on? Look up further antonyms yourself. Or save yourself the trouble and simply read the book.

Although *Bottle* is the sequel to *Nails* it can be read in its own right.

Deutschisch

What starts out as a routine task of collecting the body of a German national murdered at a Turkish resort becomes an emotional odyssey for *Oberkommissar* Dannaks (of REX: Racism and Extremism).

Intent on contributing to the investigation he is confronted by a wall of silence from the hotel staff. The Turkish police aren't giving anything away. And if that wasn't enough even his companion Reupke (from Homicide) is happy to treat the trip as a holiday. Finally, the resort begins to seduce Dannaks, culminating with the distraction of a fledgling romance.

Then when a girl, missing since the murder, gives herself up and confesses to the killing, Dannaks appears to be the only one to believe she is lying.

Back in Hamburg he unexpectedly finds himself suspended from duty. Using the time to investigate the girl's past he uncovers not only her terrible secret, but also a mistake by Reupke's Homicide colleagues. His emotional odyssey turns into a quest for truth and justice that takes him to Berlin and Central Anatolia.

...and the man who
loved cats

First published in 2012 by David M. Samson, 20 Arundel Road, Bath, Avon BA1 6EF.

Printed and bound by Lulu.com.
Lulu Enterprises Inc.
860 Aviation Parkway
Suite 300
Morrisville, NC 27560
United States of America

ISBN 978-0-9556796-4-3

British Library Cataloguing in Publication Data.
A catalogue record for this book is available from the British Library.

Cover design by David M. Samson.

www.davidmsamson.com

About the author

David M. Samson, born in Wallasey (near Liverpool) in 1957, lives with his wife and two daughters in Germany.

The author extends a big thank you to Bernie Morris for her support, advice and eagle-eye.

Contents

The man who loved cats.

(including: Girl in the lake, Belief, The Mask, Christian Soldiers)

As he swam towards the drowning girl, something peculiar began to happen. Instead of progressing he appeared to be going backwards: he did not seem to be getting any closer. But then, he had heard that under such circumstances time played tricks. Every stroke made itself felt, yet in reality he knew he was covering the distance in record time. When life and death were in question time stretched as if it were elastic. But this feeling of not progressing was accentuated by a deep belief that something was pulling him backward. It was not physical. And it seemed to have nothing to do with time. He could not feel the progress of time, but he knew that it was moving forward. He could count off the units with the crash of his arms in the icy water. It was his thoughts that seemed to be reversing. As he moved onward his thoughts went backwards. Huh, he had always believed that during such times of stress the mind froze and one had no thoughts at all. This was obviously not the case. His mind was alive and his arms and legs were thrashing.

He could hear old Sultan barking at the lake-side. His parents had often asked why he had called him Sultan and he had no answer. Funny that this thought should come now.

It was lucky that he had chosen this walk. This was the long one. And why not? It was a Sunday. He had nothing else to do. He never had anything else to do. Life was not what you made it; life was what it made of you.

At twenty years old this was how far he had come. This was the sum total of his wisdom.

He had been thinking of ending it all. Life was a gruelling and depressing thing. It was full of lonely people, never connecting, never coming together. That had been what he had been thinking. But, no, he had been mulling over a related something. Something that had been haunting him for a week.

The water exploded rhythmically in his ears. A related something?

There he was, walking along the lake-side. Thinking. Thinking what?

Then he had it. He had been thinking of it during his walk. It had caused him to mull over ending it all, and he had imagined his

7

parents' reaction, the reactions of the people at work, his friends and then some relatives. His father had read it aloud. A rare honour for the morning. It had been last week. It was one of those "what happened locally one hundred years ago" articles. On this day, a servant girl had drowned herself nearby because, they guessed, she had been desperately lonely. It was known that she suffered bouts of depression and this coupled with the fact that she had been found naked with no evidence of foul play – her clothes, in a neatly folded pile, had been discovered first – hinted strongly at suicide. And as his father read he had thought, if only I had lived then. Loneliness was not something particular to this day and age. If only I had known her. Or rather, if only she had known me. I would have shown her. I would have loved her. I am so full of love. I have so much to give. And she could not have helped but love him too. Of course he got depressed. Everyone got depressed, didn't they? But they would have helped each other. Given the chance he would have saved her. And now, miraculously some greater power had given him his chance. History was repeating itself, but this time he was there to change the outcome.

"I'm off," he had announced, knocking back the last of his tea. His father looked up from his paper and nodded. He never spoke much at breakfast. Only his mother tended to waffle on.

"Well, wrap up then. It's quite chilly out."

"Yes, Mum." She wanted to fuss about him, but she was held back by the fact that he was now a young man. Much to his father's disgust – don't pamper the boy, you'll turn him into a sissy – he let her comb his hair. He allowed her this one ritual because she felt quite lost now that he had grown up.

Crash, crash. He dug and pulled at the icy water. Ahead was glitter. He had wondered during his walk, why was it that when people attempted suicide they did so naked? Was it a rejection of the trappings of society? Was it some kind of expression of freedom along the lines of we come naked into the world and naked shall we go? Or was it something completely opposite? Namely, that they felt abused and worn down, that society – or whatever – had taken everything from them and they had nothing. That is, they felt exposed and wanted to express this vulnerability in nakedness. He did not know.

"Look, I'll get a girlfriend when I'm ready."

"Lighten up, son."

"Don't tell me to lighten up. Just mind your own business."

Of course he wanted a girlfriend. How stupid of his father to tell him to get out and about. He liked reading; he liked staying in. There was nothing wrong with that.

Fountains and foam flanked him. So many people never connect.

School hadn't been easy.

"Watch out. Here comes the toff."

"Hey, have you been frying chips in your hair, again?"

"Yeah, watch those spots. You'll get a lunar module landing on your face one day."

"Ah, leave him alone."

But he had been surrounded by so many that friendships were unavoidable. The working world was an every-man-for-himself place.

The water was so cold it was tasteless. It froze the taste-buds. And the drowning girl seemed as far away as ever; dangerously close to those treacherous reeds.

"Why couldn't I have had a brother or sister?"

"Because we wanted to have you all to ourselves. We wanted to spoil you."

Splash, splash. Was he getting any closer to the drowning girl?

"Oh Mummy, it hurts."

"Come here, let Mummy kiss it better."

It was strange: he looked up again to check his bearings one minute and the next he was upon her. It was as if she had transported herself to him.

He hurriedly grabbed at her, but was arrested by a number of things. He was aware of none of them in particular: he was half-aware of them all. The summation of them was his arrest, an arrest that quickly twisted into confusion.

In that moment he saw her smile. It was a beautiful smile. It was a smile that said welcome. There was confidence in her grey eyes. She had put rather too much kohl around them. But her beauty carried off this clumsiness. It added an exotic interest to her. Of course she was pale – curiously white. Indeed, there was a bluish hue to her skin. It was her calmness that shocked him. There was no stress. But his shock was short-lived for her welcoming smile stole him. He did not question her. He forgot the image of her near the reeds, her arms flailing. Instead he returned her smile with a weak one of his own.

The proximity of their bodies allowed nothing less than an embrace. Therefore he was aware of her coldness.

He wanted to turn her: to get her back on his chest. So that he could swim her to safety.

He was puzzled by her smile, her presence. She appeared calm and welcoming. Arrested, his heart filled as her lips neared his. At the same time he was vaguely aware of an icy thinness: a feeling akin to standing before a crevasse. It was a gaping thing not unlike that when standing before a dark cave. It was not raging or tormented like the feeling at the edge of a cliff by the sea. Here the magnitude was the same, but the feeling otherwise. There was no passion, perhaps no emotion, and certainly no warning. Here was also a precipice: a malevolent opening threatening to usurp.

He felt her arm upon his shoulder. Its wetness made it feel slimy. And although he had the feeling that she was not weak, the arm seemed to slop upon his shoulder.

Her delicious smile never vanished. It was fixed and glistening and hard like porcelain. It calmed and perplexed him. A part of him wanted to give itself up to her.

With the slopping of her arm upon his shoulder he perceived a glistening flash of oily dark green, almost black.

The thinness of the atmosphere before the chasm began to seize his thoughts. Although it was incomprehensibly still, he sensed the threat in it.

Moments before the kiss he noticed her hair. It was dark and matted, glued to her head in a slippery gloss that appeared viscous and fixed: lacquered. But the edges of her were wrong. He could think of it no other way. It was similar to a film where something is poorly super-imposed upon the background so that the edges are fleecy. More than this it was like a shimmering tear in the fabric of reality. Like a pullover becoming unstitched it was as if the substance of the world had come apart. The reek of decay came through this rip. And it was she who was piercing the structure. She who was from the other side.

And in that instant he knew he was completely alone amongst the reeds.

But he had given himself up to the irresistible kiss. Physically and mentally he found her irresistible. Her strong embrace dipped him like a Latin lover, a last tango. He flinched and shuddered as he tried to gulp down the impossibly long thick column of water.

10

Muscular and fluid, like a Moray eel, her slick tongue reached down into his chest. His last sensation was seeing the water climb the edges of his face; her lips sealed over his in an open-eyed, foul-tasting kiss that never ended.

* * *

The house was still: suspended.

High above a sparrowhawk targeted its prey.

The forms outside were not loud but their boisterousness lacked reverence. They were silhouetted and fluted, first by the sunlight and then by the frosted glass of the front door. Through the glass they resembled bizarre ant-like aliens. Their limbs and torsos were drawn and blown like glass: capillary fine in places, beetle bulbous in others.

The grating sound of the key in the lock was beak upon bone. The opening of the door was a crack of the old man's knees, a furious beat of wing and the stale air sighed like lungs expelling a last breath. An intrusion of blinding daylight coincided with the sudden plunging of the feathered predator.

"Wait," he said, not registering the mute snarling yawn of the languishing cat, retrieving the key from the lock and pushing the door inward.

The pattern of daylight dappled upon the carpet as the door was swept aside. It had been undisturbed for a number of days, shimmering with the occasional breeze. Now it was replaced by an askew square, its edges fudged by the fibres of the carpet and the diffusion of uncertain light. The light reached the skirting board that was gouged by a cruel claw.

Fresh air invaded the stale, but the latter was stubborn.

He turned to her and put out his arms; the labelled key still in his hand.

"Oh, Chris." She smiled. "You're such a romantic. But is it wise?"

"No, it's not. But I'm going to do it anyway."

She smiled and allowed him to pick her up.

He carried her merely three steps into the house. She thought he would jokingly stagger with the exertion and although her arms were about his neck she was ready to reach for a wall. Instead he was serious and his steps cautious.

"Jeez. Are you sure you're only seven months?" he groaned.

Chris put her down. Then he crunched up his face. But she was the one to speak.

"It still smells in here."

If the house had been an animal, then it had eaten something exceedingly foul. The opening of the door had been as good as a belch, the vile smell coming up from the belly of it. It was an indescribable smell, one that spoke of animal, urine, decay and festering.

"Yeah."

Outside a lone bloodied feather swung lazily to the ground.

Looking into the house the stairs were to their left. To the right was the front room. This is where he went and she followed.

He was at the windows, his palms on the sill, his eyes scanning the wooden frames.

"What's wrong?" she asked.

Completely engrossed, he did not answer.

"Chris?" He turned to her, startled.

"Huh?"

"They're bay windows. They're made like that."

"Er, yeah," – he was not there – "I, er, know."

"Chris, darling," she began, moving towards him. "I'll take back what I said."

By intentionally bewildering him she now had his undivided attention.

"What?"

"I said: I'll take back what I said about it smelling in here."

"Yeah?"

She was losing him again. The next step was shock.

"It positively stinks."

He woke with a smile.

"You didn't think it'd leave with him, did you?" Before she could speak he directed her to the windows. "But look here Terry. The silly old buzzard not only screwed the windows shut – we can do something about that – he painted the bleeding things in too."

Teresa looked over the framework and shook her head.

"No wonder it stinks in here. Him and those cats. What can we do?"

"I'll try to break a few out, I guess."

"Let's open the back door."

"Hopefully, that isn't painted in," he said tetchily.

She knew this was going to be the cost – if not more – of the surveyor they had waived because the price of the house had overstretched their purse.

She regretted the oversight and knew that saying so would inflame Chris. He was livid. Even speculating why the old fogey had painted them in was out of the question. Old people and their exaggerated need for security sprung to mind.

"Sod's law, eh?" He smiled wearily and pecked her on the cheek. Then he left the room for the kitchen.

She remained where she stood scrutinising the window frame. Satisfied that she could do nothing she turned to look back into the empty room.

"Can we open a window?" she had asked some weeks ago.

"No," said the old man. "Bones, you know."

He was sitting in the corner in an old padded chair that resembled a throne. He was not smiling. And he was not smirking. But there had been something in his eyes. A catlike smugness: a secret. His face bespoke age. The shock of close-cropped white hair drew one's attention. On another face, a crueller face, he could have been taken for an ex-military man. But something suggested that this was not what he had been: the rounded shoulders perhaps. The wooden grain of his features was set like bark, banishing expression and therefore emotion. He was not craggy, more weathered. Not that he could be mistaken for a seafaring man. But one hundred years of experience were carved into his face. What had he endured to cement his face so permanently?

That was her first impression.

Later, after the visit, she felt his environment inexplicably connected to him and the secret. And the secret bound him to the house and his cats.

The cats.

She had counted six in the room with them. Entering the house she had noticed two in the kitchen and one at the top of the stairs. And then outside she had seen one on the garden wall and another sauntering along the path leading to the back garden.

Although there was little movement from them, as if they were permanent fixtures, she was continually aware of their presence. One was curled up behind the television set, near the socket, its head not visible. It was a kind of orange-ginger colour: a living Davy Crockett hat. Another two sat upon the window sill; both were black and white. One of these watched them with wide and then contracted eyes, the other with its eyes shut sat as if it had no legs, like a duck on water. One sat under Chris's chair and another at the wall near the door. These two were of that camouflage grey-green tabby type. The last, also a tabby, was upon the old man's lap, purring now and then like a little motor boat. On entering the room after the tour of the house, this one had jumped upon Ricketts the instant he had sat down. It had circled in his lap, its claws catching his trousers, before it settled down.

Teresa had the feeling that should one approach the old man the cats would be upon them. Yet, despite this passive hostility, she did not feel intimidated. If the truth be known she was rather scornful of the entire set-up. This was his world and they were intruders.

As to the scene everything was doused in a dry brown hue. The pattern of the cloth covering the chairs was lost: faded or worn. The colour of the carpet was also hard to describe: grey, brown, patterned, plain? The wallpaper was plain and the curtains were a heavy chocolate brown. Teresa noticed that they had been put up the wrong way round. Appearances were more important. Such a setting, although uninspired, could be thought of as restful. Here it was drab and careless. The air seemed clogged. Muddy would have been a good description for the turgid feel of the room, although it was too dry. And the word musty lost the feel of heaviness. The air seemed to be warm, dry and damp at the same time. She felt that it was clogged with fine animal hairs. Light fibres of asbestos fluff – maybe they were damp? – floating in the room. They were drying up her throat, chafing her skin, making her feel irritably hot.

"Why are you selling?" Chris had asked.

Teresa had normally all but cut herself off from the weary sequence of questions. She only picked up the unusual answer; all else was merely background noise. Like on the radio, she was conditioned to its dross, but things out of the ordinary jumped out and she had attuned herself to selecting these for scrutiny. So it was Chris who went laboriously through the set questions until now; to her, they sounded so hackneyed and rehearsed, much like an uninspired DJ. But old Mr Ricketts had demanded her full attention, even her wits, from the outset.

However, the overall smell in the house had put her on edge. It demanded a certain concentration. In addition she wanted to be out and into the fresh air as soon as possible, so the quicker things went the better.

Was the old buzzard smiling?

"Stairs."

Chris waited and Teresa felt sorry for him. He was leaning too far forward for a glance at her and she knew he probably wanted her reassurance that he was not being stupid.

The answer, however, seemed to be enough for the old man, for he looked down upon the animal he was stroking at his lap.

Was he smiling?

She felt the horribly oppressive stench of the animals that was more than urine and wrapped itself about her like a heavy coat. She would take a bath later.

The child inside her kicked.

"How do you mean, er, Mr Ricketts?" Chris asked eventually.

"Too much for me now," he rattled.

She cringed at the tone of him. He was acting a main character part and, as far as she was concerned, he had not earned the right to presume such an elevated role. It was an elevation that put him on the high ground, which he already had by default because he was at home. She felt the awkwardness of distance.

"An' the hills."

"Ah, I see," Chris said, almost apologetically.

Next question.

Teresa could mouth the words with her husband. Naturally, she refrained from doing so.

"Has anybody else been to see the place?"

The old man seemed to contemplate the question.

She knew that her husband would be beginning to wonder whether Ricketts had heard him, but hoped that he would not demean himself repeating the question. That would be playing right into the old man's hands. Please Chris, wait him out, she had almost prayed.

The smell was like smoke in the room. It seemed to cloud her vision. She knew this to be the first wisps of nausea. But she could not ask for a drink of water. The two of them had seen the cracks and stained rings on the cups that hung from the wooden tree in the kitchen. They had declined Ricketts' offer of coffee or tea.

Perhaps he had not heard him?

"Aye," — oh no, did he think he was Long John Silver? — "a wee lad." He looked down upon the fur in his lap. "Interested." There was more. "Last week. Didn't like him."

She then realised that he never spoke in complete sentences. Neither did he speak in riddles. The listener simply had to fill in the missing words. Was it part of the charade?

She had hoped her husband would ask why he had not liked the boy and to her joy he did that, although a reply did not come.

"Oh?" Chris had queried. A cat appeared at his leg, pressing itself to his shin as it moved past.

"Sad to leave," Ricketts muttered without looking up.

This statement put her on her guard. Chris, however, was quite willing to play buddy.

"Yeah, you've been here a long time." The cat turned and ran the other side of its velvet body against his leg.

The sequence of questions was shot. Offers on the house normally came next. They had done problems with the house, but they had not covered the neighbours and the neighbourhood.

"Since marriage."

Now things were wide open. Where was his wife? Was she dead? Teresa had noticed a feminine quality to some of the artefacts about the house. In the bedroom she had noticed a picture of a magnified butterfly upon a leaf. And the room had the feel that nothing had changed since this date or earlier. Upon the dressing table – in itself testifying to the presence of a woman at some time – was an ornate bowl with a lip of gold and delicate primroses and violets painted upon a white background. Its style was baroque without the bloated cherubs. She had noticed an ornament in the unused front bedroom. A cast of a cluster of roses, entirely in copper green, with no apparent purpose other than to mirror the ceiling rosette. There was something neo-classical or even gothic to the feel of some of the ornaments: something that suggested death to Teresa. Whatever, these things and others in the house had been the only evidence of possible female presence; there were no perfumes, soaps, brushes, cosmetics, and not even a photograph. Almost everything pointed to a stale bachelor existence.

Small but realistic heads of rogues hung upon the walls in the hallway, stairs and back room. They were weathered, tanned characters, craftsmen that resembled pirates. Little people encased in the walls. Their realism gave them the appearance of shrunken heads;

petrified expressions, glint in a life-like eye, hint of presence behind an enigmatic smile. Indeed, Ricketts, because of his lack of expression, could be seen as a mildly animated version of one of these unsettling fixtures. Teresa found herself checking that they had not changed their expression when she was not looking.

Chris had warned not to judge the house by its contents. He had seen it once already – and along with the other they had seen earlier that day – he had selected it for Teresa's opinion. When he had seen it the previous weekend Mr Ricketts had not been present and the estate agent had shown him around. So this was also his first meeting with the owner.

"It must get quite lonely here," she probed. Despite the fact that she wanted to get out, and felt the first strains of a headache coming on, she was not satisfied.

His eyes came up to meet her. They flickered and she saw something despicable, then with a blink it was gone.

He nodded slowly.

"So where are you moving to?" asked Chris with boyish enthusiasm.

Teresa slumped back within herself.

He told them that he was moving to a bungalow – no stairs – in an area with no hills.

"Of course. Very nice."

He nodded again, almost rocking.

She felt the awkwardness of her husband. She knew that he wanted to leave but was torn by how to extricate himself.

The old man did nothing. Teresa sensed his enjoyment. Could she really blame him? Wasn't it always so with people who lived alone? They didn't want the loneliness but couldn't cope with company. She knew that he was not coping. He was all defence: a fortress. A sham. But he had tapped quite effortlessly into the vein of her husband's confidence. This was Chris' failing: he reached out in such situations. There again, to her, it was also one of his attractive qualities.

"When's the bairn due?" Ricketts asked suddenly.

Teresa was as much gobsmacked by the complete sentence as she was with the strange word for a baby. Did he have Scottish connections?

"Five months," she said.

Another silence opened up between them. She looked at her husband but he was staring at the cat in Ricketts' lap and she made ready to speak.

"So, Mr Ricketts," Chris began courageously, evidently having registered her glance. "We've, er, seen all we want." He looked to her. She met his gaze. Her expression had communicated that he had not asked all the questions. "Have you any questions, love?" he asked.

Clever, she thought. She did not want to converse with Ricketts, for she could be drawn into his game. On the other hand, she could not reproach her husband later if she did not speak up now. So be it, she decided. She would play, but she would change the rules and use familiar ground.

"Have you any children?" She had looked over the artefacts in the room. They spoke of his life. The story of him. A picture of a cricket team. Strange that there were no photographs of his wife. Mr Ricketts liked cricket, she had mused. There was a tacky pun there too. Old paperback books on the shelves in the alcove said that he had not read anything for a long time. Perhaps his wife had been the reader? The seating arrangements, the position of his armchair, spoke of nights in front of the television. The two other chairs – no sofa – spoke of few guests. And perhaps, when his wife had been around, of separate people?

He did not look up.

"No."

A sudden itchy heat took her – fleas? – and lent urgency to her enquiry. "And Mrs Ricketts? She agrees to the sale? Sorry, I mean she is alive, isn't she?" Although she felt the itchiness it was Chris who appeared to be squirming in his seat.

"Yes." What happened to Long John Silver's: 'aye'?

Then, as if on cue a cat meowed.

"The cats. Hungry," he said, gruffly.

Time to go, she thought, but you don't get off that lightly.

"Yes, they're good company for you."

Chris threw her an expression of annoyance which she rode like a boxer. Then it occurred to her that perhaps she had misinterpreted his comradeship with Ricketts and that he too wanted to get out as soon as possible. Perhaps he too felt sick? This thought unbalanced her causing her wits to lose to the rising nausea.

The baby moved again.

"Aye. Food now."

"Yes, of course, they must be fed," she said over-politely.

Then the cat upon his lap began coughing dryly, its face crunched up and neck elongated with the agony. Teresa found the sight quite revolting because it accentuated her own feeling.

"Fur balls," said Ricketts.

When they got outside the stickiness did not leave her. Even the mild breeze seemed to have no effect.

"Stuffy in there," she said, as they walked to the car which was parked some way down the street.

"Yes, I wanted to get out. But you wanted to gossip."

His tone brought her back up.

"You never asked all the questions," she accused.

"Neither did you," he retorted.

"I was getting there." She felt herself giving in to the yellow treacly sickness that had coated her.

"We came to look at the house and ask him questions about it. Not about his life. I thought–" She lurched for their car. "Are you–" With a hand on the hatchback she bent over and threw up into the road. The splashing sound alone made her retch again.

And so it was now, standing in the empty front room. This memory of being sick coupled with the cloying smell of urine and animal, made her dizzy and she staggered out of her reverie. She stumbled to the doorway, the Boa constrictor about her chest, crashed against the side of the stairs and lunged for the front door.

Chris, having heard her, called out, but she did not hear him.

When he came to her she was at the side of the house, having recovered.

"Are you okay, love?" he asked, his hand upon her forearm.

"Yeah." She smiled bravely. "I spent a little too long in the front room. I was thinking about that time with Ricketts." She took a couple of deep breaths, ran her tongue over her teeth behind a closed mouth and then spat. "The place reeks of him and those cats."

"Okay, okay," he began tetchily. He looked about and then down at her sick. By the time he looked at her his mood had changed. "I'll have another go at some of the windows. And in a month's time you won't recognise the place. It'll be ours."

She turned to him with soft eyes and nodded. He smiled.

She remembered his words after that first visit. *Did you see any cat trays? The carpets are probably soaked in urine.*

"I'll come in to get some water, but I'd like to stay outside for a while."

"I can get it."

"No. It's okay."

He nodded and led the way. In the kitchen she scooped up the cold water hand to mouth. Then she left him.

From the house she looked up to the road. The slope was such that one had to descend large concrete steps, almost stone blocks, to the front door. Going through the house to the kitchen at the rear, one met the back door parallel to the front door, through which one had to descend a metal framework of a stairway, much like a fire escape, to reach the back garden. At the back of the house underneath this stairway was the door to the cellar, itself built in the foundations of the house.

They had done well to get the house on this leafy street, apart from being detached, it was near the end of a cul-de-sac and without through-traffic it was particularly quiet. Although not quite in the countryside they could be said to be situated on the edge of the city. They were not wealthy and had slightly over-stretched themselves to buy it. For what it was worth they had got a bargain. The house had a great potential. Teresa had seen that, and although she held reservations, she let herself be carried along by Chris's enthusiasm. Until this house they had only considered semis and end-terraces. After more than six months searching and successively compromising their conditions Teresa was ready and willing to see the house's potential. However, the potential was offset by the fact that a considerable amount of work needed doing just to get it into a decent state. Not one single room was as they wanted it. And their overstrained budget had just been snapped by the state of the windows. She knew that Chris had been irked by this discovery. But the house itself was relatively sound. The repairs the old buzzard had carried out had been make-shift and cheap. Enough to hold things together. Essentially he had just let things wear out. Almost everything was twenty or more years old. There was no central heating, just sixties gas fires in the downstairs rooms and absolutely nothing upstairs. Ricketts had kept an old paraffin heater on the landing. The windows were, of course, not double glazed. The house itself was exposed from all sides and being on a hill made things worse. But the slope meant that the place was dry.

She meandered slowly down the side of the house, towards the back garden. The path here was made up of long steps of about one and a half paces. The sun was out, but a breeze regulated the temperature. Nonetheless, in her skirt and blouse she felt comfortable. To one side of her was a band of turned-over dirt with some unidentifiable bushes and other plants. The monotonous wall of the house on the other side of her was unbroken except for the little window at the top of the stairs, brightening the landing. Because of the position of the house this patch of garden saw very little direct sunlight.

As she looked away from the imposing wall, brick upon brick, she heard a thud, then another, then a crack, virtually a splintering, and then the landing window shuddered open. Chris's head popped out and she was reminded of some children's television programme. "That's one," he called down triumphantly. And his head popped in. Looking away, she smiled to herself.

Teresa stopped beside the stairway at the opening to the garden. She did not see it straight away. All she saw was the central lawn, bracketed by the turned-over dirt for flowers or vegetables at each fence. Nothing notable was growing. Lots of potential, she thought. Only at the back did the grass reach the wall. It encompassed the two small trees – crab apples? – that grew directly at the boundary. The cellar door was painted the same colour as the frame of the front door and the metal stairway: black gloss. On the metal of the steps the paint had chipped in places and the brown of rust showed. He had liberally coated the metal with the paint, laying it on so thickly that he may have used a trowel instead of a paintbrush. Maybe it had not been chipped; maybe the lumps of paint had fallen away under their own weight. On the underside of the stairway was a silken network of cobwebs of such density that it could be mistaken for the spittle-like white that one sometimes found on the underside of leaves, something to do with larvae and pupae. She knew this to be called cuckoo-spit.

When her gaze left the stairway she saw it. Its stillness had caused her to overlook it. What startled her most was that it was looking directly at her. She did not know what type it was, but for its species – she guessed it to be a tabby – she knew it to be oversized. It sat impassively on the wall, between the trees in the sunlight. Its eyes took her back to her childhood days on the street, playing marbles with the others. For the marbles were hard cats' eyes. Each a black slit, a vertical ellipse with sharp ends and a blot of lifeless colour in cold glass. The cat continued its marble-hard stare and she stared back, recovering and hardening. Then the animal did something that inflamed her. It was a small thing and under different circumstances an insignificant thing. But her mood was more fragile than she realised. What it did was close its eyes on her, like an owl blinking and turning away. This complete disregard scotched her. As if the animal, totally bored by her, had pompously said she was a mere trifle, not worthy of its gaze.

She charged as best she could at the cat shooing at it as she did. At first it merely jumped up and remained in position, but she continued coming, her determination sharpening her shooing into a hiss. Then it was off with such agility – for so large an animal – that she was taken aback. It flicked its head away from her and leapt upon the roof of the shed of the neighbour's garden, situated below their own. Then it padded along for a moment, paused at the edge of the roof, checked itself, and then leapt leisurely to the wall of the garden where it casually, flauntingly, even tauntingly, ambled along in a catwalk.

Catching her breath, feeling the baby turn in her, she looked about herself, down the row of gardens and backs of houses, for she felt rather stupid chasing the cat.

As she returned to the house she noticed them amongst the bushes to her right. They were lollipop sticks bound together with what looked like clear sticky-tape. There appeared to be half a dozen or so. Tiny crosses. Some were straight, some askew. But all were too dirty to tell whether they had ever had names written upon them.

* * *

Over the next month Chris, friends and workers virtually gutted the place. Not all of the front room bay windows were opened. Wallpaper and carpets were stripped. The walls were patched and painted; the floor was sanded down. The skirting board should have been replaced, but one of the lads handy with a spatula had filled the gouges and smoothed the surface down for repainting. Teresa spent little time at the house. The furious pace and length of time the men worked emphasised her helplessness and she felt as if she was in the way. Also, all the dust and dirt flying around was far from healthy for a pregnant woman. But she didn't sit in the hotel all day flicking through magazines. When she was not getting to know the area or visiting her new doctor, she was underway with Chris or one of the workers buying necessities for the house.

Only late evening when things had settled was she at the house with Chris looking over the day's work. On one such occasion, a day or two after work had begun they were together to discuss progress and the week's strategy. Chris said he also wanted to show her something.

He took her round the back of the house. A broom had been taken to the underside of the lower steps of the metal stairway. Higher up would require the help of a ladder.

Chris unlocked the cellar. Apart from some of their boxes stacked in a corner, brought by friends who had been storing them, Ricketts had cleaned it out as agreed. He had left some garden tools which didn't bother them. But he had also left two monstrosities. One was something Chris said he could use. It was a thick wooden workbench. Although aged and gouged, in places the petrified trenches resembling a First World War battlefield, it was so solid and bombastic that even Teresa could see its usefulness. A large brutal vice was clamped at one end and Teresa couldn't help seeing it as an instrument of torture. Bones could be cracked and ground to powder by it. The other monstrosity present, a huge oak double-door wardrobe, was far more imposing simply because it took up so much room.

"I was going to call him and tell him to take it away," said Chris. "But then I saw this." He stepped away from her to his right and she moved to him to stare in the same direction.

"What is it?" she asked.

"Can't you see? Look at the beam."

The central beam to what was the floor of the backroom rested on a small stack of wood on top of the wardrobe.

"You don't mean..."

A single stone pillar situated more centrally also met the same beam.

"I don't know. But yes, it's possible the wardrobe is holding up the backroom." They were silent for a while. When he seemed satisfied that she had digested the full horror of it, he backtracked. "I can't believe it's holding up the room, but I'm reluctant to move it without someone seeing it first."

Again Teresa heard him thinking of the money saved on the surveyor being swallowed many times over by these hidden costs. But could a survey have brought the purchase price down?

She opened the doors. The stench almost knocked her over. Apart from some newspaper at the bottom, it was empty. A rail for hangers ran the width under a high shelf. A speckled mirror was attached to the inside of one of the doors.

"Whatever died here," she said, "it died in the wardrobe. What do you want to do?"

"Nothing now."

"It's an eyesore," she said. "But we can live with it for a while."

"Yeah, well, we're not going to have our house warming down here." They had promised a party after the birth. Because of the distance for both of their parents they would see the house as soon as the baby was born.

"It also stinks of him," she said. In the house the smell had succumbed to that of wallpaper glue and paint. Down here Ricketts's presence was strongly felt.

Then right on cue a cat whined.

"Yeah, they're still turning up," said Chris. "I don't know who they belong to. If I didn't know better I'd say they're strays."

"They'll stop coming when they realise there's nothing here for them."

"John puts milk out for them." He was one of the friends working on the house.

"Tell him to stop. We don't want them here."

"Okay. But I think the old woman next door does too."

"Well tell her to stop."

"I, er–"

"Then I'll tell her."

"I can do it. It's–"

"You've got enough to do. I'll tell her tomorrow."

"I think she's a bit batty. John said he spoke to her and she ignored him. He also saw her carrying a six-pack into her house."

"Maybe it's for visitors."

"Since we've been here I've never seen anybody go to her house. It wouldn't surprise me if the old bird was a wino."

"Beer and wine don't mix."

24

"A boozer, then." He shook his head. "I think they should rename this place loony street."

"Let's see. I'll speak to her tomorrow and tell her not to feed the cats."

But Teresa forgot and didn't tell her. And when she did remember, it was too late or inconvenient and she decided to do it after they'd moved in. She would have plenty of time when Chris was at work.

They also agreed to limit what they stored in the cellar because of the smell. No fabrics or anything that could take on the stench should be brought down. And they would not fill the wardrobe at all. Chris said that he feared anything that went into it would disappear and probably end up in Narnia.

Halfway through the month she was at the bank negotiating an overdraft. The hotel and supplying food and drink for the friends, giving up their days, evenings and weekends had all been calculated down to the last penny. Unforeseen snags in the renovation incurring unexpected expenses had devoured their safety thin margin.

*　*　*

The sound of the drip from the tap into the bath water was such a satisfying plop as to be voluptuous. That and the luxurious warmth were her only sensations. Her eyes were closed. But they had been open. And when they had been open she had watched the drop forming on the lip of the flecked tap. From a suggestion, indeed a lip, to a quivering body: holding on, stretching but resisting the weight of itself, ever forming, until beautifully pear-shaped, it let go and jettisoned, free-falling it hit the water with an echoing plop, a hoof upon cobblestones, but voluptuous and round, without the hard edges. Once she had tried to stem the flow with her big toe, but it had been more indulgence than a serious attempt. However, it was not a flow in the true sense of the word, more a periodic sequence. For now she had her eyes closed and tried to predict the next plop. Such was the duration of the silence between the drops that she had twice opened her eyes to check the progress of the formation. She considered this cheating.

Teresa was aware of time and not quite on a sunny beach, but she relished the moment wallowing in the heat. She felt she deserved this self indulgent luxury. Having soaped herself she lay in a watery greyness, the thought of which, although distasteful, could not dispel her wantonness. Her knees and the tip of the dome of her belly were exposed and a little cold. She had slipped down to her chin and to cover her knees would mean exposing the upper part of her torso.

"Have you fallen asleep in there?" Chris called.

She smiled. Should she top up with a bit more hot water? Or was it time to get out?

"No."

Chris was already in bed. Tomorrow was Monday and he would start his new job. Career-wise it was a good move.

He had already had a quick bath. She had washed his back. He had worked like a trouper. For that matter she too had done her fair share. Kate, Gerald's wife, had helped her unpack the kitchen things, clean shelves, as well as occasionally directing the men and finally fetching a takeaway from the nearest Chinky for the evening.

John and Gerald had constructed the bed. It was the only thing properly finished. Boxes and bags were piled up all over the place. The majority of the cupboards, shelves and wardrobes remained virtually empty. The kitchen was almost fully operational, but the bulk of the unpacking was still to be done.

By seven everyone had left.

She looked up at the boiler. At first she had been rather afraid of lying in the enamelled cast-iron bath. The large water tank, on the wall above the taps, was as big as the inside of the bath. It was an enormous thing, the weight of which she could not begin to imagine. Rounded at both ends like a capsule she was afraid that it would fall into the bath and with cartoon cruelty squash her like a bug; perhaps a single arm, the only piece of her not crushed, would reach round to embrace the monstrosity. It had been painted yellow gloss, like the bathroom itself, save the woodwork – skirting board, window sill and frame – which was naturally in the famous black gloss. Yellow and black, what a combination. Like a bumble bee. And some mad sculptor had left an unfinished metallic interpretation of the body of a bee suspended in front of her. Yet, it was not so inspiring and belonged more in the bowels of a ship rather than here in the bathroom. The boiler room, of course.

It would have to go. The bath too. In fact the entire bathroom would have to be gutted and modernised. The chunky enamel sink had the same style-less taps as the bath. The metal was mottled; the faucet formless and tube-like. Inset in the tops were cracked ivory-coloured pieces upon which the words HOT and COLD were written in black. The boiler put the installation of a shower out of the question. For now they would have to use a flexi-plastic attachment for their hair.

All this would be done when they had saved enough to install central heating.

Not everything was negative. Upstairs the smell was all but eradicated. Downstairs it was more noticeable and in the cellar it was diabolical.

She had not wanted to go down to the cellar; she didn't like the metal stairs and that meant going the long way out of the front door and round the house. But her favourite peeler had been misplaced. Packing at the flat had begun organised, each box's contents scrawled in marker pen, but towards the end they had thrown things in. Words like miscellaneous, bits and bobs, odds and ends, and etc. began to appear as additions or even titles. Added to this was the chaos of two moves. Their belongings had first gone into storage in friends' cellars and garages. A lorry had done the rounds collecting the larger objects and their friends had transported the remainder.

For dessert after the Chinese take-away she wanted to make a fruit salad for everyone. She had quelled any protest with a statement of her craving for something fresh.

Being her favourite the peeler had been one of the last things to be packed. She had an inkling in which box it had disappeared. When Chris said it was in the cellar she couldn't back down. The peeler was one of her accepted foibles, but it now threatened to exacerbate a long and demanding day. She asked him to come with her.

Before she could gauge his mood Chris opened the kitchen door to the metal stairway. Rather than leave via the front door she followed him out. Her husband crashed ahead of her, the structure shuddering under his hasty descent. She stepped out with something akin to trepidation. The construction was firmly bolted to the house, but its clang and exposure made it feel insecure. The exposure lay in the gaps between the supporting rods of the hand-rail and the fact that the steps were metal mesh. They revealed the ground below and not only emphasised the drop, but seeing the out-of-sync movement of the ground rendered descent, especially descent, uncertain. Something akin to vertigo upset her progress.

Teresa steeled herself and ran the gauntlet, one hand finger-tipping the wall of the house, the other using the hand rail that ran the outer edge of the affair by way of a banister. A child could easily slip between the supporting rods of this banister.

The framework groaned under her weight, but essentially the structure was sound.

When she reached the bottom she had to fight a rising anger against her husband. She knew it was wrong to blame him for making her use the stairs and this infuriated further. Then maybe her anger was there to combat any protest from him about retrieving the peeler.

Chris had unlocked the cellar door but was standing outside. "All yours," he said.

When she looked into the cellar she had a job overcoming her disappointment. She had not realised how much had come down here. There were at least two dozen boxes. Luckily they were in stacks of two or three and there were corridors between them.

She went in and the stench increased. It hung in the cellar.

"We have to get as much of this out of here as soon as possible," she said reading the writing on the boxes. Unfortunately the boxes were simply stacked and the writing was sometimes hidden.

Teresa moved about and Chris remained at the door.

"I could help if you'd tell me what box we're looking for," he said.

"I'm not sure," she said distractedly.

"Great."

She cringed but maintained her composure.

Then she said: "I'm looking for classics." She was referring to their collection of classic literature.

"Why–" he began, but thought better of it and fell silent. He entered the cellar and began looking over the boxes for their writing.

"Here it is," she said, at a top box in a corridor of boxes that ended at the wardrobe. She held a broom that had been leaning against the stack in her hand.

"Are you sure it's in there?"

Her expression was the answer.

"Let's get it out, then."

"It's probably slipped to the bottom. Let's take the box. I don't want these books down here, anyway. And I can fill the front room bookcase tomorrow."

"Okay."

28

She stepped aside and he grunted with exertion as he lifted the box.

"You could have chosen a lighter one," he groaned. Humour had returned. "Take the key."

She took the cellar key from his hand. The corridor hindered his manoeuvrability and she hastily stood the broom and shouldered boxes aside.

"I'll go round the front," he said, when they were outside.

"Yeah, I don't like those stairs. They're too rickety."

Her choice of word made him laugh and she did too. "Rickety," he said, before setting off.

She turned to lock the door. As she closed it, the broom she had stood at one stack fell to lean against the opposite stack and barred the way to the wardrobe like a barrier.

Yes, it had been a long and busy day and she was glad of the solitude and peace of the bath. However, the water was getting cold and she'd already topped up twice. It was time to get out.

She thought she could get out without trouble. This was a mistake. She slid up into a sitting position; evaporation immediately chilling her bare wet skin. She shuffled forward mindful of the palpitating water and for a moment she tried to use her toes to pull the beaded chain of plug. But her grip was no match against the weight of water and she quickly gave up. With her hands on the edges of the bath she attempted, unsuccessfully, to lift her body sufficiently to bring her legs beneath herself.

The lapping of the water muffled the sound for her. But she heard enough to freeze and listen. She heard the bed springs twang. Then her husband said something about slippers and a second later she heard his yelp.

"What is it?" she called.

But he didn't answer and she recklessly turned on all fours, the water rising violently to the top of the bath. He said something but she didn't catch it.

"What?" she called; standing and making ready to step out.

"I stubbed my bloody toe!" He was now on the landing or the stairs. She couldn't tell.

When she out on the landing, having hastily dried herself and pulled on her towelling robe, he was nowhere to be seen. The cold swept up from the stairs and shot up her calves and under her robe. Behind her the sound of the emptying bath compelled her to go down the stairs. And the cold held her back. She stepped down a couple of steps to see the front door wide open.

"Chris?" she called, but not loudly.

The cold was like a living thing: an ice-breathing dragon. It was invisible and that flew into the house and up the stairs. The experience was a cold rushing in rather than the heat fleeing. A huge claw grasped her head – her hair was damp – and the body of the thing entwined her from below, starting about her ankles. Strangely, there was no wind of sorts, not even a zephyr. She was not arrested by the sensation; she was frightened.

A cat yelped viciously. Fight or flight? She couldn't tell.

The sound took her back to another time. It was a flashed image, rather than an indulgence. Then, too, she had been oddly numb to the feeling. It had also been dark. The simple romance of the Greek setting had battled with the collective boisterousness of the group. They had completed their meal and were waiting for their plates to be removed, sipping Retsina and beer and milky ouzo with water. The table told more of a ravenous party than a civilised dinner: fish and chicken bones, remnants of taramosalata, calamares, chips and vegetables devastated, husks of lemon and little cairns of olive stones. Flies tried to settle upon the scene of destruction, but they were constantly waved off. The pedestrian zone was an avenue bordered by restaurants and gift-shops. The tables – every one of them taken – spilled out into the zone and it was hard to distinguish were one restaurant ended and another started. The customers and passers-by were young, like themselves, but probably not all of them were students. Thus the atmosphere had been buzzing with life. The boys in the group had been alternately court jesters and sages and the girls accordingly giggly and sober. The cry had come from a neighbouring restaurant. People had been slow to react. Like a crowd being hailed by a speaker. But as the sound persisted so the diners grew hushed. It was a violent, tearing sequence of catty screams: an animal in the throes of death. People looked dully in the general direction of the kitten, but tried not to stare. It was in the open, spinning and clawing as if desperately trying to fend off some invisible attacker. The common consensus of opinion was that the grey waif of an animal was choking on a bone. The fight lasted no more than thirty seconds, perhaps no more than twenty seconds. It was the silence after the sudden stillness of the animal that she remembered. Not long after the death of the animal things were as before and some twenty minutes later nobody but her seemed to notice the owner of the neighbouring restaurant pick up the furry bag of bones and fling it into the dirt in a bricked surround at the foot of a nearby tree. What remained with her was not any feeling of callousness on the part of the restaurant owner, but how everyone had looked on. What could they have done? A shovel to its head? Its incomprehensible agony in its last moments would leave it forever spinning in her memory. A blur of movement. It was the same with this cold that moved about her ankles; she did nothing. She did not stamp her foot or bring down a shovel. She let it take its course.

The dull tinny clang of metal upon metal snapped her back to the present.

Teresa descended the stairway barefoot. The front entrance was empty. It was a gaping rectangle. The door was wide open. Defenceless.

And something more wholesome was entering the house. Something lasting. The ice dragon had been followed by a more sinister being. And this new, growing cold was tangibly evil. Here, near the bottom of the stairs, the smell had been dwarfed: shoved to some corner and shackled.

She heard movement outside. Somebody coming this way.

Now the cold was not so shocking. But it was still growing. Filling out the house, as if it had been exposed for a thousand years. The fragile warmth that had been was barely a memory. The Outside stood before her and the house too was becoming part of the void. The cold isolated her as if she were the only person alive. It encroached her delicate body warmth, which itself began to shrink into the very core of her.

She began to move forward.

A moth fluttered in. Hugging the ceiling, moving from point to point, it headed towards the kitchen.

She watched the fat furry thing beating its wings in a rapid, velvet droning that was almost silence. The sight of it dried the roof of her mouth. She associated the soft and yet evil fawn creature with suffocating woolly jumpers, the fibres of which filled out her lungs with a network of tangled softness. Her mouth filled with feathers and her lungs were gasping and inflamed. She was drowning in a mute scream.

Outside the scraping sound of feet upon gritty concrete saved her. There was no comfort. She remained in solitude. The frame of the door framed her vision and tunnelled her sight.

The only visible evidence of the progress of the cold was her goose-bumped skin. She could not tell how deep it had eaten into her. The cold had swamped her and she had all but abandoned her body to it. She would continue to move forward. She would step out into the night. Barefoot, she would move toward the heart of the cold, of which her own heart was becoming a part. Her heart was growing as cold as this night.

Chris suddenly appeared from the side of the frame and she jumped. But he didn't notice.

"Bloody cat," he snapped. "It jumped over the fence when I went round the corner."

He was in the house, his back to her to close the door. The motion swept the cold and more squeezed round the door and a frosty tongue shot up her legs and her eyes widened.

Her expression stopped him in his tracks when he turned.

"You're as white as a sheet," he said.

The baby moved and her hand instinctively moved to her belly.

"What was it?" she asked.

"A cat," he said, bewildered. "It must've knocked off the dustbin lid." She had passed the bin on her way to the garden earlier that day. It was a pretty bashed up affair. More than likely the bin men were not too careful about carrying it up and down the steps. Nonetheless it had taken a fair beating and consequently the lid no longer fitted but rather balanced on top. "I, er, put a brick on top." He stepped to her. "Are you alright?"

"Yes. Fine. Just a little cold." Had something evil entered her womb?

He hugged her.

Teresa had felt as if a cold lonely thing had entered the house. Chris had shut it out. As he closed the front door it had fled with a barely audible whoosh. He had heard nothing. The thing had come into the house and because he had not felt it, he was in some way immune to it, safe like a non-living thing: like the quilt cover that lay upon her, for instance. The plane of the beast was simply not within his universe. But before leaving the thing had done something. Had it merely touched her? Or had it planted something?

She knew that it would be useless talking to him about it. He would be rational and logical. And he could always fall back upon her hormones clouding her. Then, she was not sure she could do justice to the feeling in words. She had always been the more receptive of the two and therefore the vulnerable one.

As she lay in the darkness, holding herself, her mind inexplicably seeking traces of the smell in the air, such that she was not sure whether it was real or a memory, she heard the distant wail of a cat identical to the crying of a baby.

Chris was fast asleep.

And although it was their first night she began to dislike the house.

* * *

The day started badly. And it didn't get much better.

Her nights were not restful times. They were an endless see-saw of being thirsty and wanting to relieve herself. Her full womb didn't leave much space for her bladder.

That Monday morning she had barely registered Chris getting up for work. Oh, she'd smiled at his goodbye kiss and may have drowsily wished him luck.

He had been gone more than an hour by the time she opened her eyes.

She grabbed his pillow and put it on top of hers, leaning it against the headboard and then shifted herself into a sitting position. Her glass next to her bedside clock was empty and she picked up the plastic pitcher.

She was planning her day, only half aware of her action when something in the pitcher of water caught her eye. It was at the lip of the vessel and had plopped into her glass before she could react. Her shock was the freezing rather than the heated kind. She didn't hot-headedly throw or drop the pitcher. Instead she froze for a moment before calmly placing it back onto the bedside cabinet.

Teresa didn't pick up the glass. She just looked blankly at the moth floating on the surface of the water. In horror she studied the soft insect. Even wet its cushiony down repelled the water. Its spread-eagled wings were shimmering perfection. Were its colours brighter, were its body more slender, in fact, were it more like a butterfly, it could have been beautiful. Instead there was something sinister about it. Like an owl there was inherent danger in its design, in its integral silence, in its lethal stealth.

Just the thought of having drunk water in which the thing lay made her want to spit.

She took the glass and flushed its contents down the toilet. She then gave her teeth an extra long brushing.

In the kitchen the pitcher and glass went into the dishwasher. Over breakfast she browsed the newspaper. Leaving the radio on, she went to the boxes of books in the back room. There she began to fill the empty shelving. Occasionally she allowed herself to be distracted from the task and delved into a book. She could have finished in half the time, but she was in no hurry. Eventually the boxes were empty and she unfolded and collapsed them and stacked them against a wall.

She had decided to adorn some of the walls with their smaller pictures. She knew where the box was in the cellar, although she had no intention of attempting to bring it into the house. She would choose some pictures and bring only them.

Teresa left by the front door and realised that it was a shame to be inside on such a summer's day. As she walked down the side of the house she decided to put up a few pictures and then sit in the garden for a while. Maybe she could doze. It was that kind of day.

She passed the dustbin with the brick on top of its lid. There were no cats in sight. But she recalled the baby cries. Thoughts linked and she resolved to speak to the neighbour later. Hopefully she wasn't a boozer. Perhaps they could sit in the garden together?

Movement on the underside of the metal stairs caught her attention. On a large cobweb a fat orange spider with black spots, its legs moving deftly in a coordinated flurry, like typewriter hammers under the expert control of a touch typist, spun a black raisin that was once an insect. The sight made her shudder and when her gaze wandered up the underside of the black stairs she saw that this web was one of many. She knew they would be forever brushing this underside.

Then she was at the cellar door. The uneven gloss of the black paint made it look as if it were perpetually melting. Like ancient glass it was a viscous oozing mass descending the door over the decades. In this sunlight it appeared to be sweating.

As she pushed the key in she thought she heard a noise inside and she froze. She waited and listened, moving closer to the door but not turning the key. She heard nothing.

She remained poised, wondering whether or not to open the door.

Bracing herself, she turned the key and pulled the door open. All was still and she put the noise down to her imagination. She stepped forward. A Daddy-long-legs on spindly Dali-exaggerated stilts moved away in gangly, robotic awkwardness. Its comparably tiny soft bead of a body, made it appear emaciated. As she reached in to switch on the light something moved and before she could bring a hand to her mouth a cat appeared from behind a box and shot past her legs. By the time she turned it had jumped onto the neighbour's fence.

Anger bubbled up within her.

The vile smell assaulted her nostrils and inflamed her anger further.

She would get the damned pictures and go straight to the neighbour.

As she calmed she began to puzzle over how the cat had got in. Was there another entrance? She left the cellar and went round the house looking for another means of access. The cellar had no windows. Maybe there was a hole?

Despite being outside the smell lingered. Her clothes had absorbed it or her imagination was soaked in it. Whatever, it seemed present in all its cloying glory.

She went round the entire house.

She found nothing and returned to the cellar. At the box she pulled out four small framed pictures. A twinge of fear brushed the hairs on the back of her neck. A coldness seemed to clutch her heart. It was not only a physical sensation – the warmth of the day could not enter the room – it was something else that was no less tangible.

All the while she was irked.

Something was different.

Outside she leant the pictures against the wall to lock the door. As she closed it she saw what was wrong. She opened it wide and switched the light back on. But she didn't go in. She merely looked at the wardrobe at the end of the corridor of boxes. Her view was unhindered. The broom was not how she had left it. It stood against one stack of boxes and no longer leaned from one wall to the other. Had Chris been down here in the morning? Could the cat have moved it?

She stared at the thick workbench. The legs were like the beams of a sailing ship. He had left his vice. Strange that he should leave it. Chris had told her they were quite expensive. A large, chunky horseshoe clamped the side of the bench, the gripping surfaces made of metal blocks of a different material. It was a large brutal looking th–

Her eyes strained. The hush of death engulfed the room. Could she take a step forward to check? Of course she could move closer. But she did not move. Instead she craned her neck forward and tried to stare what she thought she could see into concrete reality. It was no good; she would have to move further in. So she took one step towards the vice. Again she scrutinised the device, but still she could not be certain. Before she moved again and this time she would be at the workbench, she turned and glanced at the daylight behind her. There was the day, bright and alive. Here was cold and dead. Yes, despite the spiders and other creepy-crawlies the place seemed devoid of life.

She stepped forward.

Looking down upon the vice she confirmed what she thought she had seen. There was a small knot of hair on the corner of one of the gripping surfaces. Had they been there earlier? From a distance they could have been mistaken for a crushed Daddy-long-legs, but now she was certain. They were not long or thin enough or even jerky enough to be such a spider's legs. Then again, she could not say they were human hairs. Perhaps an animal? Her imagination was lapping at the sides of her thinking. Ricketts crushing the head of one of his beloved cats in the thing. Saliva running down his chin from a grinning mouth. Ghoulish eyes about to pop out of his head. And–

She reached down and picked up the yellow pencil on the floor. It was an ordinary graphite pencil, 2H. She wanted to clear her mind and would not normally have read the type. The placing of it upon the workbench where it rolled into one of the many trenches was over too soon. Still she pushed the thing away. The pencil lay in the groove. How the surface of the bench resembled something living. The wood was so worn, gouged and scarred, almost wrinkled, that it resembled elephant hide. It was tough and somehow soft and reminded her of something like baked leather. The trenches running the length of the bench had been scratched on by elephant tusks. Her imagination refused to be ignored and to shock her from her indulgence it swelled the workbench. Indeed, she saw the surface swell as if it were a living thing: a slumped ebony rhinoceros.

She had to get out.

With a furrowed brow she locked up, picked up the pictures and returned to the house.

Try as she might she couldn't quite build up any enthusiasm putting up the pictures. What could have been a joy, branding the walls, stamping home their mark was an empty chore. She measured up, inverted the house broom to hold the frames in place, stepped back, tried alternative pictures, various positions, but nothing gelled. There was no satisfaction, no pleasure. And so she didn't put any of the pictures up.

She gave up and made herself lunch and a cup of tea.

She was sitting at the dining table in the back room when the thud occurred. She had finished eating and was drinking her tea. Her hand jumped and hot liquid slopped onto her fingers. She hastily put the cup down, knowing it would leave a ring and flicked her hand with pain.

Then she was at the window, seeing the smudge, looking outside trying to see as close to the house as possible, looking at her hand.

The quickest way down was through the kitchen and down the metal stairs. There was no time to think. She clambered down as fast as she could, hating the clumsy clang and unsteadiness. At the bottom she turned to the back of the house.

Lying in front of the cellar door was a twitching sparrow. The angle of its head was awkward. Just as she had stood before the cellar door after hearing the noise, the dilemma froze her. Of course she acted quickly. An observer would have said that she moved within seconds. But to her she seemed to stand there for an age.

The decision she had to make was literally life and death. Should she fetch a shoe box or something similar or something hard and heavy to put the poor thing out of its misery? She chose the latter and used the railing to yank herself back up the steps.

She wanted to collect the key to the cellar to fetch the garden shovel, but saw the broom and grabbed that instead.

As she went down the steps she saw the white-haired neighbour in her garden. She had her back to her, hunched over flower or vegetable beds. Teresa marvelled that her noisy descent didn't disturb her.

When she turned the corner the bird was gone. For a moment she was flummoxed. Had she dreamt the episode?

Then she saw the cat, sitting on the other neighbour's shed, the sparrow hanging from its mouth. She prayed that it was dead.

Teresa stood rigid with frustration. There was nothing she could do. The cat was too far away. Oh, she prayed that the sparrow was dead.

* * *

Although the cat had long disappeared, Teresa stared in the direction it had gone. She felt profoundly depressed as she turned to go back to the house. Through the hedge she glimpsed her neighbour and strode over. "Hallo," she called after the old woman. Teresa was certain she was within earshot, but the woman ignored her. "Hallo!" she called again, louder this time, so that there could be no doubt. But the woman didn't falter or turn and, carrying a shallow plate or bowl, went into her house.

Miffed, Teresa returned ponderously to the kitchen. Once there she could not whip up the enthusiasm to start dinner. Passing the pictures leaning against the wall had not helped her mood one iota.

When Chris entered the house an hour and a half later she was sitting in the dining room. "Hi, I'm home." His jovial frame of mind, which could be seen in the breeziness of his expression and in the tone of his voice, vanished when he saw her.

She attempted a brave smile.

"What is it?" he asked, dropping his briefcase and striding to her.

"I've had a bad day." The words were barely out before she began to cry.

"What happened?" he asked bending down to hug her.

After a moment she wiped her tear and laughed uncertainly. "It's silly really. And I wanted to be so productive today."

"I saw the pictures in the hall."

"Yes, but a bird hit the kitchen window and a cat got it. And another cat jumped out of the cellar when I went to get the pictures and I can still smell the cellar on me. The neighbour ignored me. And oh yes, there was a moth in my water—"

"What? What? Wait. Tell me from the top. But let me get you a cup of tea; that one looks cold."

She nodded and he took the cup from her.

"I wanted to surprise you with dinner too," she called after him.

By the time he had returned with the tea she had regained her composure and wanted to hear all about his first day. But he insisted that she told him about her day first.

When she told him of the cat jumping out of the cellar he could only suggest that it had sneaked in when they weren't looking.

Their financial situation stopped her from broaching the subject of changing the cellar lock. Apart from the cellar, the locks to the house had been changed during the month-long renovation.

When she had finished relating the events of her day she said she could possibly whip something up for him to eat. He suggested preparing the meal together then he could tell her about Hugh the boss, who was nicknamed 'Hug-aitch', and his secretary, Babs with the big boobs.

* * *

Teresa was in the kitchen, daydreaming at the sink, when the knocking began. But that was not what spooked her and sent her hastening to the telephone.

Once again she had missed Chris getting up for work. There had been a cat crying in the small hours and long after it had ceased she had remained awake. Consequently she had not only missed her husband rising, she had also got up later than she had planned.

By ten she had finished her breakfast at the dining table in the back room and had just finished unloading the dishwasher when she was shaken by the sound of someone banging the pipes with something blunt.

This was not the sharp tone of metal upon metal. Indeed, two things were unusual about the sound. The first was that it was not deafening or particularly loud, but penetrating. It seemed to echo in her mind. So much so she tried to will it to stop, like tinnitus or the high-pitched buzz one sometimes picks up. The second thing added to the illusion that she was imagining it. The sound defied location. Apart from the fact that it wasn't coming from upstairs, she couldn't tell where it originated.

The sound was more than a thud. It was a staccato thumping. And it was so bruising, the urge to flee the house was strong. Instead she frantically, almost in a panic, went from room to room.

She left the kitchen and stood in the hall. From there she went into the back room. Again she stood listening, turning her head, straining to hear a difference in the pitch. Seconds later she fled the room, suppressing the urge to cover her ears, and entered the front room. She pushed the door open and stepped in. The sound appeared no different, but she again turned her head in an effort to locate the source. Her unseeing gaze panned over the bookshelf, across the mantelpiece, to the wall above the television. Her distracted gaze was moving on to the bay windows when the periphery of her unconscious vision snagged on an image in the blank screen of the television. It looked like the reflection of an old woman. Teresa snapped her head to behind the door, where the person had to be standing. There was nobody and when she looked back at the screen there was nothing there too. The entire duration of the visual experience was no more than a second. But such was its impact she didn't notice that the banging had stopped until a full five seconds later. And then only some moments after this did she realise that she was hyperventilating, one palm drawn to her labouring chest, the other protecting the mound of her womb.

She was so stunned, she remained rooted to the spot, staring at the blank screen, straining to retain and scrutinise the appearance of the woman. But the details were fading like a half-remembered dream. The woman appeared small, but not frail, more tight-lipped and critical. Her white blouse was buttoned all the way up, but her limp cardigan hung open. Her hair was indiscernible: fair, perhaps white. The face was flour-white, soft and unreal in the medium. It did not transcend the medium but was firmly embedded in it, like strangers in old photographs are bereft of the dimension of personality. So too then, this person was steamrollered into the medium, the edges ill-defined, fuzzy. Only by contrast did the face manifest itself.

The realisation that the banging had ceased sent her rushing to the phone.

She was thrown by the woman's voice that answered her husband's number, and the moment it took for the woman to reel off the cheery company greeting wasn't enough for her to recover. Teresa announced that she was Chris's wife and asked to speak to him. Her tone must have given her away, because after the woman said that he was in a meeting, she offered to fetch him. Teresa's hesitation was interpreted as a yes and the woman switched on the piped music.

Whilst she waited, staring at the lounge door, she decided only to tell him about the pipes. She was recovering and had to consciously hold on to the horror as it dissipated and threatened to slip into bagatelle.

A good two minutes passed before Chris came on the line.

He did not hide his concern. "Terry. What's wrong?"

"I'm sorry to call you out of your meeting." She found herself having to feign her earlier distress. Such was the extent of her recovery.

"Never mind about that. Tell me what's wrong. You sound awful."

"Who was that on the phone?"

"That was Babs. Barbara, remember? What's wrong?"

"The pipes started making a terrible banging sound."

"I can't hear anything."

"It's stopped now." Her story was in danger of being trivialised. "I was frightened. I, er, thought they were going to explode."

"Now you mention it I remember when we were doing the place up the electrician said he had heard the pipes knocking. We never heard it. It's no wonder what with all the work that was going on..." Her silence forced him to continue. "It's probably the water pipes. Maybe a fluctuation in the pressure caused them to clang. Or perhaps there were some road works nearby, you know, drilling or something vibrating, making them knock and setting up some kind of resonance. What do you think?"

"I don't know."

"Well, unless there's water spurting out of the walls, I don't think we can do any more than keep an eye on it." He wanted to get back to his meeting. Perhaps he was wondering why she had pulled him out of it in the first place.

"There's something else."

"Oh?"

"I saw someone in the television. It was switched off. But there was a reflection."

"What?"

"Like a reflection."

"An apparition?"

"Yes."

"Is it still there?"

"I don't think so. It was only there for a split second."

"What did this person look like?"

"An old woman."

Silence.

"Chris?"

"I'm sure it was just a trick of the light. The banging probably stressed you." He prudently didn't suggest that all the hormones swimming about in her because of the pregnancy were turning her loopy. "Let's talk about this when I get home. You've got your appointment soon, haven't you?"

"Yes."

"Good. It'll get you out of the house. I'll come home early. I promise. Okay?"

* * *

Chris had used public transport to get to work, leaving her with the car to get to the doctor's for her fortnightly check-up. He would have liked to accompany her, but they had agreed that his meeting on his second day at his new place of work took precedence.

Teresa was surprised how much she missed her husband at the sound scan. Although the doctor enthused, she felt it a joy unshared.

Returning home she was locking the car when she saw the old neighbour put a saucer down on the path at the side of her house. The woman turned and headed for her front door.

Teresa called out: "Excuse me." But she was ignored and the woman entered her house and closed the door.

Teresa was determined and, after dropping off the bag of shopping in the kitchen, she went to the neighbour's house.

She rang the doorbell and waited.

And waited.

She rang again, this time noticing that there appeared to be no sound. So she tapped the knocker resoundingly.

She waited, her determination dissipating by the second.

The bell was given another longer press.

She was just about to leave when she sensed a change in the light beyond the closed door.

She pressed the bell again and tapped the knocker and then she heard movement.

There was the sound of a chain being slipped into place and a muffled voice saying: "Just a minute." Then the door opened an inch or so. "Yes?"

"I'm your next door neighbour," said Teresa to the partial face.

"Yes. I've seen you."

"I, er, wonder if I could talk to you?" She could see the conversation continuing on the doorstep. After all, there was no reason the old woman should let her in.

So she half-expected her to answer something along the lines of: "you are." Instead she again said: "Just a minute." She then closed and reopened the door without the chain. "Please come in."

"Thank you." Teresa walked past the woman who closed the door behind her.

"Please," said the woman, ushering her into the lounge/dining room. At some time the separating wall had been knocked down. At the far end of the room, terrace doors looked out upon the back garden. Because of the position of this house on the slope of the hill, it was possible there was no cellar.

Teresa could see that she wore a hearing aid.

The woman noticed and Teresa apologised for staring.

"I've not always been deaf," she said. "It's age. But it has its advantages. I often switch it off to get some peace and quiet. Of course—" she chuckled "—it saves the batteries too." Then she caught herself and with a worried expression asked: "Were you at the door long?"

"No," she lied.

"The bell is that light over there, but I don't always see it during the day, I'm afraid."

Before sitting they introduced themselves. Pleasantries were exchanged in the form of enquiries about each other. Ruth asked about Teresa's pregnancy, then her husband and his work. Teresa discovered that Ruth now lived alone. Her husband had passed away some years ago.

Ruth brought in tea and biscuits – there was no offer of a pint. Teresa was at the terrace doors viewing the immaculate garden, as tidy as the room, and asked Ruth whether she had done landscape gardening.

The old lady laughed and said that she drew a lot of her ideas from magazines. Gardening had always been her hobby.

Inevitably they spoke about the house and Ricketts.

"His cats did a lot of damage. Were you ever inside?"

"No. They kept themselves to themselves. It's a quiet neighbourhood."

"Yes, I noticed. I haven't seen the neighbours the other side of us."

"You won't for a while. They're on a six-month cruise."

"I see. Well, we only really moved in this weekend. We had a month doing up the place. You should have seen the result of living with all those cats." She paused. "The skirting board and wallpaper were in a terrible state. And the carpets too. You should have seen his chairs. The cats had plucked the sides to death. It was nothing but tufts of fabric in places. And everywhere, if you looked close enough, there were tiny hairs."

"It sounds dreadful, dear."

"The place still smells despite ripping out the carpets and sanding down the floorboards. Oh, it's undoubtedly better. The cellar is the worst."

"Maybe something died down there?"

Teresa was shocked; although she couldn't say the idea hadn't already crossed her mind. "I don't like going down there."

"Well, I don't want to be forward, but my husband was a great one for facing fears. He didn't like heights, so he did a bungee jump."

"I do go down. I can't really see where anything could have died..." In the ensuing silence she remembered the trapped cat.

"Do the cats bother you?" Teresa began. "They still keep coming to the house."

"I see them now and then. But what exactly do you mean bother?"

"Do you hear them whining at night?" The image of a cat with a plump baby's head, a cherub's head with a cat's body, a mythological creature straight out of the pages of a weird gothic comic, shuddered her thoughts.

"I wouldn't really, would I dear?"

"No, I suppose not. How silly of me. It's driving Chris mad. He's not sleeping at all well. And neither am I, but at least I can get something of a lie-in. I wouldn't go so far as to say that we're under siege, but it's getting that way."

"Is it that loud?"

"No, I suppose not. But it's irritating. Like a mosquito in the room. I don't know where they come from. Can you get strays?"

Ruth shrugged.

"I don't know how he could have lived with so many cats. I've nothing against pets, but there are limits."

"I don't know either, dear. He probably got used to it."

"What do you mean?"

"The cats were *her* thing." Teresa's expression said: give me a moment to digest this information, but Ruth added: "Mrs Ricketts was the animal lover."

"Is that why she married him?" It was a knee-jerk reaction.

Ruth was stunned and then she laughed. And Teresa chuckled.

"No, seriously," said Ruth. "The cats were her thing."

Teresa had decided not to tell her about the apparition. She didn't want to give the wrong impression. But the laughter had eased the politeness and was a big step towards friendship. The talk of Mrs. Ricketts was too good an opportunity to miss. "What did she look like?"

"Oh, I don't know. She was old like me. But not as – how should I put it? – rounded as me. She was small, but thin, no wiry. Yes, wiry. Sinewy if you like. Do you remember *Old Mother Riley*? No, I suppose not. Before your time. She reminded me of her, although her face was not long; it was round like mine."

"Did she wear make-up?"

"Well yes. She powdered her face quite heavily. When my husband was alive he used to call her snow-flake. He thought she was flaky too... Why do you ask?"

"No reason. Did she wear lipstick?"

"Funny you should ask. She had thin lips and a small mouth. She had a loathsome habit of putting her lipstick on beyond the edges of her lips. I think she thought they looked more passionate or fuller. From a distance they looked bigger, I'll admit, but close up they looked ridiculous."

Teresa hadn't noticed."Sounds ghastly."

"Her lipstick was like a red dash on a white sheet. Oh, I'm becoming cruel. I didn't really know her. But she struck me as a person with a severe temperament."

"You think she bullied Mr Ricketts?"

"I don't think Ricketts had an easy time of it. But I don't really know. As I said they kept themselves to themselves."

"What happened to her?"

"She upped and left him for an old childhood sweetheart."

"Huh."

"He may have been the hen-pecked husband. But when she was gone he was not any happier."

"Maybe he got used to being bullied."

"Maybe... There was a kind of bitterness in him."

"How long ago did she leave him, then?"

"About two months, I'd say. More or less."

"Wow. He sold rather quickly."

"Yes, he did."

"I'm sure we didn't make him an exceptional offer. Naturally, we knocked his asking price down." Pause. "Seems strange that he sold so quickly. Perhaps the place reminded him of her or something."

The conversation seemed to have dried up.

"One last thing, Ruth."

"Yes, dear."

"We, er, spoke about the cats."

"You said you wanted to speak to me. You're getting to the real reason for your visit, aren't you?"

"Oh, I wanted to meet you. We–"

"It's okay, dear. What is it you want to say?"

"I was hoping to persuade you to stop feeding the cats."

"I only do it on occasion."

"But just now–"

"The bowl?"

Teresa nodded.

Ruth laughed. But because Teresa could only smile awkwardly she cut herself short.

"I put out bowls of beer to catch the slugs."

"I don't–"

"I don't want them chewing up my garden. The beer draws them and they drown."

"I see." This explained a lot.

"A friend of mine was also a gardening enthusiast. She's passed away now. She used to cut them in half with the gardening shears. I think this is a much more humane way of killing them. If you can talk about humane killing?" She laughed. "You can tell I'm not a Buddhist. But ask any true gardener and they'll tell you that it's not just about growing; it's as much about killing."

* * *

Although she had plenty of time Teresa set about preparing dinner. All the while she thought about her conversation with Ruth. Her post-mortem served as a basis for what she would tell Chris. Her thoughts were in freefall; words associating. She's not an old bird. Or a wino. She was like a favourite aunt. And she would be a good neighbour. We must invite her to dinner as soon as possible. As soon as possible. He had sold as soon as possible. Ricketts. The smell and Ricketts. He was not a ghoul after all; he was just an old man. A sad old man who had turned a mite peculiar. At this she glanced at the cellar key upon the wall. *My husband was a great one for facing fears.* Resolve thinned her lips. She stopped what she was doing, wiped her hands on a tea towel, snatched the key and went in search of the torch.

She left via the front door.

There was a chill in the air. The cold of the evening was encroaching upon the warmth of the afternoon. She didn't hesitate with the cellar key. With the cellar door flung wide open, there was a moment when the wardrobe stood alone at the end of the avenue of boxes. Her shadow was a stunted, knobbly finger pointing to it. She reached in and fumbled for the light switch. Had her frame of mind been less set and unyielding, this fumbling would have unsettled her; instead she was merely nettled.

When the light came on, to the cluck of the old man's false teeth, everything was rendered hazy. It was as if the air was thick with particles – much like in a sandstorm, but not nearly as bad. This was merely a trick of the weak light.

She clicked on the torch and the beam was a scythe that cut away the haziness and returned detail. It was her sabre and, armed as she was, she strode to the wardrobe. She moved to the far side of it: the other side of the bench. There she put her cheek as near to the dirty wall as she dared; the fingertips of her right hand upon the brickwork maintaining her balance. She moved the light up and down

47

the length of the wardrobe in the gap between it and the wall. All she could see was a few inches of wall and then blackness. The back of the wardrobe was placed too close to the wall. The resultant angle was simply too steep. She turned the knob with her right hand and pulled at the door, but all she achieved was a heavy rattling and her nerves took to the air like a flock of birds shaken from the safety of the trees. Teresa felt a subterranean stirring. From the movement of the latch she realised that it had a strong spring mechanism and that it needed substantial turning. Her palm grew sweaty and she looked at the bench which was the back of a crocodile. The aim of her torch wandered to the object on the workbench. It was the pencil she had picked up. She was drifting. Her resolve was abandoning her. She found herself clinging to her impression of Ruth as she applied more pressure to the latch. Click and it was open. Open, slit vertically, like the plastic eye of the crocodile, fooling one into thinking that it was weighty and docile, only the knowing smirk hinting at its insect agility.

Teresa unconsciously held her breath as she pulled the door wide, letting it carry itself towards the end. Everything was in shadow. But she could see that within the half that she had exposed there was nothing but a yellowing newspaper at the bottom. She curled her hand tentatively round the other door, reaching up, searching for the catch. Finding it, she pulled, felt the door ease (there was evidently no lower catch, or it had not been applied), gave it a touch of momentum and rather dramatically stepped back. She watched with bated breath as the wardrobe revealed itself. As the door opened, a mirror on its inside tried to distract her with its reflected motion. But she would have none of it: she shoved aside mirrored apparitions of a manic-looking Ricketts or a pale Mrs Ricketts. Such things were the stuff of a cheap shock in a film. Only the corner of her eye checked for reflected irregularities, of which, there were naturally none. The bulk of her attention remained set upon the interior of the wardrobe.

The smell was here. But was this the source?

The door swung open stopping just short of the bench.

To her disappointment, other than the newspaper there was absolutely nothing inside the wardrobe. The left hand door held a mirror and underneath a small tray-like shelf for apparel such as cuff-links, brooches, or tie pins. The central rail that had obviously run across the wardrobe was gone: the two wooden blocks secured high up on the facing sides, their cut-out U-shapes testified to its absence. The back was made up of two panels, one supported an unobtrusive metal coat hook, and the other displayed a discolouration showing that it too had once had a similar hook. That was all.

Nonetheless, she felt an unnatural stillness. A stillness that bespoke of impending action. Like the dormant crocodile in the workbench. It was as if the wardrobe were a trap, or the opening to such. Once again, she could not pinpoint the source. But she felt that her next action would be important. There would be consequences. The wardrobe was the entrance to a vast silence, and yet not a silence, because the silence was a restraint. Something was there and now that she was this close, it chose to be still.

She moved closer.

Where the doors met the body of the wardrobe there was a lip of wood so that the doors were built into a front frame, but despite it being dark in inky black shadow she could see that there was nothing hidden.

Perhaps the feeling emanated from the text of the newspaper itself? Maybe it said something of Ricketts or the house or the smell? It seemed unlikely that it could be significant. But she had to follow up all possibilities. Would she read of child murder? Or would she find something superficially less sinister: a dirty old man stalking the area.

Looking about herself, she knelt down and peered at the newspaper. It was a single folded, double-page sheet, reaching the back and front of the wardrobe, but with space at either end of its length. Another sheet of similar sized newspaper would be required to cover the remaining area. She scanned the text. It was a local rag. The upper half of the page was devoted to some kind of children's corner. And the lower half reported local weddings. The passage of time lent an element of melancholy to the passport-size photographs of the happy, smiling couples. They suggested questions such as, had they remained as happy as depicted by their smiles and were they still together? She checked the names of the marriages and she drew a blank. She began to look over the children's section. She was not looking for anything in particular. She was merely taken by an obscure interest in happenings long past. Indeed, judging from the age of the paper, most of the contributing children would be middle-aged with children themselves. There were puzzles and events listed and there were some poetry certificate winners. None of the names meant anything to her, but she found herself reading the winning entries. There was one in the middle of the page at the fold nearest the back panel, and because her shadow fell upon it she could not read it. Having read the others, she felt obliged to read this longer one. So she reached in, having clasped her hands at her lap all this time. Perhaps because her hands had been in the warmth of her lap she found the inside of the wardrobe icy. The chilled air was pure fear similar to that which surrounds a bear-trap: cruel metal jaws, taut and waiting to snap, waiting to bite through flesh and grip raw bone. Her fingertips touched the aged paper. It was crispy like fresh pound notes. But it was also crinkled and slightly buckled. Too dry to be the source of the smell. Sliding the sheet forward, it grated upon the grit underneath. Using the torch she read.

<u>The Loch Ness Monster.</u>
My name is Tom MacKay,
And it happened in the month of May.
I was at Loch Ness
With my cow named Bess.
Suddenly I heard a loud swish,
But I only thought it was a big fish.
I thought something had come out of hell,
When I heard a loud roaring yell!
Bess jumped up and went "Moo",
And I jumped too!
It was huge, ugly and green
And it was the worst thing I had seen.
It towered above Loch Ness
And it frightened me and Bess.
It had two round eyes,
As big as steak and kidney pies.
It had two large fins
As big as large dustbins.
Bess and I ran for our lives
As the monster's teeth came down like giant knives.
I dived for the ground
As the monster gave another roaring sound.
It twirled and splashed
As Bess and me dashed.
I ran and ran for my parked wagon
As the thing roared like an underwater dragon.
I got away,

But I'll never forget that day,
And no one believed I saw it,
And everyone said I was a nit.
But I'll never forget that day
In the month of May.

The poem caused her to smile. It was sweet. She re-read the boy's name. Hmmm, he would now be in his thirties. Then she glanced over the page again, just to check that she had not missed anything. No, it was just a sheet of paper at the bottom of a wardrobe.

She pointed the torch to the inside upper corners. Nothing.

Teresa slowly rose. For some reason she felt weary; as if maintaining the crouching position had drained her legs of energy, making them feel thick and heavy.

Grabbing the side of the door with the mirror she began to close it, the mirror once again reflecting the background with a nauseatingly rapid distraction.

The face in the mirror was such a shock that her heart missed a beat.

"What are you doing down here?"

She caught her breath and spun round.

"Sorry, love," he began, "did I frighten you?"

"Yes," she answered, becoming limp.

Chris moved towards her. "I'm sorry. I said I'd be back early. I saw the light and came down. Didn't you hear me? What are you doing in here?"

Weakness overcame her. It had debilitated her physically and now she began to feel it impair her reasoning.

"Er, nothing..."

"Nothing?" He took her by the shoulders.

She could not answer him.

"Terry, look at me. Are you okay?"

"Yes, yes," she said, the life coming to her eyes.

"You had me worried for a moment. I thought you were going faint. You still look awfully pale."

She smiled. "No, I'm okay."

He looked hard at her, as if examining her appearance. "Have you been speaking to the great white telephone again?"

"No." She smiled. She realised that she would have to cut the conversation and so reassure him. "No, I've not been worshipping the porcelain God or up-chucking anywhere else for that matter."

"Alright."

"It's cold down here and I haven't started dinner."

"I'll make it if you like."

"No, that's okay."

"We'll do it together, then."

They left the cellar, switched out the light and locked the door.

As they ascended the stairway, Chris asked about the visit to the doctor.

The evening was subdued and they felt tired. So they agreed upon an early night.

They were climbing the stairs, both somewhat fragile, when the sound of a cat started up. Chris, on the stairway behind her, exploded, cursing loudly.

"I mean it. I'm going to ask Gerald for his gun!" he said as he made for his shoes near the front door.

Teresa did not smile.

He pulled on his shoes and without tying the laces he opened the front door. The crying stopped.

She remained on the stairs and although she could no longer see him, she heard him cursing the cat under his breath.

"Come on, you little bastard, where are you?"

She guessed him to be at the side of the house near the dustbin.

Sighing, she was about to turn when the little head appeared near the bottom of the doorway. A paw dipped upon the threshold and then the black cat entered the house its body curving about the entrance. Teresa did nothing. She merely stared at the creature. It watched her and surveyed its immediate surroundings as it padded languidly into the house. Its movement was grand. There was no other way to describe its sleek feline motion; its tail erect and moving independently as if testing the air and its padding forward with unbent forelegs stretching ahead in soft steps. This was a royal inspection. Still, she did not move. But her will hardened against the creature. She tried to meet its eyes with her own despising slits. And although it saw her and probably felt her anger – if all that was true of cats and their sentience was to be believed – it chose to supremely ignore her.

Chris appeared at the doorway. He had said something that had alerted the cat and, although it was facing away from him, its head was turned to him. He stopped mid-sentence, glanced at Teresa and then went for the cat.

Teresa was as surprised as Chris by the action of the animal. Chris was stunned into position and the blood drained from his face. He was visibly stricken. The shock of it was heightened by Chris's reaction and Teresa felt her heart freeze. It seemed a foregone conclusion that her husband would scare the cat out of the house. The cat had taken up the challenge. It had turned and with rigid legs and a humped, compressed back, it had snarled at him. The snarl itself had mesmerised Teresa. It had been a hiss, long and cruel. The incisors too, looked long and cruel.

Chris moved forward and Teresa brought a hand to her cheek. The cat was on three legs, its fourth was a raised claw.

"You spiteful little shit," said Chris, bringing up his own foot.

It snarled again.

"Yeah," said Chris, defiantly.

In what seemed a split second before he was about to kick it, it made a lightning movement past him and through the doorway into the night. It was very fast and yet she observed that its movement was liquid. The cat actually flowed past his legs. Somehow – and to Teresa this was almost supernatural – it managed to nick him with a claw as it went by.

"Shit!" he yelped.

Chris leapt to the door but the cat was gone.

Teresa went to him. He, however, deflected her attempt at comfort, by cursing and saying that that was it. She was unsure what he meant by 'it'. In any case, he ignored her and went to the telephone that topped the up-ended empty cardboard box. On the sill next to the door they had stuck the little piece of note-paper upon which Ricketts had written his telephone number and address, the latter for forwarding post and the former for any emergencies. Chris clearly considered this an emergency. He pointed an index finger of one hand as he dialled with a finger of the other.

"What are you going to say?"

He ignored her. Then he was standing looking vacantly at the wall before him.

"It's late, darling. Perhaps he's already gone to bed?"

He glanced at his watch. It was shortly before ten.

"Tough."

* * *

Early that Saturday afternoon they returned from their shopping spree to the ringing of the telephone.

They had risen early and done the week's food shopping and after returning and packing it away they had gone out again and bought a lawn mower and a waist-high dresser topped with a plastic coated sponge mat to change the baby.

Teresa had taken the call and feeling steamrollered handed the receiver to Chris. He floored the box that contained the parts of the dresser and relayed the conversation to her. The Jamesons were inviting them to dinner. Their original guests had just cancelled because of illness. Teresa could tell Chris was keen to go and nodded her consent when he hastily explained.

Barbara and her husband were a well-suited happy-go-lucky couple. Their primary interest was to have a good laugh. And Teresa and Chris couldn't help getting whipped up by their inexhaustible effervescence. From the very start, when Larry introduced himself, saying that Babs and he were happily married; adding that Babs was happy and he was married, the ice was cracked. As the evening progressed any suspicions that the driving force behind the humour was founded in nervousness, bitterness, frustration, or the like were dispelled and the ice melted and vaporised. Babs and Larry were an in-your-face genuine and lovable couple.

"How many months?" asked Babs.

"Eight, but it seems a lot longer."

"One to go," said Chris.

"We spoke on the phone the other day," said Babs.

"Oh yes," said Teresa. She knew she should elaborate.

"You sounded upset."

"Both our nerves are raw," said Chris. "The previous owner was a cat lover."

"Yes, Chris told me about the cats."

"I think the house still draws half the cats of the city," said Teresa, grateful that her husband had come to her rescue.

They touched on Ricketts but didn't dwell. Neither Teresa nor Chris was in the mood and their tone conveyed this fact.

"Now, talk of cats is a banned subject for the entire evening," said Larry.

Teresa enjoyed letting go. She was swept along with her husband's ease, which was slipping out of control. Not least because of the vulgar size of the red wine glasses. Larry joked that the goldfish were in plastic bags for the evening.

As they talked Teresa unconsciously scanned the furnishings. Many of the objects were African. Simple carved-animals, some wild, some beasts of burden, and sag-bellied women carrying infants or pots, proud, stiff warriors and masks. They were replicas of ancient things of a strange and primitive clumsiness, concomitantly brutal and beautiful.

The evening remained with Teresa because of the stories. And they remained because they seemed in some way connected with recent events.

The dinner was over and with it the manic exuberance.

For a moment Chris and she were alone. An air of satisfaction and contentment bound them. And they took the opportunity to kiss. Teresa expressed her liking for Babs and Larry, adding that she thought the former's breasts were not so prominent as to deserve such a nickname. Before Chris could speak the said Babs returned.

Larry followed with a tray of three glasses of liquor. He wore a monster mask.

Chris laughed and after a moment's hesitation Teresa smiled. Babs either relished Teresa's uncertainty or wanted to reassure her. Whatever, Babs's laughter broadened Teresa's smile. "We're Halloween fans," she said.

Larry put down the tray and pulled off the mask. "Phew. It's hot in there." He sat down with them. "Yeah. Every year we have a party."

"Strictly fancy dress," Babs added.

"You must come."

"We will," said Chris. Although Teresa nodded, her expression said otherwise and he caught it. "Assuming we can, er, get a sitter."

"I love a good scare, don't you?" said Babs, sipping her liquor.

"Sometimes," said Teresa, feeling she was being addressed. She recalled the banging and the image of the old woman.

"How about a ghost story to round off the evening?" said Larry.

"I know all yours," said Babs.

"I've got a new one."

"I'm game," said Chris.

"I don't want to be a spoilsport," said Teresa. "But I don't know any."

"Everyone knows a ghost story," said Babs.

"What about your teacher?" said Chris.

"That's not a ghost story," said Teresa.

"Is it horrible or uncanny?" Babs asked.

"Uncanny, I suppose."

"Let's hear it."

"It's not a story. It's, er, an incident."

"I'll tell you what," said Larry suddenly. "I'll tell mine first."

Teresa nodded and they all settled down to listen to Larry.

He began by saying that his was a local ghost story, which he called 'Girl in the lake'. In the late 1800s a beautiful servant girl, abused by the gentry, became pregnant. Sent forth to avoid a scandal she aborted the baby. She was then spurned, gang raped and finally drowned by the lads of the village. Because she had been an orphan nobody was made to pay and it was as if she had never existed. Even the womenfolk, openly jealous of her beauty, readily kept quiet. The lake in which she was said to have drowned was a short drive from Ricketts's house. Every few decades a life was claimed. Almost invariably it would be that of a young man trying to rescue someone in distress near the reeds. Witnesses on the bank say they too see someone waving in the lake. Of course, only the lad's body is ever recovered. These deaths have kept the story alive.

"It's probably a trick of the light in the reeds," said Chris. "And who knows what currents there are."

They were silent for a while.

Then Chris told his ghost story 'Christian Soldiers', which was new to Teresa. After this Babs told her tale called 'The Mask'. This left Teresa ample time to suitably embellish her story.

"Since you're all giving titles to your stories I'll call mine 'Belief'. As I said, my story happened to me. So it's more a haunting incident than a story." She checked she had their full attention. "My secondary school was an all girls' school. But in my second year it went comprehensive. There was a boy in our class. Junior Wilson was his name. He was from Jamaica and he was really black. I mean most people of African descent are brown, but Junior was as black as ebony. And his teeth were as white as the whites of his eyes. So when he widened his eyes and bared his teeth the contrast was quite frightening." She expected a bogie man comment, but her three listeners remained silent. "But Junior wasn't unusual because of his appearance."

"I suppose it's the same in all racially mixed schools. Crossover existed so that it appeared that everyone played with each other but racially defined cliques existed. Junior wasn't truly accepted by any clique. He was a true loner. He was unpredictable and inaccessible. I think this is what made many wary. Most of us were there to learn, despite our derision. Junior was on another planet. He had absolutely no interest in school. I can't say he wanted to have fun. And I can only believe he came to school because he was forced to. I can't even tell you whether he was intelligent. He didn't fit and really needed to go to a special school." Teresa stopped suddenly as if unsure how to proceed. Her listeners didn't prompt her in any way, but simply took the opportunity to sip or top up their liquors. Teresa too sipped her orange juice.

"But my story is not about Junior – yes, I know I've waxed lyrical about him – but he's not the main character." She looked to them for reaction. Receiving none she continued. "Mr Higgins, our English teacher, was one of the few teachers who commanded respect. He didn't wield an iron hand and he rarely got angry. Even Junior knuckled down and was not his unruly, disruptive self. The best way to describe how he became is sulky. Mr Higgins wasn't imposing in stature. His hair was thinning and he wore round NHS spectacles. So how did he command respect? He did it by enthralling the class with his anecdotal style. He was a great speaker and his knowledge seemed encyclopaedic. You just didn't want to miss a nugget of information. Despite this he had a flaw." She stopped and drank some juice. "I must admit his flaw had to be pointed out to me. But once I was in the know it seemed blatant. And I did wonder how Junior held himself in check. You see, Mr Higgins was racially prejudiced. He was so clever that his thinly veiled attitude was always delivered with ambiguity. In fact some of us thought the targeted kids were being over sensitive. But as I said his wording did not always leave much room for doubt. That said, his prejudice was not continuous, but it was always lurking under the surface.

"I remember his last lesson. Not simply because it was his last, but because of its content and how it related to what happened a few weeks later. The topic was religion. I suppose it was more an excursion into belief. I forget the real point of his story. I think it was along the lines of the power of belief.

"He began by saying that some would relate to the story more than others. Some may even remember such African villages. I remember him glancing at the darker skinned pupils including Junior. But he didn't linger.

"The story was that of the village witch-doctor, a very respected and much feared man, second only to the chief. The latter had asked him to discover the identity of the man who had made one of his wives pregnant. It couldn't be the chief himself because this wife had been out of his favour for a number of months. The woman had claimed she had been raped by a jackal, but the witch-doctor had persuaded her to drop the lie. He had however failed to get her to disclose the identity of the lover.

"The witch-doctor couldn't accept failure and was as angry as the chief about the situation. An ultimatum to the lover with an offer of leniency came and went. This further infuriated the two most powerful men of the village and they said that now the only fitting punishment was death.

"The witch-doctor said that he would use his most powerful medicine to call on all the spirits to yield the culprit. All the eligible men – married or not – were made to line up in the centre of the village facing the chief's spoiled wife. The witch-doctor said that he would call on the unborn to call to his father. Then, under the blazing African sun, he began an elaborate dance. After almost an hour of this the witch-doctor confided in the chief before turning to the stony-faced men and saying that the baby needed waking. With that he struck the pregnant woman across the belly with his cane. She buckled and everyone flinched. The witch-doctor turned to the congregation and said that the father would feel the same pain but a thousand-fold. The witch-doctor struck the woman on the back of her legs. A man fell, a streak of purple on the backs of his legs. The witch-doctor looked at the chief triumphantly and the other men moved away. A thousand-fold, repeated the witch-doctor, who then poked the woman in the arm. Blood erupted from the man's arm and he fell to his knees pleading for mercy. The witch-doctor's answer was to scratch the woman's abdomen, causing the man to scream and clutch the sudden rip across his stomach. The woman sobbed as the witch-doctor poked and scratched and tapped her. He only stopped when the man, a bloodied mass, stopped moving."

"Oh Teresa, what an awful story for school children," said Babs.

"I haven't finished."

"If I may say so," said Larry, a little slurred, "you've told it very well."

"Yes," agreed Chris, also tipsy.

"Thank you." She waited until they were ready. "The next English lesson was taken by a substitute teacher. But that wasn't all. Junior was absent and his desk had been replaced by a new one. At the next assembly we were told that Mr Higgins had died. Although we, the children, were not told how he died the general consensus was that it was a heart attack. I don't know, but I felt as if we'd lost the library of Alexandria. We also learnt that Junior had been transferred to a school for troublesome children." Pause. "A couple of weeks later I was with a few of the girls in the storeroom. One of them spotted Junior's desk. We had those old fashioned wooden desks with the slanted flap top you could lift to put your books in. They even had a small well in the top edge for ink. You know what I mean? A girl called us over and showed us the carving on the underside of flap. It was a caricature of Mr Higgins. I must admit it was quite good. The thinning hair and glasses gave him away. When Junior was able to do this I have no idea. The thing about the carving was that there were a multitude of gouging lines criss-crossing the area of the heart."

* * *

"Now, where are you going with that?" asked Chris looking up from the upturned lawn-mower.

Teresa had appeared at the side of the house, the moulded plastic chair in hand.

"Don't worry," she returned with a smile, "I'll move when you get near."

"It's a dog's life, eh?" he muttered to the blade he was adjusting.

The weather had held for the weekend. It was Sunday afternoon. And it was the end of their first full weekend in their own home.

They had risen late, not least because of Chris's hangover. And Teresa had not stayed up so late on a Saturday evening, without dozing off on the sofa, in ages.

Teresa planted the chair squarely in the blazing sun. "You want me to plug that in?" she said, before sitting.

"Could you?"

She picked up the plug at the end of the orange cable and carried it to the cellar door.

Not a single cat was to be seen. If any were near then they were sitting in the shade.

Thoughts of cats brought her husband's call with Ricketts to mind.

Of course she had only heard his side of the telephone conversation that Thursday evening. But he had filled out Ricketts' part later on. In bed she had questioned him, trying to wheedle out as much tone and inclination as he had comprehended. Then, she had put flesh upon the bone, mentally piecing the conversation together and giving Ricketts a voice.

Chris had started with a curt apology for phoning at such an hour and then introduced himself. Teresa imagined Ricketts grunting at this.

"Some post has arrived for you." True. "I just wanted to check your address." Untrue. "Is that an 'e' or an 'f' at the end of your road name?" Chris smirked at his own cleverness.

"An 'e'."

"Okay. Good. Thanks." He took a breath, but didn't quite pull off the casual tone he wanted. "By the way, quite a few cats keep coming to the house. They make a hell of a noise at night. And they're really bothering my wife." Teresa was momentarily irked at being used, Chris was disturbed by them too, but then thought that it didn't really matter. "She's pregnant, you remember?"

"I don't see what I can do."

"You know about cats, though."

"Yes, I have a lot here."

"So you don't have some trick or something to make them quiet."

"Feed 'em."

"I don't want to encourage them. We'd like them to stop coming."

Silence.

"There's, erm, also a kind of graveyard at the end of the garden. Can—"

"That was her."

"Who?"

"My wife. I never did that."

"What shall we do about it?"

"Whatever you want."

"You don't mind?"

"It's your house."

"Yes."

"About your cat problem. Feed them. Make friends with them."

"Yes. Thank—"

"I haven't got them all here. I miss some of them. They will be missing me. Not as much as they miss her. Her favourites were never my favourites, you know. She can have her favourites. They don't care for me. So I don't care for them. She can have them." On reflection, Teresa imagined all his sentences incomplete, as was his way.

"Yes. Okay. Mr Ricketts."

"Feed 'em. Make friends."

"Yes. Thank you for your advice. Goodnight." After hanging up Chris had said he thought the old buzzard was going senile. Maybe he was lonely too. He had been relatively talkative.

Teresa had pressed him about the tail end of the conversation. What had Ricketts meant by his wife having her favourites? She can have them, he had said. But Chris had no idea and dismissed it as babbling.

At the cellar door, a glistening petrified oil slick, Teresa plugged the lawn mower cable in the socket on the wall under the light switch.

In her flimsy summer dress, which she referred to as a tent, the stark iciness of the cellar was all the more noticeable. The day literally could not penetrate this frigid room.

But Chris was nearby. The day was warm and annihilating. And she dismissed the potency of the cellar. It could not touch her. It was not haunting. It would not dare touch her. It had no power.

Teresa's skin tingled with the cold. From a crack at her eye-level in the brick-work the wall sweated a cold black drop, a tear in the form of a bead of a shiny beetle. She shifted her position as it rolled downwards nearing the socket and her hand.

She would not be unnerved. Yet, to consciously harden herself meant that she was being worn down.

Clicking the switch she called out to Chris that he could 'hit-it' and the motor buzzed into life.

Now she could leave the cellar and get to her book and the sunshine and Chris and life. The back of the beast startled her and she did not move. An unblinking insentient fish eye sat in a knot in the wood of the workbench. And she saw the malign grimace of a rogue Orca.

Teresa moved to her left, so that she could see more of the bench. There was no splinter of yellow. The stillness grew immeasurably. It turned her legs to lead. She clung to the sound of the lawn-mower. Chris was behind her. Nothing could happen. Yet, she could not turn and check his whereabouts. There was no splinter of yellow. She stepped forward. The air was heavy and musty.

She strode up to the bench and scanned its length. Nowhere. It had not buried itself in the leathery crags. The pencil was simply not there. Had it ever been there? Had she picked it up? Could she have imagined it? Was she going crazy? It had been there last time. Had the folds of ancient aboriginal skin absorbed it?

The wardrobe was closed but the smell was present.

"Chris!" she called, remaining at the bench. Had he heard her?

She turned and practically charged to the entrance.

"Yeah, what is it?" he asked as the motor died away.

"There was a pencil on that work bench."

"And?"

"Well, it's not there. Did you pick it up?"

"No," he answered, making a move to restart the mower.

"Wait."

He looked at her impatiently.

"Have you been in the cellar since Thursday night?"

"Well, I had to get this," he said, nodding to the lawn mower.

"I think we ought to change the lock." Only the cellar door lock had not been changed.

"What for?"

"Let's just do it."

"Because a pencil's gone?"

"For me, let's just do it."

"Ahh, maybe I did pick up the pencil."

"Did you?"

"Yes."

"When?"

"Oh, I don't know." Pause. "This is silly."

"Did you pick up that pencil?"

"Maybe?" he said in a small voice and putting on a winning smile.

She glared at him.

"Okay, no–" his smile vanishing "– no, I didn't pick up any blooming pencil."

"Let's change the locks."

"Are you sure it hasn't rolled off and fallen underneath?"

"Yes." She went back to the bench and looked underneath. Chris started up the lawn-mower again.

Of course it was dark and she could not see the pencil, but she was absolutely certain that it could not have rolled off. It would have had to literally jump out of the groove in which she had placed it. Had it existed? Yes, and it had been a 2H. She was not going crazy.

Teresa returned to the entrance. Her husband looked up but ignored her. She went to her chair and sitting heavily opened her book, but she did not read.

He cut the motor.

"Well?"

"It's not there."

He walked over to her.

"Don't laugh," she began quietly, "but I feel evil in this house."

"I'm not laughing."

"It's not just the cats."

"Oh?"

"Well, if I didn't know any better I'd say Ricketts murdered his wife and stuck her under the floorboards."

He wisely chose not to ridicule her proposal of murder.

"You don't want me to get the floorboards lifted, do you?"

"No. But the smell and everything. It'll all fit."

"Have you forgotten all those cat trays he had in the house? That smell is in the woodwork."

They had ripped out all of the downstairs carpets. Some of those upstairs she had shampooed four times. She had littered the house with vases of flowers and bowls of dry aromatic pieces of wood, leaves and petals: autumnal bits and pieces. Scented drawer paper lined their drawers in which she had added miniature sacks of potpourri. She had even resorted to the occasional use of an incense burner. At times, during the day when the windows were open, it was hard to tell whether the smell was replaced by a complex aroma or whether it was truly disappearing. "The smell's lingering a bit. Or do you think, maybe, we've just got used to it? It's hard to tell. But, it's definitely coming from the cellar."

"So he murdered his wife?" He knew before he said it that he would regret it, but he could not help himself. "Darling, really, you've been watching too many movies. Yeah, that's unfair. But, didn't you tell me that Ruth said that his wife had gone off with another man?"

They were bordering dangerously on an important difference between them: a difference that could easily lead to an altercation. Teresa considered herself open and receptive. Chris never said he thought her gullible, but she knew he thought her vulnerable and susceptible.

"Yes," she replied, having known this flaw to her argument all along. "Change the lock, for me, please."

"Okay. Come on out." She stepped away and he closed the cellar door. He moved the unused latch of the door over the loop in the frame. "I've got a padlock somewhere."

"That's not going to hold. The paint is probably the only thing holding the latch on."

"It'll do for now." Then, giving her no time to protest he added: "We'll get it changed by the end of the month. I promise."

She nodded.

"Look, it's a nice day. I was going to build the cabinet, but when I've finished the lawn, let's get away. We'll go for a walk around that lake. What do you think?"

"You're not thinking of leaving me for another woman?"

"One with a reedy voice," he laughed.

"And a hell of a kiss."

* * *

Teresa embellished Babs's story, filling it out with detail and substance, most of which came in the form of digressions by Babs, herself, or interruptions from Larry. In Teresa's mind the ditties from the couple's China trip were incorporated into the story so that it flowed seamlessly.

Babs's story was called 'The Mask'.

When the girls came upon the village they were quite exhausted. They had been walking for the best part of the day. There was no public transport to where they were going. Although they were by no means unfit the journey was made arduous by its uneventfulness and commonplace scenery. Furthermore, the accumulation of souvenirs during their month-long tour had brought their rucksacks up to the bearable weight-limit. This was the last leg of their tour and, although in the middle of nowhere, it promised to be an edifying highlight.

Culturally they were already mentally saturated. They had visited the Wall during their first few days in Beijing. The Forbidden City, Tiananmen Square, old and new summer palaces, and the various tombs and temples and other well-known sights had been subjected to their scrutiny and cameras. The lesser known sights were also soaked up. Ultimately it was the incidental, the way of life, most often off the beaten tourist track, that was more fascinating than the well-known objects and sights. These, the two girls agreed, were what made the holiday; they were the memorable gems seldom captured in a photograph. But they had wondrous photographs too. For instance they had been continually astounded by the applications of that ubiquitous form of transport, the bicycle. There was the bicycle as service-wagon: stacked high with trays of bottles, burdened with mountains of vegetables, loaded with baskets, or piled up with materials. It was used for house-moving with cupboards or chairs tied to it. Two had been tied together with a board in-between and the affair had been used as a make-shift ambulance. They had seen the same arrangement used as a hearse. The rule was quite simple, no matter what one wanted to transport, no matter how big or cumbersome it was, if it could be fixed to a bicycle or a combination of bicycles this would be how it would travel. Inventiveness was bounded only by the imagination. And the driving force behind it all was people. This was people-power, something one could not help noticing in highly-populated countries. The sheer numbers and activity impressed the vitality of human life upon them; the place was teeming with life, and they felt like interlopers, an alien species in a hive of bees busying themselves.

So far the trip had been rather hectic. Their itinerary and planning had been so meticulous they had left little room for flexibility. The only way to find room was to drop a planned excursion. They had tried to include a margin of time for hidden factors and eventualities such as missed connections, small detours and illness. There was even a contingency plan should they be robbed. But true to Murphy's Law: the more time they had in reserve the more time they used up. There had been so much to see and with a "this could be a once in a lifetime opportunity" attitude, they had crammed in as much as possible. Once they had agreed that all the dashing around was getting silly, but after a day of recuperation, which both of them could not help feeling was squandered time, they donned their rucksacks and charged off again. In fact, after this day of relaxation it only took them a few hours to get back into the hyperactive state they had been in before the break. When they realised this they could only laugh.

This was to be the last week of their holiday. Then it would be a direct route back to Beijing for a long flight back to England. They were to stay with Judy's mother, an archaeologist, who was the centre of some kind of mild sensation in the archaeological world. How she had wangled her way past the Chinese authorities, which were notoriously isolationist when it came to poking about in their land, was not explained. According to Judy the furore was associated with lost masks of some dynasty or other her mother had found.

"Jeez, talk about back of beyond," said Alex, as they reached the crest of the track and found themselves looking down upon a dusty collection of huts, without the characteristic skirted roofs, nestled at the foot of some terraced fields. It was not a particularly inspiring scene. It bespoke hardship and toil: a pitiful scratching upon tired earth existence. Near the Mongolian border the way of life was probably unchanged since the time of Genghis Khan.

"I told you," said Judy.

Without further word they set off down the slope.

Alex wondered about her companion's feelings. She was not certain whether they were joyful or fearful. She suspected a little of each. All she had heard from Judy about her mother made her sound like a woman of great fortitude and character. For here she was out in the middle of nowhere in a foreign land doing what she enjoyed and wanted to do. Undoubtedly this had been at the expense of a marriage. Judy's parents were divorced.

The arrival of the two girls generated no interest at all. The peasants glanced their way but went about their work and showed not the slightest hint of curiosity. They did not even nod. The girls couldn't pinpoint any unwelcoming signals. Equally there was nothing in the manner of the peasants to say that they were welcome.

Nobody said anything to the two girls as they walked through the centre of village. They kept walking until they reached the end of the collection of primitive buildings. Then, having run out of village, and beginning to wonder whether they were in the right place after all – having listened to the man in the town who had said follow the track until you reach the village – an old woman, squatting by a large bowl of rice, looked at them with impassive eyes and raised the back of a hand and waved them on with a limp wrist. The gesture was not dismissive, but an indifferent communication of direction.

The track disappeared up the hill.

Silently the two trudged onward.

Having climbed the hill they came upon another, wealthier, but not wealthy, set of buildings.

Alex was the first to break the silence.

"If this is not it, let's stop for some tea. I need a rest."

"Ditto."

As they neared the buildings a Caucasian woman in a dirty brown smock emerged ahead of a collection of Chinese men in similar attire. It was a shabby scene. The shrubbery too was autumnal without the yellows or fire. Dirty brown people descending upon them from a dirty brown landscape.

"Hallo darling," greeted Judy's mother theatrically, giving her daughter a big hug, the exaggerated warmth of which bordered on insincerity. "And you must be Alex," she said, abruptly ending the embrace and extending her hand. "I'm Harriet, but everyone calls me Harrie."

Alex saw a weathered woman. She did not look worn-out, but flushed with exertion. Her facial skin was taut like a drum and was beautiful in a hungry kind of way. She wore no make-up.

"Hallo," Alex returned, shaking her hand.

The Chinese were now fussing about the girls, helping them get their rucksacks off.

"It's quite a walk," said Judy.

Harrie smiled and looked at her daughter. "Yes, of course, you must be tired. Have a rest and then we'll have dinner and a long chat. Don't expect five star cuisine. It'll be something along the lines of broth."

"Oh, we've been on a frugal budget," said Alex. "No five-star hotels for us."

Harrie gave Alex a second look and in that moment Judy knew that the relationship between the three of them was fixed. Her mother liked someone who spoke their mind. How often when she was little had she been told not to act like a mouse? Squeak, squeak, her mother had goaded in her attempts to make her buck up. But her feuding parents had merely increased her timidity.

"There's no space for you in my room, I'm afraid," Harrie explained as they all walked towards the buildings. "And you can't stay where the boys live." Only two Chinese men had remained to carry the girls' rucksacks. "So I'm putting you in the relics' room. There're a couple of camp beds there."

As Harrie unlocked the building she warned them not to touch anything. Alex wasn't impressed by the security. A determined thief would need little effort to break down a wooden wall. Inside, nearest the door, were the tools of her trade: shovels, picks, trowels, an assortment of hammers, knives and brushes. Upon sheets on the floor were labelled bits of dirty stone and pottery and metal. And on a number of benches at the walls were further oddities. What caught one's eye immediately were the masks. All were damaged in some way, some were little more than a cheek, shards of faces – all that is, but one.

At one end of the rectangle of space in the centre of the room two camp beds had been erected. Washing and toilet facilities were in another building.

Harrie left them to doze and returned cleaned up in a fabulous kimono, two hours later to give them half an hour to freshen up before dinner. She said that they would not dine with the boys tonight – she always called them boys, although it was impossible to discern their ages from their faces and one or two of them could be in their late fifties – instead the three of them would eat together in the relics room. Then she could tell them something of her work.

In the remaining space near the camp beds, the three of them sat upon cushions about a blanket that served as a table. They ate like natives: bringing bite-sized balls of clumpy rice to their mouths and using wooden spoons for the broth.

By now the light of the day had gone and despite growing uncomfortably cold they felt cosy huddled about their picnic scene in the middle of the room. To stave off the chill Harrie introduced them to something she called mash, which was a local rice-based spirit, the Chinese name of which she also imparted but which was instantly forgotten.

The conversation, suitably lubricated, began with the two girls speaking of what they had done and seen on holiday. Harrie listened with amusement that could have been interpreted as condescending had it not been for her occasional interjections which supported or filled out what the girls had deduced but not known. All the while the two of them were itching to hear about Harrie's work and short-changed themselves.

Eventually the conversation petered out and there was a small silence.

"Now, it's your turn Mum," said Judy, pouring some mash into her small earthenware chalice.

Harrie looked at each of the girls.

"I don't want this to turn into a lecture."

"Mum," Judy began, "it doesn't matter. A potted history would make more sense than all the dry facts we've read."

Harrie nodded. "Yes, you'll need a basic background to what I have to say. Without it, all this'll be just shards of dirty pottery and stone and bits of rusty metal."

Harriet ladled out another helping of the broth and stirred it with her wooden spoon.

"My specialty is between the Han and Tang dynasties. It was a time of social misery and chaos called Southern dynasties period. But let me give you some time-scales to all this. The Han dynasty was between 206BC and AD220. And around AD618 the Tang dynasty began." She ate some soup. "During the unrest of the Southern dynasties the people tended to make statues of fabulous beasts baying at the heavens for help. More often than not they were combinations of conventional animals, and people, ministers, warlords and warriors. You know what the animals represent?"

"Some of them," answered Alex.

"Tell us anyway," said Judy.

The girls had finished eating and Harrie took the opportunity to eat some soup, rather than snatching the occasional spoonful as she had been doing.

"The dragon is such a potent symbol I could bore you for hours. Its colours are important. It symbolises happiness, longevity, even immortality, fertility, procreation, protection against evil spirits. Oh, there's really too much."

"Tell us about the other animals, then," said Alex.

"The horse, then?" The girls nodded. "Since the Han time the horse symbolised protection against demons. It was the watcher over graves. The elephant represented peace but it was also used to guard the palaces. The lion was for power, the animal that could do wonders. The tortoise for long life, the crane for luck and elegance and the peacock for beauty. I have simplified everything, but from there you can get your bearings."

She finished her bowl of soup. Then she looked at each of the girls.

"I'll take you to the site tomorrow. It's not far from here. Shall we take a look at what we've found?"

The two nodded.

"We'll start with the least significant and work our way round."

The two girls followed her about the room, crouched about the finds as she pointed out the finest details, some merely grooves upon shards that made the piece important. Taken alone the girls admitted that they would pass over them. But Harrie linked everything. And the whole talk took on the mantle of detective work. There were clues, suppositions and hard evidence. Some connections seemed tenuous, but were backed up with a wealth of indirect evidence, circumstantial or otherwise, and it seemed safe to assume the connection. Harrie drew upon her knowledge with the ease. She opened the world of archaeology to them and they were so enthralled they craved for more and felt an urge to take up the profession themselves.

They were interrupted by two Chinese men who began to clear away the food. Harrie evidently told them to leave the earthenware bottle of mash and the three chalices.

"And now, to my babies," announced Harrie. "But first a drink." It was impossible to tell how much mash was in the bottle, but it seemed to contain an endless supply. None of them were drunk or even light-headed. They had drunk three or four chalices, but due to the size of the vessels this did not amount to much. "To the intrepid travellers," she said as they stood about the blanket.

"To the intrepid archaeologist," said Alex.

The three smiled and sipped their mash.

"Before looking at the masks themselves I'd better say something of the history that surrounds them. Okay? I can call it history now; before it was myth.

Of course, masks have always been an integral part of Chinese culture across the entire spectrum of society. I'm not talking just of theatrical masks, but sorcerers' masks, Shamanic masks, exorcising masks. The list is endless.

"I told you that during the time of the Southern dynasties from the third to the sixth centuries the people made statues pleading for help and peace. Magic and superhuman powers were the simple beliefs of the time. This is where a little bit of myth creeps in. But you might as well have it all and then you can decide. There are many legends of great warriors, warlords and magicians. But there was a group of magicians who turned their energies to freeing the spirit. That is, they searched for ways to escape the torment of the time. Their cause was more religious than hedonistic. Some say they developed masks that were said to have powers beyond the imagination. They could release the spirit, by freeing the mind. They were said to unlock parts of the mind and endow the wearer with insight: allowing them to see into the past or the future. Others say the masks were used as disguises or protection to sneak into the next world... Whatever, as I've already said, this was a time of chaos and unrest and the sect along with the masks disappeared. Some of the Khans and various warlords through the ages are recorded to have searched for the lost masks. But until now they have always been considered mythical things. I must admit, these could be imitations. Even so, they are certainly a find because they are old. Carbon dating will verify their age. Shall we take a look?"

It was a stupid question.

The girls stood at the perimeter of the laden sheet that lay in front of the bench upon which the remains of the masks lay. Harrie gingerly stepped between the items. At the bench she half-turned.

"How many did they make?" asked Alex.

"Nobody truly knows. Magical numbers have been suggested, but as you can see, more than one.

"We'll start with the bits and pieces and work our way to the complete one. I'll let you handle the complete one, but you're going to have to take turns coming over here to hold it.

"All the masks are terra-cotta and shatter easily. They are all similar in structure, only the faces are different."

Firstly they examined the pieces from afar. And then they took turns in carefully stepping forward and cautiously handling the complete mask. Harrie pointed out that they all had the same hinge structure. This was surprising, she said, because she had expected pieces of cloth or gut to tie the front and back pieces together. Instead there was this hinge made of two loops on the face and a single loop on the back piece that fitted between these two; a piece of bone or wood wedged through the three loops fixed the two pieces together. The unfixed edge was the same and apart from the fact that the bottom loop of the front piece was broken the needle of bone remained in the top loop. The inside was dirty but dry. The outside was damp, but not glistening.

They all agreed that the face did not look pleasant. At one time it had been brightly coloured. But the patchy red had turned brown like blood and what may have been gold had become a faded yellow. Its expression was one of shock or horror rather than peace or contentment. Alex said that it reminded her of the masks she had seen in some Indian restaurants. Judy elaborated by saying that it resembled the type of masks people brought back from Indonesia. The face was not human, but it was not that of any one animal. It seemed to be a mixture of bull, man and lion. Tiny shell-like coils suggested a beard. And these seemed reminiscent of the sea. The nose was negroid, flat and flared like that of a bull. The mouth line was pushed down by heavy pouches for cheeks and it looked like one of the two masks of the theatre: the simple white clown-like masks of tragedy and comedy, and this was the former. The mouth line was the only opening in the face. Flames or waves fringed the sides and the crown of the head. But it was the intense stare of the eyes that suggested shock or horror. They were on cones that protruded from the face, extending a little beyond the forehead and pouches. Harrie said that it looked as if the fellow had a thyroid problem. For all the severity and owl-like intensity there was something of a smile to the face; a smile that was manic rather than ecstatic.

"It doesn't look as if he's found the secrets to the universe," said Alex.

Harrie smiled.

"Well girls I think we'll call it a night. I know it's only ten o'clock but we start early around here and I'm sure you didn't really sleep that much earlier. I'll leave the bottle with you. There can't be much left–"

"Maybe the secret's not in the mask but in the bottle," proposed Alex.

"Maybe," smiled Harrie. With that she left them alone.

The two of them settled on the floor about the blanket.

"I reckon this stuff's stronger than you think," said Judy as Alex poured the mash.

"Yeah. I'll tell you what though, I wouldn't mind taking some of this back to the Uni."

"I doubt you'll find it at Duty Free."

They sipped in silence for a while. Inevitably they talked of Judy's mother and then archaeology, agreeing that in all honesty it was not for them. They liked their comforts and the company of others. Undeniably it was interesting, fascinating, but it looked painstakingly hard work.

"I'm not in the least bit tired," said Alex, emptying the bottle into their chalices.

"Neither am I."

"Aren't you intrigued?" asked Alex, with sparkling eyes and a wry smile upon her face.

"What do you mean?"

"The mask, of course."

"It's an interesting story."

"No, I mean trying it out."

Judy was silent.

"Well?"

"I don't know," Judy began.

"Oh come on, it'd make a great photo."

"Yeah, but–"

"What harm could it do? Your mum let us hold it."

"Let's do it when she's around."

"Why? I'll be careful."

"It's old, Alex. And if anything–"

"What could happen?"

"No. I'll put it on," said Judy. "You take a photo of me."

Alex was stunned. It was unlike Judy to be so forthright. And certainly it was unlike her to be so daring. Maybe she felt responsible in her mother's absence.

"Okay," Alex acquiesced.

"Get your camera," she said brusquely, and stood up.

Alex suppressed the reflex of saluting. "It's in my rucksack."

But Judy may not have heard her. She was heading for the mask.

Alex felt uncomfortable with the pace of activity, but got up and pulled open her rucksack. She was rummaging through her stuff when Judy called her.

"You're going to have to help me." She was standing with the mask cupped in her hands.

Alex hesitated. The mask looked small in her friend's hands. Maybe it wouldn't fit.

She rose and went to her friend.

"Be careful where you step," said Judy.

"Go over there with it," said Alex, pointing to a camp bed. "It's better than doing it amongst all those things."

Judy went to a camp bed and put the opened mask face-down upon the stretched canvas. Then she pulled back her hair and tied it in a pony tail with a hair band she always carried on her wrist.

"I'd like to have a go after you," said Alex.

Judy didn't answer.

She picked up the open mask and pushed her head into the face and tried to close the back piece. "Can you close it?" she said in a surprisingly muffled voice.

"Okay, but I don't think I'll try to seal it. It looks too small for your head."

Alex helped her hold it closed. "I'm going to have to get my camera. Can you hold it?"

"There's still some light coming in. Close it properly."

Now it was Alex's turn to be uncertain. "I don't want to break it."

"Don't force it."

"Your head's too big."

"Don't be silly, that's just my hair."

"Tell me if it hurts."

Not without some difficulty Alex closed the mask and forced the piece of bone into the loops.

"Is it too tight?"

"A little."

"What can you see?"

"Blackness."

"Yeah, right... Let me get my camera." Alex stepped away and went down on her haunches at her rucksack, her back to her friend.

"It smells of dirt." Her stifled words were barely discernible.

"Well that's a—"

"Wait—"

At that moment Alex's fingers touched the casing of her camera near the bottom of her belongings.

"There's something..." Her voice, dampened by the mask, seemed deeper.

"What?" asked Alex, her fingers walking over her camera to grasp it.

"Hey wow."

"Very funny," she said triumphantly pulling the camera out.

"Yeah. Hey. Ahh."

"I've got it," said Alex rising and switching her camera on.

"I want it off."

"Just a minute." Although Alex was facing her friend she was setting the camera to portrait.

"Get it off."

"Don't piss about." Alex raised her camera. As she did she thought she heard a thud. The thought of her friend not being able to breathe flashed through her mind, but by then she had raised the camera and was framing up. Judy was standing. Just as Alex squeezed the button and the camera flashed she saw the face of her friend. The mask looked different. There was that same look of shock. There were the protruding cheeks, the down-turned mouth line, the terrible bulging eyes, everything cast in an exaggerated expression no human being could hold. Yet, the mask looked alive.

Alex lowered her camera and her eyes fell upon the mask, in pieces on the floor.

* * *

After mowing the lawn they had driven to the lake and walked for a while before sitting on a bank-side bench. They had looked out at the reeds, trying to spy a drowning figure, and agreed that they didn't find the place sinister. In fact Teresa pointed out the aesthetically pleasing bulrushes.

After watching some television they retired for the night.

Chris had taken to plugging his ears. If the alarm didn't wake him Teresa would give him a nudge. She was not bothered with earplugs. Her sleep was always fitful. The baby inside her would be active, kicking out for more space. Even if the cats did wake her, she could lie in, or take an afternoon nap.

Chris had turned out his bedside light and was a slumped heap under the quilt; merely a bunch of tufted hair showing. Teresa was on her back holding her book to her bedside lamp. Her eyelids were becoming heavy as she urged herself onward to the end of the section.

It was almost a quarter past twelve when she put out her light and plunged the room into darkness. Then one of those silly situations sprung up. Her eyes felt tired, but she realised that her mind was not in the least fatigued. At first she searched for sleep, seeking it in a physical position. This, of course, was not enough and she found herself in combat with her mind. She wanted sleep but her mind pursued thought. Attempting to wipe her mind clean – the old think-of-nothing-strategy – was flawed by her own lack of confidence in such a ploy.

Consequently, in this half-awake state, having incorporated the cry of the cat into her dreamy thoughts, she focused in on the wail of the animal. In so doing she became more awake and alerted to another barely audible sound, also outside. Because it was barely audible, she honed in on it to verify its existence and then its source. The sound was a gritty scratching. It was a frustrated sound. It was the dull sound of metal upon metal. Then there was silence. Silence, long and drawn, broken by the seductive and envious rhythmic susurration of her husband sleeping. A cat gave a single cry and she sharpened her attention, seeking the inexplicable sound and beginning to doubt its existence. When she heard it, her eyes snapped open with disbelief. The sound was that of a crack of wood. A slow, crack, crack, crack, much like somebody creeping on the stairs. But this was outside. She waited a moment when it stopped. When it resumed she turned to Chris and shook him. Shushing him, she told him in an urgent whisper that she thought somebody was trying to break into the cellar. They both lay still and listened and predictably heard absolutely nothing. Just as he was about to speak she arrested him with a movement of a hand. The intermittent cracking began again.

Chris leapt out of bed and moved gingerly to the window. In complete contrast to this sudden dynamism he tentatively parted the curtains.

"I can't see anything," he whispered.

"They're right up at the door," she answered.

"Okay, don't switch the lights on. I'm going down."

"Don't you think we should phone the police first?"

"Not yet. Let me take a look first." By now he had tied his dressing gown and was picking up the baseball bat.

"Are you sure that's a good idea?"

By way of reply he looked at her, but it was too dark for her to see his expression. He slipped on his house shoes and left the bedroom. She heard him move down the stairs and thought that the noise was enough to alert the slowest of intruders. The cracking had stopped and although it was hard to tell, the sound swamped by the wind rustling the leaves of the trees and bushes, she heard a shuffling movement upon the concrete area at the cellar door.

Teresa was up and pulling on her dressing gown when she heard her husband open the front door. Her heart began to pound. He could have gone down through the kitchen and down the metal stairs, but by the time he would have reached the bottom the intruder would have had ample time to flee. She looked about the room for something with which to arm herself. There was nothing suitable and she grew a little frantic. Finding nothing better she picked up one of Chris's shoes.

At first she tried to move silently down the stairs on her slippered feet, but then realised that Chris was presumably confronting the intruder at that very moment. She then hastily went to the front door, which showed a chink of the outside. Changing her mind she went to the kitchen and tried to peer into the garden below. As far as she could tell it was empty. Whoever they were they were apparently too close to the house for her to see them. Possibly directly under the stairway. She returned to the front door, but not before placing Chris's shoe on the work surface – on reflection not such a hygienic idea – easing out the cutlery drawer and fetching the rolling pin.

Opening the door the first thing she saw was a cat on the front wall silhouetted by the lamp-light behind and she could not make out its features.

Rather than move down the length of the house she stood at the corner and called her husband's name. He did not reply. The night hissed something incomprehensible.

There was no alternative; she would have to go to the back garden herself.

Cautiously she moved down the side of the house, wishing she had chosen a knife rather than the rolling pin. She could hear nothing except for the penetrating hiss of the breeze irritating the foliage: an icy shoal of razor fish cutting through cold vegetation.

Just before she reached the corner to the rear of the house, where it opened out onto the garden, she heard her husband's heated voice. The vacuum that was the night swallowed their voices and they sounded as if they were murmuring.

She lowered the rolling pin and turned the corner. The two men looked over at her.

Teresa gave Ricketts an exaggeratedly perplexed expression. The darkness made exaggeration necessary. She then ignored him, noting however, the large sports-like holdall at his feet, and turned to Chris.

The scene was colourless: a mish-mash of hushed shadow and pale light. Greys and black. A sickle moon cut the inky black sky. And when they spoke their words vaporised as quickly as their dry-ice breath, itself a poor mimicry of the thin wisps of cloud that drifted in a virtually cloudless sky. The old man's snow white hair showed at the edges of his dark flat cap that sat limply, like a pancake, upon his head. But it fitted with the rest of his attire. He wore a dark – perhaps olive green – fisherman's jacket that gave away no details of the form it protected: it was baggy making him look formless; his head too, appeared too small for his body. His trousers and boots were equally featureless. All was black and grey-white.

"What's going on?"

"Ahh," exclaimed her husband in disbelief. "He was trying to get into the cellar." Chris proffered the door with a wave of the baseball bat for her inspection. There were a few small twigs, broken, wedged in the door near the padlocked latch. Apparently he had tried to prise the door open with the sticks.

"What for?" she asked the old man.

But it was her husband who answered. "He says he wanted to use the vice."

"What? At this time of night?"

Then he spoke. "Don't sleep much. Comes with age."

When he spoke she noticed his sharp little moon-white teeth: child's teeth in a man's head. There were too many like a ventriloquist's dummy's teeth. A light glinted in his eye.

"But you've no right to be here. Why didn't you ask us?"

"Afraid you would say no."

"Too right."

"There's no harm."

He was an old man out in the cold of the night: small and hunched. In spite of the fact that he was the most well-wrapped-up of the three of them, he appeared vulnerable and weak, but not quite frail. White and exposed, he did not have the high ground. He was displaced and at a disadvantage. Yet, he did not appear to be that frightened. Was he play-acting?

"That may be," said Chris. "But I've got to go to work tomorrow and—"

"Why didn't you take the damned vice with you?" she interrupted, all steel and frost.

"Couldn't get it off."

Teresa could tell that his confidence was returning. There was something in his voice and the way he spoke. He knew he was going to get off. But what could they do? She wanted to punish him, but her husband just wanted to get back to bed.

"And what's in there?" she demanded, pointing to the zipped up holdall.

"Tools." He pulled his collar to himself. His white exposure was turning dark and concealed. He was slipping back under his stone.

"Well, I'd like to take a look – if you don't mind – at your *tools*," she said emphasising her last word with disbelief and some ridicule.

Ricketts faltered, but her husband missed it.

"Oh, come on," Chris countermanded. "I've had enough of this. Ricketts—" no longer Mr Ricketts "– if I see you around here again, uninvited, I'll call the police. I mean it. Do you understand?"

He nodded meekly. His eyes were cast downward and he would not look at Teresa. Of course, there was no real reason to check his bag. He couldn't have taken anything. He had not got into the cellar.

"Come on, I'm freezing out here," said Chris. "On your way."

There was movement at the end of the garden and the couple looked over and saw a cat stroll towards the back wall.

Something snapped in Teresa and shoving the rolling pin into her husband's fumbling hands, she bent down and unzipped the holdall before Ricketts could move. She only managed to unzip a quarter of the way before jumping back in horror.

* * *

Teresa hadn't heard the story Chris told at dinner that evening with Babs and Larry.

Bryn was on his fourth pint when he realised that someone was sitting in the old headmaster's place. The position of his seat and the location of the bar meant that he could only see the faintest shadow of the person on the far wall. There was no reason why this place should not be occupied. The headmaster had died many years ago. In fact he had died when Bryn was a boy. It was his father who had told him that the corner by the bar, under the fox-hunt picture was going to be empty for a while to come. Few would remember him now. And, as for his place in the pub, only some of the older members of the community would avoid taking it.

Normally, he did not drink so much at lunch time, but this was not normal. He was a big man and could hold his drink. Nevertheless, he had been debating whether to have another or to head back to the hotel. It was the form at the dead headmaster's seat intrigued him and gave him a feeble excuse to get up for another pint.

He rose and ponderously lumbered towards the bar. Although he squinted at the form under the picture, he could not make out his features. An arm propped up his head bunching his cheek to his hair and effectively concealed his face. No overcoat or raincoat was in evidence and he appeared to be drenched from head to foot. Bryn glanced outside. The clouds were heavy, but it was not raining, despite threatening to do so all morning. That would have made the funeral unbearable. Being the only relative at the grave-side had made it dreary enough. There were others: local people, the vicar and the parlour staff. The latter, including the driver had made up the pall-bearers. The others were ancients. He vaguely recognised a shopkeeper. The postman was there too. In all, some half a dozen people had offered their condolences. The rest of the village had stayed away.

Bryn surmised that the soaked man was an outsider. The absence of appropriate attire was a sign of someone foreign to these parts.

"Okay, Bryn?" enquired Llewellyn, from behind the bar.

"Yes," he answered, in a preoccupied manner.

"Same again, eh?"

Bryn nodded.

Nothing else was said. The landlord had already asked about the funeral. Courtesy had demanded at least that much.

The landlord knew why he was here and although Bryn was now a stranger he was treated as a local.

He carried his pint back to his place. He was glad he was a stranger. At least he was not mouthing words like the poor old dear in the corner. Had he stayed, he could have ended up that way.

Apart from the old woman having a silent conversation with herself, jutting her false teeth out with such ferocity Bryn expected them to fly across the pub at any moment – he allowed himself a weary smile at this thought – the landlord, the person in the corner and himself, the pub was empty.

Bryn drank his pint within half an hour.

He wondered how quickly he could sell her house. The local people would not buy it. Perhaps some hot-shot city-type would take it as a holiday home.

In places as remote as this people never forgot. He had even felt the underlying hostility from the locals at the funeral. But they could not touch him. Some sharp-tongued old woman might have a go at him, but his imposing physical size and a suitable glare would silence even them.

He also wondered how his aunt had fared all those years alone in such an atmosphere of hatred. Of course he had received letters from her, but she had been such a tough old bird that she had never so much as hinted at finding the place unbearable. The family had lived there for generations and she was not going to run away. The departure of his parents had been a blow. She had never truly forgiven them. Or she had never truly forgiven his father. Ultimately, his father had been the driving force behind the decision to leave. But she had missed Bryn the most. The last time he had seen her was at his parents' funeral. Ironic that only another funeral could bring them together. Why had he never visited? He knew jolly well why. He had travelled the world, faced many dangers, but this little village was the last place he wanted to be.

They had virtually ostracised his aunt, but they could not touch him. The landlord was one of – what Bryn termed – the indifferent lot. He had not been directly affected. Very few of the villagers had not been directly affected. The indifferent lot had not taken sides. In any event, the result was that his mother's sister remained isolated. And all because of a smoke in the toilets. Funny, he had never smoked since.

Bryn looked outside through the top half of the window. The lower half was of frosted glass. The folds of lead in the sky looked like layers of grey plaster slopped upon the ceiling by a drunken plasterer.

When he rose, deciding to return to his aunt's house before the heavens broke, he noticed that the figure in the corner was gone.

The drink had increased his hostility. He would not be accepted by the village and he had no intention of giving them the satisfaction of thinking he wanted to be accepted. The indifferent people were also legitimate targets. So he did not take his glass up to the bar and he did not say goodbye. He simply got up, heaved on his overcoat and left.

When he was outside he could not shrug the feeling that he was being watched. The streets were deserted.

He had always trusted his gut feeling even over his training. So he remained wary.

The petrol roofs were hardened forms of the depressing slate sky. The brickwork was mean and small. A tourist would see it otherwise. A tourist would see something twee and quaint. Bryn saw mean small houses which he knew to harbour mean small people. The tourist would see the smiles and hear the helpful tips, indeed a bit of folklore might be imparted, but the people were a tightly-knit suspicious group. They would not give anything away.

Bryn hated them. He hated them more, now that his aunt was dead. His father had always said that he had two mothers. His rightful mother and her sister.

His features turned to granite in the cold and he pulled up the collar of his trench coat as he headed into the wind.

The village was closed to him, but like his challenge to the wind, he was steel to it. He was granite to their pettiness. Like his aunt he threw down the gauntlet and simply dared them, just dared them. And not one of them would stand up to him as not one of them had stood up to her. This was a family trait of which he was fiercely proud.

He had been there three days, engaged a funeral service from a neighbouring village and all but isolated himself. Maybe the neighbouring village had forgotten the incident. It did not matter. By necessity the vicar too was one of the indifferent people. But even with him the past was taboo. Bryn would not bring it up, but he could feel it simmering behind their words and eyes.

During these three days he had always felt that they were watching him. But when he left the pub this feeling was more acute than ever. Such was the acuteness of the feeling, he could not help himself and turned around. There was nothing. Nobody. Then he reproached himself for giving in. And he became bitter.

"Hey Bryn, slow down, man. Where's the fire?"

He spun round and there not more than five feet away was a man hurrying towards him.

"I thought I'd never catch you." He smiled.

Bryn eyed him suspiciously.

"You remember me?" he questioned.

The big man nodded.

"I'm Lloyd. Remember?"

"Lloyd?" This was the figure in the pub. Bryn recognised the jacket and paisley cravat.

"Yes. I didn't expect you to really recognise me. We must be talking about twenty-five years."

"No. You can't be him."

Lloyd smiled. "Why not?"

"Because I heard from my aunt that Lloyd hung himself."

"Oh that." Again he smiled. "Yes, I did." Bryn was taken aback. "I couldn't face it. You left with your parents. But I stayed. Like your aunty my parents were isolated. It broke their hearts. I got quite depressed. It was years afterwards, but instead of getting better I got worse. I was in my early twenties when I tried that. They saved me. After that my parents took me away. We went to Hastings. We had some relatives there—"

Big drops of rain began to fall.

"Shall we get going?" he asked.

"Where are you headed?"

"The same way as you."

Bryn found this odd and although his suspicions had not been alleviated they set off together.

"When my parents were killed in a car accident I decided to come back. I don't know why. I had to face it. And you'll never guess what." Pause. "I became a teacher. Can you believe it?"

"No," said Bryn, cruelly and almost uninterestedly.

"Oh?"

"My aunt told me that Lloyd hung himself. She said nothing about him surviving."

"So what do you think?"

"I think you're an imposter."

"Don't I look like Lloyd?"

"Yes, you look like him, alright. But you look too young. I don't know who you are or what you want. And I don't particularly care. Perhaps you're Lloyd's younger brother?"

"Remember stealing Fatty Owen's homework, copying it and then burning it?"

Bryn stopped in his tracks and looked hard at the smirking man.

The rain was falling constantly in big soft drops.

"You'll get as soaked as me if we stand here much longer."

"Where?"

"Where what?"

"Where did we do it?"

"Up on Hatter's farm."

Bryn smiled uncertainly. He smiled more at the memory than at his old friend. He remained suspicious. Nevertheless he decided to play along.

"What do you want?" he asked, as they set off once again.

"After all these years I guess I couldn't expect friendship in the space of a few minutes. But I dearly want to show you something."

"What?"

"It's not far. We just have to turn right here."

"What is it?"

"Where I teach."

"And why should I be interested?"

"Because I think it'll help you face it, as I have."

Silence fell between them.

Bryn admitted to himself that it would have been like Lloyd to sit in the old headmaster's place in the pub. He was always brash with something of a crazy streak in him.

The rain fell consistently, but not heavily, as the two marched up the road. It was a grey scene. The sky overcast. The village empty. The fields and hills too, devoid of life. Bushes huddled in scrums. Brittle trees striking upward like arthritic beggars' hands.

The decision tore Bryn. As the corner drew nearer he remained undecided. His arrogance eventually won him over. He thought that it could do him no harm. He was big and strong enough to face anything. He had no excuse not to go. Running away was something he had never done. Well... No, back then it had been his parents who had fled.

An iciness that was nothing to do with the weather began to engulf Bryn as they walked on. It was trepidation. He had put himself in many dangerous situations. He had killed two men in his life, wounded many others and seen a number of comrades killed. Why had he become a mercenary? He had not done it for the money. Each and every one of them had their reasons. Many of them had already been wounded in some way. Others were simply crazy. Up until now he had never known the reason for his chosen occupation. He had been asked and a few times he had asked himself, but he had either made up an answer, joked or shrugged. When he had been feeling especially perverse, he had answered such an enquiry with a load of rubbish about being on a crusade and it having something to do with his favourite hymn they had often sung at school assembly: *Onward Christian Soldiers.* If he was drunk enough he would babble something along the lines of not being a mercenary but a missionary journeying into the heart of darkness to bring civilization to the darkies with a Bible-black Kalashnikov. Now he began to suspect the true grounds for his choice. He had put himself in danger as a form of death wish. It had been his way of facing the incident. Lloyd had unsuccessfully attempted suicide. But Bryn had chosen the life of a mercenary. Perhaps there was some truth in him being on a crusade. He had been purged from this village and sent forth to cleanse the world. And that was what he had done. Naturally he was not so naïve as to believe that none but the guilty were cleansed. When you put down poison some friendly mice went inevitably with the rats.

As they descended the hill it came into view and his mouth dropped. The rain washed the scene in greyness but it was clearly there; perhaps a little smaller. He remembered it being bigger.

He looked at Lloyd in astonishment.

The man in the jacket smiled and nodded. "Yes Bryn, they rebuilt it."

"But she never said anything about that," he said referring to his aunt.

"Why should she?"

Silence.

Bryn felt cold. The cold prickled his neck. He felt its breath upon his face. He felt it circle his ankles.

"Are you pleased?"

He wanted to stop. He wanted to turn around. But the two men walked on.

"You teach here?" asked Bryn.

Lloyd nodded.

It was only when they neared the railings and the gate that Bryn allowed an element of panic to show.

"I've seen where you work. I'll—"

"Ah, Bryn. I said it'd help you face it."

The big man eyed the other.

"Why don't you come in?"

Bryn looked to the assembly hall and classrooms. The lights were ablaze. A yellow glow was warm in the dirty weather.

"What for?" he managed.

"To get in out of the rain, for one. And secondly, I thought you might like to give a talk."

"Give a what?"

"A talk. You're an old boy. Like me, you're a rarity. We bridge a local gap, you might say. Anyway, it'd be interesting for the children."

"What shall I say?"

"Tell them about your life."

The rumble of thunder rolled across the valley.

He was cold inside and no matter how hard he pulled his heavy overcoat to himself he could find no warmth.

"Come in. They're all waiting. The headmaster has already called a special assembly for this afternoon."

Bryn gave him an astonished look.

"I knew you'd come."

"But my life has been a violent one," he protested.

"You don't have to tell them everything."

Bryn was not convinced, but had no excuses. He had killed one man with his bare hands. He had felt the other's breath, felt his life warmth, heard his own heart thumping and sensed the thumping of the other's heart. And then he had heard the grunt and rattle. The grunt had been the death shock and the rattle a gathering of the life-force and the last expulsion of air that was life leaving the body on the merest wisp of breath. But in an incomprehensible way, talking in front of a hall full of open-faced children was more menacing.

For the first time in his life Bryn felt a flood of emotion over which he had no control. He could not steel himself against it. He could not squeeze off a clip of bullets. He could not bash somebody senseless.

How many times had he wondered about the school and how many of the boys would have become Christian soldiers like him, had they had the chance?

In the building Bryn took off his coat and slung it over his arm. Neither spoke.

They walked into the hall, or rather, Lloyd held the door open and Bryn walked in. The entire school had been waiting for him. In the moments before the eruption of applause he could feel their expectation in the air.

He turned to Lloyd for instruction.

"They've been expecting you," Lloyd nodded.

The big man ignored all the little bright faces. As he climbed the stage and went towards the lectern, he ignored all the weathered teachers seated behind it. Before he got to the lectern he saw an empty chair and casually, but with great aplomb, as if he had rehearsed the part, he tossed his coat upon it.

He could not help noticing the shininess of the floor and stage. Everywhere was wet. The boys had been outside in the playground and had probably brought it in with them.

Bryn cleared his throat when he got to the lectern and gripping its damp sides he began to speak in a great booming voice. Before he began, however, he glanced at the door through which he had entered and noted that Lloyd had gone. This unsettled him and although he continued to introduce himself without seeming to falter, his thoughts were in turmoil.

His method of getting through public speaking, or speaking to some kind of group, was not to look at anyone in particular. That is, not to catch anyone's eye. His method was to look ahead, unseeing. So, he ignored everybody as he related why he found school important and how it had helped him later in life.

He wondered whether these children sang 'Onward Christian Soldiers'.

As he spoke, almost unthinkingly, he felt the coldness tighten about his ankles and his throat. He looked over to the door and then to the windows. All of them were closed. But a breeze was coming from somewhere. Undeterred he went on, saying that what they did

87

today would affect tomorrow. It was when he talked of today and tomorrow that he found himself becoming side-tracked. He told them that he was not proud of some of the things he had done. He said that he had attended a similar school, but then realised that they knew he had attended this school and in correcting himself he found himself irreversibly heading towards an explanation of the incident.

The cold was seizing his knees. He could no longer feel his feet. And his glistening fingers were turning to ice and he increased his grip on the lectern to warm them.

No, he said, he had done many bad things in his life, but none had left such a mark upon him as what had happened at this school.

Why was he telling this story? What could he say after telling it?

But he went on. He said that it had been on a day similar to today. Wintry, stormy, wet. Saying these words he let go of the lectern and clenched his fists so that his fingernails dug into his palms. The pain in his fingers and toes were slipping into numbness. Many years ago when he was thirteen. Yes, it had been many years ago. At this he tried to smile, but it came out twisted with bitterness and he hoped that the children had not seen it. He told them how his friend Gareth and he had decided to skip the school assembly that morning. They had agreed to skive-off. Probably a different phrase was used today, bunked off or something. He said this to lighten the story, but this time he made no attempt to smile. They arranged to meet in the toilets for a smoke. The cold seemed to be eating him up. He felt it at his elbows and he was up to his waist in it. It was as if parts of him were closing down. His heart laboured against it, but it too was slowing, giving up. He felt fixed to the spot, as if the cold were a physical thing and he was mired in it. He had managed to slip away as his class filed into the hall after registration. When he told them that Gareth had not been able to get away from the same class Bryn found himself crying. He found that he could not wipe his eyes because the cold held his arms down. This he ignored, wanting to end the ordeal of the story and hoping that the children thought his face was merely wet with rain. Then he sensed someone nearing him from behind, but he remained steadfast and continued his story. Gareth had attended the doomed assembly whilst he sat in the toilet – a separate building – smoking a cigarette. Then it had happened. The fateful landslide had slammed into the building it, swamping it and bringing down the roof. Parts of Bryn's body were dying as if he had been dropped into liquid nitrogen and by degrees his body was turning to marble. The majority had been killed. Apart from five lucky survivors – who were not subject to the same singling-out and persecution – every schoolchild in the hall had perished. Lloyd survived because he had stayed at home with stomach-ache. He had later confided in Bryn, before he left the area, that he had faked the stomach-ache so as to avoid a geography test. Bryn did not tell the children this, but he did say that many people in the village thought it unfair that the wicked should profit. He said that he had devoted his life to carrying forward a righteous banner of good and just and therefore Christian. The big man felt heavy like gun metal and cold like gun metal. He was no longer sure he was talking and felt confused. He had been weeping silently but now he was composing himself, trying to stand erect, instead of leaning forward over the lectern. Or was he? He was widening his eyes to clear them when he heard the vaguely familiar voice.

"Well done, Bryn."

He thought he turned his head. The rest of him seemed to be fixed. How tired he felt. A figure was at his side. Applause exploded and there were even some cheers. Bryn blinked to view the figure who was smiling at him. But his lids were heavy. It was only when the man spoke again telling the children to turn to the hymn number indicated on the board that Bryn momentarily cleared his eyes to see the man.

It was his old headmaster.

His eyes were closing, but he looked to the board and then to the honours list that hung a little further away – gold print upon wood – and although he could not read the names he could make out the year of the last entry. It was the year of the disaster.

His respiration was growing irregular.

With widening eyes from one last flare of energy he looked to the children and scanned the faces. They were all wet. They had been outside in the rain. But they were dripping wet. Lots of little boys. He was barely breathing as he recognised an occasional face, too perfect for memory.

They began to sing.
"Onward, Christian soldiers,
Marching as to war,
With the Cross of Jesus
Going on before."

Bryn was fixed amongst the ruins of a school that had never been rebuilt, a monument to those who died. His core body had dropped below thirty degrees centigrade. He was sinking in a gully, engulfed in a thick muddy coat entering the final stages of hyperthermia.

His delirious mind scanned a row of familiar faces, faces petrified in time and place.

There was Gareth, smiling and looking not at his hymn book but directly at him.

"Christ the Royal Master
Leads against the foe;
Forward into battle,
See, His banners go!"

It was the boy beside Gareth, sharing the hymn book that stopped Bryn's heart. It was him as he had been as a boy.

* * *

That Monday morning Teresa checked the cellar door. Apart from a loss of sheen to the paint at the edge of the door there was no real damage.

Before leaving for work Chris had evidently also been here. The sticks were gone.

She unlocked the door and stepped in. The smell assaulted her.

Maybe the growing life inside her was sapping her, but she felt that since coming to the house she was dying. Her energy was waning and she felt fragile.

Something gripped her heart and she looked up at the floorboards. With mounting fear she backed away from the guts of the room to the mouth, looking upward all the time, as if something was about to fall. Now she was certain. She had suggested this as a possibility, but until now she had not looked closely at the planks and realised that there were gaps between them. She felt the presence. Her eyes searched the shadowed cracks.

She chose to stand in the doorway. Having given the cellar a cursory sweep with the torchlight, she ran the light systematically along the overhead floorboards. At any moment she expected to discover a stony eye looking down upon her, or perhaps the merest tip of a finger. Of course, unless she ran the torch the length of the floorboard, positioning herself to look down that particular length, she saw nothing but the edges of the wood or blackness. Indeed, the boxes restricted her further. Uncomfortable though she was about the idea she had to move into the cellar.

Once or twice she found herself scrutinising what turned out to be a knot in the wood or a piece of rubbish. As she neared the end of her search the possibility of finding something diminished, so a profound disappointment or depression grew.

Before she came to the end of her fruitless search her mind was working away on other avenues of investigation. The feeling of imminent terror, an encroaching jungle of twisted dread, remained with her, but some of her thinking lashed at it and in the pocket of breathing space she produced she was able to devote the rest of her thinking to the problem at hand. Indeed, the mundane running of the torchlight itself offered some distraction from her feeling of trepidation.

Turning to go back to the house she heard her neighbour filling a watering can from a tap at the side of her house.

She called out a greeting, but Ruth didn't hear her and moved deeper into her garden.

Rather than chase after her Teresa returned to the house.

Inside she looked at the two boxes in the baby's room, but couldn't bring herself to open them, and surprise Chris by assembling the cabinet. Thoughts of Ricketts and his bag skewered any thought of applying her brain. She chose to do washing and ironing instead.

The locksmith came early that afternoon and then it was time to make the dinner.

And so the day was whittled away. With respect to Ricketts's Sunday evening visit and the events of the days to come this Monday was indeed lost.

* * *

She looked at the kitchen clock the moment the banging started. It was ten twenty three. The sound numbed her, rooting her to the spot, but she fought back. It was Tuesday. When had it occurred last week? Her fingers galloped as she held her arms down to stop her hands rising to her ears. Somebody was banging the pipes. She knew she was on the verge of panic, a scream growing in her throat. The clang reverberated. It happened on the day of her doctor's appointment. She glanced at the calendar. Tuesday. Tuesday, last week, just after breakfast. Just after ten.

Teresa strode down the hallway. At the last moment she veered away from the lounge and what she might see reflected in the television and opened the front door.

As best she could she ran to Ruth's house.

Her neighbour did not take long to open the front door, but it seemed like an age.

"Hallo, d–"

But the woman didn't get any further. The urgency in Teresa's face was enough. "Please, please, come with me."

"Let me get my shoes–"

"No, come now. In your slippers." Teresa was still in her slippers.

"I'll get my keys–"

"Leave your door," she said, beginning to back away. "Please come now."

"Oh dear, what is it?" said the old woman, stepping out of her house. But Teresa had turned and merely glanced back without answering.

Nearing the house Teresa called back to her to raise the reception of her hearing aid.

In the end it did not matter. The knocking had stopped.

"What is it dear?" Ruth asked at the door.

"It was a knocking," Teresa said wearily. "It's stopped now."

Ruth glanced back at her house.

Teresa ignored the fact that she was worried about leaving her door open.

"Can you do something for me?"

"Of course."

"Can we go into the lounge together?"

"You are frightening me a little, dear."

"I'm sorry. But please. That's all."

The woman stepped forward and Teresa moved to the lounge door. She put a hand on the handle and looked at Ruth. "Look at the television." Then she pushed the door open and they both looked in.

The screen was blank.

Before Ruth looked at her the tears had formed. "I'm sorry," she spluttered, before breaking down completely.

"Oh dear," said Ruth at a total loss. She stepped forward and held Teresa. Because she was a head shorter Teresa couldn't rest her head on her shoulder. Their embrace was ludicrous and Teresa smiled and a chuckle, as much through embarrassment, broke her sobbing.

"I'm sorry," she said again, straightening and wiping her tears with the heels of her hands.

"Don't be silly, dear. But you shouldn't be upsetting yourself in your condition."

"I– I know." Another sob was swallowed back into a sigh. "I'm sorry."

"Don't be. That's enough. Now, what was this noise?"

Teresa huffed.

"I'll tell you what," Ruth began. "Lock up and come over for a nice cup of tea."

Teresa felt on the edge of hysteria. The suggestion that the proverbial nice cup of tea could wash away her worries was too bizarre. All she could do was nod.

The kettle was boiling when Teresa entered the house. Ruth had left her front door open.

"If you apologise again," Ruth said, "You're not getting a chocolate digestive."

Teresa smiled. "My lips are sealed."

Only when they were settled in the lounge with the tea and biscuits and after perfunctory talk did Teresa begin to explain. She spoke about the knocking first, adding that there were many things that had upset her and that she would like to tell Ruth about it all. Taken individually they were almost insignificant incidents. Indeed Chris had dismissed all her worries with logical explanations or doubt. And in her state, a state that was growing frail by the day, she doubted herself. But Ricketts's visit on Sunday had left no doubt for her. Something was very wrong. Something at the house was not right.

"I thought I was going crazy before he turned up. And when I opened his bag, I knew I was right."

"Go on. What was in the bag?"

Teresa saw it in her mind's eye before she spoke. Black fur, an ear, a milky plastic slit for an eye and a long fang unnaturally showing in the closed mouth. For such a tooth would only be bared in a snarl, not a closed mouth.

"What did Ricketts say?"

"He said he wanted to bury it with the rest of her cats."

"I asked him why he was trying to get into the cellar."

Ruth waited.

"He said he wanted to get a shovel. Of course he was lying. He would have brought his own shovel, had that been true."

"What did Chris say?"

"What could he say? He sent Ricketts on his way."

"I mean what did Chris think about it all?"

"Ricketts is loopy."

Ruth nodded.

"That's all," said Teresa.

They sipped their teas.

"He was quite wobbly when he left. He was pale and shaken. He staggered with his bag. We didn't see his car. But I didn't care and Chris didn't either. We just closed the door and went to bed." They had lain awake for some time trying to figure out what had happened: talking and thinking themselves into complete exhaustion. Quite a few times she had thought Chris was asleep until he spoke into the darkness.

They were silent for a while.

"Tell me Ruth, how do you know Mrs Ricketts ran away?"

As if caught out, the woman didn't answer immediately. "Ricketts told me," she admitted.

Teresa nodded.

"You think Ricketts killed her?" said Ruth.

"It would explain the smell. And why he sold so quickly."

"And the noise?"

Teresa didn't answer.

"You think the place is haunted, don't you?" said Ruth.

"What do you think?"

"About him killing her or the house being haunted?"

"Killing her."

"He could have, I suppose. But why did he sell? He could have just stayed in the house."

Teresa brightened at a realisation. "Because the place *is* haunted."

"You said the knocking happens once a week. And you've only heard it twice. That's hardly haunting."

Again the penny dropped for Teresa. "It's the time he killed her." She imagined the tapping of shoes in death throes.

Ruth shook her head. She was not convinced. "I don't know, dear."

It all seemed so obvious to Teresa and she was perplexed that the older woman could not see it. But then she had not experienced these things.

"I do," she said quietly, almost to herself.

* * *

With hindsight she could claim many things but Teresa swore vehemently that she felt that something – almost physically – would happen that Wednesday. Perhaps it was an accumulation of events over the past few days, or indeed that very morning, but the result was the same. She had the feeling that despite having visited the cellar on a number of occasions and, to all intents and purposes, seen all there was to see, she would today discover something.

She had finally decided to tackle assembling the baby's cabinet. She had opened the boxes and laid the various pieces out. Then she had checked that it was all there. Finally she had glanced over the instruction sheets to make sure she was picking up the correct sides. She was struck by how the back panel was slipped into place. The panel was pushed up into a deeper groove in the underside of the top surface before slotting into the lower groove of the base. That meant it could be removed at any time by shifting it upwards.

Teresa was not sure what she thought as she collected the torch and new cellar door key. She knew she was weak. But a faint defiant streak propelled her. She wanted to know.

Ominously, as she stepped into the garden, an ashen cat moved out from the bushes at the graveyard. It walked across the grass towards a tree. Unexpectedly, it paused mid-stride, as if flash-photographed or strobe-lit. All the while it concentrated on some unseen object ahead and did not look at her; although she was in no doubt that it was aware of her. Then it bounded up the tree, like a squirrel, for a moment clutching the trunk. The ominous thing was that it settled itself in a position that overlooked the cellar. When it was settled its head swivelled like an owl and it began watching her.

Teresa shuddered and uneasily turned her back on it to open the door.

Opening the cellar door revealed the usual yawning stillness. Yet, this time the place was holding its breath: a breath that was beyond human. This feeling was not manifest, it was obtuse and all the more poignant.

Added to this was her diminished strength of mind. Since moving into the house the subtle attrition had worn her down.

Once again she left the day behind her: outside. Naturally she left the door ajar. With an eggshell-frail hardness she steeled herself and moved down the corridor of boxes to the closed doors of the wardrobe.

She took in a long breath through her nose. The smell was there. But she had not taken in this breath for the smell. She had done it unconsciously because the wardrobe was the thing she most feared.

She opened the door and stepped back as if something could jump out.

Uncertainty was eroding her determination. Fissures of fear were trickling through hairline fractures in the wall of her will. She had the sudden feeling that someone was behind her and swung round sharply. Nothing. Vulnerability shook her and some of the fractures split open becoming cracks. Fear was beginning to flood her thoughts. She knew that if she did not act soon it would be too late.

She reached in and pulled the catch that would release the other door.

As it swung open she realised that she was staring at the askew newspaper. The old paper with the children's corner on it. Her lids were heavy. Were her eyes burning? If so, was it sweat? She could not tell. She seem divorced from her body and only seemed to be catching snatches of its signals.

She sought the boy's poem. There it was. "The Loch Ness M—"

"The Loch Ness M—"

The yellowed paper was askew. The edge, and the remaining letters that made up the word Monster, was folded underneath.

Ricketts had been there at least once since she had read the poem. The pencil had disappeared after she had read it.

The paper was askew, caught in the lower half of the back panel.

There could be no doubt.

Was she breathing?

Inexplicably, she became both cool and frantic. An icy apprehension cooled her and she moved with some deliberation. At the same time she grew frantic with fear: a fear founded on adrenalin, and indeed, she wanted flight and fight.

She reached down and gave the paper a tentative tug. It was ensnared where a back panel met the base.

The frightful noise of a choking cat began to spin in her head.

The only handle that offered a grip was the hook on one of the back panels. Before touching the hook she gently but firmly pressed the panel with the tips of spread-eagled fingers. It remained steadfast. Clenching her fist with the bent index finger protruding beyond the other fingers she tapped the panel. Of course this was silly because she had nothing similar with which to compare. In any case it sounded hollow.

Teresa was swimming towards something. She was heading towards something despicable. Diabolically drawn by the girl in the lake. And she was being drawn into a quagmire like a big man pulled down by a childhood disaster. Was her face a mask? She daren't look in the mirror.

She watched her hand reach into the wardrobe. She saw her fingers grasp the hook. Part of her awareness registered the upward shift. The panel was slotted in. She put the torch down. Her other hand came in support of the first and she felt the thing lift. It left the lower groove and uncontrollably crashed against the wall and upon the ground behind the wardrobe.

Teresa let out a breath of exertion. The baby kicked.

The stillness was awesome. She no longer held her breath, but something else did. There was the sound of a wind that did not exist, currents that did not flow. And there were stirrings too. Scuttling. Movement.

But she saw and heard nothing. For the scuttling and movement were things in her mind. Things becoming unhinged, like the panel resting against the wall were she knew a hole to be.

Panting with dread she put her hands to the edge of the panel and began to shift it aside in short sandpaper jerks.

What would she see?

Trepidation and triumph brought water to her eyes, but she was not sure whether she had begun to cry.

The bottom of the panel caught and it became unbalanced. It slid with a horrible scratching sound to a forty-five degree position where it wedged itself immovably; stuck behind the bench. The sound and the revelation caused her to step back. But this was not all. At the moment of exposure everything and nothing happened. On the one hand a hole in the wall was exposed. And that was all: a physical fact.

On the other hand a gob of smell was spat at her. But it was not merely the smell that sickened her; it was the awareness of scampering. Exposing the hole had set a chain of events moving, a chain of events so remote that she barely registered its beginnings. And then it was upon her. First they were murmurs, but then they grew to a cacophony of screams and cries: the shrill call of a cockatoo, the trumpet bellow of an elephant, piercing squeal of a bat and much more. She experienced these things. Outwardly everything was passive, perhaps shock-still, but inside an appendix burst its poison, a tumour devoured the last of a ravaged organ, a heart palpitated, something haemorrhaged, a stroke ripped through the side of her. To her an entire zoo of beasts was stampeding, they were fleeing a forest fire, escaping something quite hideous.

The gap was waist height and although it was too dark to see inside, she could see that the floor moved off at this level too. This construction was probably something to do with the support of the house and how it married the slope of the hill: two tiered. The hole, although almost square in dimensions, was irregular, the bricks at the sides jutting back and forth: gaping teeth in a mouth on its side.

The yawning silence had returned. The flight of the wild animals was over. Only a column-rigid cloaked vampire stood behind her to her right. With vulture-like patience, seductive vulture-like certainty, the creature, that was outwardly a pillar, was waiting. And then a mouth of stagnant and foul breath awaited her too. Whatever was inside awaited her.

Teresa remained fixed to the spot. She seemed incapable of action. Eventually, she managed to retrieve the torch, but not without first feeling the torture and pain, the intense years of suffering of the furrowed brow that was the bench. She took the opportunity to glance about herself and check that she was alone.

She was now in no hurry. A part of her wanted to forget the whole thing and wait for her husband to come back.

The torch had remained on all this time and it was a simple matter of pointing it into the hole. But she let the light rest upon the newspaper.

She was aware that something horrible lay before her. She wanted to find out what it was. But her mind was frozen. She was physically cold too. It was almost as if she had died. Macabre inquisitiveness held her in place. She felt nothing. There was no triumph, no fear, nothing. Was this shock?

She wiped her eyes.

Then she followed the torchlight as it rippled over the brickwork towards the gap. Then it brightened the hole, but it exposed nothing. The beam had hit something. It had hit something regular: rectangular in form.

Teresa knew that she would have to step closer to the wardrobe; she may even have to put her head into the hole! This latter thought caused her great anxiety. If she put her head inside she would never come out the same. A mask would be fixed in her mind.

She remained at a distance squinting at the shape. There was another to its left. She extended her arm and peered.

But she was still too far away.

She stepped forward. The torch at the end of her extended arm could now touch the brickwork of the hole.

Suitcases. They were suitcases.

The light wandered the width of what she could reach from her position. But within this arc were only a pile of old bricks and some pieces of wood and some bits of cable. These things appeared to be leftovers that the builders had not bothered to remove. Or more likely, they had used this area to dump superfluous materials. The outcome was the same: other than the suitcases there was nothing to be seen.

She would have to move closer.

Again she hesitated.

After some moments she stepped up and into the wardrobe. She refused to put her hand right into the hole and of course putting her head in was out of the question. The smell was amplified. It reeked. For an instant her stomach tightened and cheeks bulged in readiness to retch – the stench was that strong – but she held it down.

Panning the light to the right revealed a further suitcase and to the left more pieces of rubbish and some clothes. She scanned the clothes. A couple of coats and then dresses, jackets, blouses and so on. Women's clothes. She swung the light back to the right and caught something dark near the hole. A fur stole or a jacket? It was hard to tell and she leaned into the hole.

She caught her breath as she recognised the slack thing to be an animal. She was not sure, but she thought it was a cat. Moving the torch over the limp thing she caught something else. It was a glint of light. The fang in the set snarl of another dead cat. Then there was another and another, all in various states of decomposition. The nearest, being the best preserved and therefore the most recent. One had a dried lump of brown blood at an ear. Another appeared to have a broken head.

Teresa felt dizzy. Her heart was pulsing in the wrong place.

When she was retrieving her head from the hole she happened to glance to her immediate left. Although the torch was not pointing at the form, the light was sufficient for her to recognise what it was. It was in the corner in a sitting position the legs extended. The arms hung lifelessly at the sides. In the dullness one could have mistaken it for a life-sized doll, but she knew that it was no such thing. The form was irresistible and she brought the torchlight to meet it.

She moved the light up the form, towards the head, fairly rapidly, and yet the details her brain registered were far beyond what would normally be observed in such a short length of time. The duration was therefore extended and as if with some morbid relish she appeared to move the light slowly. But there was no savouring here. The horror was not compelling; it was debilitating. Physically she was sick and weak with fear. She had no energy. Some miraculous reservoir from the very dregs of herself kept her going. Parts of her were lifeless. And other parts of her were shutting down. Put simply, the parts of her that had not abandoned her were themselves dying. At the same time she was conscious of a background of dark activity. A wealth of images invaded her mind, such that during these moments she had no actual thoughts. She didn't recognise the images. They hinted at distant childhood fears. When she paid attention to them they seemed childish. But like childish things they had a purity to them. They were not shocking or curious. They were disturbing. They were not the images an adult conjures up, but those a child might. An insect sprung upon her head and munched her skull: the bone crunching like dried leaves and the insides soft but firm like a poached egg. And the snake, dead shark eyes, flick of insect rapid tongue, inexorably and slowly squeezing the life from her heart. A rat snarling: pure and contorted and irrational. The capillary needles of leeches siphoning the warmth from her body. Flies fussing about the tops of her legs, maggots waiting in the wings, wings waiting in the maggots. All were alien: things with which she could not reason. Things that knew nothing else. They inhabited a different world, a world she could not compromise. A world without reason; a world without conscience. A world apart. And the form had skipped out of her world. It had sprung over to the cycle, treadmill, that these alien creatures inhabited; the world she set herself above but could not deny. Such ascension was arrogant and illusory, but acknowledgement was too distressing to be dwelt upon. The parallel between these worlds was life and death. At this moment, travelling the body, that she was reminded of the swirling leaves of that morning. With it came the realisation that the image did not belong to her. The dream was beyond the realms of her imagination. It was not her dream. She had felt something that did not belong to her. The torchlight flowed unevenly over what was once an arm and hit a broken watch, the face of which became luminous with the passing of the light. She barely registered the time as just after twenty past ten and moved the torch on. A mask of death greeted her when the light reached the face. Reminiscent of one of the ornamental shrivelled heads that had adorned a wall when Ricketts had occupied the house, this head did not look real and she knew that it could only be real, that it was all the more repulsive. She had travelled the slack legs that lay with the points of the dark high heels pointed outwards: a Charlie Chaplin stance. The light had moved over the skirt that rippled so slightly over the thin legs that one could take the ripples to be folds in the material. Probably because the body was propped up in the corner the torso seemed impossibly caved in. The shoulders were uncomfortably rounded. And then the sloppy head: a carp grimace, dark stretched skin constricting shrivelled flesh, staring insentient lifeless pits, miniature ears, scraggy chicken-brittle neck, straggly colour-drained hair. The broken watch on her wrist showed just after ten twenty. All this alone was frightening enough, but it was the red lipstick that slammed the final bolt of fear through her. No heinous trick such as a centipede or beetle crawling across the corpse's cheek and into the darkness of an eye socket was necessary. A grin of red lipstick had recently been smeared across her face. The lines that made up the hideous smile went beyond the lips making it grotesquely outsized. It was abhorrent, a disfigurement, rendered all the more frightening because of its freshness.

All this took almost no time at all. The torch was dropped and the back of her head banged cruelly against the wall. She began to stumble out of the wardrobe, pain searing her wounded head, the newspaper betrayed her and slipped, and although she reached out for the pillar to her left, she fell onto the concrete floor. This too was against her and was a potato peeler to her living skin. She badly grazed her elbow and knee.

The gush of wetness was the last straw and she collapsed amongst the boxes.

Unthinking, all she could do was call out hysterically.

"Ruth! Ruth! Ruth!"

* * *

Ruth had not come. Teresa had staggered to the house and called her husband to call an ambulance.

The baby was premature, but not in danger. Teresa could not have any more children.

The couple were interviewed by detectives and heard that they had broken into Ricketts's place. He had apparently died a few days earlier. He had suffered a heart attack and wounded himself whilst falling. Although they didn't explicitly say so, it was obvious that his cats, locked in with him, were lured by the wound and had started devouring him.

Crime scene technicians descended upon the house and all but evicted Chris. He relayed their conclusions to Teresa. Ricketts had cut his wife's throat in the kitchen.

On Tuesday Chris had waited in the house until eleven o'clock before going to work. There was no knocking.

They discussed selling the house and agreed to see how Teresa felt when she returned with the baby.

* * *

The bench and wardrobe disappeared. Although Chris was reluctant to part with the former. They had the cellar gutted and plastered.

And they remained.

* * *

Their son was a sickly child and grew into a timid boy.

* * *

Teresa had resisted buying a dog, arguing that it would be an added burden, but when she returned to the house she relented.

The dog, successfully putting paid to any visits by cats, died when the boy was ten.

* * *

For his eleventh birthday he received an Alsatian puppy which, for reasons he could not explain, he decided to name Sultan.

Skin

Darkness. Pitch black velvety darkness. Darkness punctured by brittle clinical sounds echoing in his mind. He could sense someone in the room. He must be in a room because the sound of birds was muffled. They were outside. But why were they chirping at night?

Then he remembered the broken bottle to his face. A flash. The memory was so vivid – the broken bottle coming towards his eyes – that he cowered and then flinched. With the spasm came the pain. The person in the room must have heard or noticed his movement because he sensed a sudden stillness.

Hurt, dull and sharp in strange places where he normally didn't feel, probably should not feel, tormented his entire body. He wanted to open his eyes, but couldn't.

The effort needed to move his right hand horrified him. A tube was attached to it. The swish of stiff starched material reached his ears. As his fingers touched the bandage, his arm feeling the tubes that entered his nostrils, his ribs aching, his left side screaming, he sensed the proximity of someone. The smell told him it was a woman. She was not perfumed, but smelt lavender pleasant.

"Don't worry," said her voice. She would be standing over him. He tried to pick the edge of the bandage to lift it off his eyes and she put a hand on his. "You're still healing," she said.

Her accent said that she was not a native speaker.

"I–" he began, his cracking voice strange in his head. To steady its uncertainty he overcompensated and his words came out harsh. "I'll be able to see."

She gently guided his hand down to his side. "I'll call the doctor."

He sighed and heard her leave. Her caring tone irked him and made him wary. His irritability warranted curtness not sympathy. The number of strides she took to the door made the room little bigger than his bed. The window would be to his right.

He let his left hand wander in the air, moving in an arc past his shoulder. His ribs protested again and the searing pain in his left side yelled at him to stop. He hit something hard and awkwardly investigated it with his fingers. A bedside unit. The tinkle of glass froze him. Then he moved his hand more cautiously. A pitcher and glass.

By now the pain was unbearable and he was sweating. The moment he rested his hand the agony didn't disappear, it receded.

The door opened and no-nonsense strides defined by swishing material came to his ears. He smelt the nurse enter. A man cleared his throat.

"How are you feeling, Leon?" The masculine voice, from the end of the bed, was like the man's gait: no nonsense.

"Fucking brilliant," he said bitterly.

"Yes, well, what do you expect?" The doctor was nearing him. He was unfazed by Leon's hostility.

Leon replied with a grunt.

The doctor held his wrist. Breakfast fried eggs and coffee hung on his breath. "Any headache?"

"No." He took a deep breath. Then, magically, he was aware of his throbbing head. "Just give it to me straight. Will I be able to see again?"

The silence could have been interpreted as reluctance, but when the doctor spoke, his tone was clinical, emotionless. He told Leon that he would never regain his sight. Before he could digest this fact, the doctor added that there was only a slim chance that he would ever walk again. Only after the swelling had gone down, and the pressure taken from the nerves of his lower back would they be able to tell how much damage had been done.

"But," Leon stammered, "I – I can feel my legs."

"Okay. Wait a minute."

Leon heard the movement of bed sheets.

He felt their presence at the end of the bed. What were they doing?

"You didn't feel anything, did you?"

"What? I... No."

"I just poked the soles of both your feet with my pen."

Something warm and wet dampened the bandage of his right eye.

The doctor said something to the nurse, but Leon was too wrapped up in his own thoughts and missed it.

"I'll see you tomorrow, Leon. But just remember one thing." He was using that same stern emotionless voice, contrasting that of the nurse. "We're here to help you."

He pressed his lips tight for fear of losing his grip and spewing a vile retort. He'd wanted it straight and had been suspicious of the nurse's caring approach, but now he wanted her sympathy.

The door clicked shut. Had the nurse left too?

He reasoned that he had nothing to lose speaking into the room.

"Can't anything be done?"

"I'm sorry. You heard the doctor. But this is a special clinic."

"Where am I?"

He was glad when she said that he was more than two hundred kilometres from home. It meant the gang wouldn't see him like this. What about his mother and step-father? Ha! They'd disowned him years ago. If they were even thinking about him it would be gloating with a told-you-so attitude. They wouldn't come. He didn't want to see them. He didn't want to see anyone. And then he realised the unfortunate wording of his thoughts. He wouldn't 'see' anyone ever again.

"I have a flannel and a bowl of warm water here," she said. "If you'd wash your face I could give you a shave."

He wanted to snap at her, but there was something about the gentleness in her voice that soothed him. "I, er, I've had a shock. Could you do it for me?"

"I've been doing it since you arrived." He remained silent. "Okay. This once." There was a smile in her voice. "If you promise to do it for me next time."

"I promise."

"Shave my head too."

There was a moment before she spoke. "Why, Leon?"

"It's how I like it."

"It's very short still. And it looks so golden. Let it grow. We can always cut it later."

Again he found himself on the verge of snapping, but then he thought what did it matter and acquiesced.

She spent a long time shaving him and he savoured her touch and her aroma.

Of course he had no intention of washing or shaving or doing anything. There was only one way out now.

After wiping him dry she led his hand to the alarm switch at the end of a cord near his head. She also guided him to the radio switch on the panel in the wall.

She told him he would enjoy physiotherapy. They had a wonderful pool. And he'd be able to join the Braille class too.

He asked how long he'd been unconscious and she said that he had been in a coma for almost two weeks.

As she made ready to leave he asked about his things.

"Your clothes are in the cupboard. The police confiscated your weapons."

"Could – could I have a cigarette?"

Her hesitation told him that it was possible.

"It's not allowed."

"Please." The unaccustomed word sounded unconvincing even to him.

"I don't smoke."

"There should be a packet in my jeans."

He heard the sound of hinges of a cupboard door. "If they're not here, you can't have one." She could lie to him and tell him there weren't any. How helpless he was! "I've found them. The packet's in a sorry state."

"Thanks." Another infrequently used word in his vocabulary.

She opened the window and remained in the room until he had finished.

"I'll pop in from time to time. Lunch is in two hours."

"Can you close the window before you go?" He hated the cheerful birds.

If she did pop in he was asleep and he missed her.

The two hours seemed an eternity as he dozed in the gaping silence. Five minutes radio was enough. Like the birds it chirped joyfully and only served to impress upon him that life went on in its mundane Technicolor way.

In the two hours he mentally ticked off all the things now denied him. Play computer games, drive a car, walk, see a film. Marry, for who would marry a blind wheelchair-bound cripple? He wasn't just finished, he was fucked and finished. Good and proper.

Lunch arrived with the news that now he was conscious the police would be notified. He declined the offer of a lawyer.

Nothing mattered.

The nurse with fathomless patience wanted him to try to feed himself. But like the shave he refused, this time saying that he wasn't hungry but sounding like he didn't care. She fed him, but he ate slowly and very little, the food on the last forkfuls was cold.

If the two hours before lunch had seemed long, the afternoon lasted aeons.

A different nurse brought his dinner. She said her name and that she was the late shift. Her hint of perfume assaulted his nostrils. Unsympathetically she refused to feed him. Instead she made him sit up – searing pain flaring from the small of his back – and feel the edge of the tray and the items on it. He asked when she would collect it. She said seven and he had to ask what time it was. He decided to wait out the hour. His back was aching when she collected the untouched tray. She scolded him, but he stayed tight-lipped, hating her for her brusqueness and blaming her for his backache.

"If you want anything you know how to call."

"I want to sleep," he said gruffly.

* * *

A week later he was not only stronger – on solids, his pain reduced and by and large, unplugged: no tubes up the nose or into the back of his right hand, although a plastic valve remained attached to the latter – he also knew the nurses' routine.

After collecting the dinner trays they looked in about ten o'clock and then again around five in the morning.

That gave him plenty of time. Seven hours, in fact.

He chose Lavender's day off. She had told him her name, but he had taken no notice. Let the brusque nurse of this shift find him.

By coincidence that very morning a gang member phoned. Most of them had been taken into custody. A couple were still being held. Now, he and some of the others wanted to visit. Leon said he was starting a new life and that they should save their money. He had no intention of returning to that life. In fact he had no intention of returning. Full stop. They could keep his belongings. He had no use for them. He didn't want to see them and he wouldn't admit them.

He waited until the ten o'clock look-in had passed. Then he waited some more. He had no idea how much time passed. Had it been an hour or two or three? Seven, certainly not. His preoccupation with time upset his composure and lent urgency to his resolve. Yet, he moved with slow deliberation, as if trying to delay the action. He held the cord above his head and located the call-button, taking care not to press it. He fingered his way further along and gripped and tentatively tugged. Then he pulled, gathering the length on his chest. When it resisted he gave it a jolt to check its firmness. He was pleased with the length. Mindful of the call-button he fashioned a running noose. Shuffling into a slouching position, pangs of pain shooting up from his lower back, he rested before continuing. How much time had passed? An hour? Two? He craned forward, his back again shrieking, and pulled the noose over his neck. After pulling it tight he again rested. Before he could doze off he reached over for the glass of water. The effort of collecting the cord and sitting up had been gargantuan and he was soaked in sweat. The glass almost slipped from his damp hand. That wouldn't do. The sound of smashing would bring the bitch running. He held the glass on the bed, bringing it to his lips, sipping carefully. Eventually his thirst was quenched and he returned the glass to its place. The most strenuous part of his action now lay before him. Pressing his lips together against the pain, he manoeuvred his upper body to the edge of the bed. He then yanked free the well-tucked bedding from under the mattress. Using both hands he grabbed the pyjama trouser of the leg nearest the bed edge and half-lifted half-pulled it to the edge. His hands heaved his other useless leg. He used a hand to check the overhang of his hip with the frame of the bed. Satisfied, he dragged the material of the outer trouser leg. His back protested and he grunted back a scream. It sickened him that he could only tell that his leg was off the bed, his foot probably touching the floor, when his hand felt the bend in what was his knee. He went back to moving his upper body, thinking his other leg would follow. He reached down with his leading arm, but couldn't feel the floor. In the light of what he wanted to do he smiled at the thought of hurting himself with the fall. Before using his elbows and shoulder to move over the edge he tightened the cord. He was precariously close to falling when he realised that he was too high and his head would hit the bedside trolley. So he tried to push himself down. By the time he understood that his leg on the floor was hindering him, his squirming at the edge made him lose his balance and he fell, his head hitting the trolley, his neck awkwardly bent against it, his shoulder cracking and more than all this his back screaming. The noose was tight and he was wondering whether he could breathe when he lost consciousness.

* * *

Darkness. Voices. The hushed voices of men. A frustrated edge in their hasty speech.

"If we'd known we wouldn't have travelled all this way."

"He was only discovered early this morning," said the doctor. "My first priority is his health. And by then you were well on your way."

"And?"

"I think he's fine. The cord was too loose to cut off his air supply. He just banged his head."

Leon felt there were more than just the two speakers in the room. Was it their respiration or body warmth?

He was also aware of another sensation: a physical sensation that puzzled him.

"So it's not a wasted trip." It was more a statement than a question. "We can talk to him when he wakes up."

Leon surmised that the speaker was a policeman.

The doctor maintained his authority. "When he regains consciousness I'll examine him and then we'll see."

"You just said, you think he's fine."

"Yes. I think he's fine. But I won't know until I examine him. At the very least he's had a shock. He may not be capable of being interviewed. Now, if you'd please leave us alone, I think he's coming out of it."

How did the doctor know? He hadn't moved.

There was a lot of movement. Then silence.

Somebody picked up his left wrist.

"How long have you been awake?" It was the doctor.

There was somebody to his right too.

"Leon. It's okay they are gone. You can answer me."

He was considering replying when the nurse spoke. "Doctor." It was Lavender.

Leon felt the bedcovers being lifted.

"Well, Leon," said the doctor, "This is a good sign. Maybe the damage to your back wasn't so extensive. Can you feel your friend here?"

"Yes," he croaked.

Something hard touched the end of his erect penis and he flinched.

"Sorry," said the doctor. "I had to be sure."

"Does this mean I could walk?"

"It's too early to say. But it doesn't put it out of the question." His voice took on its customary less friendly tone. "How are you feeling?"

"Great."

"Sarcasm doesn't work in here. You should know that by now. Just straight facts. That's the only way we can help you. Have you a headache?"

Leon answered the barrage of questions at the end of which doctor said that his actions meant that he would be strongly recommending psychological treatment. Then he said that he thought he was well enough to be interviewed by the police and that he would send them in.

"Could I have some water?" said Leon as the doctor moved to leave.

"Nurse," he said. "I'll be in later."

When he was gone Lavender adjusted the level of the bed so that he was in a half-sitting position. "I'll hold the glass," she said, bringing it to his lips.

He was drinking when they entered. Nothing was said until the nurse left.

The detective who'd spoken earlier introduced himself and his underling. Leon relished giving the man no acknowledgement. Although he had to nod his agreement to waiving the right to legal representation. The man came close enough for him to smell his cheap aftershave. When the detective again spoke his voice hard a hard edge to it. But it didn't matter. Leon would give them nothing. He steeled himself against all their approaches. This man would have the uncompromising weight of the law behind his every word. Bad cop. His underling – should he have to speak – would go for empathy. He'd be younger, more streetwise. They may even play the left-alone-in-the-room-card: where the senior office has to leave on the pretext of going to the toilet or something, taking his officialdom with him and paving the way for a more appealing route. The good cop. Leon despised the good cop even more than the senior cop, because his approach was the more insidious of the two.

The senior detective gave it to him straight, pausing vainly for response, the pauses growing longer with time. Leon said nothing. He didn't even give them the benefit of a smile. Expressionless. All they had were their voices. At this moment blindness was an advantage.

They wanted to know what he had seen. Who had killed the spiky-haired youth? Of course he was named, but the name meant nothing to him. Only their descriptions. He teetered on the verge of asking them to fill in some of the gaps, but in time they eventually did.

They had pieced together most of what had happened.

Leon and his friends had gone to the abandoned house, a renowned left-wing hangout full of dropouts and drug addicts. With the intention of purging the town of the scourge of society they had gone armed. Trapped, the Lefties had fought back with surprising ferocity.

Leon had gone for Spiky himself, for he represented the worst of the parasites, what with his piercing and chains. He was an abomination. But somebody had taken Leon down. He suspected the big lad. As he turned to rise a bottle had hit him in the face. His head had been kicked and then somebody had torn the iron bar from his grip and used it on his back. Another kick to his head and he had lost consciousness. That was it. He really didn't know how the others fared or what had happened after going down.

These cops wanted to know what he saw. Ha, he didn't even know that Spiky had been killed.

Predictably the senior cop announced that he was popping out for a cigarette.

The underling didn't speak for a long time and Leon began to grow intrigued by the possibility of a new tactic. But he did speak and his streetwise attitude was tiresome.

The good cop even hinted at sympathising with right-wing ideals. Lefties didn't respect order. They had no pride. Drug addicts too were vermin.

The senior officer returned and although nothing was said Leon imagined the younger man visually communicating his failure.

The senior officer was above the desperation of threat, but somehow he managed to talk for another half an hour.

It didn't make any difference. They should have known that a Skin never talks to the police.

Eventually they gave up and left. A parting empty shot of you'll-be-hearing-from-us almost made Leon break his deadpan mask with a smile.

* * *

"How do I look?"

She was redressing his bandages and he could feel the air cold on the damaged skin about his eyes.

He was being clever. His ploy was to dupe them into thinking he cared. He would feign keenness for life until he could put an end to his miserable existence with certainty. Why, he even knew that Lavender's name was Maria and that she was from South America.

"You're healing nicely," said Maria.

He knew what that meant about his appearance but didn't press it.

His ploy was to be sickly polite: a good lad. How else could he get his daily cigarette? Yes, although it was against the rules she allowed him a single smoke during the day. She even bought his brand. His own had been exhausted more than a month ago. He especially appreciated her purchases because she was a foreign nurse, undoubtedly earning a pittance.

No, Maria wasn't a problem. She was the best thing about his incarceration. He could even say that he looked forward to her entering the room. Her days off were barren ones for him.

His problem was the psychologist. He was snide and Leon had to keep his wits about him. Without sight it was terribly difficult to gauge whether the man was taken in by his lies.

Their talks had covered the cowardice of suicide and the wonder of life before delving into his past. He had been forced to talk about his childhood. And the psychologist, the cunning bastard, had a knack of prying at the right crack, not necessarily easing it open, but poking at it long enough for him, Leon, to be aware of it. Were these small faults in his personality? Contradictions in his thinking? Unseen crossroads at which he'd blithely taken the wrong turn?

Others were to blame. Yes, his guardians, especially them. A whoring mother and a string of stepfathers, some of them pimps, the majority of them abusive. No, he couldn't call them parents.

His truancy stopped when he left school and moved out to share a flat with an older lad. This lad was a neo-Nazi, who had long taken the schoolboy Leon under his wing.

The psychologist agreed that others were to blame, but added the word partly. For he, Leon, shared responsibility for who he had become. To all the situations he had chosen how to react. He was, and still was, responsible for his actions, for who the person called Leon was.

At some point he chose to react extremely, tightening the shell about himself, slapping cement in the faults, presenting the right to silence card. Yes, he was up to the challenge. This man wouldn't get to him. He wouldn't turn him soft. He was a Skin.

By then silence wasn't an option. The psychologist knew too much. He had a wealth of material at his disposal. And whether inadvertently or on purpose, Leon found himself compelled to correct some of his understanding and suppositions.

Then the man tackled his ideology.

"I don't deny that what I believe is full of intolerance and hate. But that's the only way to fight a weak government, letting all these foreigners in to take our jobs and women."

"They do the jobs many nationals don't want."

"Maybe, but working for peanuts is destroying the market"

"Surely the employers are to blame."

"Yes, they're all Lefties..."

"Everyone knows that the victors write history. Why, concentration camps were a British invention from the Boar War."

"But they weren't intended as extermination factories. It was internment that went horribly wrong..."

"I know invalids were killed under the T4 Program. It was a form of euthanasia."

"Really? Tell me how a two-year-old's consent was obtained."

"Okay, it was a form of mercy killing."

"You don't think simple economics might have been behind it? Get rid of the expense of feeding extra mouths and free up the staff for the Cause..."

"No, no, I'm not one of military-fascination types. And I'm not one of those simpletons or social outcasts in it for the comradeship."

"But you admit your childhood lacked a sense of family. So there could have been an element of sanctuary involved..."

His sessions with the psychologist were mentally exhausting. The man chipped away at his personality. If he hit a fault-line a chunk of him would fall away.

Leon was convinced the man could make him believe black was white.

Afterwards Maria's presence and invariably the day's cigarette was a balm. At first he'd give her up to half an hour after the psychologist left before pressing the buzzer. Nowadays she appeared within a quarter of an hour. Again, her days off were devastating. But he'd managed to rearrange the psychology appointments to coincide with her schedule.

The very best of days was when she gave him his bed bath. Although his legs were not responding, what was between them had a mind of its own. "You are a naughty boy," she would say as she rubbed him down with a damp flannel. He so relished the way she said it, that he sometimes made a conscious effort to impress her. "I've got no control," he would then lie.

Despite these small joyful moments he had not abandoned his resolve. He would end it all.

* * *

She was washing between the toes of his left foot with a damp flannel. He neglected the fact of his hard-on in favour of its cause: the sensation of her fingering his toes.

"Maria," he said, "you're washing my little toe." She froze and when she asked him which toe she was pinching he told her.

He could barely move his legs and she said that the reason was the wasting of his muscles. Her regular lifting and bending was of little use in that respect.

From then on, for the last six weeks, she had encouraged him to move his legs. His left was doing far better than his right. He could raise it a centimetre or so off the bed and he could wiggle all the toes. Although he could feel his right leg and foot, he could hardly move either.

His upper body was fine. He had small hand-weights for arm and chest exercises. Using the metal rail at the top of the bed above his head he could sit up unaided.

Some five months after his suicide attempt he was lifting his legs off the bed whilst shakily holding the wheelchair to the bed. Its rattling annoyed him. And then Maria's encouraging words added to his annoyance. And he harshly shunned her offer of help. After a struggle he crashed into the chair. "It almost beat me," he said when he'd straightened himself.

Maria wheeled him outside and he felt the breeze on his face, the faint warmth of the sun, heard the birds clearly, heard other sounds too, vehicles, the rustle of foliage, voices.

A gust blew a lock of his hair into his face and she tied it back in a ponytail.

Part of his negligent attitude was to humour her and let his hair grow long. She called it his golden mane and said that it was a shame that he had always kept it so aggressively short.

He wondered whether this nurse and this psychologist were providing the care and guidance he had missed in his childhood.

The psychologist chipped away, sculpting him into something unrecognisable. For he wasn't Leon. He wasn't sure who he was. And somewhere during the chipping and sparring, the ducking and diving, the round-the-house blows, the psychologist said that he would break right down, but that he would help build him again. Help build a new Leon.

One afternoon the inexhaustible hammering unexpectedly shattered him. Like some brittle statue he was smashed to smithereens. Leon was recalling a minor incident, something to which he had given little weight at the time, when the emotion rose up within him and gushed out with him blubbering.

Later when Maria came into his room he remained fragile. But there was victory in his defeat. Leon the Skin was broken, the newborn, unknown Leon, on the verge of sobbing confessed to her that until this moment he had harboured suicidal intentions. He wasn't sure why he told her. But he thought she, more than anyone who knew him, would have felt most betrayed should he have killed himself. He silently waited out her reply. The whiff of lavender gave her proximity away and he braced himself for a slap across the face. Instead she kissed him on the cheek. But rather than leap with joy he began to cry. His right eye watered, the tear ducts of his left were shot, and shudders racked his body. She then hugged him and he embraced her and kissed her on the neck.

After a time she eased herself away. She placed a palm on his cheek and he covered her hand with one of his own.

Maybe she didn't know what to say. He certainly had no words.

* * *

He needed three weeks to master getting in and out of the wheelchair. Towards the end of the third week he was regularly going out on his own. He was also able to get to the physiotherapy room unassisted.

If the sparring with the psychologist had taken him to his mental limits, the physiotherapy sessions took him to his physical limits. At first both his legs were caged in callipers and he would stagger, dragging his legs, especially his right, using all the muscles of his upper body straining to hold himself up between the parallel bars. It demoralised him that his staggering was mostly a jutting motion from the hips.

During this gruelling period the police returned to question him. A lawyer accompanied them. Armed with the knowledge of his progress and that he was no longer a Skin they hoped he would talk. But he had nothing to say. Before departing they told him that in the light of his injuries criminal charges would be dropped.

A further three months passed before the callipers were removed from his left leg and he could walk jerkily with the aid of a stick.

His right leg did not recover, but with the callipers he could walk. His gait wasn't pretty and the awkwardness exhausted him and he flopped in the wheelchair.

Somebody came and presented him with a white stick. He assumed it to be white.

"Flick it out like this," said the man. "Don't wave it about like D'Artagnan. Think of mine-sweeping. And that is what you'll be doing. Sweeping for objects that obstruct your path, or worse, can cause you harm."

His affection for Maria was unbearable. It had gone beyond innuendo, beyond cheekiness, deepened to something of substance. When she could she would steal a kiss. Why, she would kiss his scarred eyelids. Her presence filled him with warmth. Of course touching and secret kissing wasn't enough. On one of her days off, having made an arrangement with the night duty nurse, she came to his room. Before mounting him she said: "You are such a naughty boy."

* * *

His day of departure arrived. By then the entire hospital knew of their clandestine affair. So nobody was truly surprised when he moved into Maria's flat.

There was a waiting list for guide dogs, but through her he could see. She was not only his eyes, she was his light. She not only built him up, she kept him buoyant. Of course their relationship wasn't continuously rosy, but she was the better person and he was the one with the mood swings. Most of the time she supported him, but sometimes he was too demanding. He became adept at understanding her by virtue of the inflection in her voice. So he knew when to ease off and give himself over to remorse.

When she was at work he rarely ventured out alone. Instead he'd spend hours perfecting his Braille. Before going blind he could count the number of books he read on one hand with fingers to spare. Now he couldn't read enough. He discovered a gratifying connection in reading. Audio books were something he also enjoyed. Many of them were lent free by various societies and charities.

They went for walks. She took him shopping so that he could choose. Maria made a routine of these, as far as her shifts would allow, so he got out as much as possible. They had talked of him getting a job, but he wasn't ready to face the challenge of work yet.

Now that he was blind he saw the mediocrity of his previous existence. Life could be rich if one filled it with joy. Love opened you up to receive. It was something multifaceted; upon it you could build and explore other emotions. There was joy in giving and sharing. Hate, the fulcrum of his past, was monotone. By its all-consuming destructive nature it destroyed the hater. They felt nothing but hate, could only hate, could not see, let alone receive, the richness of the world. It was selfish.

Leon vehemently opposed his past philosophy and regretted his wasted youth. At these times he had the urge to light up, but at Maria's behest he had long ago weaned himself off cigarettes.

* * *

Maria had chosen a new walk for them. She parked the car and arm in arm they set off along the path into the woods.

The sounds were new and exciting to him. The earth soft underfoot. He adored the song of birds and sounds of nature.

"I'd like to write a book," he announced.

"What about?"

"Me." He gave a little laugh at the thought. "I want to write my story. You know, being a neo-Nazi and seeing the light only after being blinded. Maybe I can reach out to some of them."

He heard their voices and she stopped. He couldn't hear anyone else. Just the youths. He could measure their distance by sound. It was too late to speak. He smelt Maria's fear. Could he talk to them? He had just spoken about writing his story to that effect. But their boisterousness alone made him realise the pointlessness of speech. He saw himself in their eyes: a long-haired blind cripple. They fell silent and he felt the presence of four maybe five of youths – in their stale clothes, reeking of schnapps and nicotine, with body odour added to the mix – surround them. Talking to them would be akin to trying to reason with rabid dogs. What chance then a book?

"We've got a double-whammy here lads," said the venomous youth in front of them. "A blind hippie crip and his nigger bride."

Connections

When he sat on the bench he did not immediately go to his briefcase and so to his book, rather he paused to look about himself. The opposite platform under the shelter was already sufficiently dark because of the blinding light of the summer's day, and the haze veiled the waiting passengers further. The sky itself rose from a wash of greys and whites through a magnificent, flawless canvas of turquoise to a deepening passion of royal blue. The sun that hung way up with uncanny poise brought out the true colours of everything with an uncompromising ruthlessness. It almost stole their colours: turned them pastel. Then the gravel about the sleepers took on a fireside golden tone, the grey shadows of the rusted pillars and beams of the shelter seemed as sharp as the objects themselves, and the faultless parallel lines of the rails with their polished silver crown moved off luxuriously, curving out of sight towards infinity. The wood panelling of the walls bared their notches and swellings and the weathered corrugated roofing betrayed its discolouration. Everything about the scene – save the foliage way off, which defied the fading property of the sun and appeared greener than ever – was tinged in a kind of sepia. All this, all this and the majestic sweep of the hills in the background, was stripped naked, blessed and tortured by the brilliance of the day.

He had taken the morning off work – one of the advantages of flexitime. The routine had been broken and he therefore savoured this indulgence all the more. How good it was to be off work. It was like borrowed time. And on such a glorious day.

A breeze nudged a crumpled cigarette box that lay near his feet, and stroked the back of his neck, highlighting the strangeness of his hair. The breeze itself was refreshing and the coolness on that part of his neck pleased him and yet, because it was an unaccustomed feeling, he felt uncomfortable. The keen awareness of his haircut made him uncomfortable. He suppressed an urge to rub the back of his neck. The sensation was not unpleasant and moreover it was not merely physical. No. He felt cleaner or refreshed. The hairdresser had massaged his troubles, rinsed and cut them off and finally he had seemingly blown them away. All the anxieties and worries of life paled into insignificance. Like the sun fading the colours. And like the initial effects of alcohol it precipitated a state of levity. He could only assume that it was the continuous, uncomplicated conversation with the barber that caused the feeling. The talk was invariably trivial, because the hairdresser could little more than recognise his regulars. In addition, there was hardly the opportunity for building foundations for deeper conversation – especially in such a public place – and knowing this neither tried.

Other factors contributed to his mood. Firstly, he was not one of the faceless, scurrying commuters. Secondly, he was in no particular hurry to get to work. Ordinarily he would be anxious to get to the office, clock in time 8.1 (decimalised), but right now he did not mind waiting for the train. In fact, he welcomed the chance to feel the harmony of the day and allow its gold to shine on him.

He noticed a cluster of metallic silver-grey pigeons busying about some find, heads bobbing, nervous beady eyes, bodies strutting on twig-like feet and the coo-cooing. He then noticed the splash of droppings about the station, some like flowers, others like scars, but all like congealed white paint, as if some sloppy painter had been at work. This thought caused him to smile. What pests they were!

After taking another look about the station, to check all was tranquil, he fetched his book, opened it in his lap and placing the marker randomly between some earlier pages, he began to read.

> The semi-detached house, being on a slope, was some steps down from the road. At the gate Mary paused. She wanted to view their first home and preserve the moment. Of course, she had seen it before, twice in fact, and although it was unoccupied, from the outside it looked inviting.
> "The garden needs attention," noted Roger, after locking the van and coming to her side. He had misinterpreted her pause for scrutiny.
> "Hmmmm." She smiled, and to communicate her feeling she squeezed his arm.
> "Come on," he said.
> She followed him down the great blocks of steps to the front door. As he dug into a pocket of his denims for the key, she peered along the side of the house to the back garden lawn.

A porter appeared on the opposite platform from behind a door marked Private.

As he pushed the door open, he said: "We'll give the door a new coat."

She returned to him and acknowledged his remark by touching the paintwork.

In the hallway the emptiness was accentuated by an abundance of light, mainly from the bare kitchen window at its far end.

The porter picked up a wide broom that had been leaning against the rail in the sunshine.

Here was a house that had been emptied. But it was more than that. It was almost as if it had been stripped. Here was a shell, something stripped to its bare essentials, so that it remained what one could call a house. And this house seemed to yearn for the dignity of possessions. It needed possessions to restore its character, if not to give it character. The carpeted floors – not all the rooms had carpets – were out of place with the bareness and gave that odd feeling one gets on seeing an otherwise naked person in shoes and socks. If one had to attempt to sum it all up, the overall atmosphere within the house, with or without carpets, was that educed by a new-made bed: lonely, yet tidy and immaculate, but all the while wanting and awaiting occupation.

The couple moved down the hallway to the kitchen. There they looked through the window upon the back garden and the valley beyond. The rear of the house commanded a panoramic view of the city.

The sound of the porter brushing the dust in the heat with the steel hard bristles of the broom.

"Beautiful, isn't it?" he said unnecessarily. And he put his arm about her waist and squeezed her to him.

"Yes," she agreed.

A sweeping scratching sound that was in some way satisfying.

The city sat like a collection of sandstones on a bed of moss. Only suggestions of the buildings that climbed the far slope could be glimpsed through the greenery. Everything seemed miniaturised before them, even the foliage resembled broccoli. Distance made the city appear as one might imagine an English country village: quiet, with nothing much going on, the bobby on his bicycle on his way to fetch grandma's cat

121

down from the big oak, as usual, the vicar pruning his roses, and the postman – who incidentally doubled as the local solicitor – doing his rounds. And every day was a Sunday. But in reality it was a bustling city brimming with tourists. Nonetheless, to them it was peaceful. This apparently tranquil scene was crowned by a huge mother-of-pearl cloud and, although it carried the threat of a possible shower on this spring morning, it hung protectively, like the palm of a hand. The very seagulls were respectful of this peace and swung silently with an effortlessness and independence that reminded Mary of the albatross.

Roger moved to the pantry and checked the shelving and Mary remained at the window, glancing over the worktops, draining board and sink, but always returning to the seagulls.

"Yeah," he began to himself. "New shelves."

A young lad came up the steps and after wandering about a bit, leant against a pillar.

"Pardon dear?" she queried, turning from the window, an expression of bewilderment upon her face as though she were returning from some far-off world.

He too took on a bewildered look, because the words had been for himself and he was not sure what he had said.

The brushing stopped. An old lady had interrupted the porter—

His speech was therefore somewhat mechanical and not representative of his happy frame of mind. This perturbed him. "I, er, said: we need new shelves. These ones are rotting."

She nodded, wondering at his peculiar expression and tone. Then she began to wander from the discord and she spied how the light put an auburn halo about his dark brown hair.

—probably asking him when the next train to wherever was due.

He shook himself from the lack of contact and the growing awkwardness that accompanied it. "Come on, let's go upstairs." And then, "I still say the wardrobe won't fit in that alcove."

"Ha!" she exclaimed, jumping at the link he proposed, and then recoiling from the trap, for she was convinced the wardrobe would fit in the alcove.

The sound of voices caused him to look up. He did not notice the other woman or the two children – although it had been the sound of the children that had alerted him – he merely registered their presence. The first thing that struck the right chord in him was her overall poise: she walked with supreme self-possession without conceit. Her hair was perfect for her lovely face. Her charcoal grey suit, jacket and skirt, the jacket pinched at the waist, the skirt curving like an inverted tulip, was fitting. With a hat she would have looked fantastic, but at the same time, for his taste, ridiculous and untouchably pretentious. Although she was obviously not their mother, the children bubbled at her feet. She was their cousin or aunty or something. She was attentive to the children's whims, but not tethered to them, not enslaved and so burdened by them. This casual responsibility told him that the children were not hers. Their mother was the other woman, not radiating sunshine, consternation crumpling her brow and walking lethargically by comparison.

He was not so much awestruck as struck by a wave of admiration. Although she was pleasing to his eye, something in his mind came alive. It was almost as if he had some knowledge of her. Therefore, she was beautiful to him not by physical appearance alone. This uncanny knowledge made him feel that he could trust her. And the feeling excited him.

She glanced at him as they passed by and, though her expression was unmoved, her look conveyed no hostility. If anything there was a hint of curiosity.

The party moved far down the platform, out of the shelter and into the dazzling sunshine.

He glanced at the oversized clock that hung from a beam. Another ten minutes.

After an unnoticeable sigh, he gave the group another look and returned to his book.

As they ascended the stairway Mary ran a hand along the wall. She did this not to assert any kind of possessive command over the building. She did it out of love. And this gesture was as much for the house as for herself.

They checked the bathroom and toilet, as if they could have altered since their last visit. Then they entered the rear bedroom – their bedroom – and after acknowledging the picture-window view he put her before the alcove.

123

The call of this activity is controlled by the respective transaction.

The floorboards creaked as he stepped back. Apart from the small bedroom, the entire upper floor was uncarpeted.

"Okay, come on," he said, confidently, almost as though he were talking to a naughty child. He felt that he would be proven correct.

The old lady on the next bench began knitting.

She stretched her arms out and seeing her fingertips nearing the edges of the alcove she held herself short.

"Hey, hey." He smiled. "Stretch those arms. You know jolly well how wide that wardrobe is."

The needles fenced. Tick, tick, tick.

"I am," she lied, trying to suppress a grin and put on a strained expression.

...is controlled by the respective transaction.

He moved to her and gripping her wrists he proved himself correct.

"Ouch," she complained, although he had not hurt her. It was the aggression of him that had hurt her pride.

He was momentarily forlorn, but recovered by tickling her under the arms.

She squirmed and giggled, firstly to escape the humiliation of his triumph and secondly to offer him sanctuary from his offensive.

The proximity of their bodies demanded something from them. For either of them to move away would cause injury. So he took her head between his hands and descended to receive her kiss.

In the test transaction, this activity is not called.

A faint rat-tat-tat at the window rose up from nothingness and then died. The clouds had gathered themselves together to form an ominous leaden roof. Though, in the distance, blue skies were still visible. Now a silken haze of rain blurred the view. The tattoo upon the window increased and decreased with the wind. The clinging drops on the glass shivered and distorted with the gusts and then they were snatched by the rivulets that began to form; snaking and twisting, flexing and racing downward. As the intensity of the downpour increased, so the veins of water that had moved erratically upon the

*window fused together into translucent films that washed down
in a continuous vertical.*

Then how to test this activity?

*A chill shook the couple and the floorboards and emptiness of
the room chilled them further. Mary shivered and virtually
fled the room. Roger followed her.*

Write a driver or frig a program in test. That was the only
solution.

*In the front bedroom the lack of interest was noticeable – this
would be the guest bedroom for visiting in-laws, friends and
perhaps other relatives – and it jarred their contentment.*

*They traipsed into the small bedroom and here a welcome
affinity bound them against the unpleasant weather. Possibly
it was the size of the room or the fact that it was carpeted that
made it feel warmer? Or possibly it was the cartoon
wallpaper? Whichever, a knowledge bridged the earlier lack of
contact that had occurred in the kitchen. They knew the
changes that would be required to this little room for the
purpose it was to serve. Here, there was no need to speak, no
need to voice their thoughts. The junction was complete.*

*However, the incessant rain won through, and they were
eventually driven away. But this time they left the room
united.*

The sound of the approaching child caused him to look up.

Leading her excitedly by the hand, tugging like some animal
on a leash, the little girl was talking elatedly. Despite the child
pulling at her, she remained true and demure and yet, she was
attentive to the child's ravings.

As they passed before him, he felt her smile and although
she did not look at him – and he cautioned his own eyes by furtively
glancing down the line, to the opposite platform, at the clock – he
knew that she was viewing him from the corner of her eye.

What fine calves she possessed.

Once more he returned to his book:

In the front room they–

–but he could not read.

The increasing sound of the goods train disturbed his
concentration further. He had registered its presence way down the
line during his furtive glancing: quivering in the heat, a silent mirage,
steadily growing and somehow seeming motionless.

In the front room they realised the cheer—

The train would not be ignored. Its heavy, relentless motion was deafening. He looked for her, but she had moved from his field of vision – a shuttered kiosk obscured his view – and the frightening, rustic trucks of the train that hurtled before him, carrying tons of gravel and cement made him anxious for her. The chunky wheels turned over in some kind of irreversible momentum. They turned too fast. Surely it was dangerous? This station was not particularly big: two rails sandwiched by two platforms connected by a tunnel. The cumbersome trucks themselves were too heavy. Then there was the sound. The sound of all that unstoppable weight: a cacophony of shrill clanging and screeching ricocheting off the deafening rumble.

He was pleased when the last truck arrived and with it the return of stable shadows and quiet sunlight, for the train had caused a chaos of shadow to darken his frame of mind. The tail of the train moved away and soon it returned to its approaching state: muted and fluttering in the brilliance, almost as if it had never been.

She reappeared, the child substantially subdued, and he relaxed, although he looked down at his book.

—realised the cheer—

The cheer of what? It did not make sense.

She was getting nearer.

—carpeting—

He resolved to show his feeling and so discover her sincerity.

Carpeting?

Thus, after quickly checking the child, he uncharacteristically and yet naturally, without apprehension or assumption, with just a touch of timidity, looked her full in the face with – what he considered – a welcoming expression.

She saw his greeting and returned a hallo with the most subtle of expressions.

A scream of delight shook his mind and he knew that there was no possibility of a mistake. There was absolutely no possibility that her expression had lacked sincerity or that the smile had been that of a self-satisfied ego. No, he was certain.

Because of politeness he could not stare. In addition he was in such a chaotic state – as if she had dealt him a blow – that he needed time. Therefore he returned to his book. Still he could not read. His mind was alive and swamped. The flame that was his spirit had been doused in petrol.

She passed by.

Inexplicably, though goaded by self-doubt – which he fought with blind ferocity – he felt reasonably calmed, strangely sated and he was able to read.

In the front room they realised the cheer of carpeting, but even this apparent warmth could not give them sanctuary from the cold of the frigid rain. They discussed some of the changes they would make, but they were over-enthusiastic in their ramblings and it betrayed their growing uneasiness. So they lapsed into an uneasy silence. Each bordered on scotching the other and they hated the feeling. Furthermore they wanted to be rid of the chasm that was again opening up between them.

Write a driver...

Nevertheless, they returned to the rear room in silence.

The wind on this side of the house was weaker and had the effect of lessening the bite of the rain. In a way it was softer and not so brittle. As if the drops were bigger and not so vicious.

"Phew, it's cold," said Mary, rubbing her sleeves.

"Mmm. Shall we try the fire? The gasmen were supposed to have come yesterday."

DO I = CHARLEN BY -1 TO 1;

She looked at the fire, but did not answer. He crouched at the appliance and quickly discovered that the gas was not coming through.

Mary turned to the window. The sky was still a dirty sea of angry cloud, but the rain was now a fine drizzle. It had settled down.

REM = 0;
DHR(REM,DIV);

"I think it's stopping," she remarked, moving closer and searching for the seagulls.

But Roger had left the room. He was investigating the meters and pipes beneath the stairway.

CHARFLD(N) = 'F0' + LREM;
END;

"Ah," he called, turning a lever. "Try it now."

She was watching the struggling sun, which was trying to burn its way through the heavy folds of cloud. Slowly it torched a patch of watercolour out of the thick oil of greys. Shadows began to appear and the rain submitted and became jewels and glitter moving down invisible slanted threads.

"What?" she asked, returning from her reverie and suddenly noticing that he was no longer behind her.

"The fire... Try it now."

"Oh," escaped her lips. For some reason the fire no longer seemed important. She could not explain it, but what he was saying and doing seemed somehow trivial. This, in turn, made her feel guilty.

She crouched at the fire and turned the knob. The hiss was instant and it took her by surprise, almost snapping her back to reality. In a slight panic she pushed the stiff ignition button. With a suddenness, that also caught her off-guard, a woolly roar of soft young flames bulged out and then obediently returned to the confines of the plaster-white waffle cage.

From the hearth-side she looked to the window and the wall of cloud. The drops had grown sparse and as if to mark the end of the downpour, or perhaps to chatter about the event — and here submitted to anthropomorphism, stamping her human cognizance upon the creatures — the chirping song of birds began to mount. And the seagulls reappeared, occasionally crying their vulgar, shrill scream.

When he returned she had her palms to the fire, pressed against an invisible barrier beyond which the trespasser would find the heat uncomfortable. He was not particularly cold and wished to sit rather than be near the source of heat. So he sat beside her, his weight leaning upon a straightened arm, and giving her a smile he brought up one of his calloused hands halting at a boundary a little further from the fire than hers. She moved from her precarious and hence wearying crouching position to the permanent stability of a similar posture.

In the wake of the storm a certain electricity lingered in the air. There was a freshness outside. That new day feeling. And in this stillness a calm engulfed them.

Mary looked to the fire and accepted the warmth full in the face, like a challenge, until it grew unbearable and she was forced to turn away.

The hand of the clock clunked as it swung; then it quivered in its new position. Another five minutes.

His feeling of well-being was barely containable. At that moment he was profoundly happy. He was content with his life. Would he jump up and sing and dance? Of course not. But he smiled at the thought of it. Ha, it bordered on insanity. People would not understand. It would disturb the old woman knitting on the neighbouring bench. And the young chap leaning against the pillar would be disgusted. No, he could not show his feeling. He could not run over to the girl and confess his feeling. That was for books and movies. It was against the unspoken rules of English society. One had to have a certain restraint. One had to take hold of oneself. Get a grip and so on. Even she, yes, even she would be shaken by his approach. Undoubtedly flattered – ah, who was he kidding? – no, selfishly, she would be flattered. But it would be a contradiction in the character she would have formed of him. And then her apprehension would cause him to cower and perhaps shy away. And if she took up the aggression of him, then he would have to re-evaluate his picture of her. No, he could do nothing. Social etiquette demanded at least this humility from him.

A desperation began to consume him. On top of the frustration of his situation he realised that he would soon be in the office. He would be back within the confines of work.

There was no time for emotion in the mechanics of programming and analysis. Everything was black and white. Yes or no. Signal or no signal.

True or false. Logic had no room for emotion. The basic building-blocks were too few and cumbersome. From AND, OR NOT one could build anything... non-emotional.

CHARFLD(N) = 'F0'X + LREM;

With respect to reality this concept was flawed. What of grey and maybe, perhaps, violet? There were a multitude of possibilities, links and jumps. Rules? There were none outside basic conceptions and understandings. Even down to the simple words that made up the language of thought. Even they were for the most part woolly in definition and subject to individual interpretation.

Ah, but for him, behind his desk he was practically no better than the machine he programmed. He would clock-in on the flexitime clock and his emotive faculty would all but clock-out.

Load the job.

Access the disk.

Read the data.

Let $A = B + C$

Maybe he was being too cynical. Only if he did not have to go to work. Only if he could jump up and sing and dance. Why did society suppress emotion? Why did technology drive humanity further from the basics of humanity? Was it really progress? Surely, the more the System – in the name of progress – divorced Mankind from his basic animal requirements the more unrest there would be? Psychologically, all expression must be channelled out in some form or another. And to suppress is to warp.

He felt depressed and sought refuge and after checking her position he returned to his book.

> *Roger watched her. The glow on her face enchanted him. The unyielding softness of the carpet was alien to him. It was synthetic to his fingers. So he touched her hand to realise the living softness it yielded. She turned at the touch and he greeted her with a tentative smile.*
>
> *She saw the softness in his eyes and knew that he did not want words. Therefore she replied with a brightened and understanding face. Sometimes she was weak and a child and sometimes he was. She ignored his childlike attempt at communication, accepting the message for what it was and not how it had been transmitted, and reflected his precarious euphoria.*
>
> *A channel was created through the electric atmosphere – or rather the electricity was tethered and channelled by them. An emotion travelled between them, an emotion that melted their eyes. The ardour drove the surroundings from them and the warmth of the fire physically drove the chill from their vicinity.*
>
> *The cocoon of emotion turned their unspoken declarations of contentment into weak smiles. For their joy bordered on sadness and, as a form of sanctuary, they gathered themselves into a kiss. And this kiss was delicate and tender, because the feeling was powerful and dramatic. The preciousness of the moment began to succumb to the energy. It began to crumble.*

But to tear away would be to cause injury. They then knew that a tender kiss would not be enough to overcome the moment. Then again, too much passion would be equally harmful. Hence, the kiss continued and they grew cautiously adventurous. His hardened fingertips wandered aimlessly about her cheek and neck. His touch was fine, for although years of labour had rendered his fingers all but insensitive, he touched her as if he were exploring some priceless piece of craft-work: fine, like a wafer of etched rice-paper. She idly raked the fingers of a hand through his unkempt hair, running it behind his ear. The kiss took on more passion as the explorations grew more purposeful. He moved his hand beyond her neck and under her sweatshirt to a soft bare shoulder. What a furnace there was within the living body! Her fingers, with great dexterity, released a further button of his shirt. Her move charged him and he forced his fingers under her brassiere strap at her shoulder. After some stroking here, and as she began to twist a further button, he left her shoulder and made an entrance at her waist. There he caressed – almost tickled – her belly and side and then he slowly moved upward, dropping back now and then in a teasing way. In the meantime she had been running her fingers through the hair on his chest and circling a nipple. His teasing caused her to giggle and in retaliation she nibbled his ear. He began to weaken and his neck became limp with satisfaction. Unable to tease her any longer, and needing to bring her down to his state of dishabilitating delight, and incapable of anything else, he moved his hand under her brassiere. The contact with his hard fingers sent signals racing within her body. Tiny little pulses, glowing pinpricks of charges began to run amok. Something independent of her had been set in motion. Her mind became awash with the growing sensation. For some time now he had gone beyond the point of no return. She surrendered to the inevitability of the feeling and they dreamily and disrespectfully began to remove each other's clothing.

The couple did not hear the mad chorus of birds. They did not see the sliver of molten copper drop shafts of light through the spent cloud upon the refreshed countryside. And they missed the glory of the rainbow that arced over the valley.

He smiled at the contrived sensationalism of the writing. However, for the time and place and his feeling it had worked. It had contributed and fitted well with his mood. Everything was right. Even this dingy station was beautiful. The over-exposure caused by the daylight swept away any hint of dismalness. Such things as depression, filth and the like had fled the scene and had crawled meekly into the few darkest of cracks that even this light could not penetrate.

He looked down the line for the train and, although it was nowhere to be seen, it was due any minute. Rather than read on and risk having to stop at an inappropriate place he decided to put the book away. He ceremoniously – for he was somewhat distracted – placed the marker between the opened pages and closed the book.

The party at the extreme end of the platform began to move towards him. His composure began to quake once more. The nearer she drew to him the more he felt that he would lose control. However, some hidden strength held him together and he nonchalantly picked up his briefcase and placed the book inside.

He was having difficulty in holding down his urge to jump up and hug her. He truly felt that she wished something from him. But in the event of him jumping up and hugging her she would recoil. It would be too brash. And with her company and the rest of the travellers it would also be embarrassing. No, it was out of the question. This made everything all the more unbearable.

He looked down the line and watched the train laboriously round the corner. What could he do? Was it too late? And then, as he wearily stood, not wanting the arrival of the train he tried to convince himself that maybe the situation was better left. Why spoil the feeling? Maybe that was how it should be?

The party had stopped a short distance from him. He saw something hard in her face. Could she possibly be stricken? He felt disarmed and appalled. What could he do? The children were watching the train, once again bursting with suppressed energy, held back by a mixture of awe and perhaps a dash of fear. The other woman who had been watching the children suddenly looked past her and caught him staring. He decided instantly not to challenge the woman - whom he disliked for no reason whatsoever – for the right to his indulgence and turned to the approaching train.

Then the train was before them, slowing as it passed, carriage after carriage, carrying windows of people: indeed, curtains of people, profiled or peering out. So many isolated beings.

The train would carry him away. It would carry her away. He would more than likely never see her again. He had never seen her before. Perhaps she was only visiting and did not live in the area? Ah, but now he knew that he was searching for excuses. Oh, for inspiration. He looked at her again and knew that she was aware of him. Aesthetically there was something between them. Only if he could jump up and buy her flowers. That would be something. It would acceptably break the ice. But there was no florist. And it was far, far too late. Only if she were alone. But she was not alone. Ah, only if he did not have to go to work. Only if he had more time. But there was no more time. Only if–

With an ear-piercing squeal the train came to a halt and he moved to a door. This was the nearest point to the steps at the station of his disembarkation. He was on auto-pilot. But he did not think to enter where she was entering. Ah, he could always move down the train. Maybe he had severed something by not following her?

The train and the roof of the shelter practically overlapped and the area was considerably darkened. His feeling burst and he was flooded with anguish, the body of which was more weariness than sorrow. The bliss of the contact was greater, but the wonderful experience had drained him. Part of himself – his energy – had gone into the contact.

He was appalled by the uncaring briskness with which the passengers alighted the train. Then he realised that he too was one of these people. Perhaps he was worse than them? He was one of the morning commuters – a completely different breed.

It was customary for him to stand at the door of the train, rather than take a seat. He loathed the confinement of a compartment. It disturbed his reading. In addition his journey was short. Finally, it meant he could be one of the first through the gate and on his way. Not part of the great press of people that converged with their passes and tickets held up. This is what he did. He knew which compartment she was in. But for him to be near her would be intolerable.

At the end of his journey he knew that he would not have satisfactorily resolved the situation and that he would race to work.

Furthermore, he knew that in a couple of hours he would curse himself for not having been inspired enough to do something. But for now he attempted to preserve the experience. Then he would remember and, hopefully, the subsequent regrets would remain dwarfed when put alongside the towering pleasure. There was hope. There were fine things in life. Fine moments that defied expression. As they say, moments that make life worth living. Moments that one relishes. Inexplicably he felt that happiness alone was not enough. Even love was not enough. There was something that encapsulated it all. Something akin to contentment.

The train pulled out of the station. It left the littered platform, the torn posters, rusty beams and weathered roofs, all gladdened by the sunshine.

Der Anrufer

Ordinarily she did not travel on the upper deck, she always sensed a restless adolescence there, but the world-weary conductress, having taken her money and wound-out a ticket, had physically blocked all possibility of standing on the lower deck. This did not truly surprise her. Today was a Friday and inexplicably there always seemed to be more people commuting at the end of the working week. So many people. *Mensch.*

As she reached the top the bus lurched forward and she was pushed clumsily against the wall. This shook her composure, heightening her self-consciousness and adding urgency to her search for a place.

The stark lighting accentuated the naked functionality of the vehicle. It faded the colours of the worn fabric of the seats. It rendered the uninspired nicotine-yellow walls dull and musty, and then it highlighted the drunken graffiti. She found it oppressive and hostile. Its balmy, mustard atmosphere, crisp and decrepit like aging newspapers scotched her sensibilities. Yet, in spite of this functional hostility and being in the vicinity of so many people, such muffling body heat, cloying body odours, bad breath, she welcomed the relative warmth of light and security. Outside was pitch-black.

She quickly turned from the dead gaze of the man in the rear-most seat. *Such arrogance!* Most of the places were occupied and of those that were not, only one resided next to a woman. As she made her way along the aisle to this seat, the motion of the bus causing her to touch seatbacks to steady herself, she was conscious of the man's leer. She attempted to calm herself by noting the other passengers.

Henry VIII was not there, but Charles II was sitting way up front. Oh, and there was Mary I, good old bloody Mary.

When she sat down something within her relaxed, almost as if she had been holding her breath. For she too could become one of the zombie-like mass: expressionless, swaying and surging with the motion of the vehicle. All were perfectly detached, somewhere else, far off. They were rigid, sleeping bodies possessively clutching newspapers, bags, cases, umbrellas, thoughts – ever fearful of surrendering to sleep to the extent of losing their self-possession.

She held her handbag at her lap and stared straight ahead with unseeing eyes. However, she saw every man before her and was highly aware of all those behind her.

They'll get him tonight.

The smell of food was somewhere in the air. It was a nausea of beef, lingering, woolly like fleece, but festering in a thick gravy so rich that she could almost chew it. She'd once seen a haggis burst under the touch of a Scottish blade. Being a vegetarian made the smell worse. A man lifted the can of lager he had resting on his knee and drank deeply. *Animals.*

They'll get him tonight. Heute abend werden sie ihn greifen.

This thought twisted a virtually unnoticeable smile of crooked delight upon her lips, all traces of which instantly vanished as the man to her left rose. She jumped within herself when the bus turned and he stumbled towards her, his face coming terribly close to her own. She caught his appearance to the very pores of his skin and smelt the stale aftershave on his five o'clock shadow. And she turned away as if she had been struck. Simultaneously her fingers moved rapidly about the strap of her handbag and she adjusted its position as if it had slipped.

"Sorry," he said quietly, forcing a polite smile to drape his clumsiness.

She nodded acceptance, quickly and nervously, but only half-turning and without looking at him. As he moved away she sighed, but she remained steadfast and did not look around just in case she should catch somebody's eye. She did not even glance at the woman next to her for collusion.

As her composure returned she thought how stupid it was to be so nervous. After all, he had been the clumsy oaf. Why should she be embarrassed? He had been the silly Billy. *"Who's a Silly Billy, now?" William IV 1830-1837.*

With difficulty she tried to discern the stop they had just made. The windows mirrored the inside of the bus as if they were made of black glass. However, through the chaos of reflection she could see the lights of shop windows: warm islands of light in the brittle darkness. She estimated that she had another half an hour to go. *Noch eine halbe Stunde.*

Such a black night... Black knight, black prince, Black Death.

Huh, where was Henry VIII? This was his bus. Then again, she had not seen him in the queue that morning. The newcomer - yes, the one with that proud nose and that fine beard that would make a nice Richard I - had been there. What bus did this Lionheart take home?

She closed her eyes and let her thoughts meander.

"No," she said, pushing his hand from her.

"Why do you tease me?" he asked, furious with her for allowing him to touch her breast but go no further.

"I'm not teasing you." She was unsure of his mood, but this night he seemed more determined than ever. She would let him have her, but not yet. It was not right; she did not know him well enough. He could have her when she was certain that he wanted *her* and not her body, not her sex. So this attack and his assumption of her acquiescence was an insult and gave her determination steel. It was also too much of a barrier to cross, because she was not sure of him. She was a virgin. As sure as a chastity belt her virginity held her to her ideals. Oh yes, she wanted him to take her, she wanted to experience this thing that caused her both apprehension and tantalization – but not yet. She was more annoyed by his lack of understanding, his lack of feeling, than his presumption. Hence his chagrin, childishly obvious, jarred her. She wanted to ask him to drive her home, but she was afraid to ask, for in doing so she added finality to her position, and she did not want this finality, at least not without his understanding.

"Then why?" he asked, slumping back resignedly in his seat and staring straight ahead into the black night.

She looked at him and searched his face, her own imploring him to return to her. The moonlight complimented his manly features, highlighting their hard definition and yet softening his face with an incandescent pallor. How young and beautiful and masculine he looked, like he had earlier in the country inn.

"I don't know you well enough," she ventured eventually, hoping that he would understand but knowing he would not. She moved a hand to comfort him, for in touch she felt she may bridge the chasm between them.

"I see," he said with vicious calmness and extreme hurt. Her hand stopped, poised in mid-motion. "Two months," he stated contemptuously. And in his words, so sparse and so leaden, she knew that this was a critical mass moment. This time there was no room to side-step. All the undertones and signs came rushing in on her. *They had been working towards this point. He had been getting close to her just for sex. But wait, was he that deceitful? Was she being unreasonable? What did it matter whether it was two months or three?* Confusion and doubt began to fog her ideals.

"Yes, I know – but," she was frantic. Yes, she wanted to do it. But she knew that the subsequent recriminations would torture her with unbearable cruelty. How she would torment herself. Merely the idea of a fumbling conflagration in the back of a car appalled her. No, she could not give herself now. She went on animatedly, continuing to search his face, "– can't you see, I want to but–"

Before she could continue he turned to her. His inchoate eyes and puerile delight broke something in her will. "Well then, what's stopping you?" His aggression had been completely replaced by perplexity and concern.

"I'm a virgin," she blurted unwittingly.

He laughed and then held himself in check.

"Is that all?" he asked humorously, trying to strike up some confidence in her and so warm her to him.

"Yes," she replied curtly, hardening against him and yet totally unsure of herself.

His humour was wiped away by her curtness and he took on a sympathetic approach.

"Look," he began quietly. "I'll be careful. There's nothing to be scared of. You'll like it, you'll see." She allowed him to take her hand which had been clamped together with the other upon her lap.

"I–" she began.

He arrested her with an index finger to his pursed lips, then he hurriedly opened the dashboard compartment in front of her and fetched something.

She teetered on the edge of panic.

"Look." He opened his palm and she found herself staring at an insignificant little contraceptive.

She shrank, but he did not notice. He was wrapped up in a blasé, annihilating enthusiasm. His brilliant will paling her and his glee scooping her up. She knew that she was allowing herself to be seduced by his boyish emotion. It was so pure and uncomplicated, truly like that of a child. At the same time she was repelled by his lack of subtlety, for there was no waiting, no seductive romance, just this dark heat of enticing sin.

"Now, you be careful, daughter," had warned her father. "And I don't want you coming back after twelve." She had felt humiliated at being treated so. After all she was old enough to be out after twelve, but like her mother she had cowered.

"You study girl," advised her mother. "Then you can be your own boss and you won't have to rely on a man like I have to."

"Come on, let's get in the back," he said, lifting the rear door lock and opening his door. The overhead-light hurt her and she felt vulnerable.

"Don't you think it's a little tacky doing it in the car?" This was her last-ditch chance.

"We've got no choice."

Reluctantly she moved the handle of her door and before she had opened it he was outside.

In the chill of the evening air they glanced at one another across the roof of the vehicle. To her it was a last acknowledgement of who she was, because on entering the car she would become someone else. She forced herself to return his smile, but it was weak and embarrassed.

She seemed to have just entered and shut the door when he set upon her. He was tugging clumsily at her clothes – the green cardigan her grandmother had knitted and the frail blouse she adored for its intricate needlework – pushing them this way and that, wanting the flesh contact. He seemed possessed by some basic urge, his fingers brusquely moving upward over her quivering skin towards her brassiere. At first he had kissed her tenderly, but now he kissed her with such force that for her to relax would mean pain. She had no choice but to take up the challenge of his lips. Repulsively his tongue pushed into her mouth and for a moment she thought she would choke. Again she had no choice but to take up the challenge and she brought up her tongue to wrestle with his. His touch became an irritation and her stiffened nipple began to signal indignation at the offence. Then the clumsy confinement began to annoy her. And his tongue, his lust, added a sordidness to it all. She gripped his arms for dear life as he searched her legs. The irritation did not subside, instead it grew more intense. Then she felt the tears come and she closed her eyes. He was swept up by the flurry of passion and travelled onward, but she was not transported. She had stopped: left standing in cold reality. Perhaps he was vaguely aware that she was not with him, but it was too late, he was

139

too far away. She felt the nausea close in on her like claustrophobia. She felt his brutality casting aside her delicate ideals. And she began to hate his touch. She began to hate his selfishness. His brutality. The whole thing was dirty. It was seedy. She hated his uncaring, animal-thirst for mechanical flesh and her will gathered itself together.

"No," she whispered, as he touched her knickers.

"Yes," he said dreamily. He was abandoned to the emotion, hardly aware of her, surfing on the surge of passion.

"Mmmmm," she murmured, pleading for him to stop.

"Yes, yes," he went on heatedly.

How disgusting it all was in the back of the car. How her mouth ached. How dark and distorted everything was as she opened her watery eyes wide. How her neck hurt. How–

Suddenly he touched her and she caught her breath. She closed her eyes tightly and a tear was squeezed out. It was warm as it raced down the side of her face, but then it became icy. Her will once again went limp and she flew from herself, abandoning herself from the emotion rather than to it. As cold and lonely as the tear on her face she detached herself from all emotion.

He had been so considerate. Naturally he had been suggestive, but never forceful. That had been the Jekyll in him. Now she was seeing the Hyde. She had suspected that he had been suppressing something. That had been the mystery of him. That had been part of her fascination for him. *Was this all it was?* And here he was, Mr Hyde, in all his insensitive glory – sweeping away her existence.

His weight, his unbearable weight, against her leg as he fumbled with his trousers. His heavy bulk pressing her into the seat, forcing her down, down. It was all so awkward. Terrified her eyes widened. Another tear ran the gauntlet of her face. Its path incisively marked her cheek like a blade and the hurt brought her back to the shocking scene.

"No. I can't," she whispered quietly.

"Yes. We can't stop now." He was annoyed by his fumbling.

"Please."

Her weak tone inflamed his annoyance, and although he faltered the passion sent him on and his efforts became frantic.

"No," she said louder, disgusted by his haste and tensing against him.

He froze and she cemented the rags of her will together.

"We can't stop now," he repeated disbelievingly, almost pleadingly.

"I don't–"

He sighed impatiently and, despite the fact that he saw her distance with some horror, he waited for her to become uncertain. The realization that she was determined came long before he admitted defeat.

"Please understand–"

"Okay," he snapped. He was livid, not only at her for her frigidity, but with himself for his clumsiness. He paused. Then he quickly gathered up his clothes. Viciously he strapped the belt of his trousers, coldly he donned his shirt, all the time ignoring her as completely as when the passion had transported him. Now another emotion was carrying him off. It was a mixture of annoyance, humiliation and injured pride.

"Please–" she began once again, but it was swallowed whole by the chilling frost within the car.

On the verge of crying she adjusted her clothes.

Strange for her to think of this now, but then she was under pressure.

That was how it had happened. She had been eighteen. He had driven her home and with a customary, though this time obligatory, parting kiss he had driven out of her life.

Subsequent boyfriends, most of whom had been students, had also assaulted her virginity; one had even called her an old maid! She had lived at home during her University days. The advantage was that she could keep off the sexual merry-go-round that she constantly heard about. The disadvantage was that her father maintained his authority over her. Advantages and disadvantages. *Vorteile und Nachteile.*

So as not to alienate herself from her female college companions she let it be known that she had been raped when she was eighteen. It was too painful for her to speak about in detail, but she let out little snippets. She was not after their sympathy, more their empathy. Ultimately she got the former. More importantly, she herself grew to believe that she had been raped.

Now the two words were associated in her mind. Rape and college. *Rape and college. "A furore Normannorum, libera nos, Domine – Deliver us from the fury of the Norsemen, O Lord!"*

It was not until she was twenty-five that she decided that she should do it. Strangely enough she had not been that fond of the boyfriend of that time. In actual fact she had thought that sex with him might add a new dimension and therefore some depth to their relationship. It too proved to be a gruelling experience. It had hurt and she had hated it. And despite his pestering she had finished with him. *Where was affection and tenderness and romance? Where was love? Where was chivalry and her dashing prince?* In total she had had four boyfriends but she had only had sex with the last. Now she was disillusioned with men and relationships. She felt that they were obsessed with sex and that the phrase 'one-track mind' was a gross understatement.

She had recently been acquainted with a man, but as far as she was concerned he had not been her boyfriend. He had been rather strange, possibly over-awed by her strength of character, she thought. And he had not been suggestive. She had been with him for a few weeks and he had not passed the merest innuendo. This had made her suspicious. She had continued to see him in the hope of bringing out his true self. This contradiction within her had made her uneasy in his presence, and she had grown rather cruel and damning. Then, because he had not risen up to her, he had not been a brute; she had convinced herself that he was peculiar. Eventually her dissatisfaction with him grew to such a level that she sought fault in him and inevitably she broke off their acquaintance. It had been only then that she had glimpsed his Hyde. He had lost his temper and called her *spinsterish. Ha, such ignorance.*

There had been something genuinely satisfying in controlling this relationship, but when it was over, she had felt guilty and unfulfilled. She was back to square one: alone.

She wanted to be loved. But she wanted to be loved for her mind rather than her body. For love was a beautiful mental experience with little physical involvement.

Now, now out of all the people in this vast city, a pervert caller had chosen to pick on her.

They'll get him tonight. Yes, certainly, without doubt. Ja, sicher, ohne Zweifel.

It was her stop.

As she rose the man moving along the aisle politely stopped to allow her out. He smiled and a smile flashed across her face, vanishing as she turned from him. To her relief the man who had occupied the rearmost seat was gone.

She clambered down the steps acutely aware of the polite man's presence. She could feel his eyes burning into the back of her head and sense the smile on his face – that same polite smile – as he read the turmoil of her thoughts. Other passengers were waiting on the platform at the exit of the moving bus and she was forced to remain in the stairwell. There she stood as the bus hurtled along at an amazing speed. She felt his body near to her delicate frame, his massive bulk encroaching her space. He hung over her, close, a huge moth, suffocatingly close.

The bus screeched as it came to a standstill. There it remained, juddering impatiently, anxious to continue on its way.

She stepped off, rushing from the press of people spilling out into the night. As she briskly walked her familiar route home, she felt the man behind her mirroring her footfalls. Uncertainty took her pace and she began to break into dainty, though sporadic, little runs. When she turned the corner she dared a glance behind her. Nobody. She smiled and calmed herself. Slowly her breathing became normal and she began to relax. Then her pace settled and her mind began to put things into perspective.

Three days had passed and he had not telephoned. For three evenings the police had monitored the line. Of course her first thought had been to change the number, but that would be too much trouble. Now she wanted him to call. She would have to keep him talking for the police to carry out the trace. That would be the hardest task.

She grew anxious about the task and searched for something else to occupy her thoughts.

"Simon Jones go to the back of the class." All those precious boys turning bad, turning into men. But the real frustration of teaching was that she was unable to make them see the wonder of History: the intrigues and goings-on of Beckett, Wolsey, the Richards, Williams, Henrys and so on. Kids of today wanted sensationalism. They were brought up on sophisticated violence. There was no beautiful simplicity. Naturally, the times about which she taught were barbaric, but there was a certain romance too.

This walk was the last part of her journey home and the nearer she got the more the caller took the forefront of her thoughts. Still she endeavoured to find something else to think about.

143

She had her German homework to do before the Monday evening class. *There was that eighteen year old boy. He was quite interesting. He seemed to be full of life and yet wonderfully naïve. Perhaps? Then again, maybe he was too young. After all, she would be twice his age.*

She remembered the first call vividly. She remembered how, after the call, she had sat alone, shaken, momentarily overcome. Then she had heard the boy's stereo and rushed up the stairs to his room. With a trembling hand she had knocked on his door. She again saw the concern and confusion distort his clean angelic face as he ushered her to the settee.

Her French needed brushing up. *Yes, I'll have to practice. Il me faut pratiquer plus.*

"You study girl. Then you can be your own boss and you won't have to rely on a man like I have to."

She did not know him well, their brief meetings having taken place on the stairs or in the hall, but he had always been pleasant to her. Her inhibitions at turning to him at this time of distress were reduced by two things. Firstly, she felt relatively confident in his presence, because for all her timidity and shyness, she felt more of the same in him. He appeared to have no visitors. Secondly, because he had a baby-face, cherub-like, with a lovely fine down covering his rosy puppy-fat cheeks. He was about twenty years old, but could pass for sixteen.

He had sat her down and pressed her a glass of medicinal brandy into her hand. He too needed one to handle the pleasant intrusion.

A quarter of an hour later she had returned to her room, with the flush of unaccustomed drink upon her face. Despite the call she had experienced a certain levity.

She was almost home.

Although darkness had taken the evening rather early, the clouds of the day remained strong and bulbous. They were great billowing beings moving in common direction. On the ground there was a breeze, but above there must have been a wind for they congealed and softly rolled and raced on their way. In their silent monk-like wisdom they seemed to be mimicking the commuters. These huge mountains were in some way looking down on the insignificant little people. And these awesome creatures of the skies were somehow threatening to her, somehow suffocating. It was as if

144

they could descend and smother the world with their blanket weight and the thought was felt as the knee of a man pressing on her chest.

This last part of her journey was the most terrifying. It was like running the gauntlet. Some of the things he had said implied that he was nearby. She was also forced to ignore the large van as she turned the corner. *Hopefully, those inside were not asleep.* She knew that they would not normally invest their resources on a caller. They had taken her seriously from the start and, although they had said nothing, she suspected they were after a rapist or somebody. *They'll get him tonight.*

A few minutes later she was near the house. She looked at her car standing in its usual spot. Apart from the same weekly trip to the large supermarket along the same route, it was rarely used. Anything other than this was something of a dangerous expedition.

In spite of her relief at arriving home – she hurriedly pushed her key in the door: someone from the bushes might get her before she got in – she found that as she ascended the stairs her steps became laboured. It was as if she had never been away. A weekend was a chasm before her and the reality of waiting in the flat for his call for another evening began to gnaw at her. It would be yet another evening of watching the telephone, and if not consciously watching it, then always aware of its presence.

She knew that he would call her this evening. She could almost hear his thick, masculine voice. She could almost see his thick lips speaking heavily. To her he was a caricature of masculinity: overbearing, lumbering, unshaven and slovenly. For some reason she was reminded of Bluto, the cartoon foe of Popeye. But what he said was not comical.

Why her? Of all the women in the city, why her? Did she attract such men? Did her nature make her prone to such incidents with men? Admittedly, she was not glamorous, but she knew that she was pretty in a plain sort of way. When she was a little girl the other schoolgirls had nicknamed her the mouse. *"Mousey, mousey, you're always a little grousey. The big cats are going to cut your greasy pony-tails off." Such ignorance. Most of them were probably cash till-girls or bus conductresses now.* In any case, she felt that her appearance was a true reflection of her character.

She opened her flat door and before she flicked the light switch a shaft from the hallway cut across the room and framed the telephone. She cursed herself yet again for not moving it.

After throwing her handbag and coat on the two-seat sofa she lit the small gas fire. There she crouched trying to warm the chill from her hands, but as she did her eyes wandered to the telephone that squatted on the small vanity table beside the sofa. It was like a fat Cheshire cat, a dormant self-satisfied thing. Or an insect: a beetle. Because it was so toy-like it seemed incongruous to her that it should carry a little electronic signal. In its svelte plastic moulding it was almost a mockery of technology, much like some of the computers she had seen: featureless boxes. In any case, there it sat: smooth, insentient and infuriatingly unbreakable.

At the kitchen area she became acutely conscious of all about her. The hollow sound of the water turbulently drumming the bottom of the metallic kettle. The hiss of the gas fire: so comforting and warm in its reassuring monotony. Then the clang of metal upon metal as she placed the kettle upon the hob. The naked scratch of the match, the rush of gas and then the muffled woof when the ring ignited.

Returning to the lounge area she felt compelled to fill the room with some presence other than herself: some company to distract her from the soulless sounds about her.

The bland face of the newscaster unfolded with the picture. But by the time she had hung up her coat and seated herself on the sofa and begun to watch the set, the intimacy of the presenter had begun to give way to the emptiness. And although she sought otherwise, this box of pictures became another lifeless object. The blank screen had been snapped into activity and she contrastingly had been seduced into inactivity and a complementary blank expression.

How she hated it all. All this lonely space, all this lonely silence filled by lonely, isolated sounds. Oh, for somebody, some romantic intellectual to come into her life. Yes, somebody to hug her, to hold her tightly... Ah, not so tightly, not so heavily, not so suffocatingly. No, she was a free spirit. She needed space. She was independent.

There was Mr Davis. But he was so embarrassingly obvious in the staff room. She found him rather depressive. What he said hinted at desperation. He would be much more attractive if his jokes weren't so bitter. Only if he had a little more character about him. Instead he had to advertise the fact that he felt lonely. What was it that Schiller had said? Great souls suffer in silence. Große Seelen dulden still. Poor Mr Davis.

The kettle began to boil and unthinkingly she silenced the whistle. Routinely she made herself a drink and a few moments later she was again slumped in the sofa, but now cupping her hands about a mug of coffee.

The telephone sat at the corner of her eye and her disinterest in the consumer programme made her more aware of its presence. She was aware of the snub handset sitting rigidly upon the cradle: a stumped-legged rider in a saddle.

When she had finished her coffee about a quarter of an hour later, she lifted herself with some effort – sleep had crept over her body – to go to the kitchen area and prepare her evening meal. She had just placed the empty cup in the sink when the ring split the air. It was sudden and shrill. It abruptly slashed the relative tranquillity of the room, defied the television and shot like a bullet into her brain, decimating all train of thought. Only at the second ring were her thoughts able to gather themselves. Then, with amazing rapidity they began to gain momentum. It was him. She felt sure it was him. Yes. She knew. How calm she had been. How she had thought out all that she would say to extend the conversation so that the police could get a trace. But now she stood in disarray. She was frantically embracing herself, chewing her lip, searching for composure and throughout bordering on panic. Then she was gone and dreamlike she moved to the beckoning appliance. For a moment her hand remained poised over it, about to snatch it and snuff out the ring, about to confront the caller. Then she impulsively grabbed the handset from the cradle and silenced the machine, but it was slowly that she brought it to her ear. Slow, so as to compose herself. But even when it was at her ear she had not found the composure she wished.

She said nothing.

The caller was not recognised immediately and it was not until an anxiousness took the voice that she realised that it was her grandmother. A bubble burst and she answered her enquiry as to her health with an apology, an apology that was almost lost in a laugh of relief and then a statement to the effect that she had been miles away.

The call lasted a full five minutes and although she was pleased by the complete escapism her grandmother unwittingly offered in her jovial tone, she was equally and inexplicably anxious for the call to end. It was as if even this call was an intrusion upon her. She had difficulty coping with the casual frivolity and looked to the antique clock – which incidentally her grandmother had given her as a graduation present. It was slow. She mused that the thing was also part barometer. In the summer it was always ahead, and in winter, or at least when it was damp, it was always behind. She would have to correct it. When the conversation began to wane, she made no effort to rekindle it. Then when it came to an end and the incessant purring began – the hand piece remained at her ear, almost to check her grandmother's departure – she was overcome by a wave of grief and her lips parted in a whispering plea for her return.

The lonely television set and the hiss of the gas fire gobbled up the caller's voice and it was instantly fossilised into a memory, as if it had occurred a decade ago.

A sudden chilling shiver drove her closer to the fire and she crouched before it. But the warmth was unsatisfying. It was merely physical and therefore shallow: a superficial warmth. An urge to break free from her imprisonment possessed her. The last few evenings had seemed so long, so, so long and empty. Occasionally she went to the cinema or the theatre, but for now she was held by the caller: *Der Anrufer.* It was modern terrorism.

She decided that this self-indulgence would never do and set about making her evening meal.

Shortly after finishing eating in front of the television set she dozed with the plate still on her lap.

She awoke some time later and looked at the clock. After a while she tut-tutted, deciding that she must set it correctly. However, she was taken by the television programme and watched it to its end.

At length she rose and placed the plate in the sink. Returning to the lounge area she noticed the pile of books and papers. *Yes, in a few minutes she would do some German.*

Her hand was suspended over the telephone when she heard it ring. This time she was calm and even had time to wonder why the shattering ring did not shake her. Again it seemed to shoot across the room, ricocheting out of a corner, bouncing from the ceiling. It seemed to come from everywhere except the telephone itself. And this time her expression was deadpan, she seemed to have no thoughts and there was no turmoil, only stagnation. She was almost indifferent.

Tentatively she said, "Hallo?"

The caller spoke, his deep masculine voice petrifying her thoughts.

"Hallo," he returned, slowly, ever so slowly, as if to give her time to realise the full horror of him.

"Oh, er, it's you," she managed. She had to keep him talking. She was scrambling, nearly drowning, but she clutched at the merest strand of calmness.

"Yes, me." He laughed in his rich baritone.

"What do you want?"

"Want?" he enquired. "I want to talk to you..."

"O–okay. But, er, can't you do it without being abusive?"

He said nothing. All she heard was his breathing roaring in the earpiece like a hurricane.

Then he spoke. His voice had the devil's confidence, and yet, it was strained, that is, put-on, almost as if she would recognise his real voice. It was an uneducated voice, but it was streetwise. "I watched you today." And his words and even the silences between his words were all part of his instrument of rape. She could almost see his sharp little tongue, licking his booze-bloated lips. Her fear was almost sexual. She wanted to escape the bondage, flee, clasping the tattered scraps of her privacy, her life, to her stripped and violated body.

"Then tell me what I did," she blurted with such uncharacteristic defiance that she bit her lip at the thought of his discovery.

"Let's see," he began at length. "You took your usual bus to work. You were wearing that drab green coat." He paused for effect. "Why don't you wear something a little more suggestive?" Again he waited as if he were aware of her trembling.

"What do you get from this?" she pleaded. Had she gone too far?

"I get to talk to you. I get to hear your sexy voice." Silence.

"But why don't you talk to me nicely?"

She could almost feel his perplexity in the ensuing silence and the words *faux pas* repeated in her mind.

"Hmmm?" she insisted.

"Hah..." *Had he realised what was happening?* He seemed to be pondering. "Do you know what I'm touching when I talk to you?"

She caught her breath and he laughed. Then, by way of a perverse overstatement, he panted and she could almost feel his breath in her ear, and then his tongue pushing, pushing. She moved the handset a short distance away but refrained from throwing it down in disgust. His laughter became small, an electronic unreal laugh, crackling and cackling, like one of those tiny laughing boxes or a carnival doll, with row upon row of vicious little teeth.

She looked at the clock. It had no second hand, but she guessed that she needed to keep him on the line for at least another thirty seconds for the trace.

"You need help," she said.

"Well, why don't you come over?" He laughed.

"You're sick," she said in a whispering contempt of him.

"Yes, but isn't it nice?" How his voice was slurred with a digestive thickness. It was so guttural, so masculine.

He was silent and she knew that this was a critical time. And she panicked.

"Why don't we meet? Why hide?"

"Meet?" he exclaimed incredulously, but he retained his confidence. "No, we can't do that."

"Why not?" She estimated another twenty seconds.

"Because..."

Eighteen seconds.

"Hmmm, why not?"

"I like it like this." She sensed a slight rush in his words that signalled that he knew something was wrong.

"How, er–" she floundered.

Ten seconds.

"Wait!" he snapped.

Nine seconds.

"You're trying to trap me. I know..."

Eight seconds.

She was so flustered she did not even attempt a denial.

"Why you–" The sound of the clunk and pip came to her ear and then the purring going on and on.

"Eight seconds," she whispered, looking at the antique clock and dropping the hand piece into its place. She waited for the minute hand to move and confirm her eight second estimate. After what seemed more than eight seconds the hand moved.

She was so abstracted that when the telephone rang a half a minute later she was shaken.

"Miss?" It was the police technician.

"Yes. Yes, was it enough? Did you get him?"

"We, er," he faltered and was silent for a moment. "We'll, er, be right over."

Taken aback, she said nothing and he reassured and frightened her by adding: "Okay miss. Just wait there."

"Er," she began, "yes." He signed off. "But—"

She stood, totally confused by the strangeness of his order. Every time she bordered on any structure of thought, any forming idea, the words: "We'll be right over" crashed into them.

What did he mean? Why hadn't he told her whether they had traced him? "We'll be right over". *Why were they coming here?* "We'll be right over... Just wait there". *Why did she have to wait? Why put her through this?* "We'll be right over". *Why hadn't he told her over the telephone? Was it because the caller could hear them? Why had he been so abrupt?* "Wait there. Wait". *Why should she wait there? Was he nearby?* "We'll be right over..."

As she moved to fetch herself a gin – since that first call she had taken to having alcohol in the flat, used under strict self-supervision, of course – the stereo of the upstairs flat burst into life.

"Wait there". *Stay in the room.* "We'll be right over". *Stay there.* She stopped halfway to the chest of drawers on which the supermarket bottle stood.

"You'd, er, better have a drink," the downy-faced youth had said, after she had taken a seat in his flat.

Her eyes widened as she recalled sitting in the same room as him. His lack of confidence had caused her to take him completely into her own confidence. It was unbelievable. Furiously she searched for some proof that it could not be him. But the more she thought about it, the closer she was drawn to the terrifying conclusion that it could only be him. Horror gripped her as she pictured herself, all shaken and tearful, being consoled by him. Yes, it all fitted snugly together. The boy's nervousness, his weak voice concealed behind the confident, sickly one. Bah, she could almost vomit.

"Him... Upstairs," she said quietly. Trembling she moved to the bottle. She poured herself a good measure. The neck of the bottle tinkled annoyingly on the edge of the glass, such that for a

moment she thought she would succumb to the fit of blind rage
that she teetered upon and throw it all at the wall. She managed to
contain herself and at the refrigerator added a comparably small
amount of tonic. Returning to the centre of the room, near the
telephone, she drank viciously, wincing at the strength of the
mixture. All this time the noise of the television was drowned in the
maelstrom of her thoughts, of which there seemed to be so many
and in such confusion that she was unsure whether there was one
complete thought amongst them. And therefore was she thinking at
all? Steadying the glass with both hands she looked up at the ceiling.
Only then did her thoughts take on some reasoning.

He was up there. Was he scared? For some reason she thought
not. *He was probably quite satisfied with himself. He was probably quite
satisfied with the call. One might say gratified. The little pervert. What perverse
enjoyment had he got out of her fear?* She could see him on the sofa
listening to his music with a self-satisfied smile on his face. *Ahhh.*

*Only if she could get him back. Ah, the police would get him. That is,
if they had traced him. Perhaps they had just traced the call to the house and not
his flat? She caught the stranger's appearance to the very pores of his skin and
smelt the stale aftershave on his five o'clock shadow. "Sorry." Yes, only if she
could strike back. She could telephone him. No, that was not strong enough.
She wanted to scare him. Yes, scare the living daylights out of him. No beating
about the bush with half measures. But what could she do? He was a weakling;
dare she confront him?* She tried to picture herself at his door, but she
could not see it. All she saw was his downy face and his eyebrows
arched with concern. *He was undoubtedly a coward. She was probably
stronger than him. But things could turn nasty. No, she would wait for the
police. The gallant knights. But what was taking them so long? They were only
round the corner. Were they waiting for back-up or reinforcements or something?
"Look."* And for the hundred thousandth time he opened his palm and she
found herself staring at an insignificant little contraceptive. *Oh, to shake him
up. She had no doubt that verbally she could run circles round him The
ignorant little waif. Yes, to give him the taste of fear. And for safety – and
added pleasure – she could tell him that the police were on their way.
Nonetheless, things could turn nasty, she would have to protect herself. And you
never know, if he tried to be smart or played dumb, she might even threaten him
into confessing. Now that would be rather delicious.*

Incongruously, she did not immediately do anything. She
finished her drink, her eyes afire. Then she hastily poured out
another. Extenuating circumstances and all that. She needed the

courage. Knocking this second drink back, she went to the kitchen area and pulled out the utensil drawer. There, she picked out the largest carving knife she possessed.

She was ready.

She climbed the stairs, each step deliberately taken. At his door she made a fist out of her free hand and paused. She reflected momentarily and then knocked sharply.

Her nerves were alive to the thrill as the volume of the stereo was turned down and she heard him approach the door.

Then it opened and he stood there, concern etching his face, but nonetheless with a ghost of a smile in his mouthline. *Smiling!*

"H-hallo," he greeted.

Her grip on the knife behind her back tightened.

* * *

The rear door of the van juddered open.

"Hi," said the man seated inside at the controls. "I thought I'd wait till you got back before going up there. I told her to wait for us."

The man with the plastic bag of tin-foil containers climbed in. "So, something's happened?" he asked placing the Indian-takeaway on a shelf.

"I told you there was something funny about her. I set the trigger to pick-up." This meant that the equipment went into action immediately the receiver was lifted. "Have a listen to this," and the police technician at the controls flicked a switch and after some mechanical sounds a woman's voice was heard.

"Hallo?"

No reply. The line just purred.

"Oh, er -"

The purring raced on.

"- it's you."

"Shit," exclaimed the officer.

The recording continued.

"What do you want?"

Nitrogen Narcosis

The glug-glug of the *dhow's* engine – a furious mechanical bursting of bubbles – deadened his thoughts. Its very monotony, an ordered and yet strangely rounded, guttural sound that hinted at something organic was so unique as to defy vocal imitation. It was loud, but not deafening, merely thought-deadening. Thus, this unfaltering noise was not sent to the rear of his consciousness.

Looking about himself he noticed the wearied bodies of the others. They were languid, almost lifeless figures, not basking in the heat, more subjugated to the insistent lulling noise and the journey. All of them seemed to be endlessly seeking a comfortable position on the wooden deck. Then again, they remained motionless, as if the lack of motion could ease their discomfort. Towels, cotton jackets and dive-bags were used to protect them from the hard floor. Over their heads were T-shirts and towels and *gutras* and folded *habiyas* and occasionally a baseball-cap. Nevertheless, their limbs seemed awkwardly stretched out or bent-up. Yes, even their limbs were extraneous like an irritation, an extension to their lack of comfort.

Contributing to the general mind-numbness was the endless blue sky and the unbroken flat sea. It was a primordial day, a first day, and although not a young day, but a full day, it was a day without passion; it was too stretched too thinly and bland and uninspiring for passion.

And the noise of the motor isolated them in their clutter from this brutally raw day of sun, sea and sky.

The three Saudis had the best place of course: a covered area at the raised stern. For the *dhow* was akin to a miniature galleon: romantic and aesthetically pleasing. Although the rear was the best place, by virtue of its luxury of space when compared with the sheer clutter of bodies and gear elsewhere, it was little more than a wooden platform or box covered by a thin, aged carpet. But these men possessed that Indian knack of finding rest on a hard surface. And yes, they looked more like Indians than Saudis: their colour being a rich chocolate brown and their features somewhat Caucasian. Maybe they were no more comfortable than their passengers, but a simple acceptance surrounded them – he didn't see them speak but he felt sure that they spoke to each other simply and in quiet tones – and their long-practised ability to remain still for hours on end added to this aura of contentment. Therefore, although they had ignorant faces, dull eyes and heavy foreheads, their demeanour possessed calmness: something one associated with age rather than with these men in their early twenties.

Naturally, he tried to imitate them, for they were at ease with the sun and the water. And he was troubled. He was troubled. The twitching and endless shifting westerners about him troubled him further. They were like fidgeting children. And ah, to his disgust, he too had to move.

Few spoke; the effort was too much for most, what with the noise. Then there was the blistering sun and the rocking of the boat. Groups were small, most of the people were sprawled out on deck, and thus conversation had all but stopped within the first hour of travel.

He jumped down from his seated position on top of the hold. Balancing, twisting his feet between the languid lumps of bodies, he made his way past the hot, iron-black pipe that billowed a vapour-fine trail of fuel-reeking smoke, to the cool-bin. Removing the lid he drove his arm into the painfully cold ice-water and fetched a can of cola. The icy-burning encounter was too cold to be refreshing, but it did jolt his mind from its torpor.

Naturally he did not know the full story, but he did have an idea as to when it had begun. He felt that the irony of it all was that he had been the instigator of the entire thing.

Ever since their arrival he had tried to entice her to learn to dive. Here he had renewed his efforts. She could no longer fall back on excuses of it being too cold and not wanting to struggle into an awkward wet or dry-suit. In the Gulf one could get away with a T-shirt and a swimsuit – and the T-shirt was worn merely to stop any abrasion by the straps. At most – for instance a night dive – one needed a shortie. Furthermore, internal flights were company-paid and on the other side of Saudi Arabia was the Red Sea. Even she had caught her breath at the beauty of the coral and the abundance of colour and life at the slide-shows they had attended together in England.

Colin understood it all now. Now. He mused, however, that Saudi was a spawning ground for such happenings. The great sandpit. Or was it Saudi? Was it not the expatriate environment that was the spawning ground? A veneer of 'civilization' coated upon an alien environment? Then was it not true of all expat environments? Nonetheless, in the Middle-East such an environment was something of a smelting pot. Everyone was cooped-up on the camps. Of course, they could travel outside the camp; they were not prisoners. The fence and security was to keep unauthorised people out. But they had to return. And naturally they had everything they could want when they returned to its confines from the Outside. There it was: the contrast. Therefore they were always conscious of a certain confinement. There were boundaries and beyond the boundaries they were Outside, and Outside the rules were different and strange and thus dangerous. So most were content to remain housed in the camps – venturing once a week on a set bus route to a set shopping route in a nearby town. Why not? Everything was there in the fenced-in estate. Relationships and inter-relationships were rife in the isolated, clinically green, tree-lined, swimming-pooled, sun-drenched town slapped upon the wasteland. All of them were living on top of one another in the bland searing heat. All of them were warming up, simmering and disregarding the sham with parties and dinners and outings and dressing up for the theatre. Ignoring the fact that these things were all forms of distraction from the reality of their position, the folly that was their situation. 'Make the best of it, it's not so bad, don't let them get you down, stiff upper lip,' were all phrases that ran through his mind. So it went on: a kind of continuous superficiality. A superficiality that required energy that seemed to taint the sensitivity. It went on and on until this high-life became as season-less as the weather. They warmed-up under the endless blaze of the day and the suffocating oven-warmth of night. But once or maybe twice you would hear a snap. Usually it was an insignificant crack, but occasionally it was something more shocking. They were cracks in the sham, emotions warping the superficiality, disturbing the equilibrium, rocking the boat. Once in a while an expat would go off the rails, if only for a moment. He would issue a sharp brittle crack. It could manifest itself as an unreasonable burst of temper at a party, some peculiar behaviour in public: perhaps an eccentricity outside the camp, an attempt to entice danger, to risk a little for a thrill, or much more significantly a fight or a stabbing, or finally, less harmful to most of the others, a suicide.

Despite this insidious downside the material world was excellent. Almost everything was within reach. The world became so much smaller: frighteningly smaller and the scope of choice became correspondingly larger. Strange to say, it was unsettling. Money put everything within one's grasp. All one had to do was choose. Thus things lost value...

In the beginning he had been oblivious to the fact that she had been taken by Ralph. After all, he himself was so much better looking than him. So much for looks! Then again he was much more outgoing, much more fun, than Ralph. Hmm. In retrospect it all fell into place. Hindsight rendered all the glances, movements, inflexions – those he had seen and dismissed – glaringly obvious. But when he was honest with himself he had to admit that he had not seen that she had been drawn to him.

Like him, Ralph was also a dive-instructor. Perhaps more importantly, he was the branch diving officer. But Lynda and Colin had agreed long ago that should she decide to take up diving he would not teach her.

Colin now saw an odd inevitability in it all.

But he only grasped half of the story.

* * *

"Here he is," said Colin, when she opened the front door.

"*Merhaba*," said Ralph. "It's nice to meet you at last."

Lynda was invariably ill-at-ease when meeting people for the first time.

"I seem to be constantly meeting people," she said, smiling uneasily, and shifting her gaze to her husband, who stood slightly behind their visitor. She wondered why he hadn't used his key.

Colin grew on her uneasiness and the way it put Ralph on edge. "Come on in," he said, assertively moving past him and leading him past his wife; leaving her to close the door.

"Take a seat," she heard him say, and then to her, "he can't stay long."

"Oh?" she managed, unbalanced by her husband's gargantuan presence.

"No. I promised myself I'd get some novice papers marked up by tomorrow. See, it's not all play for us divers."

This easy conversation from him touched her and offered a route circumventing her husband's monstrous intimidation. He was in the kitchen at the refrigerator, but due to the proximity of the kitchen he was as good as in the lounge with them. "We haven't got much to offer," he called.

"We've only been here a little over two weeks," she added, by way of excuse.

"Yes, I know," returned Ralph, immediately regretting saying so, for it was an effacing remark and he sensed that he may have crushed her with his clumsiness. He went on hurriedly, in an effort to arrest her from possibly falling into the black abyss of herself. In addition, he wanted to combat any suggestion of his own awkwardness. "I know exactly what it's like. When I came here two years ago – huh, has it already been two years? – I..." And he explained his arrival and detailed his early days in the Men's Camp: a camp for single men and newcomers; they were now in the Family Camp which was much more civilized and open to the male westerners – single or otherwise – after a period in the Men's Camp. "It's rented from the army and little more than row upon row of demountables. There's about five thousand men there."

"Really," she exclaimed.

He nodded and took the opportunity to sip his drink.

"Sounds good to you?" Colin asked her, having brought their drinks in during Ralph's discourse and seating himself in the other easy chair. He could have chosen to sit next to his wife on the sofa and it was not so much as to dispel any unease Ralph might have felt – he occupied the other easy chair – as to retain his own now flagging dominance. His size seemed to diminish in direct proportion to his wife's mounting confidence.

In reply Lynda forced a smile. Unfortunately she could not conceal her hostility to what she felt was his brutality and the smile was insincere.

Ralph registered the discord and promptly ignored it. Politeness decreed that he blatantly feign ignorance of such undercurrents. Nevertheless, the discord unsettled him.

"Yes, but I'm afraid that women are not allowed in."

"Oh," she exclaimed, not knowing where she was and instantly becoming over-attentive after the encounter with her husband.

Ralph was bewildered and continued mechanically. "Yes, they're forbidden. Ahh, you're not missing anything. Just pool tables, table football, TV room and that sort of thing. Of course, you get to become an excellent table-football player, or Bridge player, or whatever... Anyhow, that's where I was housed first of all." He sipped his drink. "I'm glad I'm on Family Camp, now."

"Yes, it has been a surprise," she began, sensing her husband's retreat. "Although outside the camp I had expected the beautiful – Lawrence of Arabia – rolling sand dunes, but instead we've got this terribly, bitty wasteland."

"You can find the dunes," Ralph assured.

"Oh, I'm sure you can," she acknowledged, warming to his easy manner and obliterating all speculation on her husband's silence. She was beginning to enjoy the conversation. "And then there's this. It's so green. Okay, it's not a luscious green, because it's too dry. But everything is so clean. Huh, I guess it could be Beverly Hills or something." Then, with a winning, endearing smile: "Not that I've been there, mind."

Ralph nodded. He could dash her joy by telling her how the Indians and Filipinos were treated and how hard they toiled for a pittance. It was a lot of money for them, but still it was little more than modern slavery. He decided against doing so for it was not the time or the place.

Lynda was not sure whether she had seemed enthusiastically naïve for he had fallen silent. Did he think her a fool? It was at that precise moment that she sensed his depth of knowledge and she was instantly electrified.

During this brief silence the three of them sipped their drinks.

Without looking at him she noted his poise. She had already inspected his appearance. He was not particularly good-looking, his face being too rounded, but in the light of his character it was an interesting face. His green eyes bespoke of a strong spirit and the general plumpness of his cheeks anchored him to a sailors' tavern: all noise, joyful and brash. Then the way he carried himself, the arch of his brow and the thinness of his lips hinted at a wise, if not sad, demeanour. But it was in the way he talked that added the interesting dimension to him. A dimension that spoke of hours of quiet contemplation in total contrast to the loud tavern.

The nick in the collar of his shirt – a sloppy bit of ironing – testified to his bachelor existence.

Colin was better looking. He suited the moustache and goatee he sported. Initially it had been a mess, but now, ah now, it was a dashing swashbuckler's appearance. An adventurer's look with the flashing teeth and the cutlass wit and the laughing eyes. It was Errol Flynn, Douglas Fairbanks Jnr. and Burt Lancaster leaping from the rigging from starboard to port and then from port to port a hair's breadth from danger: the enraged husband, the governor's soldiers, rival pirates. Here he was, a wayward man with quick eyes and a strong heart; a man, Lynda knew, who was attractive to other women.

Both men were tall. Both were strong. They were big men. Yet, between them there was a world of difference. Colin was a man's man. He had a man's strength: instant and obvious. Even his supposed wildness was predictable. That aside, he was immediately attractive to women and thus could be called a ladies' man. Here, before her, sat a man similar in build to her husband, but that was all. Already she felt that emotionally he was at the other end of the spectrum. She was intrigued because she could not call him a man's man, even though his outward appearance leant in that direction. Oh, he was undoubtedly brave and all that, but there was a woman in him. There was a tenderness, an element of sensitivity that she would normally associate with a woman. Her husband was no brute. He was quite a romantic at times, but this and all such actions were conscious efforts for him.

She wondered how she appeared to Ralph. Did he see a tall – for she was above average height for a woman – gangly woman? Or did he spy something sophisticated in her?

The conversation started up again with the two men talking of diving and it afforded a good opportunity for her to silently scrutinize them. Yes, she scrutinized her husband too.

She scrutinized her husband too because she was inwardly reassessing everything. There was no question of her love for him and she was not disillusioned. But of late, in the region of the last year or two of their four year marriage, she had grown complacent. More disturbingly, she felt deep down in the well of her soul that she had had the child to stave off the possibility of boredom. Naturally she shunned this horrible thought. Nonetheless she had suspected that something was amiss with her to feel such boredom. Now she knew that nothing had been wrong with her and that the truly shameful thing was to have had the child for such a reason. Ah, she had wanted some form of purpose. She was an ambitious career woman without a career; for she had never established a working vocation. For a time she had found occupation in her husband and then in a family. Currently she was utterly forlorn and worse she believed that her face – or her eyes – betrayed this fact and that consequently her husband was becoming more and more speculative about her sincerity. This, in itself, could explain his warped manner. But how to convey to him that she had not fallen out of love with him? That she was merely disenchanted with her life at the moment? Simply to say it would risk him assuming a burden of blame. Furthermore, it had gone too far.

Colin was not a bad man. He loved her: purely, simply and totally. It was this purity and simplicity that confused her. For it was as if his love was not enough for her. She was not insatiable or anything like that; it was that she suspected the depth of his love, almost as if it were a shallow pale by comparison. By comparison to what? To what she wanted? To what she expected? Demanded? As far as she was concerned the well of his emotions was stunted. That is, sometime in his youth he stopped developing emotionally for whatever reason, if indeed, there needed to be a reason. Obviously she could never tell him this, but she was not completely satisfied. Incongruously, she was enthralled by the simplicity of his love. It was the very child-like aspect of it that attracted her, for she yearned for the same. His love was like that of some primitive with an uncomplicated belief in some religion: an utter, child-logic belief uncluttered by reason.

The unsatisfied love she harboured was poured into the child. Their daughter was a bright young thing, exposed and brilliant. She was pale and new, unblemished and vulnerable like freshly fallen snow. A delightful flake. Here too was another disappointment for her. Colin was not what she would call a good father. She felt that he played at being a good father. Again his love was obvious and unquestionable. But there was something in the way he liked to show-off the girl to his friends. It was his pride. In some intangible way it undermined his attentiveness – for he was attentive to the child. For him the girl was something to administer to, something to wash, to clothe and to feed, but in such a way as to give Lynda the feeling that to him the child was an elaborate living plaything; undoubtedly a wonder. Succinctly, she felt that his love for his daughter was also without depth.

Lynda herself was attentive to the child. Sometimes she was overly attentive. No mistake could be made here however; she did not spoil the child with attention. In actual fact, she knew that the child unwittingly displayed more respect for her than for her father. Children needed limits.

They were not staying together for the child's sake. But their relationship had changed. Their love had been complemented by the seductive, unconditional love for and from the child. For a number of years she had gone into a state of suspended animation at the expense of rearing their daughter. Time had flown with such speed that her inchoate mind now tricked her into believing she'd undergone a form of time-travel. Years had passed and she seemed to have little to show for them.

Sometimes Lynda fantasised Colin falling out of love with her and running off with some young thing – or then again some attractive old thing! Such an occurrence would devastate her, yet in the pit of her soul she knew some burden would be eased.

In addition to all this deep soul-searching was another thing that tormented her. This was that she was more intellectual than him. In this respect, and much to his chagrin, she could be something of a wild horse. It was the one aspect of her against which he had no standing. Intellectual pursuit was something she drank up. She adored a good strong debate. And, if the truth be known, it thrilled her to be wrong, to be brow-beaten, because that meant progress, a revelation of some kind, a new flavoured morsel to savour and mull over. Here before her sat a potential feast. Could he handle what her husband could not stomach? Thus she was excited. Although she loathed the initial meeting – always so banal – she looked forward to the subsequent friendship.

This contributed to the boredom in her eyes and the deliberate ease of her gait: something one associates with the very intelligent or the very relaxed. There was a restraint about her. Like there was a greater potential within, suppressed and barely contained. It seemed evident in her aplomb, the precise tone of her speech, the insecurity of her lop-sided smile. Yet it was supremely confident. A confidence based upon knowledge, almost soul-like. And it was in a state of dynamic conflict with something. Perhaps it was her spirit that could not find ease in this social world? So there it was, the beast that was called intellect, just under the surface, tethered but straining at the bit. It set her apart, maybe elevated her, but ultimately it alienated her.

It had been as recent as six months ago that it had dawned on her that her husband acted as a father rather than was a father. It was a subtlety, something intangible that had so far eluded her discovery. She had wondered whether all his efforts outside work were channelled into scuba-diving. But she could find no evidence to substantiate such a curbing of his paternal energies. Still she hardened against scuba-diving. More frightening to her was that this was not the crux of the matter and that she was using it as an excuse. She was excusing him for his lack. She was excusing him because he was no more; she had all he had to offer. This thought brought a sickness to her heart, a mourning in her soul against which she fought tooth and nail.

So she sat listening to the two men talking of diving and the general running of this particular BSAC (British Sub-Aqua Club) branch. She was aware of their easy conversation, of the child sleeping upstairs, of the fact that she was actually in Saudi Arabia, married to a man who loved her totally and was earning pots of money for their future comforts, aware of all this and – at that very moment – totally withdrawn from it all.

"And when are you going to put on a mask and snorkel?" asked Ralph, feeling that she had been left out of the conversation long enough.

"Oh I don't know, soon maybe," she replied, perplexed by her own perversity. She had been only just prepared for speech, for her husband had disturbed her thoughts by rising to fetch fresh drinks. "When's the next beginners' class?"

"Five or six weeks' time. I had heard that you weren't so interested." Seeing that she did not want to reply – she merely smiled – Ralph went on to talk of the diving club and the facilities available. He even presumed to give her confidence in the swim test. Everything to him was so reasonable and delightfully straightforward. Then he seemed to dash it all with a careless remark. "But I suppose he has said all this already?"

The drinks arrived and idle conversation was assumed, testifying to the fact that the evening was drawing to a close. After a short time Ralph left.

"You were quick to say you might do it?" said Colin, referring to the diving. They were in the kitchen area together. "Huh, all the times I've tried to persuade you..."

But he did not say this in an angry tone.

"Yeah." Then, "I couldn't really say I wasn't interested."

"Why not?"

"I don't know him well enough."

"What's that got to do with it?"

"Everything."

After a pause she added, "Anyhow, I may do it."

He laughed cruelly and then shook his head with exaggerated exasperation. "Women."

A flame of hatred shot through her, but she smothered it with a dead-eyed blanket of calm resolve.

* * *

When she announced that she would enrol for the novice divers course Colin was happy. His glee made her happy too and there was headiness in the unit that evening. For a short time the burden within her was eased. Simultaneously she was wounded by this harmony, for it was a veiled blow. She knew that he would see that this harmony betrayed the complacency with which they had come to accept the disharmony. Although, here disharmony was the wrong word and it was more a lack of harmony. In any event, the cut of joy was a double-edged blade – not a razor-sharp Turkish scimitar, but a wieldy, two-handed crusader's broadsword – a welcome sweeping relief and a blunt acknowledgement. This unspoken awareness heightened their joy to almost frenzy-level and it seemed to surpass itself in a love-making session and so precipitate a more profound mourning.

The subtlety of their predicament was infuriating to both of them. They argued, but not vehemently. They fought, but not with hatred in their hearts. They laughed, but not with all their humour. They held each other, but did not completely embrace. Everything was not quite whole. Not quite complete. Yet, almost... Almost... Of course their relationship could not always be afire with passion. Love did not move on a single plane; it undulated, and this was undoubtedly a lull.

Having decided to join the diving course she began to practise for the swim test. Whilst she did length after length her friend Maureen watched her daughter in the kiddie pool. She was training and the idea of a goal was stirring music to her ears. At the bottom of her heart she knew that such intense training was unnecessary. Regardless, she was committed and pitted herself at the exercise.

"Will y'be wearing y'self out on Thursday too?" asked Maureen, an Irish nurse.

Lynda had found in Maureen a true companion. Although she was not on the same intellectual plane, Maureen was a character. Were not all the Irish? And Lynda adhered to this strength. She was also amused by it. Not in a cruel way. For instance, she was amused that nearly all of Maureen's statements were turned into questions in the future indicative tense. "Will we be having fun now? Are we settling down, yet?"

The commissary, or as it was colloquially known, the Comm, was something of a cliché. It was such an archetypal western food store that it was almost laughable. Was this Saudi Arabia? There was the mundane music smoothed to a creamy consistency so that it was impossible to tell whether lyrics were spoken. Then there was the general layout of the place: row upon row of consumer goods clinically organised upon sterilised shelves; a blaze of colour to attract the eye, flawlessly identical boxes and cans that urged one to possess them – yet, when you had one, the magic of the mass vanished and it was merely a carton or a tin. Yes, it was a veritable Warhol-wonderland. Added to this were the dead-moronic looks of the staff, so hushed and self-restrained and polite, all coated in the same characterless uniform of indifference. It was the staff that highlighted the incongruity of the shop for they were Arabs. Possibly a delicatessen counter selling Arab foodstuffs could have lifted it from the obvious "little western society" sham. But no, this was a shop for displaced persons to feel at home. So too, it was a displaced shop. Even the shopping bags were of the rigid, American, handle-less brown-paper type.

Lynda had come to meet Colin from work, but she was early so that she could shop in the Comm. It was here that she had her first encounter with Ralph since their initial meeting.

"*Sallam Allacum*," he greeted, appearing as if materialising next to her.

"*Allacum Sallam*," she reacted.

"What goodies are you collecting?" he asked good-naturedly.

His suddenness meant that her thoughts were in disarray. Nervously she looked away from him to her daughter who was fingering some colourfully wrapped delights a few metres away. This nervousness caused her further embarrassment.

"Oh, nothing much." She smiled, feeling the redness of her neck.

Once more her embarrassment made him uneasy and he toppled over the edge. Colin was not here and therefore her embarrassment tantalised him for it was a communication. He almost revelled in the effect of himself. However, he was in strange waters so he moved cautiously. Looking away from her he glanced at her trolley of goods.

"What have we here?" he asked, picking out a tin of chocolate milk-shake powder. He had successfully turned his uneasiness around and found escape in enquiry. "You or the little one?"

She hesitated; about to ask why he did not think it was for her husband, but then re-evaluated and decided that she did not want to mention him.

"Me." She was pleased with her delivery for it was also a recovery. Looking past him with supreme confidence she checked on her child, who evidently had not noticed her talking with a stranger. Her daughter had never seen Ralph.

"Naughty, isn't it?" She smiled. And with the smile in her eyes she plucked it from his fingers.

Her sparkling eyes caused his heart to swoon and he ached to flirt with her, but astoundingly something held him back. Was he afraid? Had it been too long for him? So his heart swooped down like a bird over a lake. His fragile heart sweeping above the depths of her: the unknown. Unable to attain the ultimate abandonment required for the leap into the unknown, afraid to take the plunging commitment.

Then he realised that a silence had sprung up between them. "Yes," he managed.

She smiled weakly; both intrigued and upset by his sudden reticence.

"I'm no better," he confessed, shrinking away from her and no longer wanting the connection.

"Oh?" she enquired, unsure of his whereabouts.

"Yes, I'm a bit of a chocolate fiend myself." He wrenched himself away from his shrinking self, all the while he soared above her, circling further and further in the distance. "I always have a good stock in the fridge."

"Best place." She wondered at him, sensing his receding self and the conflict within, thrilled that she could affect him so.

He had overstretched himself and was in an uncomfortable state of limbo. He raced on, desperately clinging to the flagging conversation, whilst his inner self flew further and further away, far beyond her, high up where the air grew thin.

"I hear you're putting in a little practice for the swim test."

"A little," she conceded.

"Don't worry, you'll sail through it." He was now stretched to breaking point.

"I hope so. I'm looking forward to the course."

"Good."

Another pause caught them and something snapped within him. This time however they were rescued by a shopper wanting access to some shelves between them and then by the child returning with a colour-splashed bag of something.

In rags, he quickly announced that he had to get on, even though he was in no hurry.

She remained bewildered by the encounter. She wondered at her own faux-naif attitude. In Ralph's presence she became youthful. It was a dangerous subjugation, because it was uncharacteristic and obvious to both Ralph and her husband. And the latter would be infuriated should he see who she became with this man. Ralph would know the two Lyndas and know then that there was a Lynda for him.

A deeper worry was the shocking feebleness of her fidelity.

* * *

As with the end of night and the beginning of day, the swim test seemed forever arriving and then it was suddenly upon her.

She hated the test, not because of any particular difficulty, but because the sheer weight of numbers depersonalised it.

It had been dusk. The sky was a clear slate-blue, the stars dimmed by the wash of floodlights about the pool: painfully hazing the air and bleaching the shadows. The group were hushed by the volume of water, not merely by expectation but by the reflective properties of the pool. For the water played tricks with the sound and sent it ricocheting metallically, thin and tinny, off all the objects. And the sounds were violently savaged by the expanse of sky and the volume of water. So the only sounds were that of the murmur of voices and the patient lapping of the water, the irritating buzz of the lights high above and that of a nullified Filipino hosing down one lonely end of the pool-side. To her it was quite strange. All the familiar objects that made up the pool: the wooden and plastic loungers, obtrusive New York street-style hose-points, umbrellas and white plastic tables, were quite distinct. She was used to the place during the day amid the shrieks of children, fussing and gossiping mothers, a wealth of activity destroying all and so enveloping the place, bringing it all together in a dispelling insignificance. The activity killed the existence of the individual things by its very boisterousness and in so doing took them to its bosom and warmed them. Now there was no such atmosphere. Everything was noticeable, almost cold, and on top of it all every sound was an individual scream. Thus it was not the test that jarred her nerves and caused her ill-humour, it was the unfamiliar lack of ambience.

Along with the others she went through the test. Yes, it could have been routine. It was not difficult. Although, it could never have been fun. But for her it was an ordeal.

The two-hundred metre free-style was fine. But it could have been so much better. Unfortunately she did not feel free and flowing as she did in training. This inner turmoil caused her to expend more energy than normal. Like most of the women, she chose a leisurely breast-stroke, most of the men chose an aggressive front crawl. Her one-hundred metre back-stroke was also okay, though she did go a little askew. An element of strained levity occurred when a few of them collided, even though they had set off in staggered bands. The first major obstacle – she regarded it so – was the fifty metre swim with a weight-belt. The women carried one kilogram and the men five. This hurdle was overcome with surprising and confidence-instilling ease. After this came the motionless floating on the back for five minutes. For her this was not so much a respite as a lull before the storm. This began with the one minute tread water with the hands above the head. She was wearied towards the end and a miniscule element of panic entered the fringes of her consciousness and she kicked her legs a little more energetically, which had the adverse and baffling effect of pulling her down. Obviously, this was what she was trying to avoid, but she could not help herself and gulped some hard, unwanted masses of water. Their massiveness painfully swelled out her neck and caused her eyes to widen. This event was transparent to the officials – one of whom was Ralph – and just when she thought she could not go on they called time. The ultimate and, for her, most daunting task now lay ahead. One was required to recover a weight from the bottom of the deep end of the pool six times. This became more than a chore after all that had preceded. However, it was by no means a Herculean task. But the water seemed to reject her. She had to struggle against it, wrestling with it, pulling herself into the body of it as it tried to expel her and possess her: trying to enter her mouth between her tightly pressed lips. It blurred her vision and hid the whereabouts of the weight until she was almost upon it. It pressed daggers into her ears. And it wavered and shimmered and the lines of the tiles wiggled and bulged. Its psychedelia alienated her, its sounds disconcerted her, its force disorientated her and she was repelled. Nonetheless, she steeled herself and told herself that it would soon be over. Thus she endured and the thing did come to an end. Admittedly, she felt no sense of triumph, she hardly had the energy to feel relief, but she was glad it was over.

It had been agreed that Colin should not be present – he was looking after their daughter – but she wished that he were, for he would have given her a feeling of great reward. All she received from Ralph was an impersonal: "Well done." She forgave him for he was occupied by the event. Even so, she was in desperate need of comfort and was strangely quite fragile. By the time she was home, however, she was tentatively blasé.

* * *

She had wandered off. Only for a moment. She had been watching his hands. They were strong hands, without grace: a labourer's hands, large, perhaps a little too large like those of Michelangelo's David. Like this David they too held a certain power, an underlying sinewy organic beauty. She was almost bewitched by the oyster of muscle between his thumb and index finger and its hint of big, clumsy sensitivity. His interesting face, offering unspoken depth, contradicted by these oafish hands. Their insentience added a new dimension to him: a further facet to his character.

The phrase 'burst lung' snapped her out of her reverie and she was instantly attentive: hanging on to his every word to glean their total meaning and fill out the context and in some impossible way backtrack and thus eradicate the possibility of having missed something vital.

"... if you're having trouble with this, imagine a balloon. You blow it up at twenty metres and seal it. Now, as you ascend – remember Boyle's Law – the balloon expands. If you look at the chart, er, you'll see that at the surface the pressure within the balloon will be three times that at twenty metres. Our lungs behave in the same way – if sealed, that is, if you hold your breath. The trick is, of course, not to do that. The trick is to breathe normally and make a controlled ascent. This brings us onto emergency ascents..."

They had raced through the snorkelling phase and completed the basic skills test. She had become accustomed to the aqualung and had practised her buoyancy with an Adjustable-buoyancy-life-jacket or ABLJ.

Furthermore, they had performed numerous pool exercises and even undertaken a couple of open-water dives. Naturally, these had been an adventure; a pleasure with a healthy level of anxiety: enough to adhere her to her training with sensibility and calmness.

But the real adventure was the submarine flirtation that existed between Ralph and herself. Admittedly, it had grown somewhat out of hand of late, but the emotion still thrilled her and tiny little explosions erupted within her, casting her adrift. So that once in a while she floated on the quiet subterranean currents within her. These subtle surges of emotional energy that stirred within her, the likes of which she had not felt since puberty, were wild like lust, primitive too. Most importantly they moved beyond her rationale. Their irresistibility rested in their latency, for they swelled deep within her such that their depth appeared fathomless and so she was afraid. Like puberty she was unbalanced: not understanding herself or her mood. Luckily – for she felt she would lose control or go mad if they occurred any more frequently – and frustratingly, this excitement was confined to the times when they were near: before and after the class, or when, as had happened only twice so far, he gave her a lift home in his Subaru 4WD estate.

Yet all was unsaid. They both resisted. It was not so much a feigning of indifference, that would be too childish, as an enjoyment of the parrying. But to thrust, to thrust was to plunge into the heart of it and possibly kill it. Without doubt it had got rather out of hand. The reins of self-control had begun to jerk and whip and burn. It was no longer a game. In the beginning it had been a game, albeit an adult game. Now the crisis was upon them. The crisis that was the unsaid that they had dared to tease. There was no denying it.

Even the child did not seem to bother him. Why should her daughter bother him? He got on well with her. But the rules were a little different out here.

She could not rationalise it. And she wanted to rationalise it. Why did it have to be so dark and heavy? A black heart bloated with poison. Why did it have to possess such destruction? The answer was both obvious and absurd. It was because she was married. She had a child. She had responsibility. And they had dared to fool with something called sin. Sin. Such a small horrible word, steeped in religion – much like sex – but sin was the tip of the blade that was the edge of the moral society. To go beyond was to cut away something. To go beyond was to lose something, some pillar without which other things could fall away. To go beyond was to outcast oneself. Absurd, of course! Yet in this day and age, well beyond the sixties, this morality was so deeply ingrained within her. Why could it not kiss them for a moment and then leave? Why did it have to tear at the fabric of her beliefs? It was horrid and twisted that it should harbour such irrevocable destruction. And although she was not in the least bit religious she suffered a religious guilt, something Catholic, something irreconcilable. The clandestine nature of their connection was tolerable, but the consecration of the unsaid was not tolerable. The pain of self-inflicted guilt would be unbearable. Sin was a poison placed inside her from early childhood. It was a sac in her heart waiting to burst and twist her up forever and it could only be contained through worship or a strict moral code. She knew that society was founded on morality and that people were society. Then, here in Saudi Arabia, the religious morality had been exaggerated to law. In the name of Allah one could be sentenced to death. This obviousness lay bare the subtlety of such structure in Western society.

Lynda knew that a decision was upon her. Indeed, it was more of a decision for her. She asked herself whether it was an attraction to Ralph or to what had grown between them. Was there substance behind their flirtation? And she did not know the answer. He was an interesting man, perhaps because she did not know him. Then, in a completely different way, so was her husband. She loved her husband and she loved her daughter. Ah, if sin were but a fruit. She could take the smallest of bites and taste it and extract its

171

knowledge. Then she would know. Alas, Ralph was not something inert which she could taste and discard if she so wished. Consequences.

All this caused her to question her connection with Colin. Could she love someone one hundred percent for one hundred percent of the time? Could anyone? Of course not. Naturally a relationship would ebb and flow. Was her procrastination then for the sake of the child? Or did it have its foundations in her own childhood?

She viewed Ralph subjectively. Here was a man who offered her more than a roll in the sack. No matter what he said that was evident in his manner. He was holding out a hand of heavy commitment and heartache all cloaked under a tarpaulin of frivolity and harmless fun. But his eyes gave him away: a pleading sincerity; a thirst for red-blood passion. The flirtation had been fun, but that was all. And she decided that she did not want more. Thus, the very thing that had attracted her to him, the essential sensitivity and depth of him, was the thing that turned her away.

The droplet of her decision became a monsoon. She would say something after the lecture when he gave her a lift home. The parrying was over, there would be no thrust; one of the fencers was putting down their rapier. Game over. Hopefully they could both adjust to their new positions outside the arena of emotion.

"Now, I'd like to jump ahead to lecture three point eleven and talk a little about nitrogen narcosis, carbon monoxide poisoning, er, oxygen and carbon dioxide poisoning.

"We'll start with nitrogen narcosis, or as it is sometimes called: diver's delight, rapture of the deep or simply the narks.

"As you know, the deeper you dive the greater the partial pressure of nitrogen in the air you breathe and the more nitrogen your body absorbs. This has an effect. The deeper you go the more likely you are to experience the narks. But how do you know? Unfortunately, sometimes you don't and this is the greatest danger. It is a feeling similar to drunkenness: a detachment from reality, euphoria, etcetera. Hence the term: diver's delight and so on. The danger is to act recklessly underwater and cause an accident, not realising – if at all – that you're doing so until it's too late. The classic example is that divers have been known to be so elated under the influence of nitrogen narcosis that they have offered their regulators to the fish." Pause. "Nitrogen narcosis impairs the judgement. The diver may read his depth gauge wrongly, for instance. He may endanger his buddy and himself by doing something which he considers fun without comprehending the consequences – a prank or something – and so on.

"There seems to be no consistency in people's tolerance or susceptibility to the, er, condition. The same diver may feel it at a certain depth one day and nothing the next. You've got to understand that nitrogen narcosis occurs at all depths, but that the effects are only noticeable – and increasingly dangerous – in proportion to depth. There are some statistics in the manual, but I can't emphasise enough that these figures are subjective. They can't hope to take into account the variety of physiological and psychological variables. In any case, we might say that between ten and thirty metres you might feel a mild euphoria, with only a slight impairing of your reasoning. However, beyond thirty metres we enter into the realms of overconfidence and deeper still we enter hysterical laughter or terror – it depends on the subject, because like alcohol it affects different people in different ways. Still deeper, seventy metres and beyond, well, hallucinations and the unknown." Another pause. "No doubt the lost city of Atlantis has been discovered many times at these depths." Controlled laughter.

"As I've already said, other factors affect susceptibility and it would be impossible to list them all. Has anybody any ideas?"

"Drugs," said someone. Laughter – a little less controlled – ensued.

"Yes, drugs of any sort. But of course as we don't have drugs out here – " sarcasm " – and we don't dive whilst on drugs of any kind whatsoever – " stern " – because it'd mean instant dismissal from the club. What else?"

Silence.

"Well, er, fatigue, weariness, etcetera. Others are in the book. Look them up.

"Treatment? There's only one thing to do if the effects become noticeable – and hopefully before they take a grip – and that is to ascend.

"Any questions before I move on?"

Ralph went on to relate other dangers of the deep and in time the lecture drew to a close.

Although Lynda talked with the others as he gathered his papers she was aware of his movements. Her own conversation was

173

uninspired as she followed his speech with some others. This momentary, but acute, awareness was a nervous thing, a thing putting her upon the knife edge and therefore when one of the group spoke good-humouredly, but loudly, the thing inside her jumped and she was cut because of the speaker. She hated the innocent speaker. She wanted to be brusque and cutting too. Then someone else broke in and then another, until she was awash with loathing for them all. How clumsy they were! Feeling a redness rising upon her neck she interrupted Ralph and told him that she would wait outside.

When Ralph came out into the cool black evening she was in a state. He was casual and she donned a similar mood. But as she sat in the passenger seat and he, having finished fiddling about with some equipment at the rear of the car, thudded the boot shut, she jumped again and again she was wounded. During the moments before he entered the car she closed her eyes. How she hated it when she was not in control.

He climbed into the driver's seat, although she was not ready.

"That's that. Home James, right?"

"Yes." She smiled.

This monosyllabic reply tinged his good-humour.

"I hope today's lecture didn't put you off?"

"Oh, no," she said hastily, too hastily. "No, not at all. It was a good lecture."

Puzzled, he started the car.

She sheltered behind the noise of the engine and respecting her reticence he drove her home in silence. That is not to say that his curiosity vanished; on the contrary, it increased in direct proportion to the length of the silence. So that when he came to a halt opposite her unit, he had to venture: "Is something wrong?"

She had spent the journey reiterating the key phrases over and over in her mind; all the appropriate phrasing and terminology: consideration without patronization, subtlety without connivance and so on. All for a soft splashdown. Ah, but now, confronted outright – how to start? How to sound? What to assume? Wouldn't it be silly because nothing had happened.

"Er," she began hesitantly, not looking at him: first ahead at the quiet, clean-swept street and then to the books upon her lap. "I've been thinking about us."

"Aha."

"I – " she went on quickly " – know nothing has happened, yet. But – " then she blurted " – I think we've been acting rather silly." There, it was done. It was said, and at that moment, in complete contrast to the awareness she had at the end of the lecture, she was completely oblivious to him. Then hurricane of doubt swept over her. Was he scrutinising her? Was he angry? Was he sad? What did he feel?

He nodded, and she felt his presence in the movement of his head and she wanted to read him. So she glanced at him.

There was a wicked smile on his face and a gleam caught in his eye, such that she recoiled from his inexplicable expression. She wished then that she had not looked at him. What did he think? What could he think? For an instant she pondered her word 'yet' which she felt had been a mistake. And wondered why she had said it. Had he read her wrongly? The scream was within her: "I know nothing has happened, yet." Yet.

She watched his smile vanish and saw the gleam disappear from his eyes, although it could have been a trick of the street-light. The gleam seemed to snap out like a candle. It was covered by a weak smile, that was not enough to hide the extinguished joy that smouldered somewhere in his face. Then, it seemed to her, his eyes became hard and crystalline, almost black and heartless like that of a shark: ruthless beads that gave nothing. Strangely enough, this caused her heart to fly out to him, to bring him back to her. As necessary as it was, she was pained at what she had done. Perhaps she was pained too at being unable to halt the brutal slamming of doors, old keys: large and aged with experience turning in chunky clunking locks; warmth echoing away.

She realised that he had been looking at her and had seen the guilt in her eyes – did he hope to turn it to his advantage? Would he try? His smile had turned embarrassed and yet confident. The question was whether she would yield to him should he make a play for her.

"Ah, don't worry," he began. She held her breath, hoping for a morsel of reprieve and simultaneously bracing herself for an assault. "You're right, it's for the best."

"Yes," she agreed, hoping to carry him if he was not sure. At that moment he was a martyr, but not a hero. For with martyrdom she could still attach some egotistical motive. Then, although she was happy that the worst was over, she added with a strange gravity; a gravity that ironically hinted at uncertainty, "I just don't think it's right."

He was able to nod.

The collision appeared to be over. The fog was clearing to reveal the damage: debris floating about, bobbing up and down, in and out of the turbulence between them. They would be going to different ports for repairs, superficial or otherwise – it depended upon ego and wisdom. Incongruously, she was frantic to retain the connection that she had severed.

"I enjoyed it though, our flirting." Did she have to say that? "It was kind of fun." She was adrift; regretting her words. So much for aplomb! She fell silent.

He too was quiet and she felt compelled to make things still clearer.

"Look, er, Ralph– " his name for attention and connection " –I hope we can still be friends." What was this? They had done nothing. She searched his face which was now turned away looking at the dashboard or steering wheel. "I'd like that very much."

Her words had been issued like a plea and he could do nothing but turn to her. He felt that he had to reassure her: to show her that he was not so easily destroyed.

"Don't worry," he said. Again he smiled. But the smile could not throw off its burden of weakness. If only as a way of casting a parting gift, for want of something better to say, as he sailed off, he threw her a compliment. "Colin doesn't know how lucky he is."

Her heart leapt and flew to him – and instinctively – reflexively – she placed her hand upon the back of his hand that rested at his knee. Now he was the hero.

The contact snapped his eyes and a line was jettisoned outward and after the merest hesitation, she grasped it and they kissed.

It was a long kiss.

Afterwards she smiled apologetically and turned away to look at the black hedges, the dull housing units, windows: pockets of light upon ironed sandstone, a vague warmth. Inwardly she shrugged something off and then straightened herself.

Clumsily – for she wanted silence – and so very typical of a man, he felt that reassurance was necessary. "Don't worry; I won't make anything of that."

Without looking at him she forced a smile that turned him away from her, blanched and shocked, leaving him pondering.

Somehow she sensed his wondering and straightening her papers and books, though they were already straight, she said: "Goodbye Ralph."

* * *

Glug-glug-glug-glug-

Silence.

Silence, save the lapping of the water against the side of the *dhow*. Such a peaceful, natural sound after the jarring, obtrusive engine. Yet, the loss of the gurgling, exhausted alcoholic, with the petrol-fumed breath – the ghost of whom was precipitated and rapidly receding in his mind, fading to memory – was oddly sad. It was an inexplicable loss. Naturally, it was a relief, but his mind tried to cling to the aquatic asthmatic. It had been a torture, but it had been something to which he had grown accustomed. And like torture, its sudden despicable flight had left him with withdrawal symptoms. The forever drowning machine had boxed his ears for hours, spewed noxious fumes, numbing his senses, making him punch-drunk, only to abandon him leaving him empty and forlorn.

Complementing this restful slapping of the water against the side of the *dhow* – it had a lulling rock-a-bye-baby effect – was the scene about them. The sun was, as usual, alone in the sky. It was mighty like a benign king: powerful and majestic; no longer the upstart, the wild threatening knave. Ahead of them sat the merest slip of land, a beach just breaking the surface. This was Jurayd Island: a hump of sun-baked sand with some harsh bracken-like shrubbery. A tower of concrete stood in isolated vigil, its radar pinnacle sweeping endlessly – some joked that it stopped for prayer-time (pointing in the direction of Mecca) – round and round. And apart from the baboon-like screeching of gulls there was no sign of life.

That was all.

Thus, they were intruders: intruders carrying all manner of strange equipment into a scene so primitive. Even the radar, also a symbol of modern technology, melded with the elements about them by virtue of its outward simplicity and silent, perpetual motion.

All on the *dhow* – except for the three Saudis who were active: clambering barefoot about the edges of the boat, dropping anchor, checking the oil covered engine, etc., in a simple well-rehearsed routine – were beaten into stupor and slow to come out of their suspension. A hushed and sluggish and hence cool organisation slowly started up. Gear was wearily organised, tanks brought up from the hold...

The calm fell away in layers as they dragged their drunken selves from their slumber, quiet words were replaced by suitably laconic murmurings: scraps of conversation. The momentum leapt with a shattering shriek of laughter from one of the girls in response to a humorous quip. With the tranquil bubble burst, a veritable barrage of one-liners was hurled, custard-pie-like, from one end of the boat to the other, bonding them in defiance of the still emptiness.

Colin was just returning to the buffoonery. The initial shriek of laughter had been accompanied by a joyous tossing of the head. And yes, on their first date, some five years ago, she too had tossed her head from side to side. At the time he had been more intrigued than enchanted by this strange behaviour. Her happiness had been obvious, but he had thought that the movement revealed something baited and struggling: an expression that made him feel that she had accepted an inevitability, as if she was relinquishing her independence. How could she have known? Or was it the light of current events that coloured his recollection? He thought not. He believed that he had witnessed her shudder with acceptance: a hooked fish giving itself up. But the merciless light of today, years later, with so much water under the bridge, the darkness of the bar, warm oak inadequately lit by the candlelight, made the memory seem gloomy, although it had been fun. Oh, had she been such a blighted thing? Such was the dark despair of Man plunging headlong into emotive waters.

Shrinking from everything, he removed his T-shirt, kicked off his Jesus-sandals and dropped his shorts, so that he stood in his swimming trunks. Then fleeing all, he dived off the edge of the *dhow* and into the water.

For a moment there was a rush, then a strange peace filled by intermittent aquatic sounds. And then he was on the surface bobbing up and down, the heat ferociously devouring the cool of his head. He was far from the boat, but not far enough.

Lynda tossed her head delightedly and the salt filled him with nausea.

"Good idea, Col," shouted one of the men from the boat, beginning to strip off.

Colin immediately duck-dived and pulled himself down, but the water, though clear, was heavy and rejected him. He fought against it, blowing bubbles and scanning the blurred underworld. The sea-bed was little more than six metres below, but all was a suffusion of forms.

Up he came, having to bring a palm to the wooden hull to stop the gentle swell from making him hit his head. At the same time he felt the mild drag trying to take him under and he teased the keel-haul: allowing it to take him only so far. The crash of a further diver plunging into the water made him scrutinise an obscure knot in the wood. Moments later a girl followed and the three of them bobbed up and down as if on an invisible trampoline. However, this was their only connection. He was away from their gasps and exclamations, their sniffing and blowing. Just as the body of water repelled him and offered him no sanctuary, so he could not totally escape his companions.

"This is the life," said the man.

Colin smiled, pulling a hand down his face and giving his nose a short blast. Forlorn for a moment, the other threw himself backwards and made for the girl.

A rope ladder was flipped over the side and Colin climbed.

After hoisting himself aboard, somewhat awkwardly at the rim of the creaking boat, he approached the dive leader responsible for the outing. There was a second enquiry as to his well-being – a girl had told him that he was quieter than normal and looked a bit peaky – then he was told that he was to buddy with a sports diver in the first party.

Talk was loud, almost short-tempered, as the organisation took form. At length, dive plans, depths, duration, direction and so on were established and the first group ready.

And Colin? Colin thought of his friend Ralph. Over and over again he saw them in the car in the half-light. He imagined the quiet words, enigmatic, the taught rustle of clothing, the cloying aroma of surreptitious passion, all heat and awkwardness. How long? How long had it been going on? And he saw them kiss again. It had been so shockingly unbelievable that now he doubted what he had witnessed. But there could be no doubt. They moved together. One form. They were kissing. Ah, the humiliation and betrayal. The pain and the clouds. Suspicions confirmed. Hearts broken. Lies, lies and more lies. Dramatic phrases played and replayed, some about to start playing, but all overplayed or to be overplayed, and played-out. All was frustration. All was torment.

He had been committed to this trip. There was nothing he could do. He was to be in charge when the other dive-leader was diving. Ralph was back on camp. But Lynda had said that Maureen and her husband would be visiting that afternoon. For the entire afternoon? Was it true? What of their child? Perhaps Maureen was in on it too?

She would make a cuckold of him. Funny he should think of that word. It was a word from schoolroom literature. He hated it then and he hated it now. It was despicable in his mind like a cuckoo refusing to be ignored. And then the word suggested emasculation, yes, his cock lopped off. And she had raised the blade.

Round and round he went. And in the car they moved together and kissed. Spiralling down, clawing up a little when the torrent abated and then being flushed further like a spider in a pipe: unable to reach the bath at the top and yet knowing that once there, in the glaring white openness, he would be unable to scale the senseless, smooth enamel. Down was his only option. Down with the wretch! Down to chaos and the unknown. Oh, oh the storm cloud drama of Man.

An index-finger tip to thumb 'okay' acknowledgement. Could she be lying on the bed now, as he had often seen her, as only he should see her. A thumbs down. Was he upon her? ABLJ dump hoses raised. Her face, the rapturous smile, the flush of colour on her chest. Slowly slipping below the surface. The gasping and sparkling of her eyes, wide, wide open: a window to her inner self. This intimacy, his precious gift to her and hers to him, now offered to another. It was a betrayal pure and simple. His gift devalued, tossed aside. It defiled his inner self. It – Silence. Silence, save their breathing. The sub aquatic world seeped into his mind and absorbed his thoughts.

Their hair waved to the whim of the eddies, mimicking the flow of the seabed vegetation. It was a soothing movement: natural, lulling and seductive. A calming womb-sound. The fish glided with the greatest of ease and with the merest flick of a tail, such a magnificently sharp burst of energy, they changed direction. Their gracefulness was on a par with any of Nature's adaptations. They were slivers of perfection. Sometimes the snap of energy was such that these slips of life, colourful and iridescent, instantly occupied a different space.

Although buddying, Colin felt quite alone. He watched the fish dart away and felt a connection with it all. He could almost touch the wondrous harmony about him. The only difference between the sea world and him, the slow and lumbering, but hence deliberate and rested being, was that they inhabited different times. The medium thrust a relatively sluggish time-scale upon him and he was forced to observe the swifter time-scale of the sea creatures. He had to become the passive inquisitor. Consequently, he became primitive in thought, not clumsy and ignorant, but joyful and wide-eyed with amazement. Succinctly, he became a child. Everything was laid obvious before him. It spread out in all directions, a rendition in straightforward beautiful ingenuity. He moved with long, languid leg movements. The brittle stumbling of his surface motion was not in evidence here. He was at once observer and ineffective participant immersed in an enchanted world. The unlimited, uninhibited movement made him feel refreshingly free. There were no voices, no crash of thoughts, nothing complex, merely the sound of his respiration and this underworld of muffled reality. Splendid colours and strange creatures occupied this delightful fairytale land: all manner of Walt Disney inventions in wondrous Technicolor.

In the beginning there was existence, then environmental awareness and utilisation, discovery, interpretation, invention, understanding and now self-awareness. The landscape of Man's history was brought to bear in his mind. It was not a thought. He could not contain it in a thought. It was overwhelming and incomprehensible: a frontier and at the same time the essential substance of sensation.

But of course he was part of another dimension. He was alien to this world that buzzed with the danger and excitement of the unknown. The resultant anxiety of pioneering brushed aside his terra-firma worries with the merest flick of a tail. They were reduced to puerile, obsolete things. His feeling was that akin to profound meditation.

Through his mask he interpreted the fish-eyed world. Through his flat, linear time-scale he viewed his surroundings. Like a ruler to a crystal ball he flattened their curved world to his time. And thus, he could only focus by degrees; just as science explained the Universe. Therefore he was aware of a world that transcended him. This was something beyond him. It was something to which to aspire, but never attain. Something to be comprehended and incongruously – like emotion – remain beyond comprehension. Yet, he could almost taste the connection, the key to it all: the explanation. It was the merging of time and space and all that he could possibly understand and more. It was the possibility that all dimensions could merge within him. His perception could not hope to accommodate all dimensions, but then he did not need to understand what he felt.

His buddy was in sight: a large, somewhat gangly thing suspended in this underworld. How very easy it would be to slip beyond this knoll. Naturally, his bubbles would give him away. But distance worked differently here and metres away his telltale bubbles would be lost to the watery density. How easy to slip beyond. His buddy was the last link with humanity and the torturous dirge that accompanied modern-day living. Strange to think that such a profound connection be shared with an acquaintance: much like upon a battlefield. Fancy sharing such a trip – Nature unfolding its petals (but not its secrets), the wonder of sensation, the exhilarating endorphin buzz of a workout – with a relative stranger. Yet, it was right. It was how it should be.

The dive was a high: a bolt of adrenalin. And he knew that he could magnify that high, ten-fold, a hundred-fold, a million-fold, simply. He could blow his mind away. This was the seat of the buzz. All he had to do was descend. Simply float into Nature. Just give himself unto the depths of the womb of this world. It was so easy. Too easy. Nothing could approach this ultimate high. Nature would swamp his senses, wash over his worries, cleanse his tormented mind.

Colin could see himself move away. Yes, he saw his buddy's initial wave of white-eyed disbelief. Then the calm urgency, moving in one direction and then another. The frantic scanning. Followed by the rapid, but controlled, ascent. And finally, on the surface, the shouts, again the disbelief, the flurry of on-board activity, the hasty search plans...

And he? Why, he would be flying. His mind accepting the convergence of parallel dimensions. Gripping the rough-fibred reality of tarnished gold with one hand. Feeling the beckoning drag. Awkwardly removing a fin with the other hand. Moving without effort, becoming a fish, becoming a part of the whole. Another fin handed upward: stretching, reaching. Received into the Scheme; being part of it all. Reality bobbing him foolishly against the primitive hull. And he would be immortal, displaced, empty. The mask and snorkel pushed down, hanging about his neck. Struggling, inevitably struggling, with the resumed weight of the tank and ABLJ. Passing it upward, the cumbersome action adding to his folly. Then he was free to haul himself up the ladder, to pull himself onto the boat. And he did so, the manufactured, thick plait of the rope searing and painful through the thin rubber soles of his booties.

The Samaritan

"I don't know whether I can explain it," Ted had begun, returning to the breakfast table with the crockery he had fetched from the wall cupboard. "But this is how I see it."

He had set the saucer, tea-plate and dinner plate around the cup and then sat down. "The three different plates represent three people and the cup in the middle represents something of value. It doesn't really matter what it is, gold or food or – I don't know, anything. For the sake of argument we'll say it's food." He remembered looking up at Veronica who sat opposite him. He could tell that she had been attentive, but as always, he had not been able to say whether she was interested. In any case attentiveness had been enough for his enthusiasm at that time.

He lifted the suitcase and reflected whether he should have waited before tearing ahead and trying to explain it to her. But he had been so excited. Even now, having had the night to sleep on it, it was only half-baked in his head.

"As I see it, it shows the difference between Christianity and Buddhism." He had again looked at her, to see if there was a sparkle in her eyes. There had been nothing. Regardless, he had pressed on. "The Christian way is to attempt to share the thing of value. Everyone gets an equal bit. But the Buddhist way is to ignore that it has value. Almost turn your back on it. That way it loses value. Then one can take what one wants. The bigger man, for instance," he pointed to the dinner plate, "would require more food than the saucer."

Down the hall with the case in one hand and the picnic basket of supplies for the cabin in the other.

"Yes, but it wouldn't happen," Veronica had said. "People aren't like that."

"Yes, yes, I know," he had raced, "but it's the principle."

Out into the glorious sunshine. What a day. A little too warm for driving, however.

"They're both ideals," she had said.

"Yes, you're right." It was then that he had hoped to captivate her. "But it's the way of thought. The attitude of the East and the West. Don't you see?" Whoops, that had been a mistake.

"Of course, but I don't see why you're getting so excited."

He had stopped and told himself to give up. "Yeah, I just, er, thought it was interesting."

With that they had retired for the night.

That had been yesterday evening, after his lesson. The company paid half the price of the course: for the betterment of the employees and so on.

Friday was his night away from the kids – they had been in bed when he had arrived home. Thursday was her night out.

Half-baked though it was, he now felt that he could present it much better. Certain phrases had stuck in his mind. There were a lot of questions too. If only he had not said: "Don't you see?" His mind was currently alive with the ideas. The shape of the attitudes of the East and West were there as plain as daylight. The passive, accepting East and the greedily progressive West. But then patience was a virtue and he would wait. For the time being he could do little else. Still, he kicked himself for not having thought it out a bit more.

First he shifted the suitcase deep into the station-wagon and then he placed the wickerwork picnic basket on top of it. Despite having wound down the windows and left the back of the vehicle open, inside was stifling. The warm stale air sat like a solid lump.

He stood back and touched his moist temples. What a brilliant day. It was great to be alive.

Two weeks stretched out before him. It was a shame that he was going to miss two lessons. A colleague would collect the handouts. But it wasn't the same, of course.

Just then he heard the kids squabbling in the house. Veronica said something and then a few seconds later Ellen came running out to the drive.

"Daddy," she began, out of breath from racing down the stairs. Nonetheless she carried on at full throttle. "Mommy won't let me take the Sisters. And Eddy-Junior can take five of his GI-Joe men. It's not fair."

Her little bottom lip sprung out like a cash till and the tears came to her imploring eyes.

Everything was in the balance.

Ted crouched to her level.

"Well, let's go and see Mommy shall we? But first you have to promise not to cry. Come on promise. Look at the glorious sunshine. You can't be upset on a day like this. And we're going on a long trip. We're going to Canada. On the way we can stop for your favourite:

burger on rye and fries with ketchup. And you're going to see Niagara Falls. You know what they are, don't you? Yes. You'll be able to tell Mary-Jane at school that that's what you did. Now, come on, let's go and see Mommy."

He picked her up and carried her back to the house.

Her little face was determined as he spoke to Veronica from the bottom of the stairs. She was either in the bedroom or bathroom.

"What's this about Ellen's dolls?"

He could feel Veronica sigh. "She's already taking five toys. I think it's enough."

That last statement was a warning from her to him. Dare he countermand her? Diplomacy was required.

He looked reassuringly to Ellen, even though she had left out this vital piece of information. He should have known better and asked her before charging off. "Well, is another two going to hurt?" He knew his wife would be prepared for such a question. But as always he was curious as to her answer. Could there be a chink in the armour?

"If she takes another two, then Eddy-junior wants to take another two toys and so on. It'll never end. I said five and that's that."

No chink.

He turned to his daughter.

"You heard your Mother darling." The lip and tears again. "Wait," he whispered.

He called up the stairs again. "Ah Ronny," – pet name – "let's call it six and be done with it, eh?"

Veronica groaned. "You're too soft on these kids, Ted." Pause. "Okay, six."

Eddy-junior hoorayed and announced that he would be taking his 'Millennium Falcon' star ship.

Ted looked triumphantly at Ellen, who looked confused and perhaps angry. "But I want to take the Sisters. I can't take one, that isn't fair."

Veronica was right, he thought, it would never end. "Look darling, I've done my best," he said pleadingly, "perhaps you can leave one of your others behind?" He thought for a moment. "Are you taking Patch?"

She nodded, her mouth clamped firmly shut.

"Well now," he began deliberately. "You know that we're taking Jimmy–"

"Jabba," she snapped tetchily.

"Yes, Jabba," he corrected. She insisted on calling their bulldog that after seeing *Jabba the Hut* in *The Return of the Jedi*. They had chosen Jimmy because when the dog sat up he had a striking resemblance to James Cagney – they had discarded Edward G. Robinson because there were already enough Edwards in the family. "Well he's coming with us and we'll have no one to guard the house. Now I think Patch with his cutlass would scare anyone away, don't you? What do you think? Shall we leave him?"

She thought hard and then gave a serious nod.

He smiled and hugged her to him. She hugged him back. "Give your Teddy a kiss." The kids sometimes called him that instead of Daddy. This she did and then she wriggled herself free and scaled the stairs as fast as she could, favourite leg leading.

He went to the kitchen and tore off a piece of kitchen paper-towel. Then he returned to the station wagon and the startling light.

It was almost eleven o'clock. Eleven o'clock, June 1st 1991. Too bad they could never get their act together quicker. By the time the kids were washed and dressed, despite having risen at eight o'clock, and having had their breakfast and then packed their things – two steps forward and one back – a number of hours had passed. Therefore he would have to drive in the heat. But there was no hurry. They had all day. He smiled. They would probably need all day – what with the toilet stops and food breaks. On top of all that Ellen was susceptible to travel sickness. They had tried the sitting on newspapers, lots of fresh air, looking out of the window, various foul-tasting pills, story-telling – hook and crook – all to no avail.

The song of the birds could drive a man mad if his frame of mind was not right. They were loud and of such variety that it was difficult to break them down. Of course some things were not made to be broken down. Some things were meant to be taken as a whole. Today was not meant to be broken down into its individual elements: the sun, colours of the trees and song of nature and so on. It was meant to be appreciated as a whole. Like the appreciation of a masterpiece was not meant to be analysed to the extent of whether the constituents were of the right quantity or thickness. Beauty was an end effect that disregarded the means; it was the sum of its elements.

Yo, the hood was hot enough to fry eggs. He hooked it open. "Okay guys," he said to the various components of the engine, "how are we feeling today?" Was an engine beautiful? He thought that his engine had a cumbersome and ugly enchantment: a grouchy old sea dog. He drew out the dip-stick, wiped it with the kitchen towel and careful not to touch the grime inserted it again. When he had driven it up to its hilt he twiddled it and then drew it out again. "Looking good," he said, wiping it clean again. As he replaced it for a second time he heard a starter motor whir but the engine did not catch. He turned and looked at the opposite neighbour's house. For a Saturday morning Siobhán was up relatively early. He noted that the curtains were still drawn.

Partly due to the night of rain it had been a particularly fresh November morning when she had emerged from her house in a jogging suit. "Morning," she had called. The grass glistened with freshness. He had been collecting the post from their box at the end of the drive. But he had heard her open her door and had lingered a moment checking the distinguishing marks of the letters: stamps, handwriting and postmarks.

He had returned the greeting and made a remark about her will-power. Beneath the loose colourful clothing she had a great body. Her auburn hair was tied back in a pony tail to show the full beauty of her face. He would describe her as a fantastic looker. Yes, a supermodel. Her eyes were not special except for the fact that they smiled a lot. It was her mouth that haunted him. Her lips were not particularly sensuous or full. It was the shape of her mouth that invited him. It was bewitchingly wide and always on the verge of a smile. She–

The starter motor whirred again. Longer this time. It seemed to strain with the effort and he winced.

She really ought to open the garage door first, he thought, turning back to his car. He looked at the level of fluid in the windscreen-washer bottle, but his mind was elsewhere.

The motor would whir and whir, but the engine would not catch. She would lift the garage door and he would turn as she did so, catching her stretching upward to drink in the full the shape of her body. "Having trouble?" he would ask. A banal question, but the offer was there for her. Siobhán would smile and call him over. "Of course, it's no trouble." Then she would be beside him poring over the engine. Shouldn't she be in the car turning the ignition? That did not fit. She would say something about not understanding such things and he would give her a short course. In particular, he would point out something that would cause her to lean towards him. She would have to bring a hand to his chest to balance. They would be close after she had seen the thing he had pointed out. And she would look into his eyes and he would smile back. Would she pull away? No. She was not that kind of girl. She was a go-getter. Her lips would stretch into a smile and they would kiss. He would grip her arms and she would gasp under his strength. And she would be completely swept up and lead him through the side door into the house. He–

The engine caught and settled down after a couple of roars to a gentle ticking over. He smiled and returned to checking the cable he had taped-up and despite promises to himself – like now – had never got round to replacing.

Ted did not consider himself a bad person. Let us be honest, he said to himself, fantasising did no harm. However, it was not the way of the teachings: the Middle Way. He admitted that he had some pretty wild thoughts about her. They were not bad thoughts, he would protest, they were merely impure thoughts. No, he did not consider himself bad. He absolved himself by thinking that it was a lack of goodness, rather than the presence of bad. To him, it was like hot and cold. Cold was an absence of heat. So it was with the good and the bad in him. Bad was an absence of good. It was never so total, that would border on evil, but sometimes he was not as good as he thought he should be with respect to the teachings.

She had a heap for a car. The only thing that probably kept it going was the attention given to it by her various men friends. Then she only used her car to drive to and from work. More often in her free time she was picked up by some young schmuck. He knew of one in particular. Not good enough for her, he thought. But then he suited her looks-wise. He was part of that set that he, Ted, termed the beautiful people. Nonetheless, Ted hated to see her getting into his jacked-up, chromed pick-up with moon-tyres, the tread of which he estimated to be in the region of six inches deep. She was far better than that, he thought. There again, he hardly knew her.

He knew that she worked in Arcadia Mall, up on East Street. He was not sure of her function; he had only seen her there once. She spent a lot of time on the shop-floor. Management training sounded right. In any case, Daddy was probably quite well-to-do. After all, she had a house here.

He felt that she should be among the beautiful people of nearby – two hours by bus, on a good day an hour's drive away –

Manhattan. She was displaced here in the backwaters. That was Kingston on the Hudson River, Ulster County, New York: the backwaters. It was too big to be a community and too small to be a city. One could say that it was a cluster of communities. Other than the cinemas, bars, restaurants and diners there was no real night life. But what really killed it was that it had no heart, no centre. Old Kingston was a ghost-town at night and the harbour area was equally dark. The best eating was there, but the restaurants and bars were like water-holes with respect to the distances between them. So it was a case of a light in the middle of nowhere. The rest of the city spread out in a series of similar-looking main-streets each with a surplus of half-empty, and atmospherically soulless, malls with their acres of parking space. Ted wished that some kind of planning had been involved in the shaping of Kingston. It was like a boomtown not only in the way it sprawled out, but also in the fact that it resembled a mining town. Here instead of a mine there was a large computer company. This was what kept Kingston alive. Without this company it would descend into the realms of another hick town. If you did not work for this company – Ted did, placed in middle-management – then you provided a service for its work-force and their families. For people of Siobhán's age Kingston was as good as dead.

Woodstock was not far away and he guessed that was likely where she spent some of her leisure time. He also reckoned that she worked-out at one of the fitness studios. Other than this he had absolutely no idea what she did.

He and his family took to rambling and occasionally camping in the abundant countryside, including the breathtaking Catskill forest, a little skiing – weather permitting – and then there were the U-PICK-IT fields of raspberries and strawberries in Ulster County. They sometimes went along to the various sales, shows and expositions held at the New York State Armoury. There were craft fairs, turkey shoots and boat shows. And there were quite a number of festivals during the year, ranging from the Woodstock Bavarian Festival to the Pumpkin Festival at the Maritime Centre and then of course the Sweet Corn Festival in the Hudson Valley Winery. Everything was seasonal and revolved around the great outdoors. Canoeing, kayaking and rafting, golf, tennis and riding. Ulster County was renowned for its apples and corn and in the case of the latter this gave rise to a corn culture: baked corn omelette, corn bread, corn oysters and naturally corn chowder. Finally there was the socialising with families of a similar disposition.

These events, scattered throughout the year, could be little more than breaks or distractions from the boredom for the beautiful people, who gazed enviously at the bright lights and fast living of Manhattan. The activities here were things for the settled, things for relaxation and not for people looking for Action with a capital A.

He dropped the hood down and pressed it home. Taking the soiled paper towel with him he returned to the house. In the kitchen he disposed of the towel and pressed himself a squirt of cola from the refrigerator dispenser. A film of sweat covered his brow. As he tipped his head back and closed his eyes to drink he glimpsed the wall unit which contained the crockery.

He thought of the Noble Eight-Fold Path in relation to his thoughts of Siobhán. He wanted to be good, but then he did not see that he was suffering. He did not feel that he was suffering.

He washed the glass in the sink.

Could he recite the Noble Eightfold Path? He would need to learn it first by rote, if he was to move on in the course. Later he would be able to fill it out with more depth and meaning. But could he do it now? It was only yesterday he had heard it. Right view, right thought, right speech, er, right effort, right behaviour, right mindfulness, right, er, livelihood, right effort, no, had that, right, er, come on, ah, right concentration. That said it all and he smiled to himself. He would have to think up an ideogram. Then he could recite it. The real question was could he follow it? Was he suffering because he desired Siobhán? He felt suitably ashamed of such thoughts, for Ronny's sake. But he could not say that he was suffering. In truth he did not really want anything to happen between them. What would she want with a staid old has-been like him? The lure of wisdom? The experience of age? He smiled again.

Pronounced 'Shivon' he knew it to be spelt completely and deceptively otherwise. Siobhán. Such an unusual and beautiful name. He believed it was Irish in origin. An unusually beautiful name for an unusually beautiful girl.

How far did the cleansing of the mind have to go? He had no real idea, but he suspected until such thoughts did not exist. Until such thoughts did not exist! Surely that was too far? He was not training for priesthood. His mother and father would have liked him to have become a priest or a religious instruction teacher. That would have been ideal. His schooling and the recitals at home had certainly left no doubt in his mind what they had wanted. Okay, maybe a priest was going too far, but at least a person of high religious and moral fibre. The latter he had probably inherited – although recently, since the arrival of Siobhán, he was beginning to wonder whether this were true – but the former he had all but abandoned, only to return to after he had been married. His parents had not been horrendously strict. But at the time he had been plugged into science-fiction books and comics by his school friend Paul. Such books were frowned upon at home and comics were out. The next step had been computers and then when he had been old enough he had announced his wishes. His parents had taken it rather well. Evidently he had underestimated them. With hindsight he believed that they had suspected something for a long while so that it had not been a shock.

Right view, right thought. Right thought. Was there not something similar in the Bible? That was the thing about learning something new: one was liable to fit it in with what one knew and understood and if not that, then one made comparisons. He could not remember the number but he knew it to be in Philippians. It went something like whatever is true, or right, er, or pure, and er, whatever is lovely, whatever is noble – if anything is excellent or worthy or something – think about these things.

He would have to look it up.

Buddhism lacked the evangelistic passion of Christianity. He knew of no Buddhist crusades or missionaries. It was an attitude. Was it the crux of the difference between the Far East and West in the approach to life?

Maybe he was onto something. Whatever, Ted felt excited by the new information. He felt that he had opened a treasure trove of goodies. Life was taking a new turn for him. Freshness was entering his mind and he wanted to share it with Ronny. Whether he would be able to do so was another matter. He tended to break things down in a computerised fashion; nice ordered little packages of information. This stumped his progress and he knew it. On the other hand she was more emotional and apt to famous leaps of logic such as: all dogs have tails, therefore all animals with tails are dogs. Because of his nature he found this exasperating, but sometimes she saw the meaning before he did. It was too early to say; the course had only just begun, and he hoped dearly that he would not be disappointed.

For the moment he felt on the verge of something new. As if something was about to happen and his world was about to change.

His wandering eyes and avid curiosity about Buddhism meant that he was not a devout Christian, but neither was he an atheist or an agnostic. Also he was not exactly a Doubting Thomas. He believed in a greater power. The uncertainty he felt lay in his thoughts on the way Man set down the interpretation and connection to this power. It was this setting-down that upset him. It was its certainty. The phrase Blind Faith came to mind. Was not such certainty the root of all conflict? This certainty or lack of doubt disturbed him. He felt that one should question. Questioning was the basis of learning and discovery. Conversely, he was disturbed by the question: should one question? Was it not outside the realms of questioning and in the realms of feeling? This was a challenge his enquiring mind could not satisfactorily meet.

He was two years away from the beginning of his life, that is, if life begins at forty, but he already felt change. His children had preoccupied him, because he had not been ready for them, although they were planned. He had married quite late, at thirty, and had long-established ways. He did not feel that this was bad for it had meant that he had leapt up career-wise, becoming one of the youngest managers ever. His family would be secure. However, no matter how much he had thought he had been ready for the children, he had not been prepared for the effect they would have upon his world. It was only now that he could manage his time and indulge in such thoughts. Furthermore, he had a wealth of experience seated behind him. He could investigate the avenues he wished. And he felt rather excited. His exhilaration was put on a back-burner when he heard Ellen squeal.

"What's up?" he called from the bottom of the stairs.

"Daddy!" Ellen shrieked, "Eddy-junior's taking more than six toys—"

"No, I'm not," shouted Eddy-junior.

Ted looked down at his shoes and then up the stairs. "Veronica, what's going on?"

She came to the top of the stairs, exasperation etching her face. In some inexplicable way, this was his fault. "Eddy-junior wants to take his space-gladiator set."

"So?"

193

"Well," she went on slowly, having waited for his enquiry. "There's something like twenty soldiers in the box and Ellen thinks that each one counts as a toy." Veronica smiled victoriously. She could have folded her arms triumphantly across herself, but she did not.

Ted twisted his mouth, in an okay-you've-got-me-I-give-up smile.

Ellen appeared at her mother's feet at the top of the stairs. The lip was quivering.

Then Eddy-junior appeared and poked his head between the banisters on the landing. His expression was one of innocence.

There they waited for the judgement of Solomon.

Possessions are the objects of desire. Only when desire is quashed can one be truly free. Such wisdom was not much use here.

"The ruling was five toys," he began firmly. "But now it's six. And that means six toys." He purposefully did not look at Ellen, but first at Veronica and then Eddy-junior. "Six separate toys." Eddy-junior's face crunched up. "You should count yourselves lucky that you have so many to choose from. Some children don't have any." He did not feel like breaking into a when-I-was-your-age sermon. "Now, get your things together."

With that he turned to the front box-room and as he neared the entrance he heard Veronica say: "You heard your father. Shift your butts."

"Shift your butts, shift your butts," parroted Ellen.

Meanwhile Eddy-junior protested, saying that the space-gladiators flew the space ship and were needed to fight the monsters. The monsters were presumably the GI-Joes, being substantially larger than the space gladiators.

To this Veronica suggested that he reduce the number of monsters.

GI-Joes as monsters, thought Ted, funny how times change. In his day he'd had soldiers too, but they had been soldiers. They had depicted the types of games he played. Now it was all spaceships and weird and wonderful beings. These too shaped the games of the children. The wonder and joy of fantasy and imagination was encouraged. There were no boundaries. These new toys put humans against aliens, or aliens against aliens, whatever; the important fact was that it put good against evil. He had been full of battles between armies and the cavalry and the Indians. The Germans and the

Japanese had been the baddies. He was glad that this stereotyping was beginning to disappear. Such warfare had become old-fashioned in his mind too. There was a somewhat negative side to this inventiveness being in vogue. It was namely that at its core was escapism. Escapism, that is, from the pressures of modern day living or the depressing state of the planet or simply disillusion with the future.

Although he had already filled his briefcase, which sat squarely on his desk, next to the PC, he clicked it open and checked the contents.

The course handout entitled The Middle Way sat on top.

One must endeavour to follow a path that is neither torturous, physically or mentally, and then one that is not indulgent in the desires of the body. One must choose a path between these extremities. This is the Noble Path or The Middle Way.

Siobhán. He looked to his left through the net curtains at the window to her house. Still she had not opened the garage door. A puzzled expression contorted his features.

He closed his briefcase, clicking it shut and picked it up. The expression did not leave his face when he left the room. His eyes were fixed upon an invisible moving point on carpet ahead of him. Even the kids descending the stairs with their toys, Jimmy leading, had not broken his perplexed expression.

Outside he heard her car engine still ticking over.

Almost without taking his eyes off her garage door he slid the briefcase into the back of the station wagon. The buzz of the kids, advice of his wife and panting of the dog were registered behind him.

Turning he noted that Ellen was talking to him but he ignored her and looked directly at Veronica.

"Siobhán's had her car running with the garage door shut for a while. I think I'd better go and say something."

Veronica looked past him as she nodded agreement. She promoted neighbourliness. Ted thought she took it a little far, because people for fifty miles around were their neighbours. Part of that was because Ronny, unlike Siobhán, was a Kingston girl and she knew almost everybody and almost everybody knew her. But he could take nothing away from her; she was a good person. Probably morally stronger than him.

He heard them fussing behind him, Veronica telling an annoyed Ellen that Daddy was busy, as he strode towards her house.

When he reached her front door the sound of the engine was naturally much louder and the effect was to add an element of urgency to his call. He rang the doorbell and did not wait as long as he might have before ringing it again.

The door was of solid wood with a single diamond-shaped piece of frosted glass at eye-level. Through it he could see nothing but the distorted rectangular image of light framed by the kitchen entrance. There was no movement.

He looked over at his family. They were still fussing about the car. Veronica looked up and he answered by shrugging his shoulders.

Ringing again he added another two rounds to his characteristic double-burst. He barely heard them above the sound of the motor.

After gesturing to Veronica that he was going round the back, he went down the path at the side of the house. The lawn needed mowing, he thought. A chance to lend her their mower.

He went to her back door, opened the mosquito screen and knocked loudly upon the glass of the inner door. As he waited, holding open the meshed door with a foot, he wondered whether or not he should break in. A little drastic, just to give some advice. But something could be wrong. Conflicting thoughts flashed through his mind. She could be taking a shower having forgotten about the car. But then, on a day like this she could not be warming the engine. Maybe she had been overcome by the fumes. Perhaps she was upstairs with somebody and they had been overcome by something else. Breaking in and barging in on that would be terrible.

After trying the handle Ted left the door and, mindful of the flower bed on the ground below the kitchen window, he moved along the wall so that he could peer into the house. With his hands at his temples he pressed his face to the glass.

Something was not right and at first he could not quite make it out. It was as if he had seen something and passed over it and now as he searched he could not find it. Or he was being distracted by other things that did not seem right, but required reasoning as to why they were not right. However, the thing that he had first glimpsed – if he had glimpsed anything at all – gnawed at him like a half forgotten memory.

In the background the inside of the front door darkened the hallway. At the moment it was the foreground, the kitchen that drew his attention. It was not so much that it was untidy; it was more that she had not cleaned up. There were some dishes at the sink, but sometimes Veronica and he left dishes in the sink. So that was not it. The table was laid and one place set. Nothing strange about that. There was half-eaten food on the dinner plate. And therein lay something wrong. What was it? This was one of the distracting wrongs and perversely he had to solve it before he could move on. Something was terribly wrong. Yet, his eyes did wander as he puzzled over the problem. Salt and pepper, ketchup, an empty glass, some flowers. What was wrong with that? Nothing. He saw himself in one of the science fiction comics he had read. His hero had been trying to fathom a physical enigma confronting him. Turning the page, Ted, the schoolboy, had gasped inside himself at the double-page image of his hero – resembling an ineffectual fly – staring into a huge human eyeball: a mote in the huge face of the monster. Later he had found it dissatisfying that the eye had been human in form. However, the picture had made more an impression upon him than the story itself. In fact he could not remember the story. It was the same with the problems at work: sometimes it was better to stand back to see them clearly. He had most of his brainstorms whilst sitting on the John or fetching a coffee. Then it hit him. It was not breakfast. It was yesterday's evening meal. So what, Sherlock? She had not finished. But there was something more. Alarm bells were ringing in his head and he did not know why. Then he received a jolt. It was not the big one, not the one he had expected, be that as it may, it was no less a kick. The long, tightly spiralling cord of the wall telephone hung in one direction. It did not loop back. He followed it down to where it disappeared behind the table. Then he edged his way along so that he could see the handset lying on the floor. Many scenarios presented themselves, but he did not dwell on any one of them. His gaze had returned to the inside of the front door. Ted's field of vision had of course altered and he could no longer see the side of the stairway. But he could see the dark spots on the carpet in the hall. And he could see they led to, or from, the white door of the integral garage. When the jolt finally came his mouth dropped open. There was a stain near the handle. His eyes widened in disbelief and the colour drained from his face. He could not tell what colour it was because most of it was in shadow. But even this was not the disturbing something because he could not have seen it before. He needed to recheck and he moved back to his left and looked at the banisters. There was a dark streak on the white railing. He edged a little further to his left. The fused light from the glass diamond fell directly upon the mark. It was red.

"Veronica!" he shouted.

This red mark had unconsciously registered with him. He must have seen it from the corner of his eye as he had followed his footing in the flower bed and then when he had looked into the kitchen it had been in shadow.

Did his wife shout something at the kids?

As he searched for a stone, as if to add urgency to the situation, Jimmy began to bark. At the wall of the flower bed further in the back yard were some large stones. One of them would do. They certainly looked heavy enough for the job.

He was reaching for a stone when his wife arrived.

"Ted what's wrong?"

At that instant it seemed like a stupid question and he was sharp with her.

"How do you expect me to know? Just call the cops."

But she did not move and from his crouched position he turned to her. "Now!"

She fled rather than ran away.

He tugged at the embedded stone he had chosen and it moved but did not come away. Looking closer he realised that it was cemented together with the others and he cursed.

He got to his feet and saw his son at the end of the pathway along the side of the house.

"Go to your mother," he snapped.

Only seconds had passed since his discovery of the streak, but it seemed like aeons and he had grown frantic and could hear his heart pounding.

What to do? Break in. Yes, but how? Come on use your noodles. Think.

Why was he gasping? Somebody put a cork in that mutt.

"How do you expect me to know?" It had been a harsh thing to say. He would apologise to her later.

He noticed the key in the lock on the inside and the idea of twiddling the key with a stick or something until it fell onto the sheet of newspaper he had slid under the door was dismissed. It would take too long. He remembered that he had seen someone in some film elbowing through a window through a piece of cloth or a hat or something. He decided to do likewise.

"Just call the cops." That had also been silly. He should have said ambulance as well.

He fumbled with the buttons of his checked, lumberjack-print shirt. Come on, Harry! Sweat caused the shirt to adhere to him. He was no Houdini. Before tearing off his shirt he noticed a thick, sickly-brown rag, thick like a blanket with fine threads of coloured fibres interwoven, draped over the washing line. He stepped over and grabbed it.

His open shirt hung on him and he glimpsed his chest. What a hero!

The back door behind the mesh one was essentially two windows, one above the other separated by a horizontal panel of wood. Holding the rag against the upper pane, near the lock situated at one end of the horizontal panel, he turned his back to the door and brought up his right elbow. A localised blow was required. He would not get much of a swing, but hopefully he would acquire enough force.

Crack! It hurt. A spider-web instantly appeared upon the glass, radiating from his point of impact, but the glass did not break. He adjusted the rag, although it had not moved. He had merely – anxious though he was – wanted to give himself a split-second pause before trying again. Another crack was followed by the satisfying sound of breaking glass.

Not a scratch on him.

Hurriedly, but deftly, he reached into the jaws of the snarling shards of glass. Unfortunately the rag had fallen inside. Initially he tried to pull the key out of the lock, but he could not get it straight and quickly gave up. The subsequent twisting of the key was awkward but manageable. His hand came out with equivalent dexterity and he was opening the door to the tinkling, scratching sound of the glass being swept aside. Then he stepped in and his shoes crunched glass underfoot.

It took him seconds to reach the garage door and although his mind was set upon finding Siobhán and nothing else, and in this respect his thoughts seemed to have frozen, in reality he was rapidly taking everything in. His mind was a buzzing hive of activity.

Passing through the kitchen nothing that he had not already seen caught his attention. Everything should be left as is for the police. Who had she telephoned? Had she left it hanging since yesterday evening? Why had they not come over to see her? If she had called her parents then they could be on their way. He knew they lived far away, but he did not know how far. Finally, had she made the call?

He had never been in her house, although they, Veronica and he, had been invited over twice. The first time she, Siobhán, had called it off without offering a reason and the second time they had called it off because Ellen had been ill.

In the hall his gaze momentarily fell upon the red streak on the banisters, the door to the lounge beyond and then to the door to the garage. Upon the wall to the right of the garage door hung the heart-shaped mirror. Near the handle of the garage door there was a red smear and also on part of the door frame.

He had been daydreaming at his PC when the irregular-shape of light had shot up his wall, coming to a quivering standstill where it met the ceiling. It remained there but an instant, though long enough for him to query its shape. Then it flashed across the ceiling and out of the window.

That day had been much like today, even though it had been late September. It had been a mite colder, but it had been one of those Indian summer days. And the colours of the trees had been a wonderful blaze of reds and yellows and browns and greens.

He got up and went to the window to discover the light's source. Opposite their house stood a bare-armed man carrying what appeared to be a large heart. Another two were manoeuvring a sofa at the back of the truck. She was at the front door saying something to them. That had been the first time he had seen her and he had wondered which one of the three was her boyfriend or husband. All three were undoubtedly admirers. He looked at her again before she disappeared into the house. She was beautiful. And Ted was about to fantasize when the bare-armed man turned and the light had flashed in his eyes. It had happened almost like a punishment for his admiring thoughts. In any case the heart-shaped mirror had been branded in his mind.

He tried the door handle and was not surprised to find that it was locked; almost as if he knew he would have to break in. How did they do it in those tough detective shows? Should he shoulder it? Or should he kick it in? He decided upon the latter.

Ted stepped back and kicked the door. The frame cracked and the noise of the car engine grew louder. He kicked again equally as hard and the frame ripped into spears of fibred wood. The door remained in place, although it plainly offered no resistance. Phantom fingers of blue-grey smoke curled sinisterly around the door and the stench assaulted his nostrils, yet it was not disagreeable.

Why had he not called her name again?

He pushed the door away with his shoulder and it was then that he made his mistake. It could have been because he was nearer to the source of alarm and thus his actions were hastier and reckless. At the kitchen door the danger of sharp glass had been more apparent. He did not charge into the garage. The smoke ruled out any such rush. But he had moved in rapidly and his shirt-sleeve had caught on a spike of the broken door frame. At work he had always rolled up his sleeves to a fold just below the elbow. When he had become a manager he had stopped doing this because he was no longer a foot-soldier and he wanted to be reminded of the formality and gravity of his new role. But at home it was still his habit to carry his sleeves this way. His reaction now had been to violently and stupidly jerk his arm, rather than unhook himself. The shirt had ripped but not before the protruding spike had gashed the inside of his forearm.

Ted yelped and cursed.

He turned his forearm and glanced at the long cut. It looked worse than it felt, but that could be put down to his obviously high adrenalin level. How easily he could have unhooked his shirt sleeve, but instead he had been careless and impetuous.

The smell of the smoke was no longer a pleasant tinge in his nostrils: something he could take in a small dose and then leave. The smoke had invaded his lungs before he had entered the garage. It had tickled him and he had found the sensation not unpleasant, like the smoke from a bonfire, from which he could walk away. But this seduction had been replaced by something evil, something from which he could not walk away. It was an intoxication of petrol blue. It caused his eyes to smart and it filled his throat not merely with an irritating cough, but with something deadly: something that threatened his life.

Weren't you meant to put a handkerchief or something over your mouth? He didn't have anything.

His eyes watered in the thick haze and he could hardly see. He held his breath and his lungs had begun screaming for air.

The car door was in front him, the window wound down. Somebody was sitting in the driver's seat but slumped over on to the front passenger seat. He knew it was Siobhán.

His first priority was to get the garage door open. So he did not reach in to switch the engine off. He could not waste those moments: the insidious smoke was that threatening.

As fast as he could he moved down the side of the car to the garage door. By now he was sweating, his eyes were afire and watering, his right arm and hand were a mesh of blood and he was coughing. The coughing was the worst. The wound on his arm was barely felt and he could close his eyes now and then, but he could not stop the coughing. It came from a basic need. A need to breathe. As a child he had played holding his breath in the bathtub, his face in the water, but this was different. Here he was being attacked. This was not a game. Not something he could control. He was gagging. His jaw struck outwards and his glistening cheeks were hollowed in his hacking effort to purge the choking smoke and find air.

Ted knew that his life was in danger. His position in this danger could easily slip from his control. It was real. And it frightened him.

He reached the metal door, one of the overhead swing types, and barely able to see through the scalding water of his eyes, he grasped the handle and pulled, simultaneously kicking the lower half. The large door shuddered as he raised it upward and over himself. Then he staggered out, almost on all fours, gasping, the smoke billowing around him.

"What's going on, Ted?" asked the old man, above the sound of the engine.

Ted looked up, panting and coughing. He did not speak. He was filled with contempt for the elderly couple. Such a stupid question. Had the man not spoken, he probably would not have seen them, as it was, he barely acknowledged their presence. They were neighbours from further down the road.

Ronny and the kids were nowhere to be seen. Only Jimmy stood by the station-wagon. He started to bark, but did not move. Some time ago he must have stopped barking.

Ted swung round. He wiped both of his eyes with the heels of his hands. Taking a large breath, he clamped his mouth shut, although he found his neck jerking convulsively. He had lost some valuable seconds.

The light had caused the smoke to appear less dense. Perhaps it had thinned out, but the stench remained as strong as ever. He was able to make out the car and a few of the details of the bits and pieces that littered the sides of the garage. Why was it that garages always looked littered, no matter how orderly one arranged the contents?

This time he charged in, putting his left hand over his mouth, to reinforce the holding of his breath. He moved rapidly along the same side of the car, left foot leading.

By the time he reached the driver-side door he was virtually blind again.

He reached in, found and pinched the ignition key and switched the engine off. The immediate silence was awesome. It displaced the urgency, the threat, but put something more profoundly terrible in its place. It was as if the ticking over of the car's engine had been a countdown to this small pocket of time in which he had to save her.

He opened the door, leant in and grabbing her shoulder he called her name, as if he could wake her. She did not respond.

He could see that she was wearing an oversized grey Yankees T-shirt. From the waist down, where an arm rested, it was darkly stained. A considerable portion of her thigh was showing and despite the quantity of blood over her arms it was clean. He could not see her face; it was obscured by her hair.

His mouth burst open and he began violently coughing.

With his right hand at her shoulder he reached round with his left and heaved her into a limp sitting position. Her head lolled against him and the urge to hold it and protect it was strong, but he resisted because he could not support all of her at once. He had to get her out as soon as possible. For that matter he had to get himself out as soon as possible. But it did mean that he caught a glimpse of her face. She appeared tranquil, in spite of her ghastly paleness. Was she dead?

He grew frantic and closing his eyes, he coughed incessantly into her stomach as he forced his arms about her. Ted tried to lift her and a knee crashed heavily onto the rim of the car, where the lower half of the car door met the car body. A searing pain shot up his leg and he grunted. However, from this unusual praying position he was able to shuffle her brusquely towards him.

When he had her weight, her left arm slapping his cheek and smearing his face with slippery blood, he found that his legs were bent too much and that he was unable to stand. So he leant backwards, hoping to reach the wall, straightening up as he did. And if not straightening up, then he hoped that with his back pressed against the wall he would be able to slide upwards.

What actually happened was that he stumbled backward and slammed into the wall. He did manage to right himself a little, but not enough. Then he felt her slipping from his grip and he pressed her to him. They were away from the sharp edge of the door and he pushed himself towards the car again. By now his coughing was horrendous and his chin was covered in saliva from his efforts. They hit the car, her more than him and for a split second, his eyes closed, he prayed in his mind for strength. In a frenzy of rapidly diminishing energy he gripped her excessively tightly and edged along the side of the car.

Ted emerged from the smoke, his body drenched in sweat. He was staggering as he attempted to carry her. She was as limp as a doll. He stumbled on as far as he could, his sapped energy adding weight to her and she slipped. He had wanted to put her down in a controlled way, but all he managed was a clumsily controlled fall.

The old man tried to help him, but to Ted he just flapped nearby. In retrospect, the old man had probably found the pair somewhat unapproachable. He would have hindered rather than helped. The old woman too, his wife, had been helpless. She had looked on with horror-enlarged eyes and seemed to wave her hands about as if she suffered Parkinson's disease. Then she had turned in disgust – so it seemed to Ted – and walked away.

Later Ted would realise that she had been appalled and overcome. She had reached out for support and, finding none, had dazedly turned for something to hold or lean against. But during those seconds Ted was someone else. For when they were on the ground, he in a kind of worship of her awkwardly sprawled body, and the old man trying to take over – with a "here, let me, son" – he had waved him away. Had he been closer he would probably have pushed him off. It was not ego that propelled him, it was that he had assumed the central role in the incident and was absorbed to the extent that he could not simply stop and step back.

This interruption shortened his pause for breath. Spurred on, Ted pushed himself off her. He was now sitting upon his folded legs beside her gulping great gobs of air. First he turned her head to himself and slid the hair from her face. She was pale. Only the dried brown stain of blood coloured her. It was an ugly smear. Otherwise her appearance was quite tranquil. Yet, her face was no longer human. Something had left her face. Even her wonderful mouth had lost its appeal. He could not say what had left her: spirit of life or presence or self-possession or what. Somehow this was not Siobhán, but Siobhán's body.

He placed her arms, slit at the wrists, across her stomach and tilting her head to look upward and holding it with his left hand, he pressed two fingers of his right hand upon the groove between her voice box and neck muscle to check for her carotid pulse. It was there, but weak. More importantly, he did not think she was breathing.

For a second he lost control of himself. Should he stop the bleeding at her wrists first or give her mouth to mouth?

The hideous smiles at her wrists upset him most. They caused him to cringe with physical pain. So much blood. A loss in the region of two pints was dangerous. He knew that the arms should be raised to reduce the flow, but that was not his major concern.

Jimmy ran up and down now, barking incessantly. But he did not cross the road. They had trained him well. Where was Veronica?

Mouth to mouth, of course. But he had never done it before. He had attended the company course, but there they had used a doll named Alice. Perhaps the old man had done it? No time.

He remembered the steps.

Tilt the victim's head backwards to open the airway. He had done that already. He glanced into her mouth. Then he put an ear to her mouth to feel and hear her breath. Nothing.

Alice had not been breathing either. But, even though Siobhán was limp and plastic and doll-like, this was no exercise.

Pinch her nostrils with finger and thumb and take a deep breath. Yes, yes. Then seal your lips around the victim's mouth and give four quick breaths. Why four? He had forgotten. If her chest rises the air is getting to her lungs. Yes, he was sure it had risen. Should he blow again to be sure? No.

Next? Remove mouth to allow passive exhalation. Next? Watch for her chest to fall. What next? That was it, wasn't it? Yes, another breath and then blow.

Now it was routine. Okay, but the frequency? How often? Every five or six seconds. In the course they had never mentioned the panic that freezes thought.

At first he guessed, but at the third go he began to count the seconds off the way he had learnt as a schoolboy: one chimpanzee, two chimpanzee... Funny, Ronny had learnt the same trick, but with hippopotamuses.

He was hunched over her and as he was counting, watching her chest fall, he grabbed her two wrists in his right hand – he was using his left to pinch her nose – he lifted her reddened arms up, his own laced arm with its elbow hovering above her belly. But he could not hold this position.

"Here– what– " floundered the old man.

"Reduce the bleeding," Ted explained.

Five chimpanzee, six...

Just then he saw Ronny appear from beyond the couple's car.

"Bandages!" he called.

"Let me," said the old man taking her left arm by the wrist and holding it up, letting her hand loll inwardly.

Ted took her other wrist with his free hand and raised her arm. But it was not long before he was resting his elbow on her belly for support.

Siobhán remained inert. It began to dawn on Ted that perhaps he was too late. Maybe it was all in vain. It had all come out of the vein, he thought perversely. This mild hysteria twisted a smile upon his mouth, but his eyes were tearful and he was confused.

"Come on," he pleaded, almost choking on his words.

Three chimpanzee, four chim–

Where was Veronica? What was she doing? Had she called an ambulance or just the cops? So much blood. Such a mess. He was going to lose her. Had he ever had a chance of saving her? Had he wasted too much time? He should have realised something was wrong far sooner. Why had he left it so late?

Then he heard Ronny shout something in the house. This was followed by Ellen crying.

Still nothing. Siobhán was dead or going to die. After all this...

She was not the good-looking girl he remembered. She looked girlish and being this close to her dispelled the enigma of her, that aura of attractiveness was replaced by flesh and blood.

What was he thinking? It was his job to keep calm under stress. She was going to live. He would try for hours if necessary.

The roar of a powerful car increased. Cops?

When he looked up – one chimpanzee – he saw the jacked-up truck with the huge tyres.

"Do you want me to take over, son?" asked the old man.

"No, it's fine," Ted answered, the flicker of a smile on his face as he saw the old man for the first time. He too looked different. Ted had seen him often. Ronny and he had named him Spencer Tracy. He looked nothing like Spencer Tracy, but his hair was snow white and he had a full face etched with sea-faring experience. From this close he looked less kindly and fatherly, more leathery and cantankerous.

Ted had his mouth over Siobhán's when the sun was blocked out by the presence of the driver of the pick-up truck.

"Oh, Jesus, no, no."

When Ted looked up, he saw only a large silhouette.

"Is she going to die?"

"I don't know," Ted answered tetchily.

"What happened?"

The question went unanswered and Ted put his mouth to her again.

"Have you called an ambulance?"

Ted shrunk. Perhaps an ambulance had not been called. Yet, he felt hostile towards the man and left this question unanswered too.

"What are you doing with her arms?"

"We're trying to reduce the flow of blood," Ted snapped.

Spencer Tracy looked at him and Ted closed his eyes in frustration.

"I've, er, got a first-aid box in the–"

"Good, get it!"

But just as he was about to descend again he saw Ronny at the old man's car, a roll of bandage in her hand.

"No, don't bother. My wife–" He did not finish and hoped the man would understand.

By the time he looked up Ronny was beside him.

"Do that side first," ordered Ted, looking at the hand the old man held. "Pack some of the bandage to give a little pressure. It'll help stem the flow."

Ted's own arm had hurt as if he was receiving constant injections, knife jabs, one after the other. Now it burnt.

"Don't you think–" began the pick-up driver.

His arm was on fire.

"Why don't you check the house?" suggested Ted. "There could be someone else in there."

The old man and Ronny started work on Siobhán's left wrist.

"Ambulance?" Ted asked, quietly.

His wife, without looking at him or breaking her concentration, nodded.

Despite the desperation Ted felt a strange elation.

Taking charge was another point in the class. Firm leadership. Too many leaders cause confusion and therefore delay. He was in charge. And he appeared to be keeping calm under stress. He had taken care of the trouble-maker. That was another part of the course. Occupying the well-meaning and concerned who were apt to become emotional or panicky.

But his arm. He dared a glance. There was a raw flame. The network of blood was disappearing and his arm was becoming a mass of sticky red.

A period of calm had taken him. He had found his rhythm and thoughts were returning.

A kid on a bicycle appeared near the old man's wife, who was standing next to a car. The boy was joined by another on a skate-board. Further down the road a couple of women were standing together in the drive. The smoke had probably alerted the onlookers.

He watched Veronica bandage the arm and for a split second they communicated with a fleeting connection of the eyes. She was proud of him. He was doing fine.

He would probably appear as a hero in the local rag. He would be a celebrity. Even if she died the incident would be reported.

Veronica must have noticed his arm, because she remarked upon it.

"That's a bad cut."

"No, it's not," he lied. "Most of the blood's hers."

Perhaps she was not going to live. She was still horribly pale – a shock of unnatural white. Wait– Did she make a noise? Was that her? Or was it the air coming out rather strangely.

Siobhán gave a little cough.

Ted smiled and stole a glance at Ronny.

Then Siobhán spluttered and although colour did not return, pain, pure as a new born baby, crunched up her face.

So this was it, he was not merely lending her a lawn mower, as he had earlier thought. He was doing something great, something wonderful. He was saving her life. And in some inexpressible way her life would be his forever.

Siobhán was coughing badly, her face screwed up with the agony of it.

He heard the small wail of a distant ambulance siren. The cavalry were late this time. But it did not matter. He had saved her.

He would be in the local rag after all. Too bad there would be no photograph of him emerging from the smoke open-shirted with her in his arms. Perhaps that was for the best, considering how he had looked and how clumsily he had carried her. Then again, those newspaper boys would probably want a mock up. Re-enacting the whole thing would be going too far, but they might want an action-shot. He could be pictured emerging from the smoke. The local hero. And he would be holding her firmly.

Sometimes one had to descend from the ivory tower of intellect and come down to Earth. That is, come down to the nitty-gritty of life: basic physical life. Christianity, Buddhism, it did not matter. Life. That was it.

The doorbell rang and he told the kids not to put the video on pause, but to carry on without him. The three of them – four with Jimmy – were watching an adventure film together. It was Thursday, Veronica's night out.

He opened the front door, and Siobhán's face was lit by a smile. The smile was infectious because he found himself smiling.

"Hallo, er, Ted," she began. She was beautiful – no, fantastic. "I know it's awful of me to disturb you–"

"Not at all," he interrupted.

"Who is it, Dad?" shouted Eddy-Junior from the lounge.

"Yeah, who is it, Teddy?" Ellen followed.

"Our neighbour, Siobhán."

Ted smiled to her as if to say that there was never any peace. But what he felt was something rather different. She may have registered this for her smile remained true but her eyes took notes.

"Well," she went on, "I was wondering whether you had any sugar I could borrow."

"Borrow?" he did not want to be obvious, but he felt helpless. Her smile was the key and he was an open door. He was standing feebly in the gaping entrance of himself, trying to appear together. "No, no, we won't want it back. Er, come on in."

Ellen appeared in the hallway wide-eyed with wonder, a small teddy-bear hiding her shy smile.

"Go and watch the film," said Ted. "She's only come to get some sugar."

But Ellen did not move.

Ted hid his sinking feeling by striding towards the kitchen. His daughter's presence dispersed any magic, any chance to flirt.

"I don't have it in the house," Siobhán said.

"Oh, yes, not healthy, eh?"

They were in the kitchen, Ellen following them and standing at the entrance.

"Something like that."

"Now, let's see." He opened the middle wall unit.

"It's over there," said Ellen, with authority and annoyance, pointing to the far wall unit.

Ted looked at her and then he smiled at Siobhán.

"Alrighty," he said good-humouredly.

As he reached into the cupboard, Siobhán explained. "It's too late to go to the mall. You see my parents are due any minute and father takes sugar in his coffee."

"Uhuh," acknowledged Ted, turning with an unopened packet in his hand. But Siobhán was crouching at Ellen.

"And what's Teddy's name?" she asked the little girl. But Ellen did not answer and hid behind her bear.

After the outburst about the location of the sugar Ted had expected her to answer. But perhaps Siobhán was too close and this had caused her to shrink.

He moved towards Siobhán and she rose. He handed her the packet, or rather he inexplicably presented it to her like an offering in both palms.

She smiled, almost laughed.

He wanted to say something complimentary, but he was snared by the fact that it would sound terribly clumsy, if not presuming. But what killed the possibility of any probing at all, was a sudden movement by Ellen from the entrance to his leg. As if the girl sensed a threat she needed the open display of possession of her father.

Siobhán smiled a thank you and made a motion to back off. She looked at the packet, then at Ellen. And then back to Ted.

Was she saying something? Had she said something? Had he missed it?

He expected her to say something, but she did not. Instead she turned and headed for the door. It was not until she was in the hallway that she spoke again.

He limped after her, for although he protested, Ellen had wrapped herself about his leg.

"Thanks again," Siobhán said, "you've saved my life."

A week later Veronica told him that Siobhán had given her a new packet of sugar. It was mentioned because she had not known Siobhán had borrowed a packet from them. Ted said he had forgotten to mention it.

Other than passing greetings, that was the last time, until now, that he'd had contact with her.

The wail of the siren was louder, but it seemed no closer.

Siobhán's coughing made her grab Ted's arm near the elbow. Instinctively he held her elbow with his right hand. His straightened left arm supported his weight. Veronica held her other arm, now bandaged. She had been about to do the other arm. The old man crouched rather lamely nearby. And the pick-up driver stood, statuesque and helpless, dumbly looking on.

"It's okay," said Ted. "You're going to be all right."

Siobhán continued to cough and Ted looked on pityingly. Her grip upon him grew painful. Her nails dug into his arm. So much blood. And now their blood was mingling: his burning flame and her vicious slit. Maybe they were bonding forever, mystically like blood brothers? They'd exchanged saliva too. Intimacy without sex.

Her coughing had at some point turned into sobs.

The wail of the siren was going on forever at the same level, the same distance, no closer.

"Nooooooo," she whined.

Although her cry distressed him, when her eyes flickered open and she looked him full in the face, he forced a weak and uncertain smile.

From somewhere she mustered a reserve of energy and tore her bandaged arm from Veronica to give him a damning slap on the face.

The siren was becoming ear-splitting.

His smile vanished as it occurred to him for the first time that she had wanted to die.

"You bastard," she squealed, during her crying.

Her grip on his arm became terribly painful and he wanted to tear away.

"But–"

"You don't get it," she said crying.

He was confused and she continued to cry. "What?" he asked in a voice so small that he was not sure she heard him.

Suddenly the ambulance appeared; the alarm was snapped out and faded rapidly.

She may or may not have heard him. But punctuated with sobs, she said: "I've got Aids."

Ted was dumbstruck. He searched her face, but she just continued to cry. He looked at Ronny who returned his disbelief with wide-eyed horror and then she looked at their locked and bloodied arms.

Yellow

Fresh air had not done his head any good. No good, ha, it was all no good. It was bad. Like bad bananas. Ha, he was bananas. Huddled inside a curling foetal position, sucking his thumb, turning bad, turning black. Hey, prejudice. Power. Death. Plague. Despite it being eight o'clock in the evening and relatively cool for the normal Arabian weather he was hot. He was more than hot; cellulitis was burning him up. Everything was burning and no good. He was turning into coal. He was dying. Somebody had fixed electrodes to the sides of his head and a million volts was coursing through his brain. Sentenced to death. He knew who had done it. The bitch. A flame was burning in his head and any moment his skin would peel away from its intensity, like paper, a margin of yellow curling from the growing hole. To go with it the *Bonanza* theme was playing over and over again in his head. Was he going to die? Was he going to die to the sound of racing guitars and a fire burning through the lines of agony that was the map of his face? Could he be haemorrhaging?

He stood at the open door for a moment. A moment in time. Was he really here? It was all so depressingly the same. As he had left it. The letter in exactly the same position, the central fold lifting one half off the desk in a threat of flight. Just as he had left it. A yellow moth. A yellow moth with fangs framed by the moment. A vicious thing that had bitten him and infected him with this yellow fever. His crumpled clothes in a heap on the bed. The remains of his ordered life – dishevelled. But just the same. The kink in the toothpaste tube at the bowl: just the same. A twist in the tale. A kink in the story. It was all just the same.

Everything was so normal. Normal. *NormAl.* Ꞃoꟻmɘⱡ. ⚇▢▢◯♋●🐚.

The mania of guitars emphasised the terrible silence.

Of all the shopping trolleys in all the Sainsbury's in all the world she had to bump into mine.

Only the light had changed. The soft orange at the window, almost gold upon his desk, had given out to the darkness of sundown. The meaning of time had stopped but its passage continued.

It was all just the same but everything had changed. All of it was absolutely meaningless. Still worse, for him, there was nothing left. It was all gone. His world had been taken from him. Everything he had built upon and believed in – albeit blindly – was gone. He was desolate. Without the world there was no him and without him there was no world. His world was him. It was the core of him. It was his very being. Rotten? Yes, perhaps rotten. But nonetheless the core of him had finally fallen away. Then, not fallen away, he could not accept that. No, he needed more violence. It had been ripped out. Because at the centre of his world was her. She was his core. She was his world. Yes, it was somewhat laughable to think such a thing, but this was what he felt. Come on mate, pull yourself together, it happens all the time. But it had happened to him. Say what you will, this is what he felt. Woe, woe put a sardonic smile upon his face. She was his world. Fact – and perhaps a song? And without her he was nothing. Nothing, but a sickening dog. He wanted to go over the top. "Make my day." It was how he felt. He was empty. A twenty-six year old husk. Without her he no longer existed. Gone. The love of his life. Gone. He could no longer live. Nothing. Could he kill himself? Could he put a razor to his wrist? Could he? He thought not. Then she'd know she'd broken him and she'd have to carry it around with her for the rest of her life. Then, maybe she wouldn't carry it. He had been through enough. He was worn out. To die was everything. Let it all stop.

Telephoning her would be horrible. He knew her. He knew the distant tone she could adopt. So easy over the telephone. Silence amplified by crackles. He knew the hollowness of her words. He knew his crying and pleading and desperation. He knew his hate and his writhing anger. He knew everything and he understood nothing. He had learnt very little in their five years together, three in matrimony. But there could be no doubt. It was explicit and unambiguous. There was absolutely no way he could think otherwise or turn it around.

Yellow paper. She had written it on her unlined yellow paper. The same crinkly airmail paper: flimsy; representative of how their relationship had grown. It was the same yellow stationery he had received since his arrival. The same insipid yellow stationery he had collected over all these months. His yellow lifeline to the outside world. All the envelopes were the same: pastel-yellow. The collection probably had some daft and unimaginative name like Primrose or

Buttercup. All the handwritten addresses were identical with the characteristic curl to the nine of his box number. Then, why not? Should she have electrified her handwriting with an appropriately aggressive slant?

On hearing somebody climbing the steps at the far end of the trailer he quickly entered the room and closed the door behind him. Safe.

She had made him an offer he could refuse. Go on. Pull the trigger.

Buck up. Don't be pathetic. Pull yourself together. Oh to be frankly not giving a damn like Rhett Butler. I can't. I'm wasted. It's finished. Over. Done. I haven't got the energy. I'm tired and I want to rest. Please leave me alone. I can't take any more.

Instead of entering the room he stood with his back near the door, listening first to the squeak of the hinges of the trailer door and then to the footfalls. Clomp, clomp, clomp. Fate. Inevitable, inexorable. They were ominous on the wooden floor of the trailer and as they grew in volume he grew tense.

Go away. I don't want you. I don't want anybody. I don't want anything.

Everything was chaotic and he felt the world was tumbling in on him.

Her last word was sorry, which, he had told her, was never said when you were in love.

With unseeing eyes he stared into the room – his home. His home for the last year and a half. More like a cell. Four walls, one window, bowl, desk, cupboard and bed. Clomp, clomp, clomp. The sound of a jailer or an executioner. The sound of her. He had attempted to give the room a bit of colour by hanging printed carpets on two of the walls. One was a simple beach scene, a bay with leaning palm trees, golden sands, clear skies and sparkling sea. The other was of snow-capped mountains. Despite this the room remained uninspired. Clomp, clomp, clomp. He held his breath.

False. It's all wrong. Wrong, wrong.

There was a gritty scraping sound as the person stopped at his door. The hairline fracture appearing in the wall. It could only be a man; women were forbidden on the camp.

Knock, knock. He had expected the rap upon his door, but nonetheless he jumped inside himself.

Silence.

Should he open it? It could be one of a number of people. He ought to talk to someone. Ought he? What to say? Hey mates, I got jilted? Another fine mess, Ollie.

Knock, knock.

It was too late. He couldn't open the door.

Silence.

Then the shuffle of feet on the linoleum as the person turned, followed by the same clomp, clomp, clomp, now receding. Life passing him by.

No doubt whoever it was, was calling to see if he fancied going over to the recreation room for a game of pool, darts or table football. In the latter activity he had become somewhat an expert. Great. Or perhaps to the library and coffee room for a game of *Risk* or chess or cards? A good game of poker, where one could win a pot of up to fifty rats – that was their name for the Saudi currency, the riyal. Even money seemed to have lost value. Rats. Toy-town money in a toy-town society. Or finally the TV room? Perhaps there was another edited television programme running: no touching, hugging or kissing and no scenes with alcoholic drinks? The editing ruined the flow and rendered plots nonsensical. The butchered remnants reminded them of a culture left behind.

The trailer camp was said to be formerly owned by the army. There was no smell of napalm to love in the morning. This was Stalag 13 and he was on the ludicrous set of *Hogan's Heroes*. Ve have vazes of making you tock. Tick-tock. And that was what his life out here had become: a mechanical tick-tock. He had become mechanised. He was especially clockwork during the working week, dovetailing perfectly with the bus timetable.

Then it occurred to him that he had not eaten since breakfast. Physically he was hungry, but he could not eat. His mental state quashed his appetite completely. Furthermore the thought of all those westerners chain-sawing their way through their mountains of steak – one could have as many as one wanted; he normally asked for three and ate the best from each – was too repulsive.

After breakfast he had caught the bus to work, skipped lunch, knocked off at four, picked up his post, rode the bus home, opened the bomb, gone walkabout instead of dinner and returned.

He could not concentrate on any one thing. The racing guitars had not abated.

Money put everything within his reach, but it also rendered many things valueless. That subtlety had not occurred to him until recently.

A lot of things had taken time dawning on him. He was naturally slow. Why was he still here, for instance? Had he not promised himself to stay no longer than a year? He had made his point within the first month.

Here he was in his cabin. The lonely captain. In a submarine. Submerged in a submarine lifestyle. In this alien place no one can hear your scream.

It looks like one endless party, she had remarked. He had been showing her his photographs. Her remark had set a glow of delight within him and he had made no attempt to counter-balance her belief. Could he have counter-balanced her belief at that time? And if so, would he have done it? Probably not, was the answer to both questions.

Money, the opium of the people.

Was he still in love with her? Well, yes. Okay, maybe a touch of infatuation had crept in. Masochism? Maybe that too.

It was as if for a short while he had forgotten his headache and the pain came back with a vengeance. Nuclear fission in his head. He had a bottle of headache tablets somewhere.

Had he become pathetic? Yes. Was he proud of himself? No. Could he help himself? No.

He went over to his wash bag on the dull, silk-finished metal surround of the bowl below the mirror. Fetching the bottle he opened the top with slow deliberation, almost as if he did not want to complete the action. He carefully tipped the bottle into the palm of his hand. He had wanted to jerk two out of the bottle, but the impossibility of this was one of the wonders of science and he stared down at six or more of the little things in his hand. Then he looked into the mirror, then back at the pills. He huffed. And the palm was at his lips and he was rubbing the flat of his hand at his mouth to catch all the little fellows. The chalky numbing taste mingled with his saliva as he grabbed the glass, tipping the toothbrush and toothpaste out into the metal bowl. After filling it he drank deeply, tipped the remainder of the bottle into his hand and washed these down too.

So that was it. He was being a man. He was finally doing something. The honourable way out? Was it really? He had kept on running and he had run himself into a corner, a cul-de-sac, a dead end.

Dead end. What did it matter? He did not care any more. Nothing mattered.

Pushing the clothes off his bed, he lay down and closed his eyes. He would not have to sit in the far from beautiful launderette after all.

It had come to this. Inevitability had finally caught up with him.

...found somebody else... It was such a cliché, almost a joke. It was all a joke. All a terrible joke. He was a joke.

Whoever it was, was probably upon her now. Ow! That hurt. He could do without that kind of hurt. Their sex life had gone for a Burton long ago. *What I like about you, she had said, is that you're sensitive and tender.* Too sensitive for you, baby. Who was he kidding? He was weak: soft. Soft in the head. Mushy like gone-off bananas. A slush-puppy.

No, he was not weak. He had held his ground over television and films. He had demanded silence, much to her chagrin. When they were at home she idly flicked through one of her empty-headed women's magazines or wrote a letter or something. Whatever, the result was the same. She did not concentrate on the programme and as a result she would ask stupid questions. Her questions were stupid, either because the answer was obvious to any idiot or they were unanswerable except to someone who could see into the future. The world of television and film was his realm. He demanded silence and liked to get absorbed: to escape. She couldn't understand his love of the black and white classics and said that he lived in a celluloid fantasy world.

Could she be lying to get rid of him and take his money? Was it possible that she had written it under the influence of drugs? Or with a gun to the head? Of course not. Such thoughts were the route to madness.

He was not surprised, of course. Their relationship had always been strained. In the beginning it had been fine. It had been something of a canvas. They had painted the colours of their personalities on it, built a shared collage. Gradually it had dawned on him that they saw, and had always seen, slightly different pictures. The colours and artefacts he had contributed were not the colours and artefacts she had seen and vice versa. Time had stretched the canvas and the colours had cracked, artefacts broken away. Tears too had watered it down in places. And the picture he saw was not what he had intended. But stubbornly, he, more than her, continued to see it that way and not what it was. He had explored the possibility of adding new issue, of distracting her and taking the pressure off himself, but she had been against children. She had accepted what was happening: the marriage was not working. He knew he was dreaming and even though she began to despise him, he refused to come to terms with the reality of the situation. What we have here, mister Cool Hand, is a failure to communicate. That was when he had come up with the bright idea of working here. He was no Paul Newman but his chosen exile was as good as being on the chain gang. Perhaps she would miss him? Perhaps money could buy her? Perhaps he could sort himself out? Whatever the reason it had come from him. And now all the reasons were gone. Puff! Ten sentences on a silly little piece of yellow paper had blown them all away.

Cool hand Paul Newman was an example of a failure to communicate.

He felt peaceful. For a moment he thought his headache had vanished, but it had not.

Of course she had ...found somebody else... What had he expected? He had started with little self-lies. These had grown not only in number, but also in size. Until he could no longer face himself, face their picture. The picture itself was one big lie. Coming out here was the worst thing he could have done. It had been like running away. Yes, coming out here.

Toto, I've a feeling we're not in Kansas anymore. Duh, you don't say?

It was the day after his arrival that the full impact of where he was hit him. He had been fingerprinted and photographed, one for the files, the other for his ID card. He now had a number. After which he had attended an Orientation lecture. Rumour had it, an Orientation centre, for returning Middle East workers who required psychiatric help, existed in London. One part of this lecture had particularly struck him. He could not remember it exactly, because of the fantastic amount of information that had been crammed into the half-hour speech by the American official. But the single phrase had remained in his head long afterward. "If you are caught making alcohol, you are breaking the law. If you are caught selling alcohol, you are breaking the law. If you have an alcoholic drink in your hand, you are breaking the law. If you have alcohol in your house, you are breaking the law. If somebody brings alcohol to your house, you are breaking the law. If you're at a party and somebody is standing next to you drinking an alcoholic drink, you are breaking the law." And so it had gone on for a good five minutes, like a litany and he had wanted to join in. But it had also been a numbing knock on the head. Somehow he had already broken the law.

He suddenly felt sick. His head was still in a mess but now his stomach was in turmoil. He did not know how long he had been lying on the bed. Time had absolutely no meaning. It had been vaporised the minute he had opened her letter. His stomach churned and he staggered to his feet.

His mouth filled before he reached the bowl but he held it shut. Spraying the pills into the bowl he groaned. They covered his toothpaste tube and toothbrush. Quite a few were still whole. His eyes glazed as a second heave took him. More pills.

"Shit!" he exclaimed, looking at the little things and beginning to take deep breaths.

Spittle and pills. A combination. Connected but not melding. Their collage had become an enigmatic hotchpotch, a puzzle. She had undoubtedly begun to hold back pieces. But he? He? He had continued to contribute, doggedly continued to construct the wrong picture. It was not complete. It could never be complete. She did not fit. She would never fit. The pieces she had contributed were not part of his picture. And hammer as he might, with her looking on – oh, how they had gelled at the beginning – they simply would not fit. Square peg round hole.

After spitting, he drank another glass of water.

"What a mess," he whispered, more to himself than the bowl.

As a young man he had been obsessed by Marilyn Monroe. She'd had such golden yellow hair. A golden smile. Sunshine in her spirit – on screen at least. In a dream he had seen her naked with her back to him at the window. It would have made a great poster for it epitomised what he believed she had been. Naked and alone before the public window. Dramatic. Perhaps her face was covered in Hollywood plastic? And he, like so many other men, lying in her bed, hoped to comfort and reach her. If I had known her I would have loved her and saved her and so on. Now he felt hopeless like her. Sadly, no camera to stand before. It did not matter. The story was flawed, anyhow. It was hackneyed. We've heard it before, mate. Don't give us that crap about the jilted husband, I'll tell you a story that'll make your toes curl.

He ran the tap water over his toothbrush and toothpaste tube and placed them in the glass, which he then put back in its customary position on the brushed steel surround of the bowl. All the tablets gathered at the outlet and the bowl began to fill. Using his finger he forced the little fellows down.

It was all so hopeless and he despaired.

Oh, to get drunk on yellow wine. Why did they call it white? Give me a gallon of Retsina and an olive black heart.

James Dean was crucified on his rifle. A young Elizabeth Taylor was kneeling at his feet. Of course James Dean could never be anything but young, forever martyred. As a youth he had fancied himself as James Dean. Misunderstood and romantically detached. But he had no Elizabeth Taylor. He still had no Elizabeth Taylor. James Dean's life had been short, but he had burnt brilliantly. He himself had not done so. And if he were James Dean and she were Elizabeth Taylor, then she would be the giant. And the perspective would be all wrong. A juxtaposition would take place and he would be a pendant at best. A little crucified thing about her neck. But not for worship, no, he would be a trinket. Then who was he kidding to think that she would honour his memory in such a way?

At the Orientation they had been encouraged not to mix with the Arabs. Their culture was so alien that it was considered dangerous to associate socially. What was left? The camp cinema, occasional camp theatre, camp trip and the shopping sprees. There were bargains galore to be had in the *Souks* in town. Especially from the street hawkers selling their wares, and the bootleg cassette dealers calling out "one riyal, one riyal, one riyal" so fast that the sense was barely discernible. And then insisting vehemently that the cassettes were originals. But in reality he just waited for his next trip home. Company paid, three a year. The funny thing was that when he was back and the picture presented to him, and the realities of the colours pointed out over the course of his holiday, he wanted to return to the sanctuary of his cabin.

He had genuinely lost his temper maybe three or four times in their entire relationship. It was not like him to lose his temper. She would quiver under his rage. Perhaps it aroused her? The result was that she melted before him. That had been when she had loved and respected him. Earlier. He had once asked her whether she was afraid he would do her harm when he was angry. And she had answered to

221

the contrary, saying that she was afraid he would hurt himself. Well. Her worst fears were going to come true.

He had given everything and now there was nothing left. He was empty with absolutely no energy. The very marrow of him had been sucked out by her. Like a vampire she had drained him. And he had given his consent. He had offered his neck willingly. The two punctures were there for all to see.

Eventually the bowl was empty. All the pills were gone. Evidence disposed.

Always pleasing her. Little cameo-scenes. Little chips off his self-esteem. At the shops, after work, with friends, at her parents, at his parents, in the restaurant. Giving a little more of himself. *What would you like? she had questioned.* I really don't mind. Whatever you want. If it were not so tragic, it would be laughable, but somehow, somewhere along the line, he felt that he had lost his identity. She didn't understand. She could have made him whole. He could have had class. He could have been somebody, instead of a bum, which is what he had become.

In addition to his headache he felt lousy.

Looking in the mirror he checked his anguish. His drawbridge eyebrows cast his expression in tragic-comic relief. Then his thumb pushed out a new razor blade from the plastic container. One word, Benjamin: Plastic. He looked in the mirror again. Yes, it was him and he was really there. After all that he had done. After all that he had been. After all his laughter, his tears, fears, hopes, dreams, successes. After everything. He had come to this low. He wanted to yell: "Low!" Huh, yell low. Yellow. He held the blade between his forefinger and thumb, carefully so as not to cut himself. This thought made him smile. No camera, but he could still smile.

"You talkin' to me? You talkin' to me? You talkin' to me? Well, who the hell else are you talkin' to? You talkin' to me? Well, I'm the only one here. Who the fuck do you think you're talkin' to?"

Where was the drama? Why was life an uphill struggle, a mediocre grey drudgery? Where was the colour? He had expected a better ending. A bath would have been a better idea. But there was no bath. The noble Roman-style was denied him.

And Peter O'Toole, the movie star Lawrence of Arabia, said that the trick was not minding that it hurt.

Okay people, take your places... aaaannnd action!

He did it as quick as he could. A sharp flick over his left wrist. The pain was instant and he yelped.

"Shit," he exclaimed again and again.

Okay, cut. That was awful. No ripping sound. No spectacular movie-red splashing the walls. Just a trickle and pain.

It hurt.

After some inspection and washing under the tap he realised that he had cut deep at the beginning but not deep enough near the vein. How it hurt. Ouch, ouch. He wanted screaming. And he wanted to be a child. Mummy.

In the adjoining toilet, sandwiched between his room and his neighbour's, he grabbed a toilet roll. Both had access to this room and the shower therein. Once inside one could lock the other's door with the small latch. Of course, one had to remember to unlock it when finished.

He was a mess. Everything was a mess. He was Jack Lemmon the depressing half of *The Odd Couple* trying to commit suicide and failing.

Why didn't you say something to him? she asked.

Ah, he didn't mean any harm.

He blubbered, but did not cry.

He dabbed his wrist. Then pressing a wad of toilet paper between his wound and his stomach he searched with his free hand for something more permanent. Eventually he found a dark blue handkerchief. This he tied about his wrist.

He liked this handkerchief. He liked the blue.

Yellow was nothing. Why did she have to use it? Most colours suggested something. Green was passive, blue hinted at passion or at worst moodiness and red was fiery anger, black was impossible and white was neutral. But yellow. Yellow was nothing: it was like the word 'nice', it conveyed nothing. A nice yellow. Primrose or buttercup?

Why didn't you stand up for yourself? You'll never get that promotion.

Another walk? No. Not really. It would only be a moon walk. He had explored parts of the camp he had never seen. The Indian and Filipino areas had been particularly alien to him. All just to stay out of the room.

Nevertheless, he found himself grabbing his light-weight jacket and checking that he had his ID card and keys.

Why didn't you say something earlier? I wanted to avoid an argument.

Outside in the darkness he began to walk, past the canteen the only non-trailer in the entire camp apart from the cinema which itself was a large hangar. And now? On towards the recreation room. There were a few others walking about but he only knew them by sight. He neared the recreation room, heard the buzz of voices and continued on to the library. This he passed making his way to the pool, which at this time was closed. Then he was amongst the trailers again. Row upon row of them. All the same.

You should have said that's what you would have liked.

Ah, I didn't want to upset you.

The weekends, being Thursday and Friday rather than Saturday and Sunday, were the worst. One had to fill the time.

To live one had to shut down. The Kingdom loomed overhead, occasionally dropping a depth-charge. Something to assert their authority. A raid or normally a pre-announced raid. He liked to bash away and keep occupied. Tick-tock. Many kept their lights on, although they were not at home.

It looks like one endless party, she had remarked. He had been showing her his photographs. He could counter-balance her remark now because he saw things differently. He saw beyond the pictures of beach antics and drunken people at parties and the cosmetic camp trips. The bleary-eyed, laughing faces betrayed nothing in the photographs, but he knew the people. He knew the characters. And they were characters, each and every one of them. They all had a story to tell. He had no photograph of the lonely party pooper in the darkened corner. And the photograph of the laughter that was a little too loud or a little too long was not available. He could have asked her to spot the alcoholic come to dry out. Or the broken marriage. He could do it quite easily himself. Just look at the proportion of men to women, for Heaven's sake.

A camp trip had taken them to a Bedouin market. Ten rats to sit on a camel for a photograph. Then there were the cross-legged black pawns, with a rectangle showing Ninja-aware eyes, otherwise just henna dipped hands. They were gesticulating and trying to sell western goods amongst their traditional stuff. But packaging was faded or covered in a film of sand or both. It was hard to tell in the glaring light. What struck him, however, was that they were trying to sell things in sixties packaging in the eighties.

224

He was nearing the gate and the security building. Where was he going? The empty-eyed Arab guards were inside talking. He walked past the barrier. One of the guards looked up. Going out was not a problem.

Anything for a quiet life, that's what I say. That's what he had said.

Now he could turn towards the other camp, or go over the bridge to the various villas. He decided upon the bridge. This was the vehicle access to the camps. It came from a slip-road off the motorway it straddled. The strange thing – and this he found baffling – was that returning from work by bus one came from a slip-road on the opposite side of the motorway. Therefore in a short stretch of road one had to traverse all three lanes of traffic. He put it down to bad design. He had noticed quite a lot of that here. Things had boomed and sprung up without too much care or thought.

Did he love her? Yes. Did he hate her? Yes.

If he could have turned another corner. If he had taken that girl of his youth. What had been her name? She would have loved and cherished him. If.

Carpe Diem. He had seized the day and it had bitten him.

It was true, the weekends were deadly. But he had enjoyed the previous weekend. A beach barbecue. One of the lads had a car. They had driven along the beach road, past the occasional rusting auto cadaver, strips of tyres and other abandoned bric-a-brac. Another security check for access to the beach.

They had swum and joked. Sniggering behind hands at the Arab in chic white with his women covered from head to toe in black, lifting their robes to reveal a touch of ankle so as to paddle in the water. Oh, children, oh, children.

We're having fun. Care? Obviously we care for each other. We care for each other fiercely. We stick by our friends. But woe betide should you fall. You'd be abandoned for fear of you taking them down with you.

He had taken a walk to the far end of the beach with a couple of the others. Something had been going on. Lemming-like suicide or a great accident, he was not sure, but all along the beach and in the shallows were large jellyfish. They were like half-poached eggs, outside translucent but inside opaque and milky-white.

She had once called him a spineless jellyfish. That was during one of their many arguments. Was he like a half-poached egg? See-through right to his soft, milky-white self? Yes, probably he was, but was not that a virtue? Nonetheless, it was then that it had began to dawn on him that she had no respect for him. That is, utterly no respect for him. Shortly thereafter he had suggested going to Saudi Arabia. A decision. His decision. What a man. Wasn't it nearer brinkmanship?

I'll be back.

Then one of the lads had pointed out a dolphin not far off. No, there was a pair of them. Swimming together, free and flowing. Their hunching plastic-grey backs curving out of the water and then disappearing. They had been beautiful.

He was directly over the motorway now, and he looked down upon the speeding cars, lorries and juggernauts.

Was he really there? Was it real? Wasn't he a barefoot prince on holiday in Greece? Or a young newly-wed in France? A boy in the dinner queue? Please sir, can I have some more? A child at the wedding avoiding asphyxiating hugs and musky kisses from lipsticked puffed-up aunts? An innocent in the love-scene – sack the scriptwriter? A perfect hero of Greek mythology? A son? A victor? I am Spartacus. A failure? A baddie? A goodie? A man? A boy? Or even a mountain, a sea, a river, the world, the universe, a God? Everything? A life?

She had also once called him a worm. A cowardly worm. Admittedly the colour was right, but did worms have a concept of bravery and cowardice? He smiled at the thought.

And wasn't she watching him? Wasn't a clown turning its hideously smiling face to him? Wasn't he the clown? Oh, to be! Wasn't mother telling him off? Or father looking away in shame?

The noise of the traffic hit him and made him dizzy.

Centuries of evolution had produced him. He was a product of *The Ascent of Man*. But Bronowski had never explained the concept of suicide.

Yellow. Yellow was the colour of a worm. It was also the colour of sickness. It was the colour of bile and pus and the colour of cowardice. It sounded like wallow and mellow and fellow. Backwards it was wolley – ha, it was him, a wally.

"Dave, stop... Stop, will you? Stop, Dave... Will you stop, Dave? Stop, Dave... I'm afraid. I'm afraid, Dave... Dave, my mind is going. I can feel it. I can feel it. My mind is going... There is no question about it. I can feel it."

This was a novel. And he was the protagonist. Could it be that he was not? Perhaps he didn't even qualify as a short story?

He closed his eyes. Then he looked up at the stars and shook his head in resignation. Goodbye Norma Jean. Goodbye Mister Chips. Goodbye me. I'm sorry, Mum. Hey, you too Dad. He backed away from the parapet into the road of the bridge.

"Shit!" he shouted and ran towards the parapet. He leapt up, right foot first, seemed to pause as the rest of him caught up – another moment, the universe held its breath – and then the momentum carried him onward and he was flying. Top of the world, Ma. He glimpsed the large juggernaut hurtling towards him, realised he had timed it badly and would hit the cab and then, oddly, he saw the two dolphins swimming in unison.

* * *

The nurse pulled back the yellow-tinted plastic of the tent and he looked her full in the face.

"Don't try to talk. The doctor will be here in a moment."

He closed his eyes.

After a time, curiosity caused his will to explore his limbs. He could not move and he could feel very little. Of course he was drugged and so any sensation would have been pain. But it was the fact that virtually nothing obeyed his will that disturbed him.

There was a sound at the door and he opened his eyes again.

"You're lucky to be alive," said the doctor in his American accent, looking at the chart at the end of his bed and marking it with his biro. He regarded him for a moment as if reflecting upon something. His expression was stern, possibly angry. "You've done yourself some serious and permanent damage. You're paralysed from the neck down." The man paused as if wondering whether to continue. "So you won't be doing yourself any more harm." He shook his head. "But the guy in the cab was not so lucky. That was one hell of a stupid thing to do. Why?"

He looked away, turning his head upon the pillow to look out of the window. The movement caused him grief. He felt clammy as if basted in molten viscous honey.

He didn't kill anybody. He couldn't kill anybody. It was her. She was to blame. And if she had got the news – not fish wrapped in paper – she would say it wasn't her fault. She would say that she wouldn't even swat a fly. They'd see and they'll know and say that she couldn't harm a fly.

Then he had his first sensation. But it was not this significance that sent a tear rolling down his face.

Sunlight streamed in, bathing him in mustard light like a spotlight at a concert; it was the same colour as the doctor's biro, the same colour as the pastel walls, the same colour as sand, and the same colour as the contents of a suspended bottle and its lifeline tube to his arm.

And the sensation? He had heard the filling of the bag between his legs and although he could not look, he knew what colour it would be.

Solitary

Spending days alone in a prison wasn't how he envisaged jobbing around South America. But then he knew things rarely turned out as planned. So expecting nothing else he had planned loosely. But his current confinement sat there at the top of his anecdotal list. A list that was already long and varied with adventures: his camera getting stolen, tales of unquestioning hospitality and back-alley enmity, his bout of Delhi-Belly and the bus journey from hell – the bus with the unforgettable name of *Destina*.

He was sitting in a camarilla, a utility room, probably little bigger than a cell. He was at a desk amongst lockers of cleaning stuff and riot gear.

Daylight burnt at the high-set window and angled a shaft of musty light onto the desk. The relative dullness of the room framed this dust-laden pillar. The amount of particles in the light disturbed him and accentuated the stuffiness, but didn't seem to affect his breathing.

"It's a crime not to be out on a day like this," he could hear his mother say. Unlike in good old Blighty, days like this were plentiful. Indeed the continual sunshine rendered the weather bland and he saw the appeal of a countryside walk in the autumn cold crispness.

This was his fifth morning session in as many weeks. Of course, he'd not expected to be doing it for so long. The novelty had well and truly worn off. Once would have been enough for an anecdote.

But today could be special. He had spotted the envelope from cell 237. From the prisoner the newspapers had coined *El Senor De Las Moscas* – Lord of the Flies. To some extent the label had stuck. Throughout the prison he was known as *la mosca* – the Fly.

As usual, almost like a school teacher, he had designated parts of the desk for the various piles. There was the unread pile to his right and the read one to his left. And like a school-teacher there was a third pile – not for the outstanding ones to be read out aloud in class – but for those containing something questionable and in need of a second opinion.

He had taken the first year of the teaching certificate, but there was no practical and the theory was basically a history lesson. He gave it up in favour of Spanish. And this was the payoff for that decision. Nevertheless he mentally awarded grades. Not marks out of ten, but As, Bs and Cs. Of course it was simply a matter of taste. The handwriting was atrociously childish and the content by and large uninspired F-level stuff.

Although he'd been told not to bother with *la mosca's* letter, he was tempted to make it his first read. Perversely he left it in place to relish the excitement, like saving the opening of the best present till last.

Also on the desk were his well-used pocket dictionary, the thick black marker; his cheap pen-fan whirring on its little wire stand and a biro and his notebook. The last complemented the dictionary with prison slang and colloquialisms. This unofficial dictionary was well on its way to becoming a prized object that substantiated his tale.

José had supplied many of the entries. His uncle Eduardo had contributed too.

Inevitably Americanisms had infiltrated the language. Weapons were mainly homemade knife-like affairs known variously as a shank, *navaja*, *figa*, blade or steel. A homosexual could be a pole smoker, *joto*, *moe*, fudge packer. A dirt nap was to die and back door parole was to die in prison.

A new entry to his notebook today was 'bus therapy'. An inmate had used it and he remembered that it referred to transferring prisoners from one institution to another, to keep them away from their property, visits and contacts.

Officially he was looking for hints to plans of escape or smuggling. However, he couldn't help being drawn into the privacy of the correspondence between the men and their kin. It amazed him that many of them wrote candidly, despite knowing that their letters would be vetted. There was rarely anything explicitly intimate, but declarations of affection were plentiful.

Eduardo was a prison guard and was proud of his nephew. For José was something of a star amongst the staff. He had cracked a correspondence that appeared to be a harmless chess game, but gave itself away when the moves went beyond the board.

José's main job was as a waiter and it was in the café that they had met. José had served him his breakfast, until he began working there himself, as a dishwasher. Within a week they were inseparable amigos.

One morning José explained that his father was dying and that he had to go to him. He didn't know how long he would be away. He had spoken to his uncle and, if he wanted, he could earn extra cash working in the prison. When he hesitated, saying that he was little more than a *turista*, José said that he was a savvy hombre. Of course he was excited by the idea. But he was also wary. He'd heard terrible stories about the prisons and inmates here. He was well aware of the trick of lavishing compliments. But he allowed himself to be seduced. The statement that swung it was: "I know you have the *cojones*". Appealing to his masculinity was so childishly simple it was endearing. Anyway, he reasoned, you didn't need balls to sit in a room reading prisoners' letters. He probably wouldn't even see a prisoner.

Reading their letters gave him a keyhole view of their world. His minor victories, decoding prison slang for streetwise recipients, were not completely satisfying. And there was an element of voyeurism to sifting through their private lives. On this level they were ordinary people. No – less than ordinary. They were pitiful.

La mosca's letter could be the sensation he needed to lift the session. And here it was before him.

Eduardo had told him not to bother reading it. He also said that *la mosca* was not incommunicado, in solitary confinement, but that he was something of a recluse, not mixing and keeping himself to himself. *Loco*, according to Eduardo. Only the psychiatrist knew more.

He slipped the letter out of the unsealed envelope. As was his method he scanned both sides of the single sheet to get an overall feel for the writer and the effort involved in deciphering the text.

The language was poor and the grammar worse. He hadn't expected anything else.

It started innocuously enough.

Hola Madre, padre, hermana,

Did it mean something that father and sister were correctly written, but after the hallo the word mother began with a capital letter?

231

I hope you are well.

How was your birthday, Sis? You should not worry about that boy at school. If he doesn't notice you yet, he will soon. You are going to be a beautiful woman.

The replies tended to be juicier than the routine scribbling of the men. For he had to go through the incoming mail too. Even the occasional streetwise philosophy of the more educated men's ponderings seemed dried up. The replies to the "Dear John" types were the best. They were almost sensational. Many of the inmates expected betrayal and even provoked it like a death wish, but it was a sledgehammer when it happened. Their replies were invariably reactionary, a mixture of threat, undying love and plea.

I am fine. I have not made any friends here. The men are not the kind you make friends with. The guards are not too bad. But they refuse to do anything about the flies.

It doesn't look like this heat wave will ever end.

The room was sticky and airless. He wiped his hands on his jeans and picked up the fan, moving it close to his face, closing his eyes and turning his cheeks to it as if under a shower.

I imagine you are still protesting my innocence. But I am here and you should forget about me. Do not take any notice what those so-called experts say. During the trail they contradicted one another with their gobbledygook. Their fancy terms made me sound like a diseased tree. I'm glad you weren't there. To them we are not people with feelings. We are just thick-barked trees.

I told you last time that the doctor helped me get over that writer's block. She can be persuasive. And now I will tell you a little secret. I think she is falling for me. I can see it in her eyes. She hasn't said anything, but I can tell. What do you think of that, padre?

I know she is my doctor and many patients fall for their doctors. But this is the other way round. She cares. She told me she cares. And you cannot really care unless you feel something for someone, can you? That sounds like you, Madre.

Hold on, there's another of those damn flies. I wish they would do something about them. Their buzzing drives me crazy, especially at night. I can hear it but I can't see it. Sometimes I search for hours.

I have to stop to find it now.

Besos y abrazos (kisses and hugs)

He could imagine what the sound of flies meant to him. Eduardo said the man now heard them in his head and swiped the empty air.

Back then he had turned up the volume of the television to drown out the sound of the flies. That was when neighbours had called the police.

For a moment he stared at the letter before folding it back into its envelope. He wondered what sort of head-game the psychiatrist was playing with *la mosca*. For the letter would go to her, never to be sent. The recipients had been his victims, five days dead, sitting with him in the lounge when the police broke in.

Vitriol

"Acid!" she exclaimed. "D'yer no wot I sed?"

She stood with her arms pushed down, the whites of her knuckles glowing at her clenched fists.

He sat at the dining table with his back to her. He seemed undeterred and passively ate his meal.

She realised that he was not going to answer and turned from him to the mantelpiece with a despairing sigh. There she attempted to contain her quaking state of mind by focusing her attention on the smooth curve of the elliptic, marble paperweight. Too beautiful to be lost in the clutter of his desk.

Calmly she went on.

"I told em ter scapa. An yer bleedin cronies said they'd leave it in the drive... What the ell are yer goin ter do wiv acid? I mean – what der yer do wiv acid?"

She fell silent once again, and it did not take her long to realise that still he would not reply. She reconsidered her position. *Did she have the upper hand? Or was he holding himself back?* She could not gauge his mood. Without knowing his disposition she was at a loss as to how to continue. *Persist?*

He continued to indulge his meal, occasionally pausing to nonchalantly sip his beer. This consumption was obscene to her. The very thought of food repelled her and his noises amplified her repulsion. The sight of his thinning hair, his body, his bloated flesh, all contributed to her revulsion for the disgusting mastication. These last few weeks she had been eating meagre meals. The menopause had taken her appetite. Really it had done much more than that. It had brought home the hopelessness of her life. Hers was a pathetic, wasted life. The rags of her hopes and dreams had wasted away with her physical decay. No children. No future. Nothing.

It could have been that during this trying stage in her life she needed to vent her frustration, but it was more than that. She wanted more than sympathy from him. She wanted to shake him into some show of concern, some show of love. His authoritarian hold had always subdued her and consequently she had imprisoned her insecurities behind self-doubt. For twenty years she had wrestled with her wants. Only now, during these last few weeks had her suppressed longings culminated in these uncontrollable outbursts. Twice during such neurotic outbursts he had lost his temper and jumped for her. Luckily she had anticipated his action and fled. However, this evening she felt something different. She could not say what was different. She was as aroused and wild as before, but this time she felt something had given way. As a soldier in the field of battle may abandon himself to the nightmare of killing and risk his life, so she was somewhere beyond herself: reckless. Like before she wanted to tempt his wrath, and then she wanted to force him to his knees. She wanted to know him. She wanted to be told that she had not wasted her life. She wanted to know that she had not succumbed to his charm. She wanted to know that she had not sacrificed herself. Racked with self-doubt she wanted to be reassured of her looks, for she felt her beauty was falling apart. The cancer of insecurity had made her ugly inside. Her saving grace, her last attribute and final pillar of self-confidence, her vanity, was being threatened.

She sighed again.

"Okay, I'm sorry, luv. But yer know wot I'm goin froo. If only yerd stay in a bit more. Cor blimey, you'd fink you were in luv wiv yer work more than me." Then clumsily, like a drunk "– or that tart yer employ." She felt him freeze and a chill went through her. When he resumed his eating after this minuscule pause her thoughts were released in a mad gush.

The unreal began to envelop her and she began to shake with the rigid tension of her rage. Again she concentrated on the paperweight. This time her look was a glare and at first she did not see the stone. After a while she began to scrutinise it.

The streamlined veins of white were beautifully fine in the rich, luminous green. It was a perfect stone, almost a jewel. Like a polished tablet of soap it was flawless. She loved the feel of its exquisite coolness in her hands. The permanency and durability in its heaviness was something she respected – no, adored – for in the feel of the stone there was a pleasure she could not describe. During her many bouts of loneliness she had sought its comforting feel. She loved to fondle it in her lap, then to hold it up and admire its uncompromising strength, like the hard feel of the ball of a bicep. Since she could remember she had always been excited by the feel of a man's biceps and had used it as some kind of measurement of masculinity and virility.

Instantly and without realising it she said: "Are you tryin ter send me potty?"

He stopped eating.

Could she make it to the door?

With a razor precision that magnified the tension to an unbearable pitch, he calmly and ever so viciously cheese-wired her with his words.

"I'll giv yer me Ollie if yer don't shut yer trap."

She was close to tears, but on hearing him swallow his beer something hard crystallised the tears.

What to do now?

The tapping and scraping of his utensils upon the plate began to grate upon her. Every time the brittle sounds bruised the taut silence they pierced her thoughts and she winced. She wanted him to stop. She prayed for him to stop. For he was plucking and twanging her nerves with a torture akin to the poor playing of a violin. And she was an antique violin, a Stradivarius, light as balsa wood with finely drawn nerves that required love, care and attention, and not this constant series of disjointed, obtrusive clawing.

Instinctively she picked up the stone. But as she sent her fingers over its surface, seeking its comfort, she found that her thoughts remained an entanglement that would not hold structure. So the object gave her nothing and she felt an urge to throw it into the hand-painted china display.

They were at the beach. So young. Laughing... Then in a restaurant eating lobster. He asked her to marry him at the top of the Empire State Building. Down the club with Vicky and Jane. Playing with the various pinball machines he had acquired. She was looking up at her mother, tarting herself up. The first time he hit her. Vicky's laughing like a seal. She was watching the eye of the cheetah. Down the alley after school. The monkey snatched her sweets again. Wondering what to do with the two hundred marble fire-surrounds... Vicky's laughing now like a donkey. The first argument over children. The time she had made him so hot that he had ripped her dress. Her mother and father having it off. Landmarks. Him breaking the other guy's nose in the pub to protect her honour. They're all laughing. When he told her that they were talking business and to get out of the room. She should have protested then; she had always been part of the business. Playing in the dirt. The time she got blind stinking drunk. Honeymooning in Hawaii.

Memories like pebbles washed smooth by the sea of time.

Lonely and deserted, she turned to him.

"I wan it all outta ear tomorrah," she said, the fear opening her eyes and accommodating the volume of water; her anger focusing her awash pupils to a point on the back of his head. His consumption remained nonchalant, but there was a hint of idleness. *Was he about to go for her?*

Vicky was laughing. Where was she now? What a strange thing to think of. She was in Australia, of course. But what was she doing at this very moment?

With uncharacteristic daring, sent on by her emotion, she continued. "Not like those discs – in the cella fur two bleedin mumfs – No, oh no, I wan that stuff owt. Tank an awl..." She let her voice trail for she saw the slight stiffening in his shoulders.

Her lips parted, but rather than speak or whimper, she took a breath. He had begun to rise. He was getting up with slow, formal heaviness. Yet, although she was panic stricken, her thoughts a tangled mess, she made no attempt to reach the door. Even a scream was held fast by the terrifying paralysis. It seemed to her as if her thoughts went down two parallel paths at the same time. One was to smash the silence, escape the grip of fear at her throat and whip him from his sluggish movement, and the other was to scream and run away. But she did neither of these things, instead she remained still and mute. It was when he turned with the proud, icy confidence of Medusa: the taking of the helpless prey, about to mesmerise her with the sweet, sexual beckon of death that something snapped in her. The last thing she saw of him were his clenched teeth and thinly drawn lips. Spitting like a cobra, her arm lashed out. The paperweight hit him at the temple. He grunted and in an unwieldy stumble, a hand hitting the back of the chair, he crashed to the ground. There he crouched. Her arm dropped and she released the stone. It thudded upon the carpet as his body began to gather itself together. "Stay down," she hissed, though neither of them heard it. He was getting up. Instinctively, she went for the paperweight and as she bent he grabbed her wrist. She yelped, but scrambled for the stone with her free hand. His grip was vice-like, all his weight was behind it, and it seemed to squeeze the very life out of her – as he had done all these years. His pull was enough to floor her and demand her subservience, but then she had the stone, and blubbering she smashed it into the side of his head. He slumped, but his grip remained. "Let me go!" And she struck him again. This time she heard him make a strange rattling noise from the back of his throat. He began to shake: his entire body vibrated. Still he gripped her. As the thing quivered inhumanly, she tore the fingers from her wrist and jumped back. The stone thumped upon the carpet a second time. She watched with wide-eyed horror, both hands covering her mouth, as the thing shivered, settled and mercifully stopped. All was still and something within her relaxed; though the tension remained. She looked about herself, at the door and then the French windows. Although she knew nobody could possibly see into the room, she sought out spies. Then her eyes were upon the body. *Vicky was laughing. Or was it a donkey?* Feeling terribly weak and sensing that she was about to fall, she took another step backward – her gaze upon the motionless figure – and reached for the mantelpiece to steady herself. *Was he dead? Why hadn't she used the poker? It was always the poker. What a strange thought. And they were all laughing.* Her hand was shaking so much that she knocked the small china donkey off the shelf. She watched it fall, as if in slow motion, as if she had the power to stop it but something told her that she could not. When it broke on the mantel surround she gasped and physically jumped. Then she laughed. And stopped herself as suddenly. Her hands came up to run over each other and cover the chewing of her lower lip. She looked at the hump. *Would the crash of the ornament wake him?* She was looking at the shards that had been the little donkey; a present from some trip to Spain. He had laughed at her buying it and she had been hurt and amused. Broken. Then she noticed a spot of redness at the side of his head, the colour spreading and deepening under the skin. The activity sickened her. Silently spreading ink expanding on blotting paper. Giving the body a wide berth, the tears running down her face, she fled the room.

Having shut the door and closed off the incident she was left rather forlorn and could go no further than the foot of the stairs. There she stood for a while. Then she sat on the bottom step. She rested her chin upon her spent fists, her elbows upon her knees. A strange confidence settled upon her glistening face and she began to chuckle. Her cheeks were aglow and as she began to laugh she cut herself short. No lunacy for her. The silent front door, built in the majestic Georgian panelled style, stood before her like a judge. From the bottom step it seemed oversized. It towered over her, intimidating and accusing. The frosted-glass windows that sandwiched the door caught her attention, or more really the fading light of evening. Outside was the world. Outside things were carrying on, just as before. Things were moving on. She had stopped. She was entombed within the anguish of her deed. It had been done. There was no undoing. No choice. Her smile was replaced by grief. *When I were a boy, I used to squabble over the window seat with my brothers.* Grief, yes. Ah, but not for him – *th' poor sod* – no, for her. He did not deserve a second thought and she would not allow him to take anything away from her. She looked sharply at the closed dining room door. Had it really happened? She could not quite grasp it. He could not really be dead. Not him. Not really dead. He was too big to be dead. Not that he was particularly big physically; just big to her. Bigger than the door. Big in character. Big in life. He was too alive to be dead. Death was for small frail things. Death was for old age to drift over to, or for youth to spectacularly leap across to. Death could not take something so big and so full of life, so simply. It had been too easy, almost pathetic. How could he have slipped away so easily? Was the grip of life so weak?

She began to strain her ears for the sound of movement and she interpreted some of the natural sounds of the house as life: the creak of the building as it settled for the night, the occasional shudder of the bedroom door as a current of air nudged it, the refrigerator juddering into, and out of, action as the thermostat flipped the motor and the stolid clunk-clunk of the grandfather clock to her left.

In spite of the mounting calmness, her thinking was neither rational nor productive and insofar as the killing was concerned it was non-existent. She thought of washing the dishes, having a bath, possibly sitting in front of the television set with a cup of cocoa, or going down to the pub.

She looked over her shoulder at the dining-room door and with a wicked, sardonic smile, found herself saying out loud: "Serves yer right... You add it comin. Yer know that." And then sorrowfully, "yer should av lissend ter me."

She began to talk as if to an invisible audience, or perhaps her speech was generated by her alter-ego; whichever, her soliloquy was delivered in a quiet, gentle voice.

"I told im, yer know. E should av lissend... Fur twenny years I've bin tellin im. It's is own fault." She stood up. "Wot a marriage, eh? Cleanin the carpets." Her feet carried her ponderously up the stairs, a hand sliding up the banister. "Slavin away... It's not fair, yer know. Wot life did e giv me, huh? I ask yer? No, no, don't say it's my fault. It's is. Yeah, yeah, cors I luvved im – in the beginnin. Huh, a long time ago. I was young. A bleedin fool. If I'd known wot I no naw, I would never av marrid im. I probably would av marrid nobody. Yeah, it's clear naw... Huh, too late." She was in their bedroom. It was immaculately kept, like the rest of the house. She had taken great pains to add a touch of romance to this room of perfumed pastel. Yes, it had been her domain. It had been agreed from the beginning. The other rooms were mostly his – oh, she had the kitchen, hall and bathroom, but their functionality tended to dispel any personality. She had hung the copper and brass-work in the hall, but in truth, the bedroom was her realm. It was her soft, fairy-tale world. Black or red satin sheets with matching valance – they were not short of a bob or two – the large mirror with the ornate golden frame, thick fluffy carpet, luxurious heavy velvet curtains... Yes, her domain. And although he never passed a comment, she felt that he had loathed it. "All these years workin away. Finking this was wot it was all about. Im goin ter work, an me tidyin up." She straightened the bed sheets, although they were already straight. "Always tidyin up. Im out there, doin fings, set-in us up fur life – but this is our bleedin life." She ran a finger along the top edge of a picture frame. There was the merest film of dust to be gathered. "Always one step a ed of ther grass. By-in an sell-in. Ah, but e weren't so clever. Naw, e juss fought e was. Wheeler-dealin. By-in an sell-in." She paused. "Bort me, I spose... Oh dear... If only I could go back an start agin. I'd scratch for a real life. Yerd betta believe it, mate. Too right. Bastard. E took me. E stole me life. Serves im right. Naw, I stole is. Ha. I should av done it years ago. Yeah. I was a fool to cave in every time e clipped me ear-oles. I should av showed im." She strolled past the dressing table and caught her reflection in the mirror. "Oooh, I say, wot a sight." A smile appeared. She loved her pearly white smile. "I was really boo-iful, weren't I? Turned many an ed. Yea, yer did... Oh dear." Then woefully, "from doll to moll. Ey I am boo-iful." She pulled out a drawer and taking a jar of cream she tried to quench the pores of her skin. However, the futility of the act caused her vision to blur. "I am boo iful. Wot about that ay-een year old down ther Black Ferret? E fancies me. Yeah, an I'm free now. I can do wot I won." She petulantly put a comb to her peroxide blonde hair. Then she powdered the soft, limp skin of her face; skin that covered the merest of flesh, as if the very substance of her had shrivelled within. "Yes, I'm free." She smiled again. This time she dipped her head, put wickedness in her eyes and moved the tip of her tongue to her top lip. After checking her make-up – which she had not altered for the last decade or so – she enthusiastically removed her clothes down to her undergarments. She pondered whether she should put on her red and black lace underwear, including the suspender belt, but eventually decided that it was too much. From the wardrobe she picked out her mock leopard-skin jacket and tossed it onto the bed, then the black leather trousers and thigh-length boots and as she moved to her shocking-pink blouse she was held by the chime of the grandfather clock.

"Wot am I doin?" she asked, as if coming out of a trance. "Ease down there. Dead. Yea, dead." A bitter laugh issued from her inner self and frightened her. "Oh dear. Ears me dressin up ter go out an ease down there. Dead. Dead as a doornail. Ha. If only e could see me naw." And this thought caused her to imagine that he could see her, not as a whim, but that he really could see her. This suspicion was founded on some deeper, inexplicable belief in an after-life. She felt that although he was powerless – was he? – he could see her. He could hear her. "I warned yer. Boy, did I warn yer. Yer av only got yerself ter blame. I warned yer. An naw yer dead." She seemed chuffed with herself, but insecurity remained in her words. "Yer can't touch me." The clock stopped chiming and her mood changed. The coincidence of her challenging words and the sudden silence made the core of her shiver. "No... You are dead. Dead... dead..."

She moved to the stairs in her undergarments and stood on the landing straining to hear movement. A top tooth caught her lower lip as she began to collect herself. Returning to the bedroom, she dressed in the clothes she had on before and religiously replaced the others in the wardrobe. She spoke for comfort.

"I'll av me a drink. Yeah..."

Stealthily she descended the stairs, not taking her eyes off the dining room door. Soon enough she was in front of it. Lightning horror flashed through her as an image of him standing behind the door came to her mind. He was smiling, a horrible twisted smile. Half of his face was a grotesque purple. This horror was so sudden that she stood for a long while. Eventually she braced herself and, in some form of death wish, ready to scream, she stepped backward and leant forward, turned the handle and gently pushed the door inwards. His body was unmoved; the photograph in time had remained unchanged. Could he be faking it? No. Nevertheless, the sight of him was no less shattering to her and she gasped as the reality of what had happened presented itself once more. She could not sweep this aside. No, a body would not fit under the carpet! And she wanted to laugh. She wanted to cry. She wanted to scream. There was no way to blotch out the terrible thing. It was there, before her, lingering, festering, getting worse. It ate at her like a tumour, sitting and waiting, sitting and waiting, not going away ah, but growing worse, feeding on time.

The tremors within her were subsiding by the time she entered the room. Just like when she fled, she again gave him a wide berth. To be near the body was something that she could not begin to contemplate. The tiniest splinter of thought of the dead body shook her. There was more than the fear of death, the fear of the still thing, there was the fear of him. For her the very aura of life had not left him. It was as if death had stunned his movement. No, it had not taken him. His dominant character lingered long after she had submitted to the fact of his death. She knew he was dead. Logically he was dead. But he was not gone. Therefore she watched him with wide-eyed expectation as she moved the hinged door of the cocktail cabinet at the other end of the room. She moved the door slowly as if its sound could stir him from his slumber. When the mirrored surface of the door was fixed and horizontal she took a glass from an inside shelf. The brittle sound of the vessel upon the mirrored work-surface jarred.

It was as she poured the liquid into the glass that her confidence grew. She was spurred on by the cool of her action and she found herself raising her glass in an arrogant toast to him.

"See, ears ter yer. I'm drinkin yer bleedin muvver's." She laughed bitterly and somewhat insincerely. Her words dissipated in the emptiness. Like talking to an answer-phone, the absence of a response was unsettling.

Instantly, the large gulp of alcohol she swallowed sucked at her very senses and she had to place a palm on the wall to steady herself.

"Oh dear."

Despite this, her tentative confidence continued to rise and she smiled.

"Well, wot yer goin ter do aboud it? I'll tell yer. Nuffin. Yer can't do a fing." She gestured wildly with a finger to her lips. "C'mon, c'mon, it me on the kissa naw."

But the body remained unimpressed.

She shuddered and then tensed herself, pushing the flat of her hand against the non-existent creases of her skirt.

"C' c'mon git up. That's enuff. You ain't dead..." her voice left her. In spite of her constant desire to be convinced otherwise, she knew he was dead. It was just that some intangible part of her would not accept the fact. She did not trust him and even now, strangely enough, he still held the upper hand. Even in death he held a hand over her to keep her in place. She was bound under his will as sure as she was committed to life. This bondage was so strong and subtle that it made her believe that he was still watching her. He had always been stronger than her. That was what had attracted her to him in the first place. Because she herself had been no weak-kneed bit of fluff. One could say that he had been brutal and insentient. Of course he had not always been like that. Nevertheless his stoicism had been attractive and she had found herself kneeling before him. Although, she had been a strong person – *broke a foo 'arts* – she found that once she had assumed the inferior role she could not rise above herself. Initially her subjugation gave her the security she had always sought. Other men had been kids or puppets. He was something strong. Something she could rely upon. She had found him exciting and, masochistically, when she had tried to rise and he knocked her down, she found herself exhilarated. She rose up to be put down. Again and again, and each time her fire was doused with a fuel that had her gasping for air. Each time this saturation was enough to extinguish her. Like a drug she lapped it up. And like a drug it burnt deeper and deeper into her spirit. It sapped her strength and wearied her, and the spirit of youth in her eyes began to dull. Only she felt this attrition. For him there was no effort, no problem. Any boredom that had crept into their relationship was simply a consequence of familiarity and marriage. Roses and rages became their way of life. Of the few occasions when she did make a concerted effort to confront him, she was let down by her lack of strength. Her efforts, no matter how desperate she felt, were half-hearted. After a time she no longer rose up. She often wondered what had become of that fiery woman of her youth. No matter, the decay had gone too far and she was weak. So she accepted her lot and wandered aimlessly along in a daze of magazines, books, television, cinema, friends, gossip and tea-parties. Once in a while she probed him, trying to understand him, but she recognised no light and wondered whether it had ever existed. The possibility of the light never having existed, although shocking, was quite feasible, for her own spirit had been quite blinding. The years went by. She had an affair. Her lover had been weaker than herself and therefore, she evaluated, weaker than her husband. However, her secret meetings with this man – an employee of her husband's – were a thrill in the barren years. When it eventually dissolved she was not disappointed. As a sort of test she had coaxed him into some sort of stand against her husband, and as she had expected he had failed her. This test had been to shame him. She had wanted him to fail. And had he stood up to her husband she would have relished seeing him crushed by her husband. Ultimately she lost, for she severed the hand that had fed her, wanting more and yet not wanting it at all. The dissolution brought relief and grief. And the years rolled by.

The frequency of her protests had increased of late, but he was always, in some way, one step beyond her. Feigning ignorance was one of his tactics; maybe it was genuine. In any case the result was the same: she came away hating herself for her out-of-character ravings and was left wondering whether she was going mad. Once she had asked him. "Am I goin barmy?" His reply had been: "Maybe." Yes, he was always one step beyond her. Above her in a rational way, above her in an emotional way – for he had control over his emotions, or perhaps he had dwarfed emotions. Whatever, she always felt that he was superior to her and thus hated herself all the more when she showed that she was beneath him. Now he was one great step beyond her. He was at the supreme vantage point when it came down to touch. Death had placed him further from her. In some inexplicable way she felt he had won. His new position was uncompromising. She had gained nothing. At least in life there had been some hope of reaching him. Now he was more detached than ever. It was unbelievable. It was unfair. She had been cheated out of everything and now he had escaped any form of retribution. Her bondage was her life. Life, life, something he had cheated from her. It had been wasted. Yes, she had killed him, but his death was not her triumph. He had deserved an agonizing end or a blissful reconciliation with her. His death assured her of a slow living death. This was his final triumph, the final nail in her living coffin. How long she had reached out and failed to touch. Wasted years. A wasted life. He had sucked it away, sucked her dry. Sucked the marrow from her bones, the flesh from behind her delicate cheeks. He had stolen her life and now he had run off into the darkness. He had won. He had ultimately won.

"You bastard!" she screamed, throwing her glass at him.

The carcass remained unmoved.

An idea ran through her mind, but in surprise and disbelief she did not acknowledge it. She tried to conjure up her time with the girls and sought Vicky's laughter, but it would not come. The idea returned and like a stalker waited in a shadowed alley. Every avenue of thought was then stalked. Awareness alone disintegrated her thoughts. She was distracted by it and although she knew where it led she tried to run from it. But the idea remained and would not be ignored. Eventually she succumbed and entered the dark alley. Her plan was to abort at the last minute: to be led so far and then to duck-out. However, as she followed the course she found herself absorbed by the idea. Everything seemed to come together in a rush. Like fate, all the pieces fell neatly into place.

Her laugh was brittle.

"Acid!"

And she laughed again.

She indulged herself and thought of the strange, morbid romanticism that accompanied the act. This thing would immortalise her with the infamous. Ah, but wait a moment, of course she would not be caught. Her fancy took her to a further demeaning of him. This act would put her in a position that towered far above his petty crimes. Ha! He had been a miserable fence, buying and selling, playing with pennies. She would be playing for higher stakes. Yes, she would stand in the ranks of the masters, the household names: Haigh, Christie, Jack the Ripper. Although, she would not be discovered. On her deathbed – oh, how delicious – yes, on her deathbed she would confess.

She would dispose of the body properly, unlike Haigh who had been too cocksure, too clumsy in his confidence.

What of the questions? Ah, he often disappeared for days at a time. He had enemies in the underworld. Perhaps she could concoct some story implicating one of his cronies, or better still, that tart? However, that required more thought.

First, the matter at hand.

She knew all about murder, although, technically speaking at this moment it was manslaughter. Her plan would turn it to murder. This act would shift it to a calculated action and change the light of the incident. No sympathy from the jury. For a moment she thought of turning herself in and pleading self-defence. She dismissed the thought. It let him off too lightly.

Nothing barred her from carrying out her plan. The thrill of this delicious thought almost caused her to wet herself and she was forced to tighten her bladder. Deep down she suspected that her sudden lack of control was not a result of her dark excitement, but fear. Somehow, she believed – no, knew – that he would get her. He had always been one step ahead of her and even now she could not quite believe that this was still not the case. Despite this self-doubt a wicked sparkle rekindled her long-dulled eyes.

Shunning the insecurity she poured herself a drink.

"You fort yerself so bleedin cleva, didn yer? Keepin outta ther bucket. Ha. You were pahfehic. No betta than those teevin ponsin oodlums yer delt wiv. Praps yer were worse than 'em. You add no real bot'ule like em."

She drank.

With her back to him she looked out through the French windows to the patio and then the swimming pool beyond. However, her calm was goaded by a voice that told her to turn around and check his stillness. At first she dismissed the voice, but then to satisfy the speaker rather than herself, she turned and looked at the body. "See." For an instant she once again imagined him standing there with his horrific grin and half-purple face. But the voice continued. Why not approach the body? She was going to have to sooner or later. That was part of her plan, wasn't it? Why not touch it? Why wait? And a struggle was born in her mind. Why wait? Get it over and done with. No, don't rush. Think clearly. And she found herself arguing with the voice. Then she was overcome by a wave of pure fear. The glass began to shake and she was forced to grip it with both hands, but still it trembled. The voice she had been arguing with was his voice. And this was the first time that she had felt his presence so acutely; almost as if he had been there whispering in her ear.

"You're dead," she murmured, concentrating her efforts on calming herself. "Dead."

Pushing the act of coming into contact with the body as far away as possible she began to organise herself.

Criminals were caught because they made mistakes. They put the finger on themselves either by omitting to do something or by doing something superfluous. She resolved to carry out every single action, no matter how minute, for a reason.

"Oh dear."

She thought of Haigh. He had been too sure of himself. After luring Mrs Durand-Deacon into his storeroom, shooting her for financial gain – simply the fur coat and jewellery she carried – he had placed her body in a forty-gallon steel tank and pumped concentrated sulphuric acid in. Three days later he had returned, skimmed off some of the fats and pumped in more acid. The following day he had emptied the entire contents outside the storeroom. Then he volunteered his assistance in the police investigation, for they had traced her whereabouts to him. He treated the whole thing as a game and the detectives grew suspicious. Finally, under questioning, he informally confessed to murder, but added that without a body they had no proof.

She had read many thrillers, both fact and fiction. She knew all about murder, indirectly of course. She knew, for instance, that rigor mortis took place some five to seven hours after death. Therefore, she knew that what had to be done, had to be done before it set in or after it wore off.

Her reverie continued and she knew she was putting off what had to be done. She thought of Sweeny Todd. He had questioned his victims in his barbershop. Satisfied that they would, or could not be sought he slit their throats whilst giving them a shave, pulled a lever that sent them to the cellar, where they would be chopped up and served in his meat-pie shop next door. A fingernail, or toenail, found in a pie had given him away. Should she chop him up? Could she chop him up? No, no, she thought not.

With her thoughts still meandering she looked at him. A wry smile tugged her mouth line and an eyebrow rose in quizzical, mock contemplation. For the first time he was an object. He was a sack of potatoes, a carcass, a lifeless thing. He could no longer touch her. He was powerless. And with this came the thought that she had purposefully picked up the paperweight and hit him. Yes, it had been premeditated. And they, the great mass conscience that was outside, could not catch her.

She was a killer. She was somebody. She had power.

Haigh had made the mistake of not removing the body's dentures. Insoluble fats had surrounded them and protected them from the acid. These had been as good as a body and had sent him to the gallows. Hmmm, the fats would pose the biggest problem. She would have to remove his clothes – everything. His dentures would have to be dissolved separately. In addition she would have to skim off the fats and pour them down the drain.

At this particular moment the thought of undressing him did not seem too frightening. True, she could not envisage herself doing it, or more likely would not see herself doing it. In any case, she would have to undress him within the next three hours. It would be quite dark soon. She would take his clothes to the car and with the folding bicycle in the boot, she would drive – his driving gloves – to some secluded spot – no mud – leave it all and cycle back to the house.

How lovely it was all turning out. She had never thought so clearly and positively in years. She had some purpose and she had not lost her impetus. There was something decidedly thrilling in the task. Even in the fear of it there was exhilaration. She shuddered. What bliss! And she smiled.

"Right, me 'arties," she exclaimed, bracing herself, "tidy up."

She left the room, this time stepping over the body in a dainty ballet-like leap, for she was determined not to get too close. As she did so her heart seemed to stop. Vestiges of his presence remained.

From the small half-cupboard beneath the stairway she fetched the dustpan and brush. Back in the room –
she had left the door open – she collected up the shards of the donkey. To her this memento was their relationship, now broken, but it too had been painted and hollow. She put the glass she had thrown at him on the table. The paperweight, her partner-in-crime, was seated upon the mantelpiece once more. Yes, it was like her, a suitable companion, hard, without conscience, stone. Alas, she knew this was not true. But to be like that, to be insensible... Then again, she would be no emotional wreck. She had been strong before and she would be strong again. He had pierced beneath her surface and drawn out the weakness in her until it was all she became. Nobody would do that again.

She took his plate and pint of beer to the kitchen. The liquid went easily down the sink. When it came to the plate, she noticed his half-eaten meal. With the plate tilted towards the open bin she realised his mark, his being, his life, and she realised the utensils he had used. This food had been attacked by the dead animal. He had been alive. Half of this stuff was inside him, sitting in his stomach, as stagnant as that on this plate. A short time ago he had been consuming this revolting stuff. The obscenity of it all, the moving of his jaw, the swallowing, the belch of beer, warm-stench of food, warm stench of

248

his life, was nausea to her. Would she throw-up? Now he was more useless than this cold stuff. He was like this cold stuff, waiting to be discarded. Lying in the dining-room was a heap of meat. Even in a cannibalistic society he would be of no more use than this food. Where was the spirit? Where was religion? A sack of meat lay in the dining-room and that was all. Her revulsion caused her to drop the contents of her hands into the bin. Her will left her and she collapsed in on herself, slumping against the wall. There she waited.

The cool of the wall upon her cheek eventually forced her to collect herself. For a time she was Janet Leigh in Hitchcock's *Psycho*, staring, unseeing, face pressed against the tiled bathroom floor.

To gain control she unconsciously took deep breaths.

"Oh dear."

The cellar keys hung on the wall behind her. It seemed strange to her that they looked different. Everything looked different and individual. All the insentient objects about her seemed to lose their functional banality and take on some kind of invidious purpose. All these dead things were no longer meaningless. No, existence and form gave them purpose. Existence without pain. Purpose without conscience. The keys were useful. They could be ancient. They could be ageless. The metal of which they were made was useful. The metal was immortal. For all her superior awareness, her consciousness, was she perhaps below these things? She had warmth, but she was soft, bio-degradable. Were they of some greater incomprehensible awareness? Were they at peace with the universe on some inconceivable plane? Could she become the keys?

She shuddered again. Dismissing the possibility of a new dimension she snatched the keys. Using the young, modern key at the door beside the half-cupboard beneath the stairway she exposed the steps to the cellar. Click and the light revealed the downward path. Like a mountain defies the climber, so these concrete steps dared her to descend. She noticed, as if for the first time, just how steep they were.

A shiver took her as she descended to the older door. She had never been so scared and went down with more caution than normal. She held both rails for she was afraid that she would slip and break her neck on the hard stone floor. At the bottom she eased the ornate key in the loose lock of the old door. The aged latch clunked heavily. The door scraped the gritty stone floor as she forced it aside. Another light was given life. But grime coated this bulb and it gave off a musty yellow gaslight that was dull and small compared to the clutter of ancient shadows and objects in the room.

The house had been modernised, virtually gutted and rebuilt, but the coal cellar, barely above the foundations, had remained untouched. Even the large furnace, fossilized with rust and stilled with age remained in the darkness.

She had never liked the cellar. The objects had always taunted the darker side of her imagination. The dullness gave them a certain unity, although they were as individual as the objects topside. Furthermore, they were like the elders, promoted to a coveted monastery. Dust and cobwebs united them as a whole. Darkness was their companion. They were the immortals, long dead, but conscious. They hated intruders.

The naïve carboys squatted near the wine rack. They were newcomers. Soon they too would be accepted and shrouded, but for now they were a party of brash public-schoolboys, hushed and awestruck. Not even whispering. They were small and seemed to crouch low as if to shy from their portentous surroundings: the home of the elders.

Her glee and vexation that afternoon, in making it as difficult as possible for the men to handle the carboys – bringing them all the way down into the cellar rather than the garage – was now her mortification. It would be so difficult to get him down here. But then what better place for the disposal of the body?

The carboys stood behind the empty tank like spectators before the launching of a vessel.

How would she get the acid into the tank? Could she pour it without splashing? How heavy were the poisonous little devils?

She moved round the tank to the nearest container. There she gripped the metal framework that caged the straw which in turn bedded the bottle. With both hands she heaved and found that she could just about lift the affair. But it was all too cumbersome to manoeuvre safely.

Sitting at the edge of the bath-sized tank she pondered her problem. She felt exceedingly drained, as if that one heave had taken all her energy. Haigh had pumped the acid into a tank designed for the purpose. It had been so easy for him. Here, she was confronted by some plastic tubing, obviously a siphon, but she knew that she would be unable to get it to work. It was all tubes and bits and pieces. And there were no instructions.

The frustration of her position caused her to whimper. Could she chop him up and drop bits of him into each bottle? No, they would have to be very small bits. Suddenly she thought of dropping his penis into a bottle and she laughed. Damn it, she would not be beaten. She would work the siphon. Gloves, yes gloves, she would need her pink, plastic washing-up gloves. Although she was not sure whether they would afford any protection, she felt that she could tear them off should they get splashed and this was protection enough.

The mustard light strained her eyes and she could not focus in the haze. She became aware of the film of sweat that covered her brow and eyelids. The impending exertion, the semi-light and the stifling claustrophobia of the cellar – an arena with the surrounding objects looking on – made her feel giddy. She wiped her eyes with the heel of her hand and sighed. The thought of the cool, sharp breeze of early evening was celestial. Perhaps she would go out for a walk? But it would have to be after the deed.

"Oh, you bastard," she snarled.

Then, in a frenzy of determination, she swung into action. She wheeled a carboy round and round like a barrel to the tank. She snatched the siphon and was again pushed to the edge by the complicated apparatus and she wanted to throw it into the corner and be done with it all. But something manic and driven took her beyond this point and she began to hum to herself. Her driven state clouded her reasoning abilities and she had even more difficulty figuring-out the functioning of the siphon. At one point, with tearful eyes, she tried to force two pieces together that did not fit. Somehow she figured it out but all the while she was on the verge of panic.

When she went to fetch her gloves from the kitchen she did not have the presence of mind to try the siphon with water in the sink.

Descending the stairway once again a wicked romanticism went through her mind. Was this not some bizarre scene from Edgar Allan Poe? The film of *The Pit and the Pendulum*, perhaps?

She pulled the bright gloves up towards her elbows. They were dulled in the half-light and seemed to lose colour. She removed the stopper and tried the siphon. At first nothing happened and mistrust began to rise in her. Suddenly it started going and then it was simply a matter of waiting and watching the seemingly harmless and colourless liquid pour into the tank. Soon the first bottle was empty and she pushed it aside.

She was sweating again as she approached the next carboy. This time she spotted a strange looking barrow and it surprised her that she had not seen it until this moment. She had certainly not seen the men bring it down. From the curve of the lower half and the grips it was purpose-built to embrace the metalwork housing of the carboys. She smiled as she put it to the test. Affixing the grips she wheeled the arrangement to the tank.

Her confidence rose. "Naw we're rollin. Ha. Rockin ana rollin." Everything seemed to be falling into place. Then, under the tedium of the job, her confidence began to wane. She began to think. She began to think of anything. Inexplicably she wanted grief, really wanted it, and she urged herself to think of him. She dug deep, searching for something to upset her, a meal, a party, a holiday, a moment in time, and then when it came she tried to suppress the tears. "Oh dear." And she cried.

At length, she had no idea how long, the tank was full – or as full as she dared have it. Five carboys remained untouched and sat heavily. Perhaps it was psychological, but the atmosphere smarted like onions and she experienced pins and needles all over her body.

Wearily she plodded up the stairs, each foot as heavy as lead. After the dullness of the cellar she was painfully conscious of the fluorescence of the kitchen. The gloves irritated her as she tried to pull them off. They highlighted her nagging feeling. Something needed to be done and she had been putting it off.

"Oh dear," she sighed. "It's all goin okay. Yes, it is... Oh dear... Phew. A woman's work is neva dun." She seemed to go into a trance. "Naw, fink... Keep carm... Hmmm...first...er – a jimmy."

When she returned to the hall, holding onto the fading sound of the cistern, she found herself again procrastinating. "C'mon pull yerself togevver. Yer not gonna giv up naw. Ease not goin ter win." It was this last sentence that did the most to set her on her way. But the demanding task caused her to start hyper-ventilating. She allowed her subconscious to do this because she knew that it was a necessary part in the preparation of her psyche.

She realised that she was at the dining room entrance looking at the body. Her eyes were wide. And a terror gripped her throat. She desperately needed something to drive her and she forced her eyes into slits of contempt. Let hate drive her. Oh, let hate take her. Still she did not move. *Was she breathing?* She was frozen and abstracted, her blank eyes staring at the body. The carcass was a sack of potatoes without any hint of latent energy, all the character evaporated. She recalled a childhood game in which one child stands apart from the rest. This chosen child faces away from the others, but may turn at will. The objective of the others is to be the first to reach the child without being seen to move, if spotted they had to return to the starting point. The game took on sinister tones in her mind and although she had not taken her eyes off the body or indeed moved, the thought of the body moving when out of her sight was a scream in her mind. It would not be him moving. He was long gone. It would be some evil force.

She shivered.

"Carm down. Carm... carm..."

She found comfort in speaking aloud, not merely because it filled the appalling silence but because it added construction to her thoughts.

"Let's see." She stopped, waiting for another thought to verbally materialise. "Yes... Okay, I've gotta do this propply." A sudden tangential stream of thought was reflected in her words. "I bet yer enjoyin this. Well, I can do it. You'll see. I know all abou this. Yer won catch me out, yer bastard. Naked as a noo born you'll go. An out wiv yer false teef too. Naw, yer won't catch me. You always fort I were pahfehic, well naw I'll show yer."

She was standing over him with her fingernails digging into her palms. Her adrenalin level was high and she glistened with perspiration. Then, before she realised what she was doing and in a state of extreme loathing, she bent down, grabbed the shirt and pulled the body onto its back.

"Ahhh!" she yelled, jumping up, as the full sightless stare fixed upon her. For a time she was stunned by the half-red mask. Then she gripped the tablecloth and pulled it towards her. She lifted the glass she had originally thrown at him. But the bullet-shaped salt and pepper containers fell onto their sides. As she dropped the cloth over the head, she followed the pepper pot as it rolled noisily across the polished rosewood surface of the table to fall onto the floor.

With a palm to her rising chest she made a conscious effort to slow her rapid breathing.

"I'll do it," she said after some time. Then again she spoke to him – not to the body, which was something he had inconsiderately left lying around in the lounge, like a hammer or screwdriver. "I got ther bottle. You jus watch me."

First she put the pepper pot back on the table beside the up-righted salt container. Then crouching over the body she began to undo the buttons of the shirt. The body wasn't cold, but its receding warmth was a shock. Overcoming the shock was a minor triumph that spurred her on. The cloth over his head helped a great deal. Without a face he was unidentifiable. He was an anonymous body of meat, another slaughtered pig, a bag of flesh. "Jus a sack o tatters." Gradually, mechanically, she undressed him. The grey wire at his chest upset her a little. How many times had she run her fingers through those hairs? Nonetheless he was not there and the body was no longer him. Then she noticed the ring on the little finger of his right hand. It tormented her. She would have to remove it and banish once and for all any possibility of his returning. "Nuffin. Yer nuffin naw, an yer were nuffin when yer wer alive."

By the time the body was completely naked, except for the tablecloth, she was kneeling quite comfortably. The fact that she had been humming to herself for quite some time went unnoticed.

She took the hand and tugged at the ring on the podgy finger. *How many times had this same hand touched her? How many times had she kissed this helpless thing?* The ring would not budge. *How many times had this very hand slapped her?* "Sod you!" *How many times had it become a fist and hit her?* "Bastard fing." Still it would not budge. Desperation caused her to whimper and silent tears ran down her cheeks.

"Cut it off," a voice suggested.

"No," she replied. "No, no, no..."

"You bastard," she quivered. "... av ent I dun enuff?" And by way of an answer, the finger was now quite soft and wet with her perspiration, the ring miraculously slid off.

She looked at the ring in her hand and laughed: the laughter teetering on the brink of hysteria. Then her head dropped wearily. She was exhausted. Unsteadily she got to her feet and moved to the cocktail cabinet. Shaking with exhaustion she poured herself a glass of whisky. Sipping it slowly she looked over her work. There lay the faceless body, just flesh: maggot-pale, blotched and senseless.

"Oh dear," she said quietly, although she did not know it.

The ordeal was far from over. Physically the next task was probably the most strenuous. She would have to drag him down the stairwell to the cellar. Again she cursed herself for her obstinacy in forcing the men to carry the acid down there. Dragging him to the garage would have been so much easier.

Aggression drove her as she tied the tablecloth around the head. She then grabbed the ankles and dragged the impotent body nearer the doorway. However, her aggression had hastened her actions and she realised that she was too close to open the closed door. Despair immediately stormed her will and her eyes brimmed with tears. A conflict was born: one side crushing her down, forcing her to collapse in a heap of tears and anguish, the other shrugging off her error, the feebleness and self-pity and resuming her aggressive disposition. For a moment she was on a razor's edge. But the voice of reason saved her: she would have to carry out the task sooner or later. She lifted the ankles to her shoulders so that she could awkwardly open the door.

Incomprehensively, for he was dead, she could not allow his legs to crash to the floor. They had to be placed, not necessarily delicately, but at least with respect. *What was this respect? She had not respected him in life, so why now? Was it the same respect she held for a good slab of meat before cooking?* She thought not. She thought that this was a respect for the life the body had possessed. In transporting from the living to the dead she believed one crossed the boundary from mortal to immortal. This respect was for the helpless, abandoned body, left to decay. The body possessed but a memory of the life that it had carried. Like a photograph pictures a moment, but seldom captures it, so then this body suggested a life. This was enough to add solemnity to her respect. "Neva speak ill of the ded." This great taboo of death resided inherently in the conscience of the living. Incongruously, although she could not harm the body without a feeling of guilt, she was about to destroy it as completely as possible.

For some reason – the tablecloth – she was reminded of the television programme she had seen when she was young *The Invisible Man*. There he was unwinding the bandages about his head to reveal nothing. "Soon yer'll be invisible too!" She chuckled.

She picked up the hands and placed them on the torso. Returning to the feet she began to pull the carcass through the doorway. "Bloody Nora, talk abou' ded weight."

But the struggle charged her. It was going to happen. It was going to work.

How was she to get it down the stairs? Lowering it before her could cause problems. The–

"Cut it up! Cut it up!"

"No."

255

"It'd be so easy to drop an arm in and then a leg. No problem."

"Yes, it was true. But wait. Wait. What of the mess? Blood everywhere."

"Get some bin liners."

"Ahhhh." Would she throw-up?

"No, no, no. I'm goin ter do this, yer bastard."

The stairs were a problem. Lowering it before her could cause the leading part – arms and head, or feet – to buckle and become caught. There again, to lead, pulling the body down after her, lacked control. But with such a dead weight, how could she fail to control it? So in spite of the inherent danger she chose the latter method. How crude and vulgar it was all turning out to be! It was definitely not thrilling. Ha, Hollywood. No, this was base and sordid. It was a clumsy deed from which she could derive no satisfaction. Where was that delicious sexuality she had read about in those pulp novels? There was nothing wonderful or exciting about this crime. It was sick.

He was to blame for all that had happened. He was to blame not simply for having driven her to murder, but also for this arduous ordeal. He was watching and via some supernatural power he was making things as difficult as possible.

At the top of the stairs to the cellar she gave another unconscious "Oh dear."

Her hands were sweating and her whole body felt clammy. She thought of the lovely bath she would have when it was over, and as she envisaged this reward another thought swept over her and she chuckled.

"Not ther kinda barf yer gonna av."

In the short ensuing pause the hand of the grandfather clock clunked and to her it was him acknowledging her with a knowing smile. *But what did he know? What was this instant wisdom in death?* No, it was more subjective: he knew something pertinent to the current situation. It was as if he knew the future, as if all the questions had been answered for him.

Once again the dilemma began to grow within her. Fear was breaking through her determination and her old foe self-doubt was flanking her, sapping her strength. She grew weak and began to shrink. Life was weak: as fragile as the embryo from which it came. Death was stronger, a brutal scythe. Life was daylight, from a quavering dawn, through a bold, brilliant noon, to maturing evening and the fading light of dusk. Death was the night. Death was final, without stages, without growth. Death completed the picture. Death answered the unanswered. She foraged for feeble defences against the tsunami of fear, which had the aeons of Death behind it. "I am alive", "I feel", "I have the gift of consciousness", but they were crippled by the onslaught of the unknown. The four horsemen. The skull in the monk's habit. The serpent, sulphur, the goat's hoof... *Would the tears come?*

"Damn you!" she cursed. "Git outta ma mind." Her eyes flared. Like some wild thing she stood defiantly, although numbly, against the fear. She allowed it to flow through her, allowed it to possess and exorcise, gave it its violent rape of her, but did not succumb. The core of her, although surrounded by ruins, was resolute and solid. "Do as you will, you cannot harm me. Abuse my mind, take my body, eclipse my spirit, you cannot touch my soul." Then the evil faded away like an illusion confronted.

Within these moments she sweated profusely. Drenched in perspiration she stepped over the body and in the hallway removed her shoes and her clothes down to her undergarments. Vulnerability undermined her physical comfort, but eventually things began to subside and she grew anxious to get the body out of the hallway. It was a psychological thing, for nobody could see into the hall, but to her it seemed public. And then again, she was standing in her underclothes.

She climbed over the body to the top of the stairwell and grabbed the cold, hard ankles. She tugged the carcass ever so slowly onto the steps, lest she should fall backwards. Then she began to drag the body downwards, the dead hands rested on the abdomen but the enwrapped head tipped to nod at every step and thud back painfully.

To her horror she felt the body slip. In that same instant an inevitability, like that when helplessly observing the progress of an accident, gripped her stomach. The body gained momentum with such irresistible rapidity that she had no time to step aside. The crotch caught her feet and she stumbled onto the belly, stalling its thumping path down the concrete steps. One of the lifeless feet caught and bent at the knee, but rather than wedge the body to halt its motion – due to the momentum – it began to lift the torso. She moved back in horror, trying not to embrace the carcass, but this merely accommodated the action. The body continued to rise into a sitting position and the clothed head butted her in the stomach. She reached for the rail with one hand, the other moved by reflex to find support at the body's shoulder. Her hand barely touched the rail before the monster took her down the steps. The yelp that she issued was lost to the crash.

Then all was still. Terribly still. She was burbling with terror, on the verge of a horrendous scream. A dull pain throbbed at her waist and somewhere in her lower back a knife was being twisted. She was pinned down by the body, the faceless head near her own. She strained to be free of the burden, away from the carcass with the mummy's head and the hidden malevolent grin.

After scrambling away she stood back, her chest heaving in her brassiere, brushing dirt and grit from her skin. She was sickened by the awkwardness of the body's position. It was unnatural. Her disgust was inflamed by the apparent repose of the carcass, despite contradictory discomfort. He seemed to be laughing. He could contort his body like a doll. He could twist his shape grotesquely. All the while he would be laughing and taunting, dancing on her nerves, feeding on her frail sensitive life. A rush, like Victoria Falls, filled her ears. Vicky was laughing again. Her disgust turned to a raging fire of loathing. "Is tha ther best yer can do?" The dull bruise at her waist throbbed like the pounding of tom-toms, supporting the mania of high-pitched twangings and screechings that were her pained nerves. A blade of magnesium-white hatred rose up in the roaring inferno and she snatched a nearby garden spade and raised its heaviness above her head. She would break the body, split the sack of lifelessness. Yes, she would burst its sleep and spill its passiveness in a glory of colour. But something held her. She remained still and the spade began to falter. Then she lowered the blunt implement and returned it to its former resting place.

"Naw, yer bastard, thas wha yer wan... Huh... Naw, matey, I wown lose ma crust."

She dragged the door open a little more and paused to look about the room. The bath was waiting. The schoolboys looked on. The elders remained unimpressed.

"Oh dear."

She moved to the body and as she bent to pick up the feet she exclaimed: "Bloody ell, almost forgot yer 'ampsteads." But the thought of having to remove the tablecloth and touch the stained head held her in check. Then the inspector described to the court how he had discovered the teeth and the pathologist continued with details of the inevitable identification. After fumbling with the cloth she pulled it away to unveil the ghastly face. It was all the more frightening in the half-light. The eyes were replaced by dark pits of sockets. She closed her own eyes to steady herself. Ignoring the discoloured mask, blemished and ashen, she pushed her fingers into the mouth. Her lips were pressed together with fear and determination, and also to hold in the yelp that squeaked in her throat. She smothered the squeak in a consciously abandoned hum.

The silence was vast. She was conscious of herself. Every movement she made was amplified. She was aware of the expectant bath behind her, a gaping vessel, like the mouth of some fabulous beast. A stinging bitterness stole the inertia of the liquid. But its relative clarity camouflaged its dissolving power. It was both beautiful and deadly, much like a Venus-flytrap. And this awareness made her weak at the knees. Oh, what luxury it would be to ease her weariness, to rest her weary bones. She was conscious of the carboys, standing now, like dutiful demons awaiting some satanic ceremony. They were the spectators. They were not alone. The spade that leant casually against the wall, the fork at its side, all the little jars of nails and screws and bits and pieces, the eyes of spiders, the sacks, plastic bags, surrealistically long-legged Daddy-Long-Legs, pieces of wood, old carpet, woodlice, old bottles, racks of wine, rusted oven, centipedes, petrified paintbrushes, even the broken, limp wheel-barrow – a sinister friar, all these things assumed a united expectancy and waited.

The performance began before the passionless objects with her placing the dentures on the step above the body.

Grabbing the ankles once again she dragged the carcass. The glassy stare that fell upon her, when the head rolled, was ignored. She was ice to it all. She was dead to the sound of the pale body grating on the floor. She had screamed herself out. She was no longer there, vulnerable in her underclothes, the last wretched survivor of the gladiators' arena.

The final and most difficult task stood before her. How to get the body into the tank without splashing? Should she have put the body in before filling it? Too late.

She followed the faint grey wisps of vapour as they rolled across the surface of the liquid. The warm, mustiness of the air began to close in on her. She was both hot and cold. The cellar was cold, but the air was full of mustard that scotched her skin. The moment was critical. She knew she could no longer put it off, every moment drained a little more of her meagre energy. *Method, that was what was needed. Method in this terrible madness.*

Should she shut the door? No, something may go wrong. Did he want her to leave the door open? Did he and Fate know something that would require the door to remain open? Open or closed? Such thoughts, she knew, were nonsense. But how could she ever make a decision if she suspected he influenced her? Bah! He was dead. Gone. There was nothing he could do. She would leave the door open.

"Oh dear."

As best she could she tugged and pushed the body into a kneeling position at one end of the bath, the chin hooked over the edge.

"There yer ar, a nice ot barf. It'll clean yer ter yer very bones."

She smiled.

"Wash away yer aches and me troubles."

She chuckled strangely. But she was frightened. She wanted to laugh, but like hysteria her urge to laugh was uncontrolled and from somewhere deep down.

Let yerself go! Laugh. Her chuckle grew and she laughed. Her laughter was full, until it became a cackle that died away in a series of sniggers. "I'm a bleedin witch!" With burning tears streaming down her face, the sniggers were replaced by forced little chuckles, which in some way were meant to justify and contain the wholesome laugh.

She was completely alone. The audience were obliterated. She was obliterated.

The arms were hooked over the edge, and the hands, just beyond the wrists, went into the liquid. Incredibly nothing happened. Then as she grabbed the fatty waist she sensed some activity. It was a dull hissing, but so vague that her ears strained to realise it. When she was sure of its presence, unable to see the hands due to the milkiness of the liquid, the noise began to grow in definition. Urgency caused her to fret. With a heave the forehead kissed the liquid and the elbows were submerged into the fizzling, needle-sharp bubbles. The exertion was tremendous and despite her cautious haste she had to pause, her own body pressed against the carcass to hold it in place. She watched the sizzling liquid darken about the submerged limbs. Having mustered enough energy for another heave she grabbed the body, but it slipped down a little. As she struggled to lift it, hanging half-in and half-out of the bath, a momentary thought snapped at her. *Was the weight enough to tip the tank and drench her?* Hurry, hurry, she was almost there. It was going to work. She pushed at the fleshy animal buttocks, whimpering under the effort. With the stomach over the edge, clumsily the carcass began to slip below the surface. Because the body was bunched up at one end the legs stuck out. She pushed at the hard soles in an attempt to force the submerged portion along the tank. The dirty liquid bubbled and popped. The wisps that had rolled so effortless over the surface like threads of mist, had increased in frequency and in places rose furiously in little columns like exotic *Jinn* dancers. The warmth of the bath grew proportionally with the noise. The bubbling became a boiling and she began to feel giddy with the heat and noise. She stepped back, perspiration jewelling her forehead and stomach. The sound of the liquid piranha caused her to stumble backward. It was going to work. But it was too much. It was too violent. The feet squirmed and then sank into the effervescent mass. Like a fish out of water she began to gasp for air in the musty haziness. Her hand grabbed the barrow that embraced the half-filled carboy, a muzzled half-demon. "Got ter ge ouw. Got ter ge ouw." She blinked rapidly against the rough tongue of a lion licking at her eyes. Vertigo began to rock her and she began to weep. The roar of the volcanic action engulfed her as she struggled to get away. From the corner of her shrinking awareness she observed the spluttering and splashing of the drowning man. *Was he alive?* He seemed to be fighting the gouging torture. It was horrible. Far worse than she had expected. Her mouth was wide with her voracity for air – or was she screaming? Then she found herself blindly crawling up the cool steps, knocking over his dentures, her eyes tight against the caustic atmosphere.

Somehow she reached the kitchen – the neutral kitchen – and there she aggressively turned the tap with the merest strand of consciousness. The torrent of water splashed into the sink and hit her body. This startling sensation was wonderful and she frantically slapped the pillar of water into her face. Her entire body hungered – the pores of her skin agape like hankering young birds – for the chill of the liquid. It was the liquid of life, Adam's ale. Her very consciousness, shrivelled by the experience in the cellar, soaked up the cool. The water ran down her neck, over her body, the drops pitter-pattering on the linoleum. She wallowed in the sensation, running her taut hands with spread-eagled fingers all over her body. She tried to follow the rivulets as they raced down her quivering flesh. It was going to work! Her mind was awash with pleasure. The water and pleasure ran over her and she grew wild and began to moan. The emotion carried her so far that for a moment she thought she might have an orgasm. However, a peak of pleasure was attained and quickly dropped off, with the cold water becoming irritating.

There was a splat-splat from the soles of her feet as she fetched a paper towel after switching off the tap. The smarting of her eyes had subsided, although she could not tell whether it had completely vanished. Perhaps the burning was psychological, perhaps there was genuine cause for alarm, whichever, she tried to convince herself that it was just sweat.

She considered her experience. There *was* a thrill to killing. She understood now how executioners could get an erection before and during a kill.

The distant roar from the cellar approached the forefront of her thoughts. They – she – lived in a detached house, but could somebody possibly hear the roar from outside? She thought it unlikely, but... And then, it was so quiet and still up here. Yes, she decided, what was needed was some music. But what? Rock'n'Roll from her youth or something from the Swinging Sixties? No. She decided there was only one thing it could be. Opera. This was an opera. She was on stage. Whenever she listened to such music in the house she always felt as if she were on film or being observed in some way. Then she would sing or act out some piece she had seen on television, or simply do an impersonation. Naturally, she was alone at these times.

What better than Carl Orff's *Carmina Burana?*

So she padded into the lounge, switched on the stereo and selected the compact disk. *Fortuna Imperatrix Mundi* grew stirringly in the air and she sang along. Her words were la-la-la for she didn't understand what they sung. And she had only purchased the CD after hearing the piece as background music to a television advertisement.

It was all coming beautifully together. It was going to work. She was going to win. "I gotcha, I bleedin gotcha."

After a few moments, when the music had settled down, the roar again moved to the forefront of her thoughts. It was violent. Too violent? She could discern the popping and bubbling. Could there be tell-tale burns over the cellar walls? This thought gave birth to the same inquisitive inspector, this time with a mild sarcasm in his voice, a kind of 'and what have we here?' voice. Could she cover the tank with something? That too would show the tell-tale burns, if not dissolve. There was nothing. Then what else? Think. Think. Could she dilute it?

Yes, of course. Not too much, just enough to slow the process down. Huh, it might even cool the air.

The column of water drummed into the bright orange plastic bucket she fetched from under the kitchen sink. As it filled she glanced down at the kitchen floor. With a "tut-tut" she acknowledged the filthy snake-like patterns of dirty water. She would have to clean up later.

The burdensome pail strained as she lifted it out of the sink with both hands.

"Oh dear."

As she reached the doorway at the bottom of the cellar she again had that same daunting feeling that he was nearby and she suppressed her distress by quietly humming to herself.

The noise was tremendous. Through the mustard light, she could see the bubbles mushrooming beyond themselves like tiny leaping figures. In them she could see miniature atomic explosions, upright limbless ants, bloated bumble-bees, darting flies, flames, turbulent seas. All rising up to be pulled back into the turgid mass.

"I'm not afraid," she whispered.

Placing the pail on the stone floor she struggled to shut the door. It scraped the grit on the flagstones as it had on opening. And then it caught on what she thought was a large piece of grit. She left it ajar. The mild strain of doing this was a little victory and, charged, she found the detachment she sought. She picked up the palpitating bucket, as fragile as herself, and neared the ferocious chaos. In complete contrast she found herself pouring the water carefully, but hastily, into the tank. She let it slip rapidly into the dark liquid with the deliberate control with which one might decant a bottle of wine.

She'd almost emptied the bucket when the explosion occurred. For water upon sulphuric acid is water upon burning oil. She had no time to step back. No time to think. Remnants of the ravaged carcass jumped up from the body of the heavy solution. And she dropped the bucket into the jaws of the monster as it spat at her vulnerability. She fell backwards screaming, drenched from head to toe. The black heart of the liquid threw pain all over the cellar. As she moved to the door – she did not wonder why she had tried to close it, she did not think – her skin began to scream. Pain shut her eyes. The razor, needle-like teeth were all over her. Somehow she reached the door, squinting and crying through soapy eyes. Everywhere was steaming. She was in a cruel tropical forest. Tugging at the handle with smouldering hands, she managed to pull it a couple of inches before it abruptly halted. She could manage to get through the gap, but a frenzy of panic had united with the frenzy of physical pain. The hiss of the snake was at her ears, and thousands of forked-tongues were poking deep into her. The harder she tugged the more fixed the door became. It was a nightmare. It could not be real. It could not be so fixed. It could not be. Through the pain, claws racking her flesh raw, she sensed that the firmness in the position of the door that defied reason. It would move in neither direction. She half-fell, it was a kind of downward stumble and then she partially saw and partially felt the wedge that had entrapped her. It was his dentures. Him! Her scream choked itself and she wheeled backwards. The entire cellar seemed to be burning. And there was an incessant hiss of the blow-torch melting the pores of her skin. She lurched about blindly, crying, choking and screaming. Every nerve shrieked. Everything was pain. Histrionically, just for a moment, she stood legs astride, arms wide, and head tipped back. Her howl pleaded. The razors continued to strip her. She was being skinned alive. Immediately, as if she could limit and contain the pain by making herself as small as possible, she embraced herself. But there was no containment. Then she was crouching. Her brain received nothing but pain. Her mind was a mass of pain. There were no thoughts, only pain. The monster was eating her. It ripped and salted, stripped and salted, endlessly, tearing and peeling and tearing. The tiger savaged her and she became something resembling a tiger: something of black and fire. Her hand reached out from her shrivelling self for support, as she fell further and further down. It was when she was upon the floor that she pulled the barrow over.

Lying in the puddle, most of which was created by the carboy in the barrow, she was away from the turmoil. This hiss was a great distance away. The immeasurable agony had reached its complement. She was an alien thing: conscious but unaware. Was she screaming? Was there pain? Was she crying? The consciousness seemed to be in a suspended state. A stillness. The senses had been disabled. She was almost stone. Polished marbled stone. The whining of the heart of the body held out just long enough for the isolated mind to realise itself.

CSR

There, that's the registration out of the way. So, how can I help?

As I tried to say, doctor, it's not about me.

Go on.

It's about my son.

Why isn't he here?

He won't come.

Why not?

He doesn't think anything is wrong with him.

I can't see how I can help him if he won't see me.

I, er, was hoping you'd pay a house call.

I see... I don't usually... Tell me what his problem is.

Until this weekend there's been nothing physically wrong with him. Oh, he's been fidgety, always moving about. You know, ants in his pants, pacing, but, er, jumpy–

Irritable? Complaining?

Yes.

Tell me what happened this weekend.

Until now it's all been mental... I heard him sobbing in his room. I went in and he was lying on the bed with his left arm in the air, bent at the elbow, like this. He couldn't move his hand. And his fingers were bent up like claws. It was quite frightening. I tried force, but his arm was locked. I went to the neighbour and he came over and calmed him and his arm began to relax. He said he had seen it before and that it was stress-related and nothing really to worry about. But I don't know. I thought I'd better get some professional advice.

Quite right. What does his father think about all this?

I wouldn't know. He high-tailed it when I became pregnant.

Has he a father-figure at the moment?

I don't see what that's got to do with it. I've been quite capable on my own so far... He's a young man now and it's more difficult. But doctor, really, as one woman to another, surely you don't believe in that claptrap?

I'm sorry; I've got a full waiting room out there. I haven't the time to get into discussions. Please just answer the question.

...No, he has no *father-figure*.

Thank you. I can only help if I have the full picture. What else can you tell me?

I don't know. His eyes occasionally glaze over as if he's far away. He, erm, sometimes gets kind of reckless. You know, indifferent to danger.

Does he have problems concentrating?

I don't know. I guess so. Yes.

Does he suffer insomnia or have nightmares?

Both. But he doesn't want me to know about the nightmares.

Oh? So, how do you know?

I brought this.

What is it?

It's a dictation machine from work. I recorded him in his sleep. He talks... Listen.

Entering kill zone... An IED has taken out point man. He's fubar... Incoming at three o'clock... we're Oscar Mike.

I've seen this before. I have military experience, you know.

I heard. That's why I came to you.

I suppose you know what he's talking about.

I've an idea.

Oscar Mike means on the move. An IED is an improvised explosive device. Fubar means fouled up beyond any repair. It's like Snafu: situation normal all fouled up – although another f-word is often substituted... in both cases.

He calls our neighbourhood the GZ

The green zone.

Yes.

What you're describing is known as CSR. Sorry. I imagine you're sick of acronyms and whatever. Combat stress reaction. It used to be called shell-shock. And a number of syndromes are just fancy names for the same thing.

So it's like burn out?

No. It's more than that. You said his eyes glaze over as if he's far away. The military call that the thousand-yard stare...

Is there a cure?

I'm going to refer him to a military clinic not far from here.

266

I can't take him there.

Why not?

They won't see him.

I know some of the staff. I'll put in a word.

No. You don't understand. He's never seen active service.

Oh?

He's only fourteen...

... I see... My mistake. His, erm, age should have been one of my first questions.

Yes.

So what's he playing on his computer?

www.ingramcontent.com/pod-product-compliance
Lightning Source LLC
Chambersburg PA
CBHW020617260626
47157CB00003B/1057